Summer Harvest

ALSO BY GEORGINA PENNEY

Fly In Fly Out

Summer Harvest

GEORGINA PENNEY

MICHAEL JOSEPH
an imprint of
PENGUIN BOOKS

MICHAEL JOSEPH

UK | USA | Canada | Ireland | Australia
India | New Zealand | South Africa | China

Penguin Books is part of the Penguin Random House group of companies
whose addresses can be found at global.penguinrandomhouse.com.

Penguin
Random House
Australia

First published by Penguin Group (Australia), 2016

1 3 5 7 9 10 8 6 4 2

Design by Grace West © Penguin Group (Australia)
Cover photographs, girl by Susan Findlay/Masterfile
gumboots by Halfpoint/Shutterstock
Typeset in Sabon, 11pt/17pt by Grace West
Colour separation by Splitting Image Colour Studio, Clayton, Victoria
Printed and bound in Australia by Griffin Press, an accredited ISO AS/NZS 14001
Environmental Management Systems printer.

National Library of Australia
Cataloguing-in-Publication data:
Penney, Georgina, author.
Summer harvest / Georgina Penney.
9780143797081 (paperback)
Vacations – Western Australia – Fiction.
Life change events – Fiction.

A823.4

penguin.com.au

For Tony

&

*For Theresa, whose strength, poise and grace is
a never-ending source of inspiration*

Chapter 1

If Beth Poole had her way, the need to celebrate birthdays would be eradicated from the human psyche. Instead, you would be born, the doctor would give you a pat on the bottom and make sure you were breathing, and then that would be it. That would be reward enough. Life: the biggest party of all.

Unfortunately, she didn't have her way. Instead she was staring blindly out the kitchen window of her gran's cozy grey-stone cottage while tamping down a growing sense of impending doom.

'Beth?'

It wasn't the age thing that got to her. Turning thirty-one didn't bother her in the slightest. Her appearance hadn't featured high in her priorities for a long time, particularly the past few years. The frequently unpredictable Yorkshire weather had been kind to her pale skin and she had relatively manageable, short fine blonde hair that matched her light brown eyes well enough. Maybe her sturdy clothing frequently hung off her diminutive frame, but her canine clients didn't care. Most of the adults she socialised with of late needed trifocals to see the end of their nose, so why bother?

If she was honest, she didn't have a problem with birthdays as such – it was everything else. Or to be more specific, it was her irrepressible, stubbornly enthusiastic gran, Violet.

'Beth!'

At least there wouldn't be a party this year. Thank God the frigid weather and icy roads had guaranteed that much. Last year, Beth's 'surprise' birthday party had resulted in two senior citizens coming to blows after they'd learned they were both courting the same lady. It had struck Beth afterwards, not for the first time, that Violet's friends led far more interesting lives than Beth did.

So, no party, then. That just left her birthday present.

'*Beth!*'

Beth hoped her gran hadn't spent too much money. Violet Poole had to be the only octogenarian in Yorkshire who went against the short-arms-long-pockets school of wealth management. And she always, *always* went over the top, which explained why Beth had just spent the past five hours training William, the rabbit-obsessed basset hound, in freezing wind and snow instead of staying home. She was still thawing out and was quite sure her feet would never be warm again. Even so, she wished she'd taken on another client afterwards. If her day had been fully booked, she would have received her present first thing this morning and the anxiety she was feeling would be a thing of the past.

'BETH!' Violet's bellow nearly shook the rafters.

'Yes?' Beth called back, raising her voice nearly as loud. Her gran's favourite soap opera, *Summer Love*, was on and turned up to full volume.

'COULD YOU COME IN HERE NOW, PLEASE? WE NEED TO SPEAK TO YOU,' Violet roared.

Beth braced herself. The time was nigh. 'All right. Can I get you anything from the kitchen?'

'Just yourself.'

Beth poured herself a cup of tea for fortification purposes then made her way to the living room. It had last been decorated some time during the nineteen seventies, and was now comfortably frayed around the edges, smelling strongly of old books and her gran's Avon Soft Musk perfume. Beth took a seat on a threadbare orange-and-lime-green sofa.

Louis, her gran's second husband of forty years, had already dozed off in his horribly decrepit brown corduroy armchair. His large, arthritically gnarled hands rested on the curve of his stomach. He was beautifully turned out today in a neatly pressed white shirt and a winter-weight navy wool suit that complemented his leathery mahogany skin to perfection.

Just as neatly turned out and perched on her own genteelly tattered red velvet recliner, Beth's gran appeared twitchier than a bird-watcher spotting a rare warbler.

Despite her apprehension, Beth couldn't help but feel touched that Violet was wearing the red tartan skirt and charcoal grey cardigan she usually saved for church.

'Are you ready, then?' Violet demanded, her sharp blue eyes sparkling with obvious excitement and her fine halo of white fly-away curls bobbing.

'For what?' Beth asked with deliberate obtuseness, sipping her tea.

'Don't be silly. You know very well what,' Violet retorted crisply.

'I have no idea,' Beth insisted, widening her eyes innocently, going along with the game they played every year. To not play would disappoint Violet horrendously.

'Oh, stop it. I might have got momentarily distracted with my soap, but it would take more than that for me to forget your present. Louis? Louis!' Violet prodded Louis sharply in his stomach, waking him.

'What? What?' he asked, his Jamaican accent coming to the fore in his surprise as he heaved himself gingerly forward in his chair, wildly searching the room for the source of his discomfort.

'Calm down, old man. I just want you awake for when we give Beth her birthday present.'

'You know you really needn't have bothered,' Beth protested.

'Quiet. Just say "thank you".' Violet waved a finger at Beth before turning to Louis, who was fumbling around on the doily-bedecked side table next to his chair trying to find his glasses.

'Where have you put it?' Violet demanded.

'Where have *I* put it? Didn't *you* hide it away last night?' Louis grumbled.

During the ensuing argument, Beth distracted herself by allowing her gaze to drift to the TV, where the residents of fictional Radiant Bay (somewhere in Australia) were embroiled in enough drama to keep a team of United Nations Peacekeepers tied up for a century.

For the life of her, Beth couldn't understand what Violet saw in the Australian soap opera *Summer Love*. All those blond, beautiful, half-naked teenagers running around on the screen just set Beth's teeth on edge. Didn't they care about skin cancer in the southern hemisphere? Weren't they worried about shark attacks? What about spiders? Or snakes? The country was crawling with them. Beth knew all about them because for some unfathomable reason, Violet had given her a weighty *Reader's Digest* book entitled *Australia's Most Dangerous Creatures* for her tenth birthday. Arranged into chapters neatly categorised by species, the book listed all the ways a person could die in Australia, complete with terrifyingly close-up images of angry hissing snakes and spiders with huge poison-dripping fangs. It had given Beth nightmares for years and was, in retrospect, probably the reason she was dreading the gift-giving aspect of her birthday today.

No, she certainly didn't understand Australia's appeal or why so many of her fellow countrymen wanted to go there. Give her the rolling green hills and wonderfully temperamental weather of Yorkshire over burning sun and clear blue skies any day.

'There it is! Louis, it was right in front of you the whole time. I wish you'd look properly for things.'

'I would if you gave me a minute's peace, woman.'

'There. Beth. *Beth*. She's off brooding again. Look at her. Can't hear a word I'm saying. BETH!'

'WHAT?' Beth exclaimed, spilling tea onto her jeans as Violet's piercing shriek nearly shattered her eardrums.

'Do you want your birthday present or not? No, don't answer that. Just take it.' Violet gingerly leaned forward and handed her a brown A4 envelope.

'Open it!' she commanded when Beth stared down at the object on her lap with the air of someone about to receive a death sentence.

'What is this?' she asked, warily meeting Violet's excited gaze and then Louis's gentle smile before cautiously spilling out the envelope's contents.

'Oh no.' She groaned quietly. This was worse, much worse, than she'd anticipated.

'Aren't you excited?' Violet exclaimed. 'We thought you needed a little holiday, so we went to see the travel agent, Nathaniel, Tom's son. Remember him? And there you go. Two months of sun, sand and beaches. Oh, Beth, I envy you.' She reached out to clasp one of Louis's hands in her own and gave it a squeeze. 'Your flight is scheduled two weeks from now. Louis borrowed your diary and cancelled your clients for the next few months so you don't even need to bother arranging things. You haven't taken a holiday in years, so I know you must have plenty of money saved up to spend once you get there. Well? What do you think? Aren't you going to say something?'

Feeling like someone had not only pulled the rug out from under her feet but had also removed the floorboards, foundations and a good foot of soil, Beth looked into the beaming faces of the most important people in her life and knew she couldn't let them down.

'A ticket to Australia,' she said faintly. 'Wonderful. Gran, Louis, thank you so much.' She forced her mouth to curve upwards into something resembling a smile. 'This is great. Just *great*.'

It was another ten minutes before Beth could politely make her escape while Violet and Louis bickered over a lost remote control. Clutching the brown envelope with a white-knuckled grip, she climbed the narrow flight of creaking stairs that led to the second floor.

Australia? Of all the off-the-wall presents Violet had come up with, including last year's pole-dancing lessons, this was by far the most insane. And the thing was, the *thing* was, Beth had *known* that something big was coming this year. The terrible twosome downstairs had seemed far too happy with themselves this past week, and then there'd been the strange comment from the pharmacist in Skipton on Tuesday. When Beth had presented her prescription for refill, he'd told her to make sure she had all her shots. She'd thought he was just making his customary joke about her working with animals, but now she suspected that Violet had been standing in the high street on market day declaring her granddaughter's impending birthday surprise through a megaphone.

Still battling disbelief, Beth trudged into her bedroom, where she was greeted with a half-hearted *woof*. Charlie, her canine best friend of fifteen years, was curled up in his fraying wicker basket next to the radiator. He was a Pembroke corgi and had been blind for nearly two years now, but he still got around just fine and could easily differentiate each of his humans by smell. He was also nearly deaf, which was a good thing considering how loud Violet had the TV blaring in the living room directly below.

'Hello, old man.' Beth bypassed her narrow single bed and crouched down to give him a pat on the top of his flat head. He snuffled loudly and wagged his stubby tail but didn't get up. With the weather as cold as it was, he only moved away from his customary spot when he had to eat his dinner or answer the call of nature.

'Did you know what they were up to, boy? Why didn't you warn me?' Still patting Charlie's wiry fur, Beth leaned over to place the envelope on her small bedside table, inadvertently knocking over the single framed photograph she kept there. She rescued the frame from disaster and put it back, but the picture caught her eye and wouldn't let go.

She felt a familiar dull ache of loss as she focused on the image of her curvaceous, bubbly mother, her slender, balding father and her irrepressibly cheeky older sister, Valerie. They were all huddled together on a light blue sofa pulling silly faces at Beth, who'd taken the photograph with the camera she'd just received for her sixth birthday.

Beth smiled sadly. Her parents looked so incredibly young. They had only been in their late twenties, younger than she was today. Valerie had been eight.

They were all gone now.

Her mother and father had died in a car accident when Beth was nine, and Valerie had been taken by breast cancer three-and-a-half years ago.

Beth knew she shouldn't dwell on sadness today of all days. Given her own recent brush with illness, she should simply be grateful to be alive, but it was hard to celebrate her ongoing existence when her family couldn't be there with her.

She'd never forget the precise moment she learned that the tiny lump she'd found in her left breast was cancer. She remembered the smell of the hospital, her doctor's apologetic, harried expression and her complete lack of surprise at the test results. More than that, she remembered what had happened afterwards: the way her life had fallen apart when her husband hadn't been able to handle the reality of her illness and left her lying in a hospital bed only hours after surgery, feeling devastated and completely alone in the world. She had decided in that moment she would never again put her faith in a man and risk being let down like that again.

Thank God for Violet and Louis. Beth had moved back home with them a day after her release from hospital. She'd been welcomed unconditionally with warm hugs and the familiar smells of strong sweet tea, naphthalene flakes and baby powder.

Barraged continuously by her gran's stubborn cheerfulness, Beth had never been able to forget that she *did* have a lot to be thankful for. She was alive, for one thing. She had Violet and Louis, bless them. She had Charlie and she lived in a breathtaking part of the world and got to enjoy it every single day while earning a living doing what she loved. She'd been training dogs professionally for more than a decade and cherished every minute of it, even when she got stuck out in the snow like she had this morning.

And she now had an impending holiday to Australia, not to mention her next two months of work cancelled. She should be upset about that, but Louis and Violet's intentions were pure; instead, she just settled for being stunned, baffled and exasperated like she did every other year.

She picked up the envelope again and up-ended it on her bed. Sitting innocently on her no-nonsense navy bedspread was a horrendously expensive return ticket for Perth, Western Australia.

Perth? Why Perth? Beth furrowed her brow. She didn't know the first thing about Perth. Why not Sydney or Melbourne, where everyone else went? She shook her head in confusion and glanced at her dog, who was monitoring proceedings with a half-cocked ear.

'Two months, Charlie. What am I going to do with myself in Australia for *two months*?'

*

Clayton Hardy hummed along to a classic U2 hit on the radio and walked down the central aisle of his Uncle Les's dairy, attaching milking machines to udders and keeping a watchful eye out for any raised tails that would indicate an imminent splattering. He ruffled a hand through his thick crop of dark brown curls and pursed his lips in an unusually cheerful whistle.

It was five in the morning, already light outside, and noisy too with the magpies singing their wake-up call and the cows softly *moo*ing and munching on their feed pellets. Clayton's Australian blue heeler, Waffles, was bouncing along at his heels, every now and then pressing a cold, damp nose against her owner's bare leg when she wasn't sniffing the crisp air with a euphoric doggy grin on her face. The place smelled comfortingly of creamy milk, dusty cowhide and a generous helping of manure.

Clayton had spent the past five weeks dreading taking over the morning milking while Les went on holiday, but now he wasn't sure what he'd been so worked up about. Sure he had his hands full with the upcoming grape harvest at Evangeline's Rest, his family's winery, but this was peaceful. So peaceful it drew his attention to just how wound up he'd been of late. He'd been antsy for months – ever since his family's hired hand of twenty years had unexpectedly quit, leaving Clayton, his dad and Les doing the work of four men.

If that wasn't enough to set his teeth on edge, the builders working on his new house were slower than geriatric snails, which left him still living in his family home at age thirty-four. The whole set-up had been barely tolerable for years, but now it was painful.

A month before, Clayton's little brother, Stephen, and his new girlfriend, Jo, had temporarily moved down to Evangeline's Rest to set up a microbrewery. Normally Clayton wouldn't mind additional family members hanging around, especially since he was already sharing the house with his dad, his grandma, Angie and his sister Rachael. What he did mind was the sound of creaking bedsprings coming from the room next door to his every bloody night.

His face briefly contorted into a fierce scowl as he strode outside the dairy, his wide-set, dark brown eyes narrowing on a pen of loudly bawling calves waiting to be handfed. The least his little brother could do was show a bit of consideration. Not everyone in the house was enjoying sex on tap. Some people were experiencing a serious drought.

Even though it was tourist season and the region was crawling with attractive single women, Clayton had been too busy lately to meet any of them, let alone get them horizontal.

With luck, that was about to change. If the young bloke he'd interviewed yesterday for the farm-hand job turned out all right, Clayton would have a chance to track down his missing social life and make up for lost time.

Bloody hell it was hot.

The road stretching out in front of Beth's rented Toyota Corolla was shimmering, actually shimmering, with heat. She'd always thought that was something people just wrote about in books.

She gripped the neckline of her too-heavy, long-sleeved cotton shirt and pulled it away from her chest to allow a bit of cool air to circulate. Maybe she should have stopped in the city long enough to buy some summer clothes. She frowned in thought. No. She'd been smart to get her journey to the south of Western Australia immediately underway. She'd never felt comfortable in cities and didn't find them relaxing in the slightest.

After her initial shock at Violet and Louis's gift had worn off, she'd made the decision to embrace her first official holiday. That meant she would do it the way she wanted, even if the location wasn't what she would have chosen.

It turned out that her gran hadn't chosen it either. Beth laughed out loud at the memory of Violet's outrage when she'd discovered that the tickets Louis had purchased were for *Western* Australia, not the east coast where *Summer Love* was filmed. Violet had been truly spectacular in her indignation, bellowing from her couch at Louis for making the mistake and getting even angrier when he retreated to read his paper next to the heater in his small potting shed.

Beth had finally calmed her gran down with the promise that she wasn't devastated over the mistake and that she would enjoy herself anyway. Since she had promised to have a good time, that's what she would do. Or bloody well die trying. Which is what would happen if one of the kangaroos that the Avis man had warned her about jumped in front of her rental car . . . or if a snake bit her . . . or a spider . . . or a jellyfish . . . or a shark attacked her.

For the life of her, Beth couldn't understand how Australians could be so blasé about living in a country in which every living thing was lethal. Even more inexplicable, every Australian she'd met in the past twenty-four hours had delighted in telling her in detail about their native country's killer wildlife, and how they'd once almost died from being bitten, punctured, scratched or stung. Obviously the information she'd read as a child in *Australia's Most Dangerous Creatures* had been devoid of exaggeration.

The only explanation she could come up with for the locals' relaxed attitude in the face of so much impending danger was that the heat had sent the lot of them bonkers. It had certainly affected the landscape. She spared a moment from her inner reflection to really take in her surroundings.

She had never travelled outside England before and the first thing that struck her about the Australian countryside was the space. It was everywhere and completely unnerving. A far cry from the snow and sleet she'd left behind in Yorkshire, it was the middle of summer here; the endless expanse of land bracketing either side of the road was a sea of bleached-blond dry grass. Trees thickly lined the roadside, but after that they merely dotted the landscape here and there. They weren't the lush, vivid green she was used to. Instead they were variations on olive and khaki, and quite straggly. It was as if the heat had sapped the energy required for any effort they might have put into their appearance.

Based on the information Beth had read online, the holiday cottage she'd booked near the small township of George Creek in the Margaret River wine region would be in similar surrounds and feel just as isolated. The thought of being on her own, away from people for two months, was both worrying and surprisingly pleasant.

Beth had never really enjoyed time to herself before. She had always had someone else to think about, whether it was her gran and Louis during her teens or later, her ex-husband Greg.

She'd married Greg when she was twenty-one and had spent the seven years of her marriage supporting him through university while building her own business reputation. Then Valerie had died. Four months later Beth was diagnosed with the same cancer that had killed her sister, and it became readily apparent that the solid foundation underpinning her marriage was made of glass.

Not that she was going to dwell on all that right now. Instead, she was going to enjoy thinking about the coming days ahead despite having no idea what one *did* on a holiday in Australia.

What did people do to have fun here besides getting bitten by something and dying, or talking about getting bitten and dying? She really hadn't done much research before she arrived other than booking her accommodation in a wine region, reasoning that would be a good place to start, and buying a *Lonely Planet*.

Her eyes alighted on the car's sound system. Maybe listening to a local radio station would provide her with some answers. A quick search through the available stations left it clear that answers wouldn't be forthcoming but the boppy, happy music on a top-forty station caught her attention and lightened her mood anyway. It didn't take long before she was determinedly singing along in her notoriously off-key voice, chasing away the spectre of her unhappy marriage and most of the local wildlife as well.

An hour later Beth's pleasant mood had evaporated under the scorching midday sun. Moments earlier she had run over a small, innocuous coil of wire. She had thought nothing of it until her car listed to the left and she'd been forced to pull over onto the soft gravel shoulder of an extremely narrow road lined with tall, rough-barked gum trees and low scrub. A close inspection revealed that the harmless piece of wire had half-inch barbs on it, a few of which were embedded in her deflated tyre.

Of all the luck.

Here she was worrying about the indigenous beasties, only to be attacked by an inanimate object. If the bloody tyre had waited another five minutes to deflate, she would be at her destination and able to change it safely.

Instead she had to worry about snakes in the roadside leaf litter, spiders in the trees and another car coming around the nearby corner and flattening her to an overheated pancake. Why hadn't she been smart enough to make sure her phone was charged?

'You're an idiot, that's why,' she wheezed, while heaving out the shiny spare tyre and dropping it onto the ground before rubbing her hands on her jeans. Now, if she could just get her head around the instructions for operating the car jack, she'd be fine. She felt a rivulet of sweat trickle down her back and grimaced. If it wasn't so hot and if she wasn't dressed in such inappropriate clothing, things would be a lot easier, but they weren't, so she may as well get on with it. She pushed up her sleeves and got to work.

Chapter 2

'Fred, you there?' Clayton waited the thirty seconds it took his new farmhand to realise it wasn't Jesus talking to him, just a voice on the phone.

'Yup.'

'You moved the cows in the stubble paddock yet?' He turned his faded red Holden pick-up out of Evangeline's Rest and pulled out onto the main road heading towards George Creek.

'Nope,' came Fred's enlightened reply.

'You gonna get to it anytime soon, mate? I need you to go fix the fence near the road this afternoon, too, and the day's getting old.' Clayton gritted his teeth while waiting for his words to work their way through the haze of the five or so joints Fred had inhaled for breakfast that morning.

'Okay.'

'Okay as in you're going to get on with the job?' He gently pushed Waffles out of the way as he reached for the gearstick. Unfazed, the dog moved to the other side of the cab and tried to poke her head out the small gap in the window as Clayton waited for Fred's reply.

'Yup.'

'You wanna repeat to me what I've asked you to do? Just for my peace of mind, you understand, mate.'

'Move cows and . . . move cows . . .'

'And fix the fence near the road.'

'Yeah.'

Briefly closing his eyes in exasperation, Clayton almost didn't see the white Toyota Corolla parked on the other side of the blind corner he'd just come round. It was a good thing he swerved at the last minute or the car and its mentally impaired tourist driver would have become one more holiday-season statistic.

Gesturing furiously, adrenaline pumping, he honked his horn. 'Bloody *idiot*!'

'Hey man! That's a bit harsh,' Fred protested in an injured tone.

'Not *you*. Gotta go. Cows out of stubble paddock and fix the fence.' Clayton hung up then checked his rear-view to catch sight of the dickhead who didn't know better than to park in such a dangerous spot.

Instead he saw a woman no bigger than a kid wrestling with a tyre. That changed everything. He planted his foot on the brake and reversed back up the road, parking at a much safer distance from the corner than the woman had.

He climbed out of the cab and felt the scorching temperature hit him hard. Waffles tried to follow but he told her to stay. She was due to have puppies soon and he didn't want her out in the heat any more than she needed to be. Speaking of heat, the woman had to be cooking in those heavy winter clothes. It was the middle of summer, for Christ's sake.

'You need a hand?' he asked, crossing the road.

'I'd appreciate it,' a surprisingly youthful, out-of-breath voice replied from the other side of the car followed by a low murmur, no doubt to herself, but the trees and scrub along the road edge acted like an amplifier and he heard every word. 'Please don't be a serial killer or homicidal maniac.'

'Left my torture devices at home today, but I can go a quick strangulation if that takes your fancy,' Clayton replied, sarcasm lacing his voice. He wasn't over the shock of nearly running into her and was still irritated after his futile efforts at communicating with planet Fred.

'Oh.' She bobbed upright like a meerkat spotting a hawk. 'I'm sorry, and no thanks to the strangulation. Just help with the tyre would be fine.'

The first thought that struck Clayton as he approached was that she wasn't local. He removed his battered green baseball cap and ran a hand through his sweat-damp hair before putting it back on. The movement gave him the chance to study her out the corner of his eye.

She was a little bit of a thing, coming up to his shoulder or thereabouts, a serious pixie playing grown-ups in a baggy mud-brown shirt and old-lady jeans. Flighty, short blonde hair and huge honey-brown eyes set in a little heart-shaped face only added to the impression.

Clayton's eyes crinkled in amusement at the incongruous sight of a large wrench clutched in her small hand.

'What's wrong? Am I doing something wrong?' she asked, two little creases forming between blonde brows.

English, Clayton thought. She had to be a Brit with that accent.

'Dunno yet. Can't see.' He moved closer to inspect the tyre sitting at her feet. Standing less than a foot away, he caught a whiff of her perfume. It was a vanilla scent that reminded him of freshly baked cupcakes. The corners of his mouth twitched in a smile.

Obviously uncomfortable with his proximity, the woman swiftly stepped backwards, her foot landing in the shallow ditch littered with leaves and twigs bordering the roadside. She didn't stay there long. After one horrified look down at her feet, she made a squeaking noise and plastered herself back against the car with the tenacity of a limpet.

Clayton didn't bother commenting on her strange behaviour, figuring she was just worried about getting those ugly boots of hers dirty. Instead he studied her handiwork with narrowed eyes. 'You've set the jack wrong.'

'Oh.'

'Wanna give me that wrench?' He held out a hand and the item was promptly thrust into his palm.

'What's your name?' he asked, jacking up the car correctly and beginning to undo the lug nuts on the flat tyre.

'Beth.'

He waited for more but she didn't elaborate. He peered sideways at her. She was busy eyeballing the leaf litter behind him like it was about to grow teeth and bite her. Maybe it wasn't her shoes she was worried about after all.

'M'name's Clayton,' he said, trying to draw her attention.

'Oh.'

'Clayton Hardy. I live just down the road from here. Can you move a sec? I have to put the flat tyre away. Thanks.'

She shuffled out of the way, keeping herself pressed up against the car. He could tell she was trying to appear casual about the whole thing but it wasn't working.

Maybe there was something not quite right upstairs with this lady. Maybe she was another Fred. Anyone who'd wear so much heavy clothing in this heat had to be a bit fruity. Pity, considering she wasn't hard on the eyes – well, as far as he could see. He noticed her left hand was absent of a wedding or engagement ring.

He swiftly bolted on the spare tyre and straightened up. 'Should be fine now.'

'Thanks.' She briefly met his gaze. 'Sorry for the trouble. You have to be hot.'

'Yeah. It's boiling out here.' Clayton scrunched up his face to punctuate his words then waited for her to say something more. Nope. Nothing forthcoming. 'Right, then . . . I gotta go. See ya.'

'Thanks again and see you later,' she said distractedly before skittering around to the driver's-side door like her pants were on fire.

Her car was started and she was gone in a matter of seconds, leaving him staring down at the wrench in his hands and the car jack at his feet. He shook his head.

'Bloody tourists,' he growled to himself, picking up the jack and walking back to his idling pick-up. Now he'd have to track her down.

If she was staying anywhere around George Creek there was a very good chance she'd drop in to the Evangeline's Rest cellar door or his sister's restaurant at some stage, so he'd just leave her things there with a description for Angie and Rachael to keep an eye out.

If this was any indication of how poor his ability to charm the ladies had got of late, he was up the proverbial creek in a leaking boat without a paddle.

'Beth Poole, you are a colossal twit,' Beth moaned once she got half a kilometre down the road and realised two things: first, how unforgivably rude she'd just been, and second, that she'd just left half her rental car's toolkit on the side of the road.

Bloody ridiculous country. The heat must have already fried her brain.

She wasn't sure what had contributed to her idiocy the most. It was a toss-up between her completely rational and reasonable fear of creepy-crawlies and the winded feeling she'd experienced on catching sight of the rural god who came to her rescue. His face had looked like something someone had carved out of granite with a blunt knife. He'd been all broad planes, deep grooved lines, high cheekbones and a slightly off-centre, once-broken nose. She'd caught him studying her with a set of thickly lashed, deep brown eyes that were disconcertingly pretty in contrast with the rest of him. She had experienced genuine heart palpitations.

He was obviously from the area and had been wearing a dust-streaked, faded blue short-sleeved shirt that fit tightly across a solid set of shoulders. His tan, no-nonsense shorts revealed thighs the size of tree trunks and equally muscled, hairy calves leading to a pair of battered brown leather boots. The man could pass as a world-class rugby player – bull-like, stocky. He'd smelled nice, too. A combination of earthy male sweat with a hint of freshly laundered clothes.

'Listen to yourself.' She snorted, chagrined that she'd just spent so much time daydreaming about some random man she would probably never see again, who no doubt thought she was a rude cow, or a mad cow, more like it. Grumbling under her breath, she did a twelve-point turn on the narrow road and drove back to collect the jack and the wrench – only to find them gone.

'It's like the inside of a daffodil!' Beth exclaimed twenty minutes later as she explored the small, wonderfully welcoming cottage she'd booked for her stay.

Everything was decorated in white and yellow. The combined kitchen and living room featured white walls and had warm polished wood floors and yellow laminate bench tops. The overall effect was enhanced by solid country pine furniture and cheerful yellow gingham curtains. Off to one side, a large bedroom, painted in pale yellow, featured a beautiful white wrought-iron double bed. It was covered with an intricate white-and-cream patchwork bedspread and a whole pile of pillows that invited reclining and, above all, sleep. Beth immediately fell in love with it.

Laura Rousse, the cottage's vivacious dynamo owner, grinned widely, displaying a lot of straight white teeth. 'It is, isn't it? I never thought of it like that, but now you mention it . . .' She whisked past Beth and opened the refrigerator in the kitchen. 'I've left you all the stuff you need for breakfast: bread, bacon, eggs, milk. You're not vegetarian, are you? No? Oh, that's good. I didn't think to ask but if you are I could accommodate! I've also put a few bottles of wine in there and some of the local beer – I thought you might like that since you wouldn't have had a chance to try anything yet. You flew in this morning, didn't you? Do you need anything else? Silly question, of course you do. You must be tired coming from England. You probably need sleep, right? Do you know anyone in the area to show you around or are you here on your own? Aren't you warm in those clothes? Oh, and I know that you've already said in your emails that you were fine with there being no wi-fi yet, but we should have it for you soon. That's still all right, isn't it?' Her interrogation came to an abrupt halt and she paused expectantly.

Momentarily stunned by the barrage of words, Beth took a moment to catch up and then unexpectedly, involuntarily, began to laugh. Here she'd been thinking she was travelling to somewhere exotic and she'd arrived to find her gran's Australian, much younger, double.

'What? Did I say something wrong? Am I talking too much?' Laura's cheeks flushed and her pale blue eyes widened with worry.

'No, no. You didn't say anything wrong in the slightest. You just reminded me of someone I know,' Beth replied gently, wiping a tear out of her eye. If Beth's gran and Laura ever managed to be on the same continent, there'd be a good chance the Four Horsemen of the Apocalypse would saddle up and ride into town.

'Really? That's a relief.' Laura exhaled loudly. 'Because I often get told I talk too much, which isn't very good for someone in my industry since people want to relax on holiday not have their ear talked off. You know you're my first guest? We finished building three months ago and it's been quite hard to get everything —'

'You know . . . I've just arrived and I know you probably have to work this afternoon, but would you mind having a cup of tea with me?' Beth interjected quickly, forestalling another avalanche of words with a warm smile.

'A cup of tea?' Laura's mouth fell open, her expression saying Beth might as well have suggested they strip naked and do the hula. 'Really? Yeah, that'd be great. Do you want me to make you one? Because I can. If you need me to.'

'How about you sit down and direct me. I'll have to work out where everything is anyway.' Beth knew where she was with tea. She might be in a strange country, talking to the first woman her age she'd met in a semi-social context for months and feeling immensely disoriented, but the least she could do was make a cup of tea. It always relaxed Violet. Maybe it would work on Laura too.

'Oh. In that case, thanks.' Laura took a seat at the kitchen table and gave Beth pointers on where everything was while Beth put the kettle on and scooped out tea from an earthenware canister sitting on the kitchen counter.

'How do you take it?'

'Take it? The tea? White, no sugar.'

'So do I.' Beth poured boiling water into a squat white teapot. She brought two steaming bright yellow mugs over to the table moments later.

'Ta.' Laura watched Beth expectantly, visibly fighting the urge to say more.

'So,' Beth said, sitting down and feeling immeasurably relaxed now that such a familiar ritual had been dispensed with.

'So?' Laura prompted, leaning forward with a puppy-dog-keen

expression on her face. Beth fought the urge to smile. If the lady had a tail, it would be wagging.

'I'm wondering if you could help me?'

'Of course. What do you need?'

'I got a flat tyre on my car this morning . . .' Beth relayed the story, glossing over her reaction to the beefcake farmer, while Laura listened intently with a thoughtful expression.

'Clayton, you said?' Laura asked once Beth had finished.

'Yes.'

Laura started to chuckle. 'I'm going to tease him so much over this. He's my brother's best friend. How about I let him know where you're staying so he can drop your things off?'

Beth didn't relish the idea of running back into the wall of a man since she'd been so rude, but she owed him an apology and she needed to retrieve her things or pay a hefty penalty with the rental-car company.

'That would be fine.' She took a sip of tea. 'There's one other thing. Could you point me towards a good place to buy some summer clothes?' She ran her hands over the knees of her heavy, baggy jeans self-consciously. 'I didn't get a chance to shop before I left home and I'm boiling in these.'

'I can do better than that. How about I take you shopping? You're small but I'm pretty sure we can find something to fit without you having to shop in the kids' department.' Laura's eyes sparkled like diamonds.

'Oh no. I don't want to put you out. Maybe just tell me the names of a few good shops and I'll take care of the rest,' Beth protested, warmed by the offer.

'You're not putting me out at all. How about we go tomorrow arvo? Can you hold off that long? I have a few things to do this afternoon and tomorrow morning, but I don't want to pass up spending time with someone who's this side of eighty and female.

My only friend here, Rachael, works crazy hours as a chef, so since I moved back here from Perth I've been stuck with my dad and his friends and my brother and *his* idiot friends.' She paused and held up both hands, her expression horrified. 'No offence, though. I don't mean you're the only option I have or anything. That came out all wrong —'

'None taken. In that context, I think I can wait a day.' Beth gave her a gentle smile. 'I've been in the same situation for the past few years myself, so I can relate. I have to admit, the idea of spending time with someone my age is a little daunting but I'm sure we'll manage if you can put up with me being out of practice.'

'Of course!' Laura beamed with relief, her smile transforming her face so she appeared no older than eighteen, although Beth gauged her real age to be somewhere in the late twenties.

They chatted companionably for another few minutes until Laura's phone rang and she had to leave in a hurry.

Moments later, Beth stood at the open cottage doorway and watched the dust kick up from her new friend's departing car. Closing the door, she turned around and inhaled the smell of sun-warmed beeswaxed floorboards and fresh linens. This would do nicely.

She quickly peeked through the curtains at the open expanse of yellow grass directly in front of the cottage and the green grapevines in the distance before peeling off her awful shirt, heavy white cotton undershirt and too-thick jeans. With a sigh of relief she threw them in a corner, reminding herself to burn them later, then collapsed on the patchwork quilt on the bed in her underwear. She'd worry about unpacking later. For now she would sleep.

'So, how's the new bloke shaping up?' Jeff Rousse, Clayton's best mate and all-round pain in the arse, asked as he walked out onto his porch. He handed Clayton a Crown Lager then took a seat and put his feet up on the wooden railing.

Clayton leaned back in his chair to better stare at Jeff in amazement. 'How's he shaping up? Jesus Christ, mate! Where did you find him? He's a total bloody stoner. Every time I talk to him he starts nodding his head and keeps going until I tell him to stop. It's like watching one of those . . . whatdyacallit . . . bobble head doll things. You know, those toys people put at the back of their cars? I'm developing neck problems in sympathy.' He shook his head in disgust and took a pull on his beer.

'Really? Well, so what?' Jeff raised a ginger-coloured eyebrow and shrugged. 'As long as he does the job, who cares?'

'That's the problem. I'm pretty sure he wouldn't reach for a bucket of water if his arse was on fire. So, in answer to your question, your recommendation was shit but I can't fire him till I find someone else, and screaming hoards of applicants are few and far between.'

Jeff shrugged. 'No skin off my nose if you fire him. I'll keep an eye out for anyone else who'd be interested in working for a perfectionist bastard. Want something to eat? How's a frozen pizza sound?'

'Perfectionist my arse. All I want is someone who can speak more than five words consecutively and obey basic instructions without hallucinating that they're the sugarplum fairy and yeah, mate, pizza would be great.'

Jeff clapped him on the back then went inside, leaving Clayton glowering at the spectacular view in front of him.

The setting sun bathed the rolling valley, golden oat fields and distant Evangeline's Rest vineyards in a dusky pink light. In the immediate foreground, a large group of grey kangaroos grazed in the dappled shadows cast by a large jarrah tree, more than likely aggravating Jeff to no end, but the sight immediately cheered

Clayton. Roos had a habit of destroying fences and trampling crops, but he still enjoyed seeing them. Well, as long as it was Jeff's oats and fences they were messing with and not his.

He envied Jeff this: having a small place to himself on land he managed and made the executive decisions for. Clayton, on the other hand, had to negotiate with his entire family if he wanted to so much as buy new boots.

Not that he was complaining *too* loudly. Evangeline's Rest was too big an enterprise for one person to handle on his own with the vineyards and the winery, the dairy, the sheep, the grain crops, the marron farms and the soon-to-be-added microbrewery. Just thinking about it all made his head hurt, so he shut it out and went back to watching the roos graze in front of him while idly patting Waffles' stomach with his bare foot.

Waffles groaned euphorically and awkwardly rolled onto her back.

'Spoiled bitch,' he grumbled affectionately, feeling the lumps and bumps under her skin that would be her first litter of puppies. She gave him a slit-eyed look of pleasure that said he could be as insulting as he liked as long as he kept up the attention. He went back to enjoying the view.

Jeff had built the cabin only the year before while his sister Laura was overseeing a holiday cottage venture on the other side of the Rousse property.

Jeff's dad had recently retired from running the family farm. His retirement had coincided with Clayton's grandma, Angie, the tomboy matriarch of the Hardy family, spending an awful lot of time away from home.

Clayton smiled to himself. Old Roussey and Angie thought no one knew they'd been getting it on for nearly twenty years now. It was the worst-kept secret in the district, but no one had the heart to tell either of them. He'd have to talk to Angie about that one day, after a few bracing beverages and maybe while wearing full body armour.

'Pizza's in the oven. Did I tell you Laura's just settled in her first paying guest?' Jeff ambled back outside with another two beers in hand. He passed one to Clayton.

'Ta. Oh?' Clayton asked. He'd missed a few calls from Jeff's sister earlier in the day and hadn't got around to returning them. He'd been too sidetracked trying to understand why Fred had moved a herd of cows into the paddock near the road and fixed the fence in the stubble paddock, the complete opposite of what Clayton had instructed. It had resulted in thirty Friesians running loose and a busload of Japanese tourists getting a unique education in the Australian vernacular when it had fallen to Clayton to round them up. When the usual run of four-letter words had dried up, he'd got pretty damn inventive in making up more.

'Yeah. Booked in for a whole month. Pretty good news, eh?'

'Yeah, great news.' With the mention of tourists, Clayton's thoughts went straight to the woman with the flat tyre. Beth, if he remembered correctly.

'Said it's an English bird on her own.'

'Oh?' Clayton's ears perked up.

'Yeah. Apparently she and Laura hit it off and they're gonna go shopping tomorrow.'

'Oh yeah?' Clayton kept his tone casual. 'Laura say anything more about her?'

'Why do you wanna know?'

'Had a run-in with an English woman with a flat tyre this morning.' Clayton relayed the story, mentioning the woman's strange, verging on rude, behaviour.

'She doesn't sound rude, mate, she just sounds selective. Probably didn't fancy your pretty face.' Jeff batted his russet-coloured eyelashes and smirked.

'Shaddup.'

'You know, there's a pretty good chance this woman Laura's got staying up at the cottage and your flat-tyre lady are the same one. She good-looking?'

'Not too bad.'

'Oh yeah? I might have to stop round and introduce myself, then.'

'She wouldn't be interested in you, mate,' Clayton scoffed.

'Why not? Sounds like she wasn't interested in you. Was she wearing a wedding ring or anything?'

'Nope.'

'So, you checked,' Jeff guffawed.

'It's not like you're not just as bloody desperate. Anyway, to change the subject, what was going on between you and Rachael the other day?' Clayton asked, knowing that any mention of his sister would immediately put Jeff off the topic.

'None of your business.'

'She *is* my sister, mate.'

'She's a right b—'

'And you can stop right there,' Clayton interrupted smoothly.

'Yeah, yeah, righto. So anyway, I'm thinking of going and seeing if our paying guest is settled in all right tomorrow. Just out of sheer politeness, you understand.'

'Yeah? I just might have to come with you,' Clayton said nonchalantly. 'If it's the same woman, I've gotta return her stuff.'

Ignoring Jeff's knowing smirk, he turned his mind to the prospect of meeting the English woman again. Maybe she'd even say more than two words this time. Now, wouldn't that be great.

Chapter 3

'Do you like them? I hope you like them. They all fit you beautifully, much better than the clothes you were wearing yesterday, which were bloody awful if you don't mind me saying as much. So?' Laura paused for breath, her expression keen as Beth peered into the bags at her feet. They were sitting in the air-conditioned comfort of a beachfront cafe in Busselton, a large town a half-hour drive from Beth's cottage. Laura was sipping a fruit cocktail and Beth was enjoying a well-deserved cappuccino after she had called an end to a truly exhausting marathon shopping session peppered with random introductions to Laura's seemingly endless number of acquaintances.

'I love them.' Beth inspected a white peasant blouse embroidered with moss green stitching, stroking her fingers over the crisp white cotton. In the space of two hours, she had managed to acquire an entire wardrobe of clothes. On top of that, not only did everything fit her shape – sometimes tightly – nothing she'd bought could be described as overly practical. Every item, from underwear to dresses to cute little cap-sleeved shirts, was brightly coloured and feminine, a far cry from the dog-hair-hiding beige and navy jeans and pullovers she'd lived in for years. The clothes she'd tried on today had left her feeling pretty, if not a little awkward, and with Laura's encouragement and a little gentle bullying, Beth had purchased the lot.

'I hope you have a decent bra to wear with that. Do you? If you don't your straps will show. Mind you, you're small enough that you probably don't need to wear a bra, unlike me.' Laura frowned disapprovingly down at her own chest.

Beth scrunched up her face at the unwelcome sharp pang she felt at Laura's words. 'I'm sure I'll make do. I can't thank you enough. The colours aren't what I would have picked at all, but I'm so happy you talked me into trying them. You know, I haven't bought clothes for nearly five years. So this —'

'*What?*' Laura screeched, cutting her off. 'Five years? How old are you? Twenty-something?'

'Thirty-one,' Beth corrected.

'Really? Seriously? Oh. Well, anyway, no wonder you needed to go shopping.' She eyeballed Beth's baggy jeans and nondescript long-sleeved shirt like they were the greatest fashion crime known to man. 'And no offence meant, but you didn't have a lot of taste or any idea of your size. Those colours are completely wrong for you.'

'No offence taken. To tell you the truth, I never really bothered with fashion, because the dogs I work with are more focused on the treats in my pockets than what the pockets are attached to, and my ex-husband used to say it wasn't worth spending money on myself in my line of work . . . so, I think I gave up in the end and stuck to being practical.'

'What a bloody missionary man.'

'Pardon?'

'Missionary position – boring, vanilla,' Laura supplied, eyes twinkling, expression entirely innocent.

Beth couldn't help herself. A startled laugh burbled up and she narrowly missed inhaling her coffee. The description suited Greg to a tee, from his favourite sexual position to his rather understated personality.

'I was right, yeah?' Laura asked with a smug grin.

'Very much so,' Beth replied and then changed the topic. 'So, tell me, what was it like to grow up here? You seem to know everyone.' She waved a hand to encompass the view in front of them: the long Busselton Jetty, the swarms of screeching seagulls fighting over food left on outdoor cafe tables and the never-ending stretch of white sandy beach and choppy blue-grey Indian Ocean visible through a scraggly bunch of shorefront Norfolk pines.

'Yeah, I do feel like I know almost everyone.' Laura shrugged. 'But I didn't grow up here at all, actually. I've just got to know people since I moved back to build the cottages. Mum and Dad divorced when I was four. I left with Mum to live in Perth while my older brother, Jeff, stayed here on the farm with Dad. I only visited here once a year during the school holidays as a kid. It was just enough time for me to enjoy the place and drive Jeff mental. You'll probably see him around the farm, but he shouldn't come too close to your cottage, so don't worry about privacy. We're just getting used to the idea of having paying guests. You *are* having a good time so far, aren't you? Is the cottage okay? I didn't push my company on you today, did I?'

'Of course not. I'm having fun.' Beth waved a hand dismissively. 'I'm not like a regular guest anyway. I doubt you'll get a lot of single women travelling on their own, staying as long as I plan to, and frankly, it's been an age since I've been able to shop with another woman. It's been all work and not much else for the past two years. And before that, I had some medical problems that took up a lot of my time. I'm okay now,' she added, quick to reassure Laura whose expression was now a picture of concern.

'Oh good. Great.' Laura relaxed back in her chair. 'Out of curiosity, why *are* you staying so long? Don't you want to do some travelling around the rest of Australia? Get out and see the sights?'

'I thought about it,' Beth mused. 'But then I thought that the one thing I've never had, that I've always wanted, was some time to myself. I live with my gran and she keeps me busy running errands and keeping her company when she's bored. That's when I'm not working, which is all the time. I'm a dog trainer.'

'A dog trainer.' Laura's eyes widened. 'Like that dog-whisperer guy? The one on TV?'

'Sort of.' Beth smiled wryly. 'Although my methods are a little different, it's the same thing. You wouldn't think that it would be a busy job, but I've never been out of work. Skipton is a large village with a lot of people who need help with their pets. Usually they're desperate when they ask me to come in and fix things. I made the mistake last year of listing an after-hours number in an advertisement, and I haven't had time to breathe since. I frequently get calls at the oddest hours.'

'Serious? Why?'

'Many reasons.' Beth shrugged, smiling. 'The silliest was because a couple's pet doberman had grown possessive of their refrigerator.'

Laura chuckled. 'What did you do?'

'Since it was two in the morning when they called, I asked why they were so desperate to get into the fridge in the first place. Then I arranged to take the dog for a series of obedience lessons starting the next morning. That fixed the dog's problems, though I'm not sure about the owners'.'

Laura's amusement was infectious and over the next little while, she managed to convince Beth to share a few more stories of neurotic owners and their long-suffering, sometimes equally neurotic canine companions.

'So, you can see how I could just want some quiet time to have a think about things without rushing here and there,' Beth concluded. 'Mind you, that wasn't what my gran intended.' She relayed the mix-up with flights and Violet's *Summer Love* obsession.

She was gratified when Laura erupted into a fit of laughter.

'If it helps you get back into your gran's good books, I can always fill you in on the gossip from around here. Sometimes I think we make Radiant Bay look tame.'

'Do tell.' A bit of juicy gossip about the local fauna would be just the ticket to satisfy Violet.

'All right, but how about I tell you all about it another day? Does Friday afternoon work for you? I'm sure you're feeling pretty tired from jet lag and it'll give me an excuse to see you again.'

'That sounds perfect. I have to admit, I am feeling a little wilted,' Beth replied while trying to catch the attention of a harried waiter, who was busy shooing a particularly evil-looking seagull away from a half-finished plate of French fries on a table outside.

Laura stayed long enough at the cottage to offload Beth's purchases before speeding off in a cloud of gravel dust.

Yawning hugely and scratching her fingers through her dishevelled hair, Beth wandered to her bedroom. She inspected the shopping bags spilling out onto her unmade bed with a satisfied smile before stripping out of her old clothes and adding them to the pile from the day before.

She wrinkled her nose at them. Maybe she really would throw them out, or donate them to charity at the very least. It wasn't as if she didn't have enough money to buy more winter clothing when she returned home. All she'd done the past two years was work and save. Added to that, her divorce settlement had been more than generous after Greg had walked out on her. Until now, the money had sat in a bank account, doing nothing but accrue interest while Beth picked up the pieces of her life and worked out what to spend it on. Getting a new wardrobe felt like a positive start.

She pulled a flirty fire-engine-red shift dress out of a bag and held it against herself, deliberating before pulling it on. It fell to mid thigh, a lot shorter than anything she'd worn in years, possibly ever, and clung to her frame in a way that made her feel both sexy and slightly self-conscious. She debated taking her bra off and seeing what it would look like au naturel now that no one was around to see, but she was interrupted when her phone rang.

'Beth?' Violet's voice boomed through the earpiece.

'Gran.' Beth smiled as she rummaged through the bags again, deciding which new pair of shoes would match.

'Well?'

'Well, what?'

'Well, are you enjoying yourself? What's it like? Have you met people?'

'Yes, fine and yes.' Beth nibbled a short, unvarnished fingernail thoughtfully. Definitely the new strappy gold leather flats. They'd do nicely.

'What? Is that all?'

'Gran, I've only been here two days. You're going to have to give me a bit longer to come up with anything better. Besides, this call is costing you a fortune.'

'That's all right. Louis is paying for it.'

'No. That's not all right.' Beth rolled her eyes. 'Louis has better things to spend his pension on. How about you let me settle in and I'll call you in a week. Okay?'

'But —'

'A week, Violet Poole,' Beth said firmly. 'A holiday is what you've sent me on, and a holiday is what I'm having. Besides, I'm getting together a whole lot of juicy local gossip to tell you and I promise you it's even more interesting than what you see on the telly, so be good and wait until I call.'

There was a pregnant pause before Violet grudgingly chuckled. 'All right. I'll let you be. I'm warning you, though – it had better be decent gossip.'

'I promise it will be enough to have your bridge-club ladies in a state of shock and awe,' Beth assured her, padding in bare feet to the cottage's kitchen and pulling a bottle of white wine out of the fridge.

'I should hope so. In that case, I'll talk to you later. One week, no less.'

'No less,' Beth agreed, unscrewing the cap.

'Love you, and Louis says hello.'

'Love you too. Give Charlie a pat for me and tell Louis I love him and that he shouldn't put up with you being so bossy. Bye now.' Beth ended the call to the sound of Violet's feigned indignation. She then turned off her phone and poured herself a generous glass of wine.

Clayton didn't get around to returning Laura's calls until the next day. He knew there was no such thing as a short conversation with Jeff's sister, so he wasn't surprised that it took her a while to get to the point. Traipsing through Evangeline's Rest's barrel room and out into the main production area with his phone crooked between his shoulder and ear, he listened to her confide her latest worries about marketing her cottages.

'We've only had a few bookings so far. I'm not sure if there's too much competition down here or if there's something we're not offering that the other guys are.'

'I don't think you need to worry, Laura. This stuff takes time,' Clayton replied while inspecting the temperature gauges on two giant stainless steel, ice-crusted tanks currently stabilising this year's chardonnay and sauvignon blanc. His family employed a brilliant winemaker, but it was Clayton's habit to touch base with this side of the business at least once a day even though technically this was Angie and his dad's side of things. Trailing after him, Waffles gave everything he touched an approving sniff. Every now and then she yawned widely to remind Clayton that it was nearly time for his dinner and her evening nap.

'I know you're right, but I'm still kinda worried.'

'Relax. It'll work out. So, what were you calling about yesterday? Anything major?'

Five minutes later he hung up and decided that dinner could wait. He had a lady's things to return. Whistling for Waffles to come along, he held the car door open for her and then climbed in, unaccountably looking forward to seeing the uncommunicative Beth again.

Smiling wryly to himself, he turned to the dog as he fished his keys out of his pocket. 'It's pretty sad when seeing some crazy tourist lady is the highlight of my day, eh?' Waffles ignored him, maybe out of solidarity with her gender. Instead she occupied herself by getting comfortable on the passenger seat, then stuck her nose out the window.

It only took Clayton five minutes to make it to the Rousse farm. As his car juddered over the newly graded gravel track leading to Beth's cottage, he wondered what he was going to say to her – well, other than *Here's your stuff.*

He was still mulling over the issue when he spotted Jeff's car fast approaching the cottage from the other direction. Cheeky bastard was off to check out the new woman too.

He made sure Jeff saw his disapproving frown as he drove by, and damned if his best mate didn't speed up and cut him off with a smarmy grin before casually extending his hand out his car window and giving him the finger as he left him in the dust.

'Bastard,' Clayton muttered to himself. Pulling up just behind

Jeff moments later, he repeated the insult, this time to his mate's face.

'Dunno what you're talking about.' Jeff ran a hand over his closely shaven head, his eyes wide with feigned innocence. 'I'm just here to see if all the electrical and plumbing works. As a concerned owner of the property, you understand.'

Clayton snorted. 'Yeah, right. Desperate owner of the property, more like it.'

'Looked in the mirror lately?'

'Yeah, and I don't see a sorry bugger like you looking back at me.'

Still ribbing each other, they walked around to the front of the cottage only to stop short at the sight that greeted them.

The English woman, Beth, was fast asleep on a cane deckchair at the far end of the porch. Her head was slumped forward, sharp little chin resting on her chest and one hand loosely hanging down next to an empty glass, and a perspiring bottle of wine sitting on the deck by her side. The last of the afternoon sun was casting her creamy skin and dishevelled cropped hair in a warm gold glow.

Clayton's first thought, taking in her bright red, very short dress, was that she definitely wasn't wearing baggy winter clothes today. His second thought was that she seemed fragile, like one of his grandma's old porcelain dolls.

'Reckon we should wake her?' Jeff whispered loud enough for aliens in the next solar system to hear.

Clayton's eyebrows beetled ominously. 'Don't be an idiot. She's here to relax and chill out, and seeing your ugly mug will give her the shock of her life. I'm gonna leave her stuff on the porch and go, which is what you're gonna do too.' He tried to keep his voice low, but he'd never been good at whispering either and his volume rivalled Jeff's. The fact that their rabbiting on hadn't even budged the lady showed just how tired she was.

He gently placed the jack and the wrench on the edge of the porch and stepped away.

'What're you doing? You're passing up a good opportunity here!' Jeff whisper-bellowed, elbowing him in the ribs, still eyeballing Beth.

'Did you eat an extra bowl of stupid for breakfast this morning, mate? What the hell are you talking about?'

Jeff didn't get a chance to reply because Waffles chose that moment to finish up her inspection of Beth's Corolla and waddle around to the front of the cottage. Spotting a new human with tummy-rubbing potential, she padded over the porch and shoved her wet nose against Beth's leg.

The effect was immediate. With a sharply inhaled breath and a loudly exhaled shriek, Beth went from a luxuriously dreamless sleep to a very real nightmare. Heart racing, she bunched her legs up on her chair, fully expecting to find the source of an impending mauling, poisoning or puncturing. Instead she met the intelligent eyes of a young, heavily pregnant dog. An Australian blue heeler if she was correct.

'Who are you?' she asked with a voice scratchy from sleep and receding panic.

The dog answered her by panting aromatically, tongue lolling out the side of its mouth.

'Her name's Waffles,' a strangely familiar male voice replied.

'Waffles,' Beth repeated faintly. Saying the name out loud earned her a doggy head in her lap. She unthinkingly reached down and gave it a scratch.

Remembering that the voice had to have come from somewhere, Beth twisted around in her chair to see the man who'd changed her tyre standing at the edge of her porch. He appeared somewhat abashed, his expression serious. Next to him was an equally weather-beaten, much more wiry but no less handsome farmer type.

This new fellow had short-cropped, flaming red hair instead of brown curls and was wearing a grin that could only be described as cheeky with a capital C. She recognised that expression – it was the exact face one of her most adored and dreaded clients, Rupert the Jack Russell terrier, pulled right after terrorising all the cats in his owner's house and cocking his leg on the sofa.

'Hi there. M'name's Jeff. I'm Laura's brother.' His pale blue eyes, identical to his sister's, shone with repressed naughtiness.

Yes, definitely a Jack Russell.

'Hello. I'm Beth.' She smiled at Jeff and then glanced back at her saviour from the day before. Clayton.

Oh, he was definitely a different breed to his friend. He was quieter and seemed more thoughtful . . . built on a broader scale . . . friendly? Definitely, given the way he'd changed her tyre. Intelligent? She wasn't sure about that yet, but something told her he was. That would make him a working dog probably, like the blue heeler at Beth's feet, which had to be his.

'Pleased to meet you, Jeff, and nice to see you again, Clayton.' The latter was an understatement if the butterflies in Beth's stomach were any indication. She was surprised she'd remembered his name. She was terrible with human names. Dog names weren't a problem but humans had always defeated her. She realised both men were watching her expectantly.

Her eyes alighted on the tools sitting on the edge of the porch.

'Oh! You returned them. Thank you so much! I'm terribly sorry for my rudeness yesterday. It must have been the jet lag. You've saved me a lot of trouble two days running now. I was getting worried I'd have to replace them and I don't know the first thing about tools. I'd probably buy the wrong ones.' Was she babbling? Oh bugger, she never babbled. And where were her manners? 'Would you gentlemen like a drink of something? I think the wine here is still cold, and I have some beer in the fridge.'

'I'd love a beer.' Jeff stepped onto the porch and held out a hand. 'Need help getting up there?' His eyes sparkled with mischief, standing out dramatically in his deeply tanned face, which had no doubt once featured freckles before the sun got to them and blurred them all together.

'Thank you.' Beth took his hand, allowing him to pull her up. 'I'll have my hand back now, thank you.'

He released it slowly with an unrepentant grin. Definitely a joker. She peered around his shoulder to address the other man on the porch, the one who sent her pulse racing. 'Can I get you a beer too?'

'That would be great, thanks.' His voice had the sort of timbre that carried – presumably a necessity in such big spaces. Beth couldn't help but notice that he was frowning at his friend with an intensity that should have ignited Jeff's already flaming red hair.

Unaccustomed to being in close proximity to so much testosterone, Beth found herself auto-piloting on some obscure reservoir of inbuilt politeness. 'Okay. Well, then. All right. If you could just move aside, please take a seat out here, I'll get your drinks.' She unsteadily inched past Jeff, only to awkwardly bump into Clayton on the way to the door.

She immediately inhaled the same scent she'd noticed while he changed her tyre. Earthy, masculine and very, very appealing. He was so warm. It was hot outside, but not that hot. The man radiated heat like a furnace. Or was that just her? Oh God, was she staring at him like an idiot? She felt her own internal temperature rise a few more degrees due to sheer embarrassment as it dawned on her that she may have drunk a little more than she had intended.

'You gonna move, mate?' Jeff asked Clayton from behind her.

'Sorry. I'll get out of your way.' Clayton shuffled aside to allow her room to open the door. Thanking him with as much dignity as she could muster, Beth straightened her shoulders and marched into the kitchen with only a tiny stumble marring an otherwise sober exit.

She hadn't thought the cottage's porch was small before, but now she wondered if she shouldn't mention to Laura that it had trouble accommodating two fully grown men who weren't tall exactly, no, they were probably only around five foot ten, but between Clayton's shoulders and Jeff's personality . . . no, no, silly idea. Laura was related to one of them, so she'd already know that. Beth unsteadily leaned on the fridge before remembering to open it and extract two beers.

Bottle opener . . . bottle opener . . . She unsuccessfully searched through the kitchen drawers before deciding manly Aussie men like the ones outside must have methods of opening beer that didn't require an artificial aid. She shook her head and sent the room spinning. It had to be the wine. Or maybe it was the heat? Either way, she remembered sitting down to a large glass, or two, before deciding to indulge in a siesta because it was so hot.

Oh God, was she sweating?

Her ex-husband had always commented that she sweated unattractively in the heat. She glanced down, checking her underarms for damp patches. There was no sweat, but she wasn't wearing her usual clothes.

Red dress. Bugger, bugger, bugger! Should she change? She was suddenly extremely aware that she had two of the most handsome – well, maybe not in the conventional sense, and maybe only because they were somewhere close to her age and not a friend of her gran, but still handsome – men she'd met in a non-work situation in years sitting on her porch, and she was showing a good deal of skin.

What would happen if the sun shone at an inopportune moment on her whiter-than-white legs and blinded one of them?

'You need a hand in there, Beth?' The Jack Russell, no, Jeff, called out from the porch.

'No, I'm . . . I'm fine.' Inhaling deeply and steadying herself against the kitchen bench, she reminded herself to act sober before snatching up the beer bottles and venturing outside again.

As she approached the door she was startled to see Clayton holding it open. Had he been watching her wobbly deliberation over the bottle opener in the kitchen? She hoped not.

'Thank you.' She smiled, relieved at how sober she sounded.

'You're welcome.' His mouth curled up at one corner and his eyes crinkled. Beth hoped it was because he was just nice and not because she was making a fool of herself.

'Your bottle of wine was still cold, so I poured you another glass,' Jeff said from where he was lounging on the recliner Beth had just vacated. He was holding out the bulbous wine glass she'd been drinking from. It was full to the brim, the outside already dripping with perspiration.

'I don't think I'll need that much, but thank you.' Beth blinked, her voice wavering. She was very aware of Clayton standing behind her, only a few inches away. She briefly closed her eyes to pull herself together but opened them again when she felt dizzy. It definitely wouldn't be smart to drink that glass of wine.

'You right there?' Clayton put his hands on her shoulders when she swayed backwards.

'Oh! Yes, yes, fine, thank you.' She tottered forward, pulling nervously away from his touch, and put the beers on the table. 'Why are you . . . why are you gentlemen here? Thank you.' She accepted the glass from Jeff and sat down heavily on one of the two remaining chairs, crossing her legs at the knee and trying to surreptitiously stretch the red dress down as far as it could go.

'Oh, I just thought I'd make sure everything's all right with the plumbing, the electrical and stuff,' Jeff answered, opening both his and Clayton's beers with a bottle opener on his key ring.

'They're fine.' Beth gave him a reassuring smile, but he wasn't looking at her. Instead he was mouthing the word *What?* over her head with his eyes open wide.

Beth twisted around to see Clayton frowning again. He was seated awkwardly on the remaining spare chair with his elbows propped on his knees. The thought occurred to her that the sight was somewhat incongruous. A man like him shouldn't be sitting on one of those things. He should be . . . be . . . Beth paused mentally . . . picking up cows and throwing them over his shoulder with his bare hands. Yes. That made perfect sense. She wasn't sozzled at all.

'Good to hear,' Jeff said, drawing her mind back to the conversation. Plumbing. Yes, that was it.

Beth took a sip of her wine before remembering she wasn't going to have any more. Maybe a little more wouldn't hurt after all. 'I think it's quite lovely here. You're both very lucky to be living in the area. Where I come from the grass never completely turns yellow like this and we certainly couldn't make wine this good. Scotch, yes. Further north of course, but wine? Sadly no. That's left for much warmer climates.'

'Where are you from?' Clayton asked.

'Me? I'm from the south of England originally, Somerset. But now I live in a small village. Well, not *that* small. It's a market village called Skipton, in Yorkshire. I train dogs,' Beth blurted then beamed.

'You're a dog trainer?' Clayton's eyebrows rose until they were hidden by a hank of curly brown hair.

'Yes. Usually to correct behavioural problems, but on rare occasions, when I'm lucky, I get to train a working dog like this lady here. She's pregnant, isn't she?' Beth gestured to Waffles, who sat panting at her feet.

'Yeah. Almost due,' Clayton replied with obvious pride.

'So, Beth, how long are you here for?' Jeff interjected. He was playing impatiently with the cap from his beer bottle.

'I've booked for one month but I might stay two,' Beth replied shyly. 'As I told your sister earlier, I'm just here for a bit of quiet to relax and unwind.'

'Peace and quiet. Hear that, mate?' Clayton rumbled from behind her.

'Yeah, but you'll want to see the sights and explore a bit, won't you? No point coming all this way otherwise, eh?' Jeff asked, ignoring his friend.

Unsure what was going on between the two men, Beth kept her gaze on Jeff. 'You might have a point, yes. Your sister has kindly offered —'

'Laura's pretty busy a lot of the time,' Jeff said cheerfully. 'How about I show you around? Things are quiet right now. Not much going on.'

There was a snorting noise from Clayton but Beth ignored it. 'Oh. That's nice of you, but —'

'Great. How about I pick you up tomorrow? The day after? When's good for you? Clayton here was probably gonna offer, but he's pretty busy at the winery.'

'Winery?' Beth looked from Jeff to Clayton.

'You're currently drinking a bottle of our best.'

'Really?' Beth took another sip and then realised she'd almost finished the entire glass. It just went down so easily in this heat.

'Yeah. I can show you around and give you a private wine tasting if you'd like. It's the least I can do for Jeff, since he's such a good mate.' For some reason the latter was said with a pointed glance at Jeff.

Since she was occupied with staring at her glass wondering how she'd managed to drink so much in so little time, it took Beth a while to process Clayton's offer. When she did, she realised there was no way she could refuse. She'd never been on a wine tour and it wasn't as if she had planned anything for her stay yet.

'That would be brilliant,' she beamed. 'I know nothing about wine but I'd love to learn.'

'Great. If you'd like me to give you a tour it's gonna have to be tomorrow afternoon. My sister is the chef at our restaurant, Evangeline's, and I might be able to get her to rustle up some tapas.' Clayton's mouth curved into a smile that completely transformed his craggy features, making him appear more boyish.

'Wonderful,' Beth said faintly. He really was very handsome. Well, if you liked men who looked like they wrestled cows in their spare time.

'Yeah, anyway, about being shown around —' Jeff cut in.

'Oh, the day after tomorrow would work just as well, wouldn't it, eh, mate? Since I'm so busy it'd be a shame for Beth here to miss out on taking advantage of me being available,' Clayton interjected smoothly.

Beth's eyes flicked from one man to the other like a spectator at a tennis match. There was obviously something going on. If she wasn't mistaken, both of them wanted her company, but that was ridiculous. No, no, it had to be something else she wasn't aware of, and right now she was far too relaxed to put her mind to it.

A yawn escaped before she could catch it and she quickly covered her mouth.

'You're tired, Beth. How about we go? I'll come pick you up tomorrow at three?' Clayton's expression was concerned.

'That would be lovely.' Beth stifled another yawn and up-ended her glass to catch the last drop. Her eyes really didn't want to stay open. 'Gentleman, while this all sounds just wonderful, I'm very tired. If you'll excuse me, I need to sleep again. Thank you.'

Without waiting for their reply, she stood up, caught herself before she stumbled, then wobbled into the cottage, blearily searching for the door to her bedroom.

She felt incredibly tired. So tired she didn't even bother to try to understand the exchange she distantly heard between her two unexpected visitors still sitting on the porch.

'You're an idiot. Why'd you pour her that huge glass of wine? She's tiny. That one glass was probably the equivalent of three or four for you and me. We should have left her alone.'

'You mean *your dog* should have left her alone.'

'And what's with the tour-guide crap?'

'What's with the wine-tour crap?'

'Fuck off, mate. Anyway, you owe me a beer. I haven't got halfway through this one and we can't stay here.'

'Done . . . my place.'

'Yeah. I'll meet you there.'

Chapter 4

Clayton spent a pleasant hour enjoying a beer on Jeff's porch before returning to his family's sprawling rammed-earth home.

He still wore a faint smile as he opened the front door, but it slid off at the familiar sound of raised voices.

'*That's just selfish, Mum. Did you ever once think of me?*'

Yelling, bellowing and generally trying to break the sound barrier were normal forms of communication in the Hardy household, but the sound of a door slamming and his father's impassioned tone indicated that this might be one of those rare instances where a genuine argument was taking place.

The noise was coming from the kitchen, so Clayton detoured into the large living room off the entrance hall, thinking he'd hide out there for a few minutes until he'd gauged the lay of the land. It was immediately apparent his younger brother, Stephen, had come up with the same idea.

Either oblivious or just plain impervious to the drama in the kitchen, Stephen was lounging in a green plaid recliner with his blond, pretty-boy features scrunched up with a frown as he read through a bunch of papers in his hand. Clayton recognised Evangeline's Rest's latest sales report.

'What's up with the racket?' Clayton asked and then raised his voice to ask again to get Stephen's attention.

'What?' It took a few seconds for Stephen to focus on Clayton standing in the doorway.

'The noise, mate. What's with World War Three in the kitchen?' Clayton asked, just as Angie's voice raised in high dudgeon answered his question.

'I don't have to answer to you, Robert Hardy! I have as much ownership in this bloody operation as you do, and if I want to hire Gwen Stone, I'll hire Gwen Stone! Deal with it, boyo!' It was widely acknowledged in the household that the ability to vocalise anything at high volume came from Angie's side of the family.

'Boyo?' Clayton mouthed at Stephen.

'Ouch.'

They shared a mutual grimace.

Angie only reverted to her far distant Irish ancestry and called their dad 'boyo' when she was deathly furious and going for the jugular.

Rob was fifty-two years old and as proud and stubborn as a constipated prize mule. Unfortunately he usually reacted to any criticism by digging in his heels and trying to convince his kids to support his cause over Angie's. It never worked. Rob always lost because no one wanted to be on Angie's bad side.

Clayton sighed. 'I should have stayed at Jeff's.'

Stephen nodded, turning back to the sales projections as his cat, Boomba, waddled into the room and jumped onto his lap, immediately beginning to purr. 'Would've been smart. I'd take a seat and wait it out if I were you.'

'Yeah, I think I will.' Clayton parked himself on a brown leather couch and pulled his socks off, his ear cocked to the kitchen door as his father started to roar again.

'*Get off your high horse, Mum! If you wanted to take things easier, you should have told me! Or Les or Clayton or Stephen. I thought one of the main deals in this operation was that we discuss important decisions.*'

'*Hiring someone to work part-time at the cellar door is in no way important, Robert,*' Angie thundered back. '*I don't know what your problem with Gwen is. You've had it in for her for years. It's time to get over it. You're a grown man, for God's sake! Act like one.*'

'Jesus Christ. She's really hitting below the belt.' Stephen's brow furrowed in disapproval.

Clayton nodded in agreement. He didn't even want to contemplate what working and living with his dad would be like if Gwen Stone was employed by Evangeline's Rest.

For reasons his dad had refused to discuss, even the mere mention of Gwen Stone's name caused Rob Hardy to foam at the mouth. It didn't make sense, but no one had ever been able to find out why he hated her so much. Rob and Gwen were the same age, had grown up in the same district. In fact, Gwen had even been his mum's bridesmaid when his parents had got married straight out of high school at eighteen. As unlikely as it seemed now, Clayton had vague memories of Gwen and his dad being friends when he was a kid. Then it had all changed. But Clayton's mum had died twenty-nine years ago, when he was five. Surely that was more than long enough for Rob to get over whatever Gwen had done to get his goat?

The string of expletives coming from the kitchen was enough to indicate that it obviously wasn't.

Momentarily tuning out his dad, Clayton turned back to Stephen, whose girlfriend was nowhere in sight. 'Jo isn't trying to sleep, is she?'

'Yeah. She's still not over her cold. Although I don't think much sleep is happening right now.'

'Hope she's feeling better soon,' Clayton replied. He had a huge soft spot for Jo. She was good for Stephen, and her former profession as an engineer working on offshore oil rigs, added to her having grown up on Evangeline's Rest as their former farmhand's daughter, had left her tough enough not to take any of his family's melodramatic crap.

'So do I.' Stephen glared at the door connecting the living room to the kitchen before turning to face Clayton. 'Laura Rousse dropped by this afternoon.'

'Yeah?' Clayton winced at the sound of cupboards being banged shut in the next room as punctuation to Angie's renewed attack on Rob.

'I don't have time for this, Robert. I raised you better than this. Who do you think you are, telling me what to do?'

Stephen continued. 'She mentioned that you helped her guest out when her car got a flat.' There was an unspoken question in his words.

'Yeah. Her name's Beth,' Clayton supplied. 'I'm giving her a wine tour tomorrow afternoon.'

'Yeah? Laura mentioned she was a bit of a looker. English, eh?' Stephen's eyes crinkled in a sly smile, which changed to a grimace when there was another loud crash from the kitchen and Rob's raised voice shook the walls.

'So, you care for your friends more than your own son? Nice to know where I stand, then!'

'Yeah,' Clayton said, ignoring his father and frowning at Stephen so he wouldn't keep asking questions.

'Fair enough.' Stephen shrugged.

'Sweet Jesus, Mary, Joseph and a donkey! What the hell's going on over here?!' Rachael Hardy, Stephen's twin and Clayton's younger sister, exclaimed from the living-room doorway. With her long curly brown hair and curvaceous figure clad in chef's whites, Rachael resembled a culinary-inclined Renaissance Madonna ready to do battle. The impression was aided immeasurably by the huge wooden spoon she was grasping in one fist and the furious gleam in her large, deep-brown eyes.

'I can hear Dad and Angie going off at each other from the bloody restaurant! We've got paying customers trying to eat in there and I don't think listening to banging doors and screaming aids digestion.' She punctuated the last statement by waving the spoon threateningly in the air. 'Are either of you going to do anything about this?'

Clayton and Stephen looked at each other, then at Rachael as if she were a screw short of a meccano set. 'Nope,' they replied in unison.

'For Christ's sake.' Rachael stomped past them both and jerked open the kitchen door just as Rob yelled over the top of his mother.

'*That's your problem, Mum, you never listen.*'

Angie didn't get a chance to reply, because Rachael's irate bellow drowned them both out.

'IF YOU TWO DON'T QUIET THINGS DOWN, WE'RE NOT GOING TO HAVE A BLOODY BUSINESS TO BE ARGUING OVER!'

She was met with a momentary stunned silence while everyone waited for their hearing to return before Rob and Angie started to yell again, this time trying to convince Rachael to take sides. They shouldn't have bothered.

Within seconds Rachael had bawled them both into submission, giving them a high-volume lecture on professionalism and common courtesy that could no doubt be heard in the next farm district.

Stephen and Clayton listened for a while in admiration and shared amusement before pasting on solemn expressions as Rachael stormed past them on her way back to the restaurant.

It wasn't long before Rob and Angie resumed their argument

again, this time in hushed, angry whispers.

Clayton ran a hand over his eyes, suddenly feeling exhausted. God, his family was painful. What he wouldn't give for one day, just *one* day, of peace and quiet. His house couldn't be finished soon enough.

Beth squinted muzzily out the kitchen window at a brilliant blue sky blanketing yellow land. She risked a smile.

She was hung-over. It was a novel experience.

It was also rather comforting to learn the world hadn't ended just because she'd had a little too much to drink. Not that she planned on doing it again in a hurry, but she had to admit she'd loved sitting on the porch, sipping wine and dozing off. Contrary to Beth's expectations, Violet and Louis had been on the money with her birthday present this year. This surprise holiday was working out nicely so far.

She waited for the kettle to boil, made herself a cup of truly awful instant coffee and contemplated what to do for the day. 'Maybe we'll go for a walk, Charlie —' she said before her smile turned rueful. No doubt Charlie would appreciate the sentiment. Right now he'd be happily curled up snoring next to his radiator in Yorkshire. As for her . . . maybe she could explore the countryside around the cottage. She loved being outdoors and spent most of her days on her feet in the elements. It was hot here, but she could get used to that . . .

The numerous terrifying images from *Australia's Most Dangerous Creatures* flittered across her mind in a slide show of hissing snakes and dripping-fanged spiders. No, on second thought, too many poisonous . . . everything, but there were plenty of other options available to her if the trip out and about with Laura yesterday was any indication.

Selecting a few of the brochures Laura had left on the coffee table, Beth wandered outside with her coffee in hand. Smiling contentedly, she breathed in a lungful of sun-baked air, took in the view, then promptly wheezed it out again when she spotted her missing car jack and wrench sitting on the edge of the porch.

'Oh bugger.' The headache she'd been ignoring ramped up a notch as the events of the previous evening paraded in an orderly, if not hazy, fashion across the backs of her eyelids.

She vaguely remembered receiving a visit from Clayton, the one who made her legs shaky, and another man . . . Jeff? Why was she thinking of a Jack Russell terrier? They'd talked about England, and her job and something else . . . She rubbed her temples. What *had* they talked about and why couldn't she remember? She hadn't drunk *that* much, surely. But she did recall feeling tired, extremely tired.

It must have been the jet lag catching up with her. That had to be it. She was notoriously useless without eight hours' sleep, and she'd been under quota for half a week now.

Had she said anything silly? She had no idea how she acted when drunk, or when tired for that matter, never having been the former and never really been awake enough to remember the latter. There had been something about a wine tour, or had she imagined that? Had she been polite? She'd be mortified if she'd managed to be rude to Clayton for the second time since meeting him, when both times he'd been doing her a good turn.

She experienced a few moments of sheer panic before her ingrained pragmatism took over. She'd never been self-indulgent in the past or inclined to wallow in worry and anxiety, and she wasn't about to start now.

Instead she'd finish her coffee, run herself a bath and wait to see what happened.

Clayton was just about to leave the house when Angie's voice stopped him.

'You're a bit dressed up, love. Anything I should know about?' She was sitting at the large knotty pine table in the spacious country kitchen that had been the beating heart of the Hardy household since Clayton's grandfather built the sprawling farmhouse in the early sixties. *The George Creek Tribune* was laid out in front of her, and her rectangular wire-framed reading glasses sat halfway down her nose as she ran her eyes over Clayton's freshly ironed pale blue shirt and tan chinos.

Clayton shifted uncomfortably from one foot to the other. He wondered for the third time if he was going overboard with the chinos, but decided that Beth wouldn't know they were out of character, even if his family did take the piss out of him for dressing up.

'Got a hot date with a sheep, mate?' His dad entered the house through the kitchen door before stepping straight back outside and taking off his boots in response to Angie's evil eye.

'Robert Michael Hardy,' Angie snapped. As expected, she'd gained the upper hand and won yesterday's argument.

'Mum.' Rob scowled like a kid instead of the successful farmer and businessman he was. 'Sorry,' he mumbled to Clayton, then gave him a glare that said no comment would be welcome.

Feeling charitable, Clayton just grunted and nodded.

His father nodded in return as he wandered to the fridge, and before long, sounds of rattling and swearing reached Angie and Clayton's ears.

'Mum! Where's the bread?'

'In the bread bin where it always is,' Angie replied, glaring at her son. She flicked her long, white plait over her shoulder so that it rested against her blue chambray shirt. At almost six foot tall, and fit from working on the farm her entire life, Angie rarely dressed in anything but jeans and plain T-shirts. She'd been the only mother figure Clayton could really remember, and years of experience told him that Rob was going to get himself a clout around the ear if he didn't watch himself.

'Where's the bread bin, then?' Rob asked, now rummaging in a cupboard, probably on purpose.

Taking one look at Angie's narrowed eyes, Clayton decided it was time to go before he became a part of today's rematch.

'I'll be bringing someone by the cellar door a bit later, Angie. Can you keep Dad off my back and give Rach a word up about a tasting plate or two?' He kept his voice low so his dad couldn't hear.

'Oh?' Angie raised an eyebrow. 'Does someone have a name?'

'Beth.' Clayton dropped a kiss on the top of her head before walking out the door. 'Oh yeah,' he said as he stopped to put his boots on. 'If Jeff comes by, tell him to piss off.'

'Like that, is it?' Angie asked, eyes crinkling.

'Where's the bloody butter?'

'Gotta go. Bye.' Clayton walked to his car, whistling for Waffles as the sound of Angie telling Rob exactly where he could find his bloody butter rang out across the yard behind him.

Beth was curled up in an armchair reading a book when she heard a car pull up outside her cottage. She'd barely had time to pull a robe over her pyjamas when there was a knock on the door.

Over the course of the day, memories from the previous afternoon had become a little less fuzzy, to the point she could almost fully recall agreeing to a wine tour.

Unfortunately, she couldn't remember if it was Clayton or Jeff who had invited her or what time they'd agreed on. In the end she'd decided the best thing to do was just wait to see what happened. By the sound of it, it was all happening now at her front door.

'Just a minute,' she called, quickly running a hand through her hair and adjusting her robe so it wouldn't be so clingy.

'Take your time,' a deep, booming voice called back.

That answered one of her questions.

'Clayton?' Beth opened the door and was greeted by a solid male chest. She peered upwards. Clayton wasn't wearing the baseball cap he'd worn on both occasions she'd seen him previously. His curly brown hair was damp like he'd just stepped out of the shower, a supposition that was collaborated by the clean scent of soap.

An impeccably ironed blue shirt stretched across his shoulders, and his tree-trunk legs were concealed by a well-fitting pair of trousers. His shoes were . . . oh damn . . . she was staring. Beth quickly raised her eyes, her cheeks heating with embarrassment.

'Ah . . . hi.' Clayton gave her a slow smile that left her weak at the knees.

'I'm sorry, but I'm not dressed yet,' Beth blurted.

'Yeah. I noticed that. Sorry I'm a bit early. It's a good time to get to the cellar door, though. All the tour buses have already been through.' He rammed his hands in his pockets, his cheeks flushing a dull red. 'We don't have to go if you don't want to. I know I sorta pushed you into things yesterday.'

'No!' Beth exclaimed loudly, then caught herself. 'If you just make yourself comfortable for a few minutes, I'll get ready. Take a seat. I won't take long.' She looked around for inspiration. She couldn't remember the last time she'd been alone like this with a single man her age. She'd forgotten what to do with one.

'Just, erm . . . just make yourself some tea or coffee if you like. I'll only be a moment.' She waved in the direction of the kitchen before beating a hasty retreat to her bedroom, accidentally slamming the door behind her.

'You are a hopeless case. Simply bloody hopeless,' she hissed to herself while frantically scrambling through her suitcase for something, anything, to wear before turning to the bags of clothes she'd dropped on the floor last night. She'd have to wear something new, but for the life of her she had no idea what.

Her new clothes were a lot more complicated than her usual loose-fitting shirts and trousers, and everything was suddenly far, far too short and tight. After an internal debate of the kind not seen outside of disarmament talks in the Middle East, she finally decided on a flowing white maxi dress printed with vivid pink and blue flowers. Laura had said it made her look pretty, and, most importantly, it was easy to put on in a hurry.

She opened her bedroom door and was about to venture back out to the kitchen when she felt the scratch of a price tag against her back.

'Bugger.' She reached around to pull it off while quickly peeking out at Clayton, who was sitting at the kitchen table thumbing through the *Lonely Planet Australia* she'd left there. The tag proved stubborn, so she began to search through her suitcase for her manicure set. Instead, she found her make-up bag, which gave her pause.

Should she put on some mascara and lipstick? More importantly, had she brought any with her? She deliberated, trying to find them, then changed her mind and resumed her search for her nail scissors, only to admit defeat when she found her manicure set empty of everything but a nail file with a cracked plastic handle.

'Everything all right in there?' Clayton called out just as she'd decided to enlist his help. It was a much better option than keeping the poor man waiting for another hour while she flailed at herself.

'No, actually. I could use some help. Can you bring me the scissors from the kitchen drawer?'

'Yeah, sure,' Clayton replied, sounding surprised but not put out. She changed her mind again about the make-up and began to search through her bags again. Surely she'd packed *something*.

'How do you want me to help?'

Beth turned around. Clayton was taking up the doorway, holding a pair of red-handled kitchen scissors in a large, big-knuckled hand.

It was a perfectly innocent question, but still it left her a little wobbly around the knees.

'Tags. I need you to help me cut them off.'

Clayton's brow wrinkled as he looked her up and down. 'Sure. Where are they?'

'The back of my dress.' Beth bridged the small gap between them and presented her back to him. She shouldn't be feeling so nervous. After all, she wouldn't feel like this if it were Louis helping her. Oh, who was she fooling? No one, that's who. Every cell in her body was painfully aware that the man standing behind her wasn't in his eighties, and was, as far as she knew, single.

She waited a few seconds, holding her breath, and then risked a peek over her shoulder. Clayton was surveying her back like it was a foreign country that he didn't have a map for.

'Here.' She reached awkwardly over her shoulder and flicked the offending plastic price tag out from where it had slipped down inside her dress again.

'You want all of them cut off?' The way he asked the question, one would think he'd been asked to perform brain surgery.

'Yes please,' Beth replied. It was still another few awkward seconds before she felt a warm hand briefly brushing against her bare skin, sending an involuntary shiver down her spine. The sound of the scissors snipping was deafening to her overwhelmed senses.

'Done.' Clayton's voice was a low rumble and Beth wasn't sure but she could have sworn she felt a whisper-soft stroke of a finger along her nape. She got goose bumps all the same.

'Thanks.' She turned around to offer him a shy smile and then stepped back, startled to find him still standing close enough for her to know he'd brushed his teeth before coming. He'd shaved, too. She could see the faint shadow of impending dark brown stubble on his chin.

Butterflies jitterbugging in her stomach, she scanned the floor near her feet. 'Now I just need to find my shoes.'

'Are they the ones by the door?'

'Yes,' Beth said, relieved someone was thinking straight. 'You'll have to forgive me, you've taken me a bit unawares. I'm ready now. Would you like to go?'

'Yeah, sure.' He stepped out of her way, walking back into the kitchen. She took the opportunity to quickly spray herself with her favourite perfume, then marched into the kitchen, where Clayton was patiently waiting.

'Shall we go?'

'No worries.' Clayton held the door open.

He radiated a solid calmness, which was strange considering the nerves she was sure she'd detected when he first arrived. It was as if the more flustered she got, the calmer he became.

The minute she stepped onto the porch, she was greeted with a smiling toothy yawn from the dog she'd met the day before.

'Hello, girl. Waffles, wasn't it?' The name-drop earned her a gentle lick on the hand and a slow tail wag. She gave the dog a quick scratch and immediately felt herself relax. She knew where she was with dogs.

'Why Waffles?' she asked Clayton, who'd just pulled her front door shut behind them and was now palming a set of car keys. At the sound of them rattling together, Waffles abandoned Beth and waddled off the porch, no doubt making a beeline for the car.

Clayton looked affectionately at his retreating dog. 'The first day I brought her home from the breeder, when she was about six months old, my sister Rachael was making blueberry waffles for our breakfast. When we weren't looking, the dog jumped up on the kitchen bench and managed to get the batter all over herself. She made a mess of the kitchen and got so gummed up we couldn't get the stuff out of her fur. In the end I just put her on the back of the ute and dumped her in the dam to swim around until it all dissolved.

After that, the name Waffles stuck.'

Beth laughed. 'It's a good thing it wasn't something else you were cooking. I don't know if "Pancakes" or "Omelettes" would have had the same ring to it.'

'Yeah.' Clayton's smiled over his shoulder as he led the way around the cottage to a shiny navy Jeep Wrangler.

'Is this a new car?' Beth asked conversationally, picking up the skirt of her dress and gingerly navigating over the gravel driveway in her new shoes.

'Nah. Just the good one. I only drive it when I'm off work. Otherwise Waffles and I get around in the old ute you saw us in the day you got the flat.'

'Ute? You said it earlier. I take it you're talking about a car?'

'Yeah. Never thought about it, but it's probably Aussie slang, short for utility vehicle,' Clayton said. 'It's a pick-up. Do you call them that in England? I know the Yanks sometimes call them trucks.'

'Oh. Well, now I understand what you mean, I think ute will be fine,' Beth said as Clayton opened the front passenger door for her and then the rear one for Waffles, whom he effortlessly lifted onto the back seat.

'She's finding it a bit harder lately,' he explained, slapping his hands together to remove the fur sticking to them.

'Pregnant ladies do tend to have trouble getting around in the later stages,' Beth said, noting the care he was taking. In her profession she saw too many people who didn't understand how to interact with their dogs. It always warmed her heart to see someone who got it right. It was obvious Waffles and Clayton were lifelong friends.

'Thanks for coming to get me.' She smoothed her dress over her legs as he started the car.

'Wasn't a problem.' Clayton steered the Jeep along a gravel track different to the one she'd used to approach the cottage.

'Is that your land just over there?' She pointed to the distant vineyards.

'Yeah. My place starts at the fence just here. Jeff and I put in a connecting gate a few years back to save ourselves the round trip.' He braked at what appeared to be a normal stretch of fence before getting out and revealing it to be a crude wire gate.

'So, what can you tell me about your winery, Clayton?' Beth asked after they were underway again.

Clayton smiled warmly, revealing a shallow dimple on his cheek. 'Where do you want me to start?'

'How about at the beginning. How long have you been in existence? Your winery, I mean.'

'In answer to the first question I'm thirty-four and in answer to the second, my dad planted the first vines in the early eighties when almost no one else thought wine was a good idea. He didn't put enough in to have a big operation like some of the early wineries in the area, but it was enough to ride on the back of their success. Sometimes I just think Dad put the vines in as a joke that backfired. Now it's turned into the biggest part of our business.' He paused as he swerved around a herd of large black-and-white cows blocking the road.

Beth held on to the edges of her car seat as they bumped over a patch of rocky field before returning to the track.

Clayton glanced over to make sure she was okay before continuing. 'We have the cows still, as you can see. My Uncle Les still runs the dairy and we grow the odd grain crop and run a few sheep, too. We're currently experimenting with marron as well. If that isn't enough, we're building a microbrewery not far away from here, just over that hill. Not that I take care of any of that.'

'Marron?' Beth looked in the direction Clayton had pointed but saw only rolling gold hills dotted with sheep and the odd cow.

'Local freshwater shellfish. Sort of like crayfish, but better in my opinion.'

'Oh? I look forward to trying them. You mentioned a brewery?' Beth peered out the window, distracted by the sight of rows and rows of dusty green grapevines coming up on their left.

'Yeah, my brother and his girlfriend are setting up a microbrewery. Well, Stephen's not doing much, just being a pain in the arse. Jo's doing all the work. She's the chemical engineer. It's her thing mainly. Stephen's our marketing director, so he's going to promote it once it gets up and going.'

'Is Stephen your younger or older brother?' Beth's mind boggled at the thought of there being more men in existence like Clayton.

'Younger by four years. The other one, Mike, is two years younger than me. He lives in your neck of the woods, in London. None of us are too sure what he does there. I've got a sister, Rachael, too. She's Stephen's twin. You'll meet her today. Did I tell you about her last night? She's the chef at our restaurant and is going to put together a few things for you to try with the wine.'

'Wonderful.' Beth didn't want to admit that she couldn't remember in the slightest if Clayton had told her about his sister, but she liked the sound of food.

With the jet lag throwing off her body clock, she'd forgotten to eat lunch and didn't fancy drinking wine on an empty stomach. She didn't want to have a repeat of yesterday. This time she was going to remember every moment, especially since she was harbouring a growing suspicion that Clayton was trying to impress her. It was a novel experience.

She and her ex-husband, Greg, had never bothered with anything really romantic. They had met young and had been short on funds at first, and Greg's idea of romance had been a trip to the local chippie for takeaway fish and chips to eat next to the canal. Beth had been fine with that at the time. She hadn't known any different. After they married, the only place they'd ever gone was the local pub for dinner when Beth was too tired to cook.

She had always wondered what other people did when they went out together. The thought of getting the opportunity to find out with a man like Clayton after everything she'd been through in recent years sent her stomach fluttering with little tendrils of warmth as Clayton continued to tell her about his farm.

'The winery is named after my grandma, Evangeline, or Angie, as everyone calls her. She doesn't answer to anything else. Dad called it Evangeline's Rest because he promised her she could put her feet up and retire when it took off.' He shook his head and Beth glanced at him, curious.

Clayton's mouth curved up at the side. 'You'll meet Angie first up. She's been running the cellar door for the past thirty years and the only way we'll get her to put her feet up for good is with a tranquiliser gun. She's finally decided to hire a part-timer to give her a hand, but we all know she won't give the whole thing up in a hurry.'

Beth smiled at his description. 'What about your mother?'

The smile dimmed. 'She died of cancer when I was five. She was only twenty-three, if you can believe it. Had me just before her nineteenth birthday and was gone only five years later . . . since then it's just been Dad and Angie. My grandfather died before I was born.' The ease with which he spoke contradicted the enormity of what he'd just shared and Beth felt her eyes well up, imagining the devastated little boy he must have once been.

'I'm so sorry for your loss.' She reached out and briefly touched his arm, registering the unfamiliar feel of warm skin and hard muscle. 'I know how hard it is to lose someone like that. I was lucky enough to get two more years with my parents before they died. I still miss them terribly and think about them every day. I lost my sister to cancer only three-and-a-half years ago.' She immediately regretted the words. They were far too intimate. Clayton must have thought so too, because he took some time replying.

'Yeah . . . right.' His voice sounded husky. He cleared his throat. 'We . . . ah . . . we're almost there, so how about I tell you a bit about the grapes we grow and the wines you'll be trying today?'

'I'd like that,' Beth said, relieved at the change of topic. Her hand flexed in her lap as the feel of him reverberated over her fingertips. 'It's probably a sin to admit this, but I know absolutely nothing about wine. I've never really had a chance to drink much over the past few years and before that, well, I didn't really get a chance then either.' She laughed self-consciously. 'I probably seem a complete philistine to someone like you.'

'Not at all. To tell you the truth, it's nice. Angie will tell you that the most painful people to have around are the ones who don't know a bloody thing but try to act like they do. Personally I find a lot of the talk about wine to be pretty pretentious. When it all comes down to it, it's all about what you like.'

Beth nodded in agreement, momentarily distracted by the view out the window. They had been driving between grapevines for the past few minutes and now pulled up in front of a beautiful earth-coloured building surrounded by rose bushes in full bloom. Their blowsy red flowers were startlingly vivid against the backdrop of green lawn and vines. There was a large car park behind the building but it was nearly empty with the exception of a campervan and a faded grey Nissan Pulsar.

On the other side of the car park was another vast expanse of green lawn leading to a sprawling single-storey house with a wide, welcoming wraparound porch and a green corrugated-iron roof. Beth wondered briefly if this was Clayton's home and then returned her attention to their conversation.

'So, if I understand you correctly, you'll be content with my company as long as I compliment your wine?'

Clayton's mouth curved in a slow smile. 'Yeah. I think I'll make do.' He held her gaze for just long enough to send her pulse racing, before climbing out of the car and walking around to open Beth's door before she had a chance to do it herself.

'Thank you.' Beth stepped down from the car. 'This *is* a novel experience.'

'I'm guessing you don't have a whole lot of wineries where you're from.' Clayton closed the door behind her before letting Waffles out the back.

'No, I mean having my car door opened for me,' Beth said, then regretted mentioning it when Clayton's expression turned serious.

'If that kind of thing offends you I wasn't intending —'

'No. No, I wasn't being sarcastic. Just teasing. I should have said it's a nice experience. It's lovely to see proper manners,' she corrected hastily. 'The only other man I know who opens doors for women is my gran's husband, Louis, who is a complete gentleman. I was giving you a compliment. Really, I was.'

Thankfully, Waffles chose that moment to sit down on Beth's foot, effectively breaking the tension.

'I'm afraid you're going to have to move,' Beth told the dog, gently but firmly nudging Waffles away so that she got the message that the little display of dominance wasn't going to go unchecked.

'Com'ere,' Clayton commanded sternly, patting his leg.

'Are you referring to me or the dog?' Beth asked and was relieved when he didn't take her teasing the wrong way. Some time in the past few minutes she'd relaxed more than she had in years, maybe since before her parents died. She felt an inexplicable, overwhelming urge to tease and prod Clayton a little, maybe to see if there was a naughty little boy hiding somewhere under his serious facade.

'The dog, I think.' Clayton gave her a wink, then turned and gestured for her to walk ahead of him down a path leading to the smaller building. To one side a discreet sign above a glass door said *Evangeline's*, and Beth caught a brief glimpse of a beautifully decorated restaurant painted in warm Tuscan colours before Clayton guided her to the other end of the building.

'This is our cellar door.' He held open another door decorated in melded glass gum blossoms.

'Thank you.' Feeling adventurous, Beth skirted past him into a small, cool, airy room and the welcoming scent of furniture polish and red wine.

Chapter 5

Swearing under his breath, Rob Hardy stomped out of the house, pulled on his battered dusty work boots, then stalked across the spiky lawn separating his home and the Evangeline's Rest cellar door.

He was in a bitch of a mood. Angie had imperiously declared over breakfast that Gwen Stone would be working her first shift this afternoon, and he was damned if he'd have that woman on his property.

He'd never expected his mum to shiv him in the back like this. In hiring Gwen she had gone too far. Too. Bloody. Far. She should have let him know she wanted to go part-time and he would've happily hired someone from town. After all, he and his kids had been trying to get her to take things easy for years.

Instead she'd arranged for Gwen Stone to take over her job without a word to him, other than telling him things had already been decided. *Gwen bloody Stone*, who was so stuck up her own backside she needed a glass belly button to see anything, would be turning up for work at Evangeline's Rest every day of the week the whole year round and he couldn't do a thing about it.

Growling in frustration, he aimed a vicious kick at a half-chewed dog bone and rammed a large callused hand through his thickly curling hair before shoving open the cellar door. He was ready for war.

'And this is our sauvignon blanc. It should be crisp on the palate with a hint of green grass and apples.' Angie poured Beth a generous sample of wine and then an equally generous one each for Clayton, Gwen and herself.

'Oh. This is nice,' Beth breathed, taking the entire process seriously. She swirled her wine around the glass, sniffing and sipping it just like Angie had shown her. She then bowed her head to study the tasting notes sitting on the rough-hewn pine bar stretching the length of the room.

Clayton shot back his sample without ceremony and returned Angie's covert wink over Beth's bowed head.

'It's not bad.' He shrugged and took a minute to appreciate Beth's compact backside covered in that somehow sexy sack of a dress she was wearing. She was barely a handful. Normally he went for women he wouldn't be scared about breaking, but there was something about Beth, something he couldn't quite put his finger on. One minute she was as jumpy as a cat in a cleaver factory, the next minute playful, and the minute after that throwing him a loop like she had in the car.

He'd nearly embarrassed himself and choked up when she'd offered sympathy over his mum. He had no idea where his reaction came from and he wasn't sure he liked it, but he definitely liked Beth.

'You're onto a winner with this one, kiddo,' Gwen murmured in a low undertone, leaning over the bar towards him, her pale green eyes sparkling with mischief.

As usual she looked like a cross between someone's pear-shaped fairy godmother and the wicked witch of the west. Her short, salt-and-pepper blonde hair was spiked up in a jagged halo, and the deep dimples in her apple cheeks and her toothy grin spoke of an indomitable goodwill. The impression was only emphasised by the loose shamrock-green silk shirt she had on.

Clayton nodded while going back to admiring Beth. 'Might be.'

'So, can I assume you've been leading me on all these years, then?'

'Gwen. The minute you give me the hint, I'm all yours,' he replied with gravity.

'Watch it, I might take you up on that.'

The sound of the door banging open interrupted both Clayton's comeback and Angie's description of the white port she'd just poured.

Clayton turned towards the door and suppressed a groan. Jesus Christ and his heavenly disciples. Was it too much to hope for to *not* have a family drama today of all days?

Clayton's dad stood just inside the doorway. If Rob's expression didn't give away his mood, the tic in his jaw did. Bloody hell.

Angie and Beth were caught up in a conversation about cellaring and ignored Rob's presence at first, but they certainly noticed when he finally found his voice.

'I want her gone. *Now*,' Rob all but roared, pointing at Gwen with a work-roughened finger, his eyes narrowed.

'Robert. It's nice to see you as always,' Gwen replied calmly, smoothly pre-empting Clayton and Angie's angry responses.

'Nothing nice about it. I want you gone.' Rob fronted up to the bar and loomed over Gwen. To Gwen's credit, she held her ground. Only her hand tightening on the glass she was holding gave away any sign of discomfort.

'Manners, son of mine,' Angie snapped, finally getting over

her shock at this unexpected and uncharacteristically rude public confrontation.

Obviously disoriented by this abrupt turn of events, Beth looked from Angie to Rob and then to Clayton as she set the glass of port she'd just been given on the counter.

Clayton felt fucking mortified. The words could barely begin to describe his level of embarrassment, so he opted to take action instead. He cleared his throat noisily then grasped his dad's forearm in a vice grip. It was either that or invent a new form of profanity specifically tailored to idiotic family members. Clayton knew that his father would feel awful about his behaviour once he calmed down, but Rob Hardy worked up was like a bull elephant on the rampage.

'Dad.' He spoke in a low voice charged with a warning that echoed in the tense, silent room. 'I'd like you to meet Beth. She's from England. I'm showing her around the winery today. She's staying up in one of Jeff and Laura's cottages.'

There was an awkward pause, then Beth held out her hand. 'Nice to meet you . . .'

'Beth, was it?' Rob took her hand in a grip that would have served him better if he were operating a pump.

Beth nodded, retrieving her hand. 'Yes.'

'What do you do?'

Beth looked momentarily speechless, but then managed, 'I'm a dog trainer —'

'Own your own business?'

'Ah, yes. I do.'

Rob loomed over her. 'So, being a business owner, would you say a part-owner of an organisation should get a say in who works for them?'

'Dad.' Clayton said in a low warning murmur.

'Well, I . . . well, yes, that does sound reasonable,' Beth said, looking from the now triumphantly bristling Rob, to Gwen to Angie, whose expression looked like it was carved out of teak.

'See!' Rob thumped the bar with his fist. 'A reasonable business owner who hasn't drunk whatever crazy juice you lot have been on can see the sense in this. I don't want her here. I'm part-owner. She shouldn't be here. End of story!' He jabbed a finger at Gwen.

'Calm down, Dad. Now is not the time. Angie, Beth and I —' Clayton began what was about to be an appeal to his grandma but he realised too late that Volcano Angie was about to blow. Her sharp cheekbones were flushed red with anger and she was gripping the neck of a port bottle in a manner that implied she would like to see it smashed over her idiotic son's head.

'Robert Hardy. There are days when I wonder why I didn't ask the doctor to put you right back after he showed you to me at the hospital. Thirty-eight hours to push you out and that big head of yours is still giving me problems and that big mouth is making just as much noise!'

Rob looked like he'd just been smacked in the mouth with a lemon. 'Nice one, Mum. Yeah, just cloud the issue by trying to make me feel guilty. Well, I'm sorry for being born but I'll be damned if Gwen is going to stand behind *that* counter every day. And I don't care if she hears it!'

'I heard you just fine, Robert.' Gwen said in a calm voice, straightening the bottles of wine she'd just been showing Beth.

'Are you hungry, Beth?' Clayton blurted.

'Well, yes. I am getting hungry —'

Rob's voice cut over the top. 'I haven't seen you in a while, Gwen. You been hiding under a rock somewhere?'

'You will *not* speak to our employee like that, Robert!' Angie roared. 'And you will *not* behave like this in front of our guest!'

Clayton squeezed his eyes tightly shut as a pounding started behind his eyes. He reached out to grasp Beth's hand. Her skin was freezing. He'd have to do something about the air-conditioning in the restaurant. 'How about I show you the restaurant?'

'Yes, that does sound like a good idea. I'll need the loo . . .'

There is a God, Clayton thought. 'Outside, on your left. You can't miss the sign.'

'Oh, great. I'll . . . I'll meet you outside, then.'

'Great. See you in a minute.' Clayton had to stop himself from giving her a gentle shove in the right direction as she started for the door.

'Angie, Gwen, it was lovely to meet you both,' Beth said. giving both women a warm, if slightly guarded, smile.

'Lovely to meet you too.' The two women both replied at the same time without taking their eyes off Rob.

'Beth, don't you think —' Rob started but Clayton elbowed him hard enough in the side to shut him up.

'I'll see you outside, Beth,' Clayton said with a tight smile. 'Welcome to the family circus.'

Clayton waited the count of five after the door swung shut and then rounded on his dad and Angie. No one was saying anything yet, but it was only a matter of time.

'Need I remind you that you just had that little scene in front of a customer, never mind that she's my guest? What the hell were you thinking? Grow up and stop acting like bloody kids,' he growled in disgust before stalking out the door, letting it bang behind him.

'Is everything all right?' Beth asked the minute Clayton emerged into the blinding sunlight. She was standing next to a clump of lavender on the lawn bordering the cellar door with her dress hiked up around her calves, exposing delicate, narrow feet. The sun was reflecting off her hair in a way that made it look like warm caramel.

Clayton felt heat riding up his cheeks. 'Yeah. Sorry you had to get caught up in that. Family argument.'

'I guessed as much.' Beth peered past him to the cellar-door window, no doubt catching a glimpse of Rob gesturing wildly in anger at a stoical Gwen. 'Please don't apologise. I take it that this is some sort of ongoing thing?'

'Yeah,' Clayton replied, fighting frustration and embarrassment. 'Dad and Gwen have some history. I'm not sure what it's all about, but it's usually pretty harmless. I know it doesn't seem like it, but we don't usually air our dirty laundry in front of guests.'

'I guess I could take that a few different ways, couldn't I? It sounds like I'm a special case.' Beth surprised him by laughing softly, her honey-coloured eyes warm. 'I'll take it as a compliment, if that's all right with you. Don't worry, I might be quiet but my family used to be loud enough to make up for it. My mum and dad had loud rows sometimes but it was all for the look of the thing. They ended up laughing afterwards most of the time. Your father reminds me of a bulldog. All fierce looks and a loud bark but he's probably quite sweet underneath. Am I right?'

'Dead on the money. What's your rate for training humans?' Clayton gave her a relieved smile then chanced a hand on the small of her back as he guided her towards Evangeline's a few metres away.

'I haven't come up with one yet, but a nice lunch could be a starting point.'

'It's about time you brought someone in here. I didn't think you loved me.' A cheerful female voice greeted Beth and Clayton the minute they walked in to the restaurant's cozy interior.

'Just in case you haven't seen enough of my crazy relatives, this is my sister, Rachael,' Clayton said from Beth's side. 'Rach, this is Beth.'

Beth turned to the voice and found herself momentarily

speechless and doing her best not to stare. Walking towards them was an intimidatingly attractive woman in chef's whites. Rachael Hardy would never be a poster girl for the svelte and skinny. Instead she was sexy in an old-fashioned way with a sweet oval face, enviably long, curly brown hair pulled into a loose bun and a lush figure that she obviously enjoyed inhabiting.

'Pleased to meet you, Beth. Wanna tell me what this big lug bribed you with to get you to spend the day with him?' Rachael's lips curved into a cheeky grin as she shook Beth's hand warmly.

Beth laughed. 'If I recall correctly, there was a promise of wine.'

'She'll need a double after the scene Dad just pulled.'

Rachael rolled her eyes. 'He still worked up?'

'Understatement,' Clayton replied.

'It really wasn't a problem,' Beth said, still wanting to put Clayton at ease. She would have been blind not to see how the scene his father had just made had embarrassed him but she had meant it when she said it didn't worry her. Rob Hardy really did remind her of a bulldog she once saw because it kept snarling at the postman. Harvey had been the soul of gentleness but he had been scared years before after being run over by the postal van. Rob Hardy had the same feel about him. He seemed to have just as much bluster as Harvey but Beth got a feeling that underneath it all he was just as much of a cupcake as her canine client. 'Clayton has told me that you're a spectacular chef.'

'Ah. Well, I am but he only says stuff like that so I'll give him freebies.' Rachael poked her tongue out at Clayton when he gently pushed her shoulder.

'Don't you have a kitchen to be in?' Clayton grumbled.

'Yeah but I couldn't miss this momentous occasion. It's not like you bring people in here every day. Don't let him boss you round, whatever you do, Beth. He's a tyrant and a half and we're pretty sure he was dropped on his head at birth.' Rachael's brown eyes sparkled as she led the way to a small table for two, bedecked with a white tablecloth, a fat white candle and a bottle of wine.

Beth leaned back in her seat, surreptitiously rubbing her full belly. She was tipsy for the second time in two days, and was enjoying herself immensely. By rights she should have been feeling the flames of eternal damnation licking at her feet, but she didn't care.

She'd just spent the past two hours leisurely eating a selection of mouth-watering food prepared by Clayton's sister, who was a culinary genius. The amazing cuisine had been perfectly complemented by a bottle of the same wonderfully buttery chardonnay she'd indulged in the day before.

Unable to resist temptation, she idly nibbled on the last of a delicious plate of hothouse strawberries that had been marinated in balsamic and vanilla sugar, while regarding Clayton with a contented smile. 'You know, you talk a lot more when you've had a little to drink.'

Clayton laughed. It was a low, pleasant sound. He leaned forward, resting his forearms on the table. 'Ah well, maybe you just listen better when you've had something to drink. And so do you, by the way.'

'What?'

'Talk more,' he replied, his deep brown eyes running lazily over her features while he swirled wine around his almost-empty glass.

'Oh?' Beth chuckled and ran her tongue over her bottom lip self-consciously. 'With the exception of your looks, your sister's your complete opposite, you know. How did that come about?'

'Yeah. She is a pest, isn't she?' Clayton spoke just loud enough to be heard in the small restaurant's kitchen.

Beth laughed when Rachael's loud snort reached their ears. 'What was it like growing up with three siblings? I only had an older sister, and she teased me enough.'

Clayton looked surprised. 'You really wanna know?'

'Yes. I do.'

He shrugged. 'All right, well . . .' Over the next little while he told her about how it felt to be the oldest son in a farming family. How he'd worked with his father since he could walk and had been expected to stay in George Creek for school while his siblings opted to attend private schools in Perth.

'Didn't you feel left out? Want more?' Beth felt a pang of empathy. She'd wanted those things too once.

'Yeah,' Clayton answered simply. 'But it wasn't really an option when I think about it.' He waved a hand. 'Don't get me wrong. I love the farm. Love the wine business too, but there are times I wouldn't mind having a bit more freedom like my brothers. Mike's seen the world, travelled everywhere, and Stephen got to pick something he wanted to do in running the marketing side of things. Hell, Rachael's even managed to travel a ton. She trained as a chef in Paris for a while and toured Europe after she finished. But me? I don't even have a passport. It's a bit embarrassing to admit. Especially to someone like you. I bet you've seen a lot of Europe . . . France, England, Spain.' He gave a self-deprecating smile.

'Er. No actually,' Beth replied earnestly, leaning forward until their faces were only a few inches apart. 'This is my first real holiday, to tell you the truth. There was just never time. Someone always needed me. Something always . . . came up. I'm a little like you, really. I still live in the same village where I went to school. I married not long after high school and set up my business while my then-husband went to university. Afterwards it was just easier to stay in the same place rather than pick up and move somewhere else.' She felt a twinge of pain at the memory. 'So you see I'm not so different.'

'You were married?' Clayton frowned.

'Yes. For a while. It didn't work.' Beth bit her lip and straightened in her chair as memories of how and why her marriage had ended reminded her that while she was having a wonderful time, she didn't want to get too used to it. She wasn't ready to face being rejected again, and given how handsome and eligible Clayton was, there was a very good chance he'd find someone with her complicated history to be too much effort, especially given what he'd told her about his mother.

'Did I just ask the wrong question?'

Beth shook her head and tried to smile again, but she knew she wasn't doing a good job of it. 'No. I'm just getting tired, I think.' She tried to come up with a way to salvage the conversation but didn't know where to start. The prevailing thought crossing her mind was that she was either going to have to tell Clayton about herself if she wanted this to go further, or leave things as they were. As it was, she'd had such a great day, she didn't want to ruin it. Better to end things here.

'Ah. I forgot you just flew halfway around the world.' Clayton reached over the table as if to touch her hand, then stopped when she put the fork down and folded her hands in her lap.

'So did I. Could you take me home, please?'

'Yeah? Sure.'

Castigating herself for ruining such an enjoyable afternoon and feeling suddenly overwhelmed, Beth pushed her chair back before Clayton could help her. The scraping sound it made formed a punctuation mark in the silence between them.

A feeling of awkwardness hung in the air until Clayton spoke as he pulled up at Beth's sunset-dappled cottage.

'Beth. Ah . . . I had a great time this afternoon. I know we only just met a few days ago but I enjoyed myself with you more than I have for a long time.' He ran a hand over his jaw. 'I'm sorry if I've upset you.'

His words left Beth feeling awful. 'You shouldn't be sorry at all. I overreacted and behaved rudely. Considering how lovely you've been, it was unforgivable.' Her lip wobbled.

'I wouldn't say that,' Clayton said softly. 'Although maybe you're overreacting now.'

'I am, aren't I?'

'Yep.'

Beth heaved a sigh and looked at him shyly. 'Well, in that case, can I invite you in for a coffee to make up for the one you didn't get to finish at the restaurant?'

'Sounds great.'

'It's instant coffee and it will be absolutely hideous,' she clarified, feeling the need to be entirely honest.

Clayton chuckled. 'With that kinda recommendation, how can I say no?'

It was only after Clayton was seated at the cottage's small kitchen table and Beth was reaching up to get two mugs out of a cupboard that she remembered that coffee was a euphemism for sex.

Or was it?

It was in American movies. Was it the same in Australia? She had no idea. Actually she didn't even know if it was in England, which showed how much she knew!

The only person she'd ever managed to have sex with was her ex-husband. Greg had been intrinsically reserved in the bedroom, so they'd never really got past the basics, leaving Beth now dealing with the embarrassing realisation that at thirty-one she was probably as experienced as the average English sixteen-year-old.

'You okay there?' Clayton's question broke her out of her reverie.

'Oh. Yes. I was just thinking that coffee is a euphemism.' Beth spoke before her brain caught up with her mouth.

'Come again?'

'Oh. Um.' *Just brazen it out*, she told herself. 'For sex. You know – in the movies. The woman always asks the man in for a cup of coffee, or the other way around.'

There was a stunned silence before Clayton let out a loud, warm bark of laughter. 'Yeah? I've never come across it in real life. Had a girlfriend once a few years back who always wanted a cup of tea before we went to bed. She always needed to pee just when I'd talked her into getting her knickers off.'

Beth giggled. 'Too much information, thank you very much!'

'Yeah, yeah,' Clayton said lazily, not looking even the slightest bit repentant. 'Mind you, I gotta wonder – does asking someone in for bad coffee mean that it'd be an offer for bad sex?'

'Oh. I never thought of it like that.' Beth fought a hot blush that started somewhere in the pit of her belly. 'So, now that I've brought it up and this conversation is getting awkward, you'll have to settle for bad coffee being a euphemism for bad coffee and maybe needing to pee later. Are you all right with that?'

'I think I can make do.' Clayton stretched his legs out in front of him. He'd taken his boots off by the door and was wearing dark blue socks. One had a hole in the toe, and Beth found the sight strangely endearing. 'Milk and two sugars, by the way. Just in case you're about to ask.'

'I was, at that.'

A few moments later Beth handed him his coffee and watched as he took his first sip. He winced.

'I warned you it was hideous.' Beth tasted hers and mirrored his gesture. 'You don't have to drink this.'

'It's a challenge now.' Clayton waved his hand at the chair on the other side of the table. 'You going to hover there all night worrying about the coffee, or are you going to relax and tell me what you plan to do with yourself while you're here?'

Beth took a seat. 'Since you put it like that, I'll tell you what I plan to do. It's going to be a short list because I don't want to do much at all.' She smiled, picturing dreamy, lazy days ahead.

'Wanna do that not much with just yourself, or are you open to company?' Clayton asked in such a relaxed voice that Beth could have imagined the fleeting frown that crossed his features when she didn't answer immediately.

She would have answered him but she'd become distracted by his legs splayed out in front of him. He was so solid and she couldn't help but remember what his calves had looked like the day he'd changed her tyre.

She'd never been exposed to a well-muscled man before. Certainly not one who habitually wore those work shorts of his. Did all Australian farmers wear shorts like that? What did you *do* with a man wearing shorts like that when you had one in close proximity? Not that she was deluding herself about doing anything, but still . . .

'Beth?'

Oh damn. She'd been staring at his legs. She darted her gaze to his face. From the way his mouth was curved up at one side, he'd noticed.

'Oh. Well. Company? I haven't thought about it really.'

'Not even for Christmas?'

'That's coming up, isn't it?' Beth was surprised she'd forgotten. It had to be all this sun and heat. She associated Christmas with snow and biting cold, not blue skies and warm days.

'Yep.'

'I don't think I was planning on doing anything. Christmas is usually a quiet day for me, other than having lunch with my gran and Louis. After that they go out to the local seniors' centre to visit with their friends who can't get around, and I stay home next to the fire with my dog, Charlie.' She held up a hand at his deepening frown. 'No. It's not as doom-and-gloom as it sounds. Really.

It's better that way – really. Christmas is for families, and mine . . .'
She shrugged. 'Mine is sadly diminished. So, I much prefer to curl
up with a good book or watch a movie than dwell on it. It's a lot
less depressing and certainly less uncomfortable than gate-crashing
some other family's celebration. Actually, I'm quite looking forward to Christmas this year. It'll be a novelty to wake up to a bright
sunny day.' She smiled warmly at the thought, unthinkingly taking another sip of her dreadful coffee, wincing and setting it down
far away enough from her on the table that she wouldn't repeat the
mistake.

Clayton didn't say anything, just regarded her thoughtfully, a
thumb playing with the outside of his mug.

Beth shifted in her chair then smoothed an errant strand of hair
behind her ear. 'I must sound strange. You've got a large family,
haven't you? Do you all meet up for Christmas Day?'

A soft expression crossed Clayton's features. 'Yeah. It's my
favourite time of the year. Dad and Angie organise a party on
Christmas Eve for everyone in the area. My whole family attends.
My brother Mike even comes back from England most years. Scott,
my cousin, usually flies in from wherever he's working if he can,
too.'

'Sounds like a serious affair.' Beth ran her index finger over a
knothole in the table.

'Not at all,' Clayton replied. 'It's really just a barbie on the back
porch. The adults all have a bit too much to drink while the kids run
around getting jacked up on sugar. Usually one of us dresses up as
Father Christmas and hands out a few presents. Dad used to do it,
but I've been roped into it this year.'

'You don't seem too terrified by the prospect,' Beth teased.

'I think I'll manage,' Clayton said, deadpan.

With a small amount of prompting Beth encouraged him to talk
about the other traditions he shared with his family, warming herself

on the glow of his obvious enjoyment in recounting tale after tale of one relative or another doing something funny or just plain silly. It wasn't until she found herself covering up a jaw-cracking yawn that she realised the sun had long since set and that it was past ten.

'I'm keeping you up.' Clayton's expression showed his concern.

Beth gave him an apologetic grimace. 'I'm a little jet lagged still. I've never felt like this before. I feel fine and then all of a sudden it hits me and my brain shuts down. Sorry.'

'Don't be.' He lazily pushed himself to his feet, holding a hand out towards her. She stared at it in confusion.

'Want a hand getting up there? You look like you're going to settle in and fall asleep on that chair otherwise.'

'Oh. Yes. I probably am. Thank you.' Beth reached out and put her hand in his. Her stomach fluttered at the contact.

His hand was warm, his skin rough. She darted a glance up at him, wondering if her touch was affecting him. Other than a slight smile, his expression was impassive as he pulled her to her feet.

She was standing only inches away from him and her eyes were in line with the hollow of his neck. He had a thick patch of dark curling hair just visible above the V of his shirt, and she was tempted to reach out and touch it. Would it be soft? Springy? She saw his Adam's apple bob in his throat as he swallowed.

'Beth. I enjoyed today.' His voice sounded deep, more gravelly than it had moments before.

'Oh?' She was very aware of her hand still clasped in his. She really should pull it away, but she didn't want to right now. The physical contact was nice. Better than nice. Unable to resist the temptation, she ran her thumb lightly over a small raised scar she could feel on the back of his knuckle.

'Beth?' Yes, his voice was definitely huskier than before. She tilted her face to gauge his expression only to have his mouth meet hers halfway.

His lips were warm and firm and their touch was whisper soft. His tongue darted out so quickly she could have missed it if not for the taste it left behind – like the coffee he'd just drunk, but on him it was somehow much, much better.

'Oh,' she breathed, leaning against him as her body overrode her brain. Reaching up tentatively, she ran a hand over the side of his jaw. It felt raspy with newly grown stubble, masculine, and so nice to the touch. She tentatively ran her tongue over his bottom lip and was rewarded with a groan as he pulled her flush against him.

Coaxing her mouth open, he licked and sucked her bottom lip, sensuously, languidly rubbing his tongue against hers while his spare hand tilted her chin, angling her mouth for better access. Beth had never been kissed like this before.

'Clayton . . .' she began, wanting to tell him as much, but was distracted when his hand let go of hers and spanned her lower back, pulling her harder against him as he deepened the kiss, tongue delving, thrusting, while his hips began a slow rocking motion against hers.

A sharp rush of sensation pooled in her abdomen, swirling up through her body and setting her nerves on fire, turning her insides to liquid heat.

She heard a whimpering noise and was only vaguely aware she'd made it as she closed her eyes, letting her head fall back as Clayton abandoned her mouth and began to trail small sucking, biting kisses across her cheek, down the side of her neck. On his way, he managed to find every nerve ending, every pulsing heartbeat with a gentleness so unbearably sweet Beth felt her eyes tearing as she tried to get closer, running her hands up and down his sides, feeling the warmth from his body, the hard muscle beneath his shirt.

Clayton groaned as he placed his hands over her backside and hiked her up against him, forcing his leg between hers. Her eyes widened when she felt him hard against her stomach, then closed again as he began to rock against her, his hard thigh rubbing her sex, sending long, languid tendrils of pleasure arcing in every direction.

This was just so good. So right.

Beth was so caught up in the sensations swirling through her she only vaguely felt Clayton's hand stroking over her shoulders, then down her arm as his mouth burned over her skin moving lower, down the curve of her neck, his hot breath bathing the skin above her collarbone and then lower, leaving goosebumps all over her bare skin.

Bare skin?

Reality crashed into the scene and lust transformed into panic the instant Beth's eyes snapped open to find the bodice of her dress bunched around her waist and Clayton's mouth hovering just above her no-nonsense white bra.

'*No!*' She shoved at Clayton's chest until he stumbled backwards, then frantically reached down with shaking hands to haul her dress back up, flushing red when its elasticised neckline caught under her bra.

'Beth?' Clayton asked in a stunned, rasping voice. His cheeks were flushed, his chest heaving. 'What the hell just happened?'

Clayton reached out to put a hand on her shoulder but she flinched away.

'I'm sorry.' Her mouth trembled as waves of mortification rolled over her. 'I'm really very sorry. Oh goodness, that was such a silly way to . . . I'm sorry, but I can't do this. You took me by surprise. What we were doing just now, I – I can't.'

'All right,' Clayton said slowly after a few tense moments, his chest still heaving. 'You want to tell me what's going on?' His narrowed eyes swept over her distraught expression then lowered to where she'd protectively crossed her arms over her chest.

'I can't right now.' Beth hunched her shoulders. 'I'm sorry.'

'Yeah, I got that,' he replied shortly. He ran a hand through his hair in a frustrated, exasperated movement before meeting her eyes. 'Do I need to apologise?'

'No! No, you don't. I think I led you on. It was absolutely awful of me considering what a lovely afternoon we just shared and how wonderful you've been.' She drew a shaky breath and lowered her gaze, only to see a very prominent and visible reminder of what had just been happening between them making a bulge in his trousers. 'Oh Lord. Clayton —'

'Ignore it. It'll go away,' he said impatiently, cutting off the beginning of another apology.

'If it's all right with you, I'd rather be the one that goes away.' Beth took an awkward step backwards. 'To bed, that is. That way I won't make any more of an idiot of myself.' She tried to smile but failed miserably. She could still feel the heat radiating off him, still taste him on her lips. This was not good. She felt like a child with her nose pressed against a sweet-shop window, desperate for something she couldn't have without paying the high price of having a conversation she didn't know how to start.

'I don't think you're an idiot, Beth. Maybe a little overdramatic, but not an idiot,' Clayton replied. This time when he reached out to stroke her cheek, she didn't pull away.

'Thank you. I think.' Beth gave him a timorous smile.

'That's better. How about we chalk this up to the jet lag you mentioned before. Work for you?'

'Yes.' Beth exhaled in relief.

'I'll be going, then. I had a great time today. Bye, Beth.' Before Beth could react, Clayton bridged the small gap between them and pulled her into a brief, very gentle embrace. He planted a kiss on her hair as he let her go, then collected his shoes and walked out the door.

Standing in the middle of the kitchen, arms wrapped around her waist, Beth listened to his car start and watched the glow from his headlights gradually dim as he drove away. Then she turned and walked to her bedroom on shaky legs, feeling more completely alone than she ever had before.

Chapter 6

If Clayton was praying for a bit of quiet time over breakfast to come to grips with what had happened with Beth the night before, he was sadly disappointed. Between his dad stomping around maintaining the loudest angry silence ever known to humanity, and his sister Rachael chattering away to Angie and Jo over a cup of tea on the porch, the presence of other people was deafening.

It would only get worse over the next two weeks leading up to Christmas. His entire family would descend upon Evangeline's Rest. All ten million of them.

Biting savagely into a slice of toast, he contemplated going to check up on the builders working on his house, then thought better of it. So far he'd had a pretty good relationship with old Luciano Gianotti's building crew, but he had a feeling that could change in a hurry if he started to throw his weight around. George Creek was a popular retirement and holiday-home spot for the wealthy, and good builders were always in short supply. He should know – he'd waited six years for these ones.

He was also itching to give Beth a call, but he didn't have her number. He knew he could always drive up to her cottage again to see her, but he had a feeling that would just look desperate. Or would it? Hell, he didn't know. He'd been working so hard on the farm trying to keep on top of things that he didn't know what the rules were any more. He had a feeling Beth didn't either, but that didn't leave him feeling any better.

Beth's flip-out fell well outside the scope of his experience. He'd lain awake the whole night trying to work out what had happened and still wasn't any closer to an answer. He'd never kissed a woman and had her turn on like a light so quickly, only to push him away just as fast.

He was pretty damn sure, almost positive, it hadn't been a matter of what he'd been doing. She'd been into it. So much so, she hadn't even noticed when he'd got her dress half-off. Not that he'd intended it to get that far.

He'd planned to take things slow and be a gentleman, but then Beth had held his hand and looked up at him with those liquid-honey eyes of hers. She'd smelled so good, vanilla-y and fresh . . . she'd been pretty damn irresistible. Now he was brooding about it like a moody teenager. He didn't like the feeling one little bit.

To make things worse, Jeff was no doubt getting himself all dressed up to take Beth on that bloody tour he'd talked her into. Clayton felt something primal and furious unfurl in his chest at the thought of his friend enjoying the way Beth's nose crinkled when she smiled and the way she made a man feel ten feet tall by listening so intently. He couldn't stand the thought of Jeff getting as close to Beth as he had the night before, her slight pixie frame pushing up against his, feeling her downy soft skin under his hands, hearing those breathy little noises she made. God, she'd felt nice. It had been a while since Clayton had been with a woman, but he couldn't remember any of his past girlfriends feeling that good. If he could just work out what had gone wrong —

'Is it my imagination or are you plotting to kill someone?' Stephen asked, breaking through Clayton's broodiness.

Clayton's brother scraped a chair away from the dining table with his foot and sat down. Stephen had a large earthenware mug of coffee in one hand and a matching plate piled high with bacon, eggs and toast in the other.

Clayton grunted and scowled in reply, hoping Stephen would get the hint and bugger off.

'Like that, is it?'

'Yup.' Clayton flicked over a page of the newspaper in front of him, blindly staring at an article about stock feed.

'Fair enough.' Stephen shrugged and slid the newspaper out from under Clayton's nose, over to his side of the table. 'Jeff called last night. Said your phone was turned off. He wanted to know how your date went.'

Clayton wondered whether or not Angie would forgive him if he got his baby brother's blood all over the kitchen floor.

'Hey, before you start, don't shoot the messenger.' Stephen held up both hands in surrender as he caught sight of Clayton's thunderous expression.

Clayton grunted in reply and snatched his newspaper back.

'If you're going to be like that, I'm off to find more civilised company. See you later.' Stephen scowled, got up, collected his breakfast and headed outside to find his girlfriend.

'Later,' Clayton muttered, glaring at his brother's retreating back.

Bloody Jeff and his bloody shit-stirring charismatic way with women. For as long as Clayton had known him, Jeff had been able to get on with women with an ease that Clayton could only dream of. The only exceptions to the rule were Rachael, for reasons no one knew, and Stephen's girlfriend, Jo, who'd famously decked Jeff when she was twelve and Jeff was sixteen. Right now Clayton wished that Jo had been a sight more violent than a simple roundhouse punch. A knee in the balls wouldn't have gone astray.

He didn't want to think about Jeff having a good time with Beth, didn't want to think of her enjoying his mate's company. Just one taste of her had left Clayton wanting more, and for the first time in his life he was wishing his friend ill. Not anything major. A debilitating head cold would be a good start.

And the thing about Jeff, the main thing, was that he wouldn't know how to handle Beth if she had a moment like she'd had last night. Maybe he wouldn't be as understanding. Maybe, just maybe, it'd be the right thing to do for Clayton to check up on the two of them today. Just to make sure Jeff was keeping his hands to himself.

Just the thought of Jeff touching Beth had Clayton pushing his chair away from the table with enough force to almost tip it over as he stomped off to the porch. All it would take was a few words with Rachael and she'd play interception until Clayton could get to Jeff's after his rounds of the farm. It was underhanded, but Jeff could take it.

'This, as you can see, is a big tree,' Jeff Rousse proclaimed as he waved his hand languidly out the window of his black Monaro.

'Interesting,' Beth replied, playing along as she had for the better part of the day during Jeff's thoroughly amusing, if unorthodox, tour of the area.

'And a cave, but you can't see it because it's – and this is important, so take notes – *behind* the tree.'

'Fascinating.'

'You like caving?' Jeff looked at her out the corner of his eye. 'If you do, you can hold my hand and take me. I'm scared of the dark. Oh and there's a cow of non-native origin, much like the others we've seen today but better looking because it's one of mine.' He gestured grandly out the window at a black-and-white bovine.

'*Very* interesting,' Beth murmured in a duly appreciative tone, enjoying how Jeff radiated pure unadulterated mischief. She really couldn't help but enjoy the man's company. He had turned up at her door first thing that morning holding a bouquet of dandelions with the roots still attached to some. Despite not wanting to go anywhere and risk making a fool of herself like she had with Clayton, Beth hadn't been able to say no. As it turned out, Jeff was different. He was too naughty to take seriously, and within moments she'd relaxed.

'I know. Amazing, eh? Don't ask me what breed of cow it is. It's my day off today. I don't work on my day off. What you *can* do is ask me about a tour of my house. I can give you that. It's usually an extra addition on the tour price, but for you I'll make an exception.' He waggled his eyebrows.

Beth appeared to consider this, brow knitting in feigned concentration. 'Tempting. Oh so tempting, but I wouldn't want to impinge on your tour service any more than I already have. I do have one request, however.'

'Anything.'

'Can you direct me to the nearest conveniences?'

'Be still my beating heart,' Jeff drawled in such an exaggerated Australian twang that Beth started laughing. 'Tell ya what, we're just driving past my place anyway, so how about we stop there for a sec? Otherwise you'll have to wait another ten minutes until your place. If you're nice, I may even have a complimentary slice of chocolate cake and a coffee set up on the porch by the time you're done.'

'You're not fooling anyone,' Beth said dryly, playing along. 'It's obvious you've got ulterior motives.'

'Damn. Am I that transparent?' Jeff theatrically slapped his forehead. 'Well, all right. How about I take you to my place, we get

naked and I give you the full bells-and-whistles tour of my excep-
tional body instead? It's a fascinating tour, lots of interesting
landmarks. Comes with high praise from Lonely Planet. Just look
me up in the index under "awesome".' He pulled in to a long gravel
driveway.

Beth snorted.

'You don't have to sound so excited,' Jeff grumbled, his expression pained.

'Oh, I am.' Beth schooled her twitching mouth into a serious
line. 'Definitely.'

'Serious?' Jeff twisted around, staring at her wide-eyed.

Beth nodded solemnly.

'Oh shit. Ah, sorry. You mean it?' He ran a hand over his close-
shaven head, appearing unsettled for the first time that day. 'I mean,
I thought you said you had a good time yesterday with Clayton
and – you really mean it?'

'Oh, yes.' Beth kept her expression serious, thoroughly enter-
tained. 'It's only the natural conclusion for the day, don't you think?
I thought it's what you had planned.'

'What? Really?' Jeff's expression was comically incredulous
as he pulled up to a large single-storey log cabin overlooking yet
another spectacular view.

'Definitely.' Beth allowed her words to sink in a few seconds
before adding. 'Given that you've plied me with a full pot of tea, a
glass of wine and have just suggested coffee, I suspected quite early
on that you were plotting to get my pants off. I have to admit I'm
happy to oblige. Actually, given how much I need to go right now,
I'd say I'm downright eager.'

'Just for that, you get the smaller slice of cake,' Jeff muttered
with such indignation that Beth started to laugh again, getting out
of the car and propping herself against its hood, still chuckling as he
stomped theatrically to his front door and opened it with a flourish.

'After you, madam. The loo's straight through the lounge room and on the left. Refreshments will await,' he said in a hideous impersonation of an English accent.

'Why, thank you.' Beth added a little extra poshness to her own accent as she swished past him into his wonderfully spacious open-plan cabin.

'At your service. Ya better give me a bloody good tip, though,' Jeff called after her.

'A tip? Look both ways before crossing the road,' Beth called back, chuckling to herself.

She reappeared moments later to the sound of Jeff's raised voice.

'How was I supposed to know?!'

'You should have known because *I told you* last week. Seriously, you need to get your ears checked because — oh, hi, Beth.' Rachael Hardy turned, her expression changing from furious to friendly in two seconds.

'Hello,' Beth said, standing in the doorway. 'Am I interrupting something?'

'No.' Rachael rolled her eyes. 'Although you can help me out here.'

'God help us,' Jeff grumbled, pushing away from the porch railing and walking past Beth into his house.

Rachael didn't seem fazed; if anything, her expression was faintly victorious. 'If you were me and *your* family was organising a huge Christmas Eve party they hold EVERY YEAR —' The last two words were bellowed into the house. 'Wouldn't you think you'd be pretty pissed off if the person responsible for sorting out the Secret Santa for the kids hadn't got his shit together enough to buy presents yet?' Rachael put her hands on her hips and looked over Beth's shoulder through the screen door, waiting for Jeff's response.

After being caught up in the last Hardy family row Beth knew better than to reply. Instead she just settled with a shrug and took a seat, watching the show. If Jeff was a Jack Russell, Rachael was a shar pei, all loyalty and sheer tenacious determination. After working with the breed for years, Beth knew better than to get in the way – that would just get her bowled over. She didn't have to say anything anyway, because Jeff stormed back onto the porch holding two plates piled high with chocolate cake, plonking one in front of Beth.

'You want some cake?' he asked Rachael.

She narrowed her eyes. 'Why?'

'Because something has to sweeten you up.' Jeff shoved the plate at her and she took it. 'If you didn't notice, I've got a guest here.'

'This cake is delicious. Did you make it?' Beth stuck with a safe topic. So much for a quiet, relaxing holiday. She might as well be mediating one of Violet and Louis's epic who-lost-the-TV-remote-control battles.

'Nah, Laura did,' Jeff answered, not taking his eyes off Rachael.

'Beth, I'm not offending you, am I?' Rachael asked.

'No, of course not —'

'Good, so it won't offend you if I tell Jeff he's the laziest bastard on the planet. How hard is it to stop by the toy shop and pick up some stuff? I bet you're not going to do it until the day of the party, are you? And then you're going to get someone else to wrap them! Well, *I'm* not!' Rachael's voice rose by the end of the sentence but Beth noticed the angrier she seemed, the calmer Jeff was getting. Something told her that whatever was going on was a lot more complex than the stuff on the surface. Her suspicion was confirmed when Jeff held out a hand and Rachael distractedly handed him her fork so he could take a bite of her cake. The entire thing was so seamless, Beth would have missed it if she'd blinked.

'And it's not like you haven't had enough time,' Rachael continued, pausing when the sound of a car door slamming reached them.

Jeff looked over Beth and Rachael's shoulders. 'It's about bloody time, mate. Can you take Rachael somewhere so I can finally give Beth the tour of my house I promised her?' He turned to Beth. 'You should really take a look at my bedroom. Take my word for it, the bed's pretty comfortable.'

Distracted by that comment and Rachael's growled, 'Charming,' Beth gave Jeff an exasperated frown before twisting around to see who was behind her – and when she did she felt her stomach drop.

Clayton was approaching the porch with a lumbering Waffles close on his heels.

He looked exhausted. His thickly curling hair was dusty, his face was streaked with dirt and his clothes were rumpled. Overall it was obvious the man had put in a hard day and his dark expression said he wasn't in the best of moods.

Beth felt the overwhelming sense of embarrassment she'd managed to displace over the course of the day come back in full force as the memory of what had happened the night before played itself in fast forward through her mind, then reversed and played again in excruciating slow motion. She felt a blush work its way from her toes up to her hairline, and she put the forkful of cake she was holding down on the plate before it ended up in her lap.

If he noticed her reaction to his presence, Clayton had the politeness not to show it. Instead he offered her a quick, almost imperceptible smile and a nod before turning to Jeff. 'Your cows in the home paddock are out.'

'What? No shit? How many? Are they on the road?' Jeff demanded, all traces of his previous humour gone.

'Nope. They're currently fraternising with my bulls. I'd suggest you go do something about it.'

'Fuck!' Jeff exclaimed. 'How? They were just behind the house when we pulled up.'

Rachael's expression transformed to pure devilry as she winked at her brother. 'I saw a few out too. I'd get onto it if I was you.'

Beth winced at the steady stream of profanity Jeff scattered into the air.

Clayton's mildly amused expression turned into a scowl. 'Steady on, mate.' He narrowed his eyes and nodded towards Beth.

Spinning around, Jeff had the good grace to look embarrassed. 'Sorry, Beth. We're going to have to cut today short. I gotta fix this.'

'Oh well, not a problem,' Beth reassured him as Waffles waddled over and sat by her foot.

'I'll give Beth a lift home, mate. You take care of things,' Clayton said calmly.

Jeff spun around and eyeballed his friend with suspicion. 'You haven't been getting Fred to fix any gates today, have you?'

Beth couldn't be sure but she thought Clayton's mouth may have twitched at the corner as if he were suppressing a smile. Patting Waffles, she wondered who Fred was.

'Nope, but that doesn't really mean much, does it, mate? It's not my fault my farmhand, who *you* recommended, might I add, is as thick as two elephants in a mud-wrestling contest.' As he said the words, his eyes met Beth's before dropping lower, taking in her bare legs exposed by her suddenly too-short shorts. Beth had to resist the urge to tuck her legs underneath her chair.

Oblivious to Clayton's distraction, Jeff threw up his hands. 'Jesus, mate! If that silly bastard has let those heifers through —'

'You'll have their calves sired by my stud bulls for free. That's unless you're going to insult my loyal employee again. Then I might charge you,' Clayton finished for him, raising an eyebrow.

Jeff swore again, then stomped over to a row of shoes by the front door. He kicked off the loafers he'd worn while chauffeuring Beth around and pulled on a pair of dust-coated leather boots. 'We'll talk about the toy thing later when you're sane.' He growled at Rachael, who just flipped him the bird while cheerfully forking up a mouthful of cake.

'I'll take Beth home,' Clayton said. 'You fine with that?' He turned to Beth again.

Beth felt the knot of tension inside her chest grow ten times larger. 'Oh, it's too much of a bother. I can walk.' She half-hoped he'd say walking was a good idea and half-hoped he'd insist on driving her.

'Too far in this heat,' Clayton countered. 'C'mon, I don't bite.'

'I do. And I'm going to take a chunk out of your arse after this, mate, depend upon it,' Jeff muttered.

Clayton ignored him and studied Beth's indecisive expression instead. 'You want to come along?'

Beth gave in. 'All right. Just let me put these in the kitchen.'

'I'll do that.' Rachael waved a hand, looking so relaxed now, the house could be hers.

'Too bloody right you will,' Jeff grumbled.

'And I'll charge you by the minute,' Rachael said sweetly.

'Bitch.'

'Bastard.'

'All right. Let's go, Beth. Before these two kill each other.' Clayton gestured for her to walk in front of him to his car.

'Just wait.' Jeff glared at Clayton before stomping over to Beth and pulling her into a tight hug, mashing her cheek against his chest. For a slim man, Jeff had a chest like a brick wall.

'I had a good time today, Beth. I'll drop by soon,' he murmured before standing back and giving her a wink that had her wanting to smack him with a rolled-up newspaper. Beth swore she could hear something growling behind her, but when she turned around, Waffles was sitting by Clayton's feet, tongue lolling with a doggy smile on her face – but both Clayton and Rachael were looking like walking thunderclouds.

The only noise in the dusty cab of Clayton's ute on the drive to Beth's cottage came from Waffles panting at Beth's feet and the stones being flicked up by the car's tyres.

Beth snuck a glance at Clayton out the corner of her eye. He caught her and she quickly looked away.

As they pulled up behind her rental car, the sound of Clayton awkwardly clearing his throat prevented her from bolting.

'Ah, Beth? Would you be all right with making me a cup of that really bad coffee again? I wouldn't mind putting my feet up for a few minutes. It's been a nightmare of a day.' His eyes flickered to hers and then to some point over her shoulder.

When she didn't immediately reply, his expression turned strained and two deep lines bracketed his mouth. 'I'd understand if you didn't want to spend time with me. Especially after last night. I'm not exactly spruced up today, either.' He looked down ruefully at his dusty, work-rumpled clothes with such obvious embarrassment that Beth immediately heard herself telling him that of course, coffee was fine.

Clayton forced himself to relax as he sat at Beth's kitchen table in exactly the same spot he'd occupied the night before while she made him another of those God-awful coffees in silence.

Tonight, Beth seemed almost brittle. For the life of him he didn't know how to proceed just yet, so he settled on enjoying the sight of her milky-white legs below the tiny shorts she was wearing. She had the smoothest, palest skin Clayton had ever seen and his hands twitched with the memory of touching it the night before.

He'd always been a leg man. Well, if he was honest, he was an everything man, but he had a special thing for legs and Beth's were particularly nice to look at. His eyes trailed over a pair of lightly toned calves leading up to surprisingly curvaceous thighs for such a slight woman, and then further up to a heart-shaped rump.

He'd felt a completely irrational surge of ill will towards Jeff when he'd spotted Beth wearing that get-up sitting on his porch. She'd looked so comfortable and relaxed despite Rachael probably tearing Jeff a new one care of Clayton telling her his mate hadn't sorted the kids' Christmas presents yet. It was a far cry from how she looked right now.

As if sensing his thoughts, Beth glanced up at him warily as she carried two mugs of coffee to the table. He noticed her hands shook a little as she set them down.

'I'm sorry. I didn't get a chance to get better coffee today.' She perched on the edge of her chair and proceeded to inspect the surface of her coffee like it held the secrets of human existence.

'That's all right. I didn't really want coffee anyway.' Clayton mentally cursed how harsh the words sounded when Beth's head shot up, eyes wide.

'Oh.'

'Beth. Ah. Do you mind if we clear the air a bit here? I would have called earlier but I don't have your number or the one for this cottage and —'

'I don't have one yet,' Beth interjected in a rush. She took a sip of her coffee then winced, echoing her movement from the night before when she pushed the cup away. 'Actually I do, but it's an English one and would be too expensive for you to call,' she corrected.

'Not a problem. Anyway, I'm here now.'

'Yes . . . yes, you are.' Beth met his gaze. 'Clayton. I'd like to apologise for my behaviour last night. You were so kind yesterday. I led you on and reacted badly. It won't happen again. Your tour of your winery and that lovely meal was more than kind enough.'

Clayton scowled. This sounded like a brush-off. 'I was gonna ask if you'd like to go to dinner with me on Friday night.' He mentally winced at the thought of trying to get a reservation at a local restaurant at two days' notice in peak tourist season, especially when he knew his family's restaurant didn't have a table to spare.

It'd be worth it if she said yes, though.

He hadn't planned on asking her out just yet. In fact, he'd not thought further than getting himself alone with her again, but dinner was as good as anything else that was crossing his mind right now.

'You were?' Beth asked with obvious surprise.

'Yeah. Although I'd understand if you didn't want to go. I didn't behave like a gentleman last night. Sorry about that.'

'Oh no. I quite liked . . . you were perfect . . . no, that's all right.'

Clayton watched in fascination as a deep red flush travelled up from the neckline of Beth's T-shirt to her face. 'Seven okay, then? I'll pick you up.' He didn't want to give her the chance to say no.

'I'm not sure —' Beth began but Clayton cut her off.

'You don't have to be polite. I don't mind driving.' He knew he was being a bully but he didn't care. He enjoyed her company. He knew she'd enjoyed his yesterday until things went pear-shaped, and he sure as hell didn't want her spending more time with Jeff.

'Clayton —'

'It's just dinner, Beth. Humour me. I know I'm a bit rusty at this kind of thing, but last I heard, inviting a beautiful woman to dinner didn't oblige her to do anything but turn up and eat.' He stood up and took the two steps to get to her side of the table, then leaned down and gently kissed her cheek before she could react. He felt hugely gratified by the way her breath hitched.

Before that busy mind of hers started to tick over again, he turned and exited the cottage with a determined stride, whistling for Waffles on the way.

He was grinning when he pulled up out the front of Evangeline's Rest. The grin got wider when he spotted Jeff's car parked in his usual spot. Jeff was leaning against it, taking a drag on a cigarette. Since Clayton knew that Jeff had given up smoking years back and only indulged when angry or stressed, he braced himself.

'Since when did one cow become *cows*, mate?' Jeff threw his barely smoked cigarette on the ground and put it out with his boot.

'There was only one?' Clayton feigned amazement. 'Thought I saw a whole lot more than that.'

'You checked your eyesight lately?' Jeff growled. 'That dickhead you hired left the gate open. That's how my *cow* got in with your bulls.'

'Oh? Fred? Nah, mate. Couldn't have been. He's a top bloke. What words did you use when you recommended him to me? Oh, that's right. "Spot on. Clued in. Showed initiative." Yeah, that was the word, *initiative*,' Clayton replied in return, running his hand over his jaw to hide his smile.

'Yeah, right. Look, mate, you owe me. And don't think I don't know about you setting Rachael onto me either, you bastard. I reckon a bottle of your finest would do.'

'As long as you're paying,' Clayton replied smugly, walking towards his full-to-bursting family home before Jeff could form a comeback.

Chapter 7

'Let me think . . . Janet Little is currently getting it on with her husband's best friend, who she used to go out with in high school before she dumped him for another woman when she went through a bisexual phase. Her husband doesn't know but his friend's wife does and she's planning on leaving him for her ex-husband who used to be his other best friend. Will that please your gran?' Laura cocked her head to one side and regarded Beth with amusement.

'Ye-eess, I think this should give Violet more than enough to go on with. I told her not to call for a week, so she's text messaged me three times a day since.' Beth tapped the notepad on her lap with her pen. The muscles in her hand were cramping. Laura was a champion talker. Beth doubted she'd paused for more than a second in the past fifty minutes.

'There's more if you want to hear it,' Laura gushed eagerly. 'I mean, in some ways I'm as fresh here as you are and all this small-town politics and hanky-panky is pretty fascinating. It must be the boredom or something because people really do get up to a lot, or at least talk about what other people get up to a lot.' She set the cup of tea Beth had just made her down on the floor by her side and scrunched up her nose. 'Am I boring you? I only planned to drop in today to bring you more breakfast supplies, and look at me. It's already been an hour since I got here.'

'No!' Beth briefly rested her hand on Laura's shoulder. They were sitting in her cottage's living room, Beth curled up on a cozy yellow sofa, Laura sitting cross-legged on the floorboards nearby, a large map of the region spread out in front of her. They hadn't even bothered with the map yet. Violet's most recent text imperiously demanding gossip had reached Beth within minutes of Laura's arrival and, giving in, Beth had asked her friend to dish enough dirt to keep her gran happy.

Beth ran her pen over her bottom lip thoughtfully. 'Laura?'

'Hmm?' Laura smoothed her white *fleur de lis* baby-doll mini-dress down over her thighs before idly playing with the lace on one Barbie-pink Converse sneaker.

'Does it ever worry you that people might be gossiping about your family like this?'

Laura shrugged. 'Yeah. Sometimes. But most of our stuff is old news. I mean, my dad's seeing Angie Hardy on the sly, but that's been going on for years. It caused a bit of drama when people first worked it out because my dad is Rob Hardy's best friend. Rob is Clayton's dad. He and Clayton's mum were crazy-young when they got married and had Clayton, so people sometimes mistake them for brothers. Did you meet him the other day?'

Beth pictured the formidable, frowning, older version of Clayton she'd met at the Evangeline's Rest cellar door a few days before and nodded.

'Yeah?' Laura continued. 'Everyone was calling Angie a cradle-snatcher for a while, but that's died down. Jeff and Rachael Hardy have been at each other's throats for almost ten years although no one knows why. And then there was the thing between Jeff and Jo Blaine. She's going out with Stephen Hardy now. When they were kids she punched him out and it took him ages to get over it. They used to hate each other, but that's changed since Stephen and Jo got together and Jeff finally apologised to her for being a shit. Now they just give each other hell out of habit.'

Beth let out a surprised laugh. 'Really? I just can't picture it. I would have thought Jeff got on with anything in a skirt.'

Laura's smile dimmed a little. 'He took Mum and Dad's divorce pretty hard and for a while there he was a bit of a terror. I wasn't around much to see it all, but Dad says if it weren't for Clayton being his mate, Jeff would have either needed jail or the army to straighten him out.'

Beth digested this. 'So, they've been friends a long time? Clayton and Jeff?'

'Yeah, since they were five. They met just after Clayton's mum died. Clayton didn't talk for a year or two after that, so when they met in kindergarten Jeff did all the talking for him.'

Beth brought a hand to her chest in reaction to the picture Laura's words painted. The image of Clayton as a little boy so traumatised by his mother's death that he couldn't speak brought a lump to her throat. She squashed it down. 'When I was out with Clayton the other day, I met a lady named Gwen —'

'Stone? Yeah? I bet that was interesting. It's going around that Rob Hardy is seriously pissed off that Angie hired her. No one knows what that's all about. Dad reckons it's something that goes back to before Pam Hardy – that's Clayton's mum – died.' Laura shot Beth a shrewd look. 'Did you see any drama? Should I be asking *you* for the gossip?'

Beth waved a hand, feeling the urge to protect Clayton's privacy. 'Nothing more to tell than you already know, I'm afraid.'

'Oh.' Laura frowned momentarily before her eyes developed the same glint of mischief Beth had seen in her brother's. 'So, anyway, tell me about yesterday. Jeff said you guys had a good time. Well, at least until Rachael came along and kicked his backside over the Christmas presents. Serves him right.'

Beth smiled widely. 'I had a great time with Jeff. He showed me around and took me out to lunch. He's naughty but I like him.'

'And Clayton?'

Beth blushed and cursed her fair skin. She'd always blushed easily. Children had made fun of her when she was little.

'Oh really?' Laura grinned when she spotted the telltale colour in Beth's cheeks.

'We had a nice time.' Beth averted her eyes back to her notes. She didn't want to talk about Clayton. She was still too disoriented and confused where he was concerned.

It must have shown because Laura held up both hands. 'Sorry. My bad. Nosy me. It's a habit I'm working on.'

Beth relaxed. 'It's all right. I'm just a little frazzled. I'm not used to all this attention. I live a fairly solitary life at home. It's usually just me, my four-legged friends at work and then Violet and Louis at home. It's sad to say, but it's been like that for a few years.'

'I'm so sorry, Beth. Is that because you live in a small town?'

'Oh no!' Beth exclaimed, surprised at Laura's assumption. 'It's not that at all. Skipton is a large village, with a lot of people coming and going. Actually . . . the illness I mentioned a while ago? It's taken me a while to recover.' She forestalled Laura's next inevitable question by quickly continuing. 'I'm perfectly fine now. So, not to worry. This trip, however unexpected, has brought to my attention how isolated I've let myself become. It's embarrassing to admit it, but I'm out of practice with people.'

'It doesn't show,' Laura replied thoughtfully. 'Although it occurs to me that between me, Jeff and Clayton, you've not had a day to yourself since you arrived. Do you want some time out? I can go now and leave you to it. The weather's nice today, not too hot, so it would be perfect to explore.' She got up to go but something about the way she stood, the set of her shoulders, told Beth she was reluctant. Beth realised all at once that Laura might be just as lonely as she'd been of late.

'You know . . .' Beth began, then hesitated.

'What?' Laura's head snapped up.

'What I *would* like is to enjoy doing something normal. When I was at your brother's I tried some of that delicious cake you made, and I'm wondering if you can show me how to make it? I've never really tried to bake before. Probably because I'm too pedantic and worry too much about getting everything right.' She smiled at the memory of her one failed attempt at baking scones for her gran when she was fourteen. 'If it's not too much trouble,' she added quickly.

The thousand-watt grin Beth received in return was all the answer she needed, and she allowed herself to be dragged out to Laura's car and swept along for what would no doubt be another busy, people-filled day. With luck, she'd completely distract herself from what she now couldn't avoid calling a *date* with Clayton Hardy the following evening.

Rob was incandescent with rage. And what pissed him off even more was the knowledge that there was no one he could take his foul mood out on without getting himself into hot water. So, here he was, imprisoned at his desk in his goddamn study, entering in stock records by punching at his computer keyboard with his index fingers and hoping to hell that someone, a specific *someone* currently lurking in his goddamn house, got the hint and got the hell out of his way.

In the next room Gwen Stone and his conniving, manipulative, infuriating mother were sharing a glass of wine and clucking about the weather or something equally boring as if nothing was wrong. As if Gwen always visited *his* house, always sat at *his* dining table and drank from *his* bloody glassware. The woman hadn't been near his residence for almost thirty years.

He didn't want her here. Didn't want any reminders of Pam dying. It was too much. Too many ancient memories were coming to the surface, becoming so painfully real again that he felt his eyes sting with tears. That pissed him off even more. Since Gwen had crawled out from under her rock again, he'd found himself close to blubbering like a goddamn kid at the slightest thing. He fucking hated it.

To this day he missed Pam like an amputated limb. It had been so unfair. They'd only been kids in their early twenties when she'd died. And it had happened so quick, so bloody quick. One minute she'd been feeling under the weather and assuring Rob she had a bad virus – nothing to worry about, she'd said – and the next minute she'd been gone and there hadn't been a goddamn thing he could do to help her. She'd just lain there in that bloody awful, sterile room in Margaret River Hospital and left him.

She hadn't given him a chance to say goodbye. She'd just left him to comfort screaming twin babies and explain to his older sons that Mummy wouldn't be coming home. Michael, only three, had kept asking when Pam was coming home, and Clayton . . . Clayton hadn't talked for a long time. Rob hadn't known what to do. He hadn't known how to help his kids, let alone help himself. If it hadn't been for his mum stepping in, he probably would have tried to go with Pam. Living hadn't felt worth it. The memory of how close he'd been to ending it all during those first nightmarish days still shook him up.

Later, the doctors told him it had been leukemia. Rare in someone her age. He'd been so young, so busy, so fucking self-absorbed working fifteen-hour days on the farm, he'd had no idea. It was only later he learned that she had refused treatment. That had nearly broken him, because he knew exactly why Pam had kept it all to herself.

Gwen Stone.

Gwen Stone, Pam's supposed best friend. Gwen Stone, who was living, breathing and drinking his fucking wine while Pam was dead and cold in the ground. And he was supposed to be polite about it? Not bloody likely.

The office door opened behind him and Rob violently spun round on his chair, fully expecting it to be his mum doing her best to make his life even more miserable.

Clayton entered the room, took one look at Rob's dark expression and held up his hands. 'Easy, tiger. I'm hiding just as much as you are. Though since you're here I'll find somewhere else.'

Rob watched with narrowed eyes as Clayton walked over to his desk on the other side of the room and picked up his green John Deere baseball cap.

Rob's chair protested with a squeak as he leaned backwards and put his feet out in front of him, glaring at the holes in his khaki socks. 'There's no bloody peace around here.'

'Tell me about it,' Clayton muttered, absent-mindedly riffling through a pile of paperwork before picking up an electricity bill, scanning it then wincing.

'Can't even go into the bloody kitchen without hearing women clucking like hens.'

Clayton raised an eyebrow at that and Rob grimaced, knowing how ridiculous he'd sounded. Angie Hardy had been called many things in her time but a clucking hen wasn't one of them. Snarling, barking, snapping and growling? Yes. Clucking? Never.

'That new bloke you've hired —' Rob began, looking for a fight, anything to vent the rage he'd been sitting on.

'Is the only one we can get right now,' Clayton finished,

effectively shutting him down.

'Les found him sleeping under the vines this morning. You *sure* he's the best you could do?'

'Yeah, but best of what I'm not sure,' Clayton said wryly. 'I'll leave you to it.' He wandered back out the door, leaving Rob to go back to taking his ire out on his computer keyboard.

Beth stripped off the white peasant blouse she'd just put on, exchanging it for a caramel-coloured sleeveless silk shirt that matched her dark green skirt. She inspected herself in the mirror on the back of her bedroom door, turned from side to side, then snorted with exasperation before hauling the top off again, causing her fine short hair to crackle with static. She really didn't want to wear anything that would draw attention to her chest or what an idiot she'd been the other evening, but she didn't want to have to resort to the frumpy clothes she'd brought from home.

'It'd help if you knew where you were going. Idiot. You should have got his number so you could find out or, better yet, cancel. Where do you think this is going to go? Nowhere, that's where. You promised yourself you wouldn't let a man get close enough to let you down like Greg did, yet here you are acting like finding the right top is the end of the world!' she admonished herself out loud, scanning the floor for the peasant blouse again. It would have to do given the twenty minutes she had left to get her hair and make-up into some semblance of order before Clayton was due to arrive.

'And while you're talking to yourself like a lunatic, this is a holiday! You're going to dinner, not deciding whether or not you'll marry the man!' Giving herself a fierce look in the mirror, she marched into the bathroom and got to work on her hair and make-up.

Two-and-a-half hours later, the dappled pink-and-gold light of the setting sun filtered through the windows and bathed the living room in a warm, soft glow, but all Beth saw when she looked down at it reflecting off her too-pale skin and too-new clothes was a silly attempt at beautification. Damn and bugger. She felt incredibly foolish and just a little bit angry.

Clayton had obviously changed his mind. She ignored the pang of hurt and disappointment that came with this realisation and turned off the TV. She hadn't been watching it anyway.

'Better this happens now than later,' she lectured herself in her firmest tone of voice as she picked up her phone and fitted it with the new Australian SIM card she'd purchased earlier that day. At times like this, she could always count on her gran to cheer her up.

Retrieving the sheet of paper on which she'd written Laura's local gossip, she determinedly pushed any disappointment from her mind and braced herself for a long, distracting conversation.

'She had them yet?' A startlingly husky female voice broke through Clayton's worried thoughts. He shook his head and grimaced in sympathy as he softly stroked Waffles' side, trying to offer comfort as her whole body heaved with another contraction. When it was over he leaned his head back against the laundry wall, rubbing his eyes with his spare hand.

He'd noticed Waffles acting strange earlier that afternoon and had asked Angie to keep an eye on her while he was working. His suspicions were confirmed when Angie had pulled him away from fixing fences with the news that his dog had holed herself up in the laundry after dragging one of his old T-shirts out of the wash basket to lie on.

He'd raced home and had been sitting at Waffles' side ever since, feeling completely helpless. As a farmer he'd assisted animals to give birth hundreds of times, but this was different. This was his dog.

Jo asked her question again. 'Clayton?'

'Nope, not yet. Have you, girl?' Clayton patted Waffles again before looking up and then up again at all six feet of red-headed Amazon. She was leaning against the doorframe taking in the scene with an equal mixture of concern and excitement.

'Shouldn't be long now,' he added.

'Mind if I keep you company?' Jo hunkered down on the floor next to him, stretching her impossibly long, jean-clad legs out in front of her.

'Yeah, sure.' Clayton looked at her sideways. 'You'll be put to work, though. See that towel over there?' He gestured to an old tattered green beach towel on the floor.

'Yeah?' Jo picked it up and looked at him expectantly.

'You're the official puppy cleaner and dryer.' He nudged her gently in the side. 'As long as you're not squeamish.'

Jo chuckled at the dig. 'Mate, I've seen more men turn green at the mention of lady stuff on the rigs than you can possibly imagine, and I bet you're gonna cry when she finally has them. I promise I won't tell anyone.' She nudged his shoulder right back. Given her height, topping his by at least two inches, the push had a bit of momentum behind it.

Clayton feigned an offended scowl. 'Real men don't cry, but I'll do the manly thing and give you a hug if *you* do,' he countered. 'I might even be able to stretch myself to offering you a clean hanky.'

'Yeah? All right, it's a deal.' They both fell silent as Waffles' body heaved with another contraction.

Ten minutes later, when the first mewling puppy was born, Clayton had to find a hanky for Jo. She'd made it truly soggy by the time it was all over and six whimpering little blue-grey puppies had entered the world.

Waffles was a trouper, alternating between trying to clean her offspring and licking Clayton's hand as her babies fed. By now

everyone else in the house had worked out what was going on and
the laundry was crowded with Jo, Rachael, Angie and Stephen, who
each watched on with a big sappy grin on their face.

For the first time in a few months, Clayton didn't feel claustrophobic with everyone around. He beamed proudly as he accepted
the hot chocolate Angie made everyone and allowed himself to relax
and enjoy the company.

The contented feeling lasted until much later that evening, when
he pulled his now tired, cramping body off the cold laundry floor,
stumbled to his bedroom and saw his good shoes sitting next to his
bed, ready to be polished before his dinner with Beth. The dinner
he'd just missed.

'*Damn.*' He gave a shoe a half-hearted kick before scooping up
his good clothes and heading for the shower.

'I was bisexual once,' Violet mused into the phone, no doubt having got into Louis's single-malt whisky for a medicinal post-lunch
tipple.

Used to statements like this from her gran, Beth waited patiently,
resisting the urge to roll her eyes.

'There were two men in the village who'd been chasing me for
some time.'

'Kevin Soames and William Peakes,' Beth supplied.

'Yes. How did you know?' Violet asked, sounding chagrined
that Beth would ruin the revelation of her salacious tidbit.

'Lucky guess. Gran, bisexual doesn't mean having affairs with
two men. It means —'

'Yes it does.' Violet sounded affronted. '*Bi* means two. Having
sex with two men means bisexual. I'm old, not stupid, Beth.' Beth
could hear some fumbling at Violet's end and then heard her call
out to Louis. 'Bisexual means having sex with two men, doesn't it,

dear?'

Beth didn't hear Louis's reply, but the sound of a door slamming on the other end of the line told her he had decided that the violets in his potting shed were preferable company to the one in the house.

'No, Gran . . .' Beth started and then stopped. What was the point in arguing? After all, she was getting what she wanted. Instead of prying into Beth's private life, Violet was now recounting her nineteen-fifties tale of two suitors with relish.

Beth scanned the crumpled sheet of paper in her lap for another piece of gossip but the sun had gone down and the faint light the moon afforded wasn't enough to read by. She pushed herself up from the sofa, suppressing a groan when her back twinged from being slouched in the same position for so long. She was about to speak again when she was startled by the sound of knocking.

'What was that?' Violet paused her story.

'Someone's at the door. I think I'm going to have to go.'

'At that hour? What time is it there? It has to be eleven o'clock, Beth. Who visits at eleven o'clock at night? I don't think you should answer it. It could be anyone. They have serial killers in Australia, you know. There was this one episode —' Violet began but Beth firmly and gently said goodbye and hung up just in time for another knock on the door.

She opened it and instead of a serial killer, she was confronted with Clayton's silhouette outlined in the moonlight.

'Beth?'

'Clayton?' Beth flicked on the porch light. 'You're late.'

'Yeah, I know it's pretty late, but can I come in for a minute to at least explain?' He looked decidedly sheepish and maybe a little worried.

'I'd like to say no.' Beth's tone betrayed the hurt feelings she'd been telling herself all evening she didn't have.

'Yeah, I'm guessing you would, but if I told you that Waffles just had her puppies, would that explain it?'

'Oh.' Beth exhaled. This changed everything. 'That's wonderful news! Is she all right? I'm assuming so. How many puppies? Were they all born healthy?' She turned on the kitchen and living-room lights and gestured for him to come inside the cottage. His hair was damp and appeared almost black as it glistened in the light. His neatly pressed clothes smelled of sunshine, laundry detergent and freshly soaped man.

'Yeah, she had six. She pulled through fine but I couldn't leave her and I'm sorry to say, I completely forgot the time.' Clayton's face fell when he finally caught sight of Beth's clothes and make-up. 'Oh Jesus. You're all dressed up still. Beth, I feel like a right bastard.'

'Oh no. No, don't apologise,' Beth said in a rush. 'Quite understandable. In this instance I'm more than happy to play second fiddle to another lady. Especially one as sweet as Waffles.'

'Yeah?' Clayton looked relieved. 'Great. Well, I know it's late, but are you tired yet? There's something I'd like to show you.' He finished his words with a sweet, tentative smile that left Beth feeling a little fluttery despite her residual bad mood.

She fidgeted with the hem of her blouse for a moment while debating her answer. It was eleven at night. What could the man want to show her this late?

'It's nothing weird.'

'A comment like that is bound to worry me.'

'I promise there's nothing to worry about.'

'So . . . if I agree to come along, what do I need to bring?' Beth asked cautiously.

'Just yourself.'

Beth felt a flush creep up her cheeks and cursed her body's instantaneous reaction to a simple statement until a thought occurred to her. 'What about bugs?'

'Bugs?'

'You know. Insects. Lethal, biting insects? And reptiles, for that matter. Is what you intend to show me outside? I know about the outdoors here and I'd rather not die tonight.' Beth did nothing to contain her scowl when Clayton started to chuckle. Even if his eyes did that nice, crinkly, sexy thing when he laughed, it wasn't so nice if it was at her expense.

'You don't seriously believe all that stuff you see on TV, do you?' Humour marred his deep baritone.

'Yes.' Beth stuck her chin out. 'Or are you telling me there isn't anything out there that could potentially kill me?'

'Not *really*.' Clayton looked thoughtful. 'I mean, you might run into a death adder this time of night. And maybe if you tried to pick up a rock you could get bitten by a redback spider but —'

'Case in point.'

'*But*.' Clayton spoke over her using a voice more suited to bellowing at livestock. 'I'd protect you. I know what I'm looking for. You've got nothing to worry about.' He offered a not-quite-arrogant-but-definitely-self-assured smile that flashed a dimple.

Beth felt herself giving in. 'Thank you, but honestly, do I need to bring anything? Bug spray? A mosquito net? A large stick? Anti-venom?'

'Nope. Just yourself.' He held his hand up with thumb and pinkie finger crossed in a Boy Scout salute. 'If I'm wrong I promise you can shoot me. I'll even bring the gun around tomorrow.' He said it so seriously, Beth felt herself softening.

'All right. I'll come with you, but I don't want you thinking I'm a pushover.'

'Never.' Clayton held the door open and gestured for her to lead the way to his car.

Chapter 8

It was strange sitting in Clayton's Jeep without Waffles making enough noise to fill up the quiet between them. To distract herself, Beth focused on calming her overactive imagination, while Clayton seemed intent on the dirt track stretching out before them as he navigated around rocks and deep potholes.

'Are you at least going to give me a hint?' Beth asked eventually, just to break up the silence.

'Nah. You'll just have to wait. I'd tell you, but . . .' He smiled. 'It'd sound stupid. Much better you see, eh?'

'Now you've really got me on the edge of my seat.' Beth stared out the window at the silver-grey shadows cast by the moon on the white-gold grass. There wasn't a building or light in sight as they followed the blue-black silhouettes demarking the rows of grapevines.

'Clayton, honestly, where are we going? Remember that comment I made about you being a serial killer when you helped with the tyre? You know I was joking, don't you?' Beth tried to keep her tone light but that didn't stop a faint edge of worry creeping in by the end of her question. Even in the Yorkshire countryside she had never felt this isolated. There was always a car or the lights of the next village shining in the distance. Out here it was just dark sky and the moon.

'Gave all that up years ago,' Clayton replied, amusement in his voice. 'The only thing I've serial-killed lately is Corn Flakes.'

Beth shot him a disbelieving look, her apprehension temporarily forgotten. 'That has to be the worst joke I've heard in years! *Ever*, actually.'

'Nah. I can come up with worse. Gotta give me a bit of time for that kind of originality,' Clayton drawled as he finally pulled over next to a row of grapevines on a bumpy stretch of road identical to every other bumpy stretch of road they had just traversed.

Beth barely had time to think before he opened his door and walked around the back of the car. She craned her head to watch him retrieve a black duffel bag from the back seat. Something inside it made a clanking sound like metal brushing on metal.

Oh God. Black duffel bag? Before Beth knew it, her brain decided to turn a corner and hurtle down a crazy tangent fuelled by the late hour and her far-too-vivid imagination. Had she just done something very, very silly? Here she was in the middle on nowhere, in the middle of the night, with a man she'd known for four days. She hadn't even remembered to bring her phone. Bugger. Bugger. Bugger.

A myriad of horror-movie plots sped through her mind as an internal checklist formed. Isolated country location? *Check.* Vulnerable, common-sense-impaired woman? *Check.* Large, attractive male? *Check.* Suspicious bag? *Check.*

Yes, she knew she was being daft, but still . . .

'If you wait here, I'll be back in a tick. I'll just set up.' With that, Clayton loped off to a location somewhere behind the car with the bag and something much larger he had retrieved from the Jeep's roof rack.

'Set up? Set what up?' Her sharp question was answered with the thud of receding footsteps.

'I don't feel much better for being left alone,' she called after him but was met with silence marred by the odd rustle of something in the vines and a sheep bleating in the distance. She waited for a reply but got nothing.

'Clayton?' she called out again, this time much louder, before unbuckling her seatbelt and scrambling out of the Jeep, hugging her arms around her body and turning around a few times.

There wasn't any sign of Clayton. He'd turned the headlights off but the full moon illuminated her surrounds well enough to see clearly. She crunched across the gravel and dirt track around to the driver's side of the Jeep and saw he'd also left the keys in the ignition. It didn't leave her feeling any better. After all, she had no idea where she was.

Beth's ears pricked up and the small hairs on the back of her neck electrified at the sound of more loud rustling in the grapevines. There was definitely something moving around in them, something large to be making that much noise. Her skin prickled as her mind frantically whirred back to all the information she'd read, seen and been told about Australian wildlife. Were snakes nocturnal? A lot of them were, weren't they? Did they climb things? Of course they did. Tree snakes. Were the death adders Clayton mentioned tree snakes?

She moved herself a good distance from the car and the grapevines just in case.

Another thought occurred to her. Maybe these death adders camouflaged themselves like the rattlesnakes she'd seen on TV. Did they have rattlesnakes here, or was that just America? Damn, she couldn't remember if she had seen a reference to them in her copy of *Australia's Most Dangerous Creatures*. All she remembered was close-up images of venom-spitting fangs.

Five minutes later she had worked herself into such a state of paranoia that she'd climbed back into the Jeep and was eyeballing the landscape through the open windows as if she expected it to rise up and gnaw her to death any minute now.

'Any reason you're still in there?'

Beth's stomach tried to jump out of her mouth. She shrieked and twisted around to find Clayton on the driver's side of the car, his arms crossed, amusement clearly lining his features in the moonlight.

'Oh, no reason,' she croaked, moving her hands woodenly from where they had been clutching her chest.

'You want to get out of the car now?'

'Not just yet. You know when you mentioned death adders and those spiders?'

'Redbacks. Yeah?' he asked with obvious confusion before understanding dawned. 'Beth. Are you frightened?'

'I might be.'

'Right.' Clayton frowned as if in deep thought. 'How about if I told you I just did a thorough check of the area and there aren't any snakes or spiders,' he reassured her with the same voice he probably used to convince the cows in his dairy to produce extra milk and tipsy senior citizens in his winery that they needed to go home to bed.

'That might help,' Beth said, not believing him for a second but still feeling soothed by the assurance in his deep voice.

'So, do you want to come out of there now?'

Beth thought about things for a moment. 'All right.' She climbed out of the Jeep and walked around to his side.

'You all right?' Clayton asked, probably thinking she was going to have another hysterical fit.

'Ah. Yes. Yes, fine.'

'Good.' He held out his hand.

She stared at it blankly until he wrapped his work-roughened fingers around hers and gently began to tug her along the rocky dirt track behind the car.

'Clayton?' Beth tried to keep up with his longer stride while madly surveying the ground around her. She'd foolishly worn her new delicate gold leather sandals and they were catching every stone and clump of dirt in the vicinity.

'Hmm?'

'Clayton!'

'What?' He stopped so abruptly at her shout that she barrelled into his back.

'Would you mind slowing down?' Beth paused to catch her breath. 'You've got longer legs than I do.'

'Oh. Sorry.' He had the grace to look sheepish before setting off again, this time at a much more relaxed pace. 'It's just down here.'

'What is?' Beth returned her eyes to her feet. Every stick on the side of the track looked like a snake, every rock appeared to harbour a giant spider. Her panic grew worse as they veered off through a wide grassy gap between the rows of vines. Their forms cast blue-purple shadows on the silver grass in the moonlight. The scene was beautiful but all Beth could think was that it was harder to see the ground.

'Almost there,' Clayton said, his mouth twitching in amusement at her distraction. She caught his smile and frowned.

'Where?'

'Here.' He came to an abrupt stop and grinned down at her expectantly.

It took Beth a few seconds to drag her eyes away from his to look around her.

'Oh. *Oh!* How beautiful!'

In front of her, sheltered between two widely spaced rows of grapevines, Clayton had erected a fold-out card table flanked by two camping chairs. The table was covered with a white cloth and next to a bottle of wine sat a large platter holding a selection of cheeses and fruit. Beth took a step closer, her eyes tearing up a little.

'It's lovely,' she said in a husky whisper.

'And to top it off . . .' Clayton pulled a cigarette lighter out of his pocket and lit a large white stubby candle, placing it in the centre. The flame flickered a little with the gentle night breeze but the vines provided enough shelter that it didn't go out.

'Makes the area snake- and spider-proof,' Clayton said with a completely serious expression.

'Really?' Beth asked, distracted. She was still caught up on the thought that someone would do something so romantic *for her*. Someone she'd only just met. Who she'd made bad coffee for *twice*. This couldn't be happening.

Maybe the man was gay.

The random, desperate, far-fetched thought popped into her mind and once it was there it didn't want to go. Weren't a lot of gay men rugged with a nice body? They always were on the telly. Okay, so Clayton had kissed her, but to Beth's knowledge and definitely to her experience, straight men *surely* did not do this kind of thing, at least straight Yorkshire men, and certainly not for her.

'I don't know what you're thinking, Beth, but I'm not sure I'm too encouraged by that expression.'

'Clayton, are you gay?' she asked before her brain could tell her mouth to keep shut.

A while later, when the silence got less deafening, Beth stopped fidgeting and sneaked a peek at his stunned expression. 'Sorry. My bad. Blurting things out like that. I'm . . . this is just so unexpected!'

Clayton ran a large hand over his mouth and shook his head as if to dislodge her words. 'Uh. Beth. Jeez. That came out of nowhere. I gotta say I don't have a problem with people being gay, so I'm not gonna say I'm offended as such, but . . .' He paused, his expression comically bemused. 'I wouldn't mind knowing what I've done that'd have you thinking I'm hitting for the same team. I'm pretty sure being out at midnight with a beautiful woman, sharing a candlelit dinner under a full moon would make my sexual preferences pretty bloody clear.' He searched her face before his voice dropped to a lower pitch. 'And I'm pretty sure I proved to you which way I swing the other night.'

Beth didn't know what to do or say to that. His words left warmth pooling through her chest and into her belly. She focused on the little table again.

'So, are we going to sit down or are you just going to stand there? I haven't had anything to eat yet tonight. What about you?' Clayton placed a hand on her hip and gently prodded her forwards.

'No . . . no, I haven't.'

'Sorry about that,' Clayton said before changing his tone so that it had a sharper edge. 'Beth, it'd really offend me if you didn't sit down and enjoy yourself.'

'Oh. Oh, sorry. Damn. All right,' Beth said, immediately taking a seat. She sunk down into the canvas chair and tried to force herself to relax.

Clayton certainly didn't appear to be sharing her dilemma as he poured them both a generous glass of wine. The liquid was black and mysterious in the half-light. 'This is one of our two-thousand cab savs. I've been saving it. Should be nice.' He raised his glass, inhaling its fragrance appreciatively. 'Fantastic,' he said with such satisfaction that Beth had to see what the fuss was about.

The dark wine flowing over her tongue tasted like black coffee, raspberries and a hint of sin. It slid down to her empty stomach like a sigh and she immediately felt her shoulders relax.

'Nice?' Clayton asked.

'Very nice.' Beth took another sip. Then another. It wasn't long before the rustle of the breeze flowing through the vines no longer struck her as ominous. The shadows flickering across the table and the land around them didn't seem threatening, and the man sitting across the table, relaxed in his chair, his knees splayed comfortably while he regarded her with a small contemplative smile, was too good to be true.

'Give the grapes a go.' He gestured to the platter. 'They're ours.'

'Really?' Beth reached for a bunch, popping a small green grape into her mouth. Her eyes widened with surprise at the delicious combination of faint sugary sweetness overlaying acidic tartness.

'Try one with the cheese.' Clayton picked up one of the crackers he'd arranged on the plate, smearing creamy Brie over it. He placed a grape on top before holding it out. Beth leaned forward and allowed him to pop it into her mouth. The mix of flavours melted on her tongue, amazing to her hungry tastebuds.

She was so caught up with enjoying the first food she'd had since lunchtime, she almost didn't notice the way Clayton's finger rested on her bottom lip a few seconds longer than necessary. He'd already leaned back comfortably in his chair by the time she registered the contact.

'Shouldn't we be having red grapes with red wine?' She took another luxurious sip.

Clayton shrugged. 'The great thing about owning a winery is that I don't have any hang-ups about wine. I like to drink it with whatever feels right, not what some tasting chart tells me. Keeps things interesting.'

'Oh? That's reassuring.' Beth relaxed a little further into her chair and munched her way through a small bunch of grapes before she could stop herself.

'You like those?'

'Hmm.'

'So,' Clayton said. He was holding his wine glass by the stem. His large, square-topped fingers should have looked clumsy, but they didn't. 'You know what I do. You want to tell me a bit about you?'

'Me?'

'It's either you or the sheep.'

'In that case, ask the sheep. I'm sure they're far more interesting.'

'Nah. I talk to them all the time. Conversation is pretty repetitive.' Clayton tilted his head, looking at her expectantly.

'Well, all right.' Beth gave in. 'You already know my job and that I live in a village in Yorkshire. It's very green. Lots of hills, famous for them actually.'

'The moors, they're called, aren't they?'

'Yes. There are moors and dales. The moors are more interesting. They send people mad. Or at least they did in *Wuthering Heights*. You know, it's a sin but I never liked that novel.' Beth made her confession with the same gravity a person would use to say they didn't like puppies and kittens.

'Yeah? I gotta say I didn't either. I read it to Rachael years ago. It was pretty bloody depressing, disturbing too if I recall.'

'You used to read to your little sister?' Beth tried to imagine the big burly man in front of her hunched over Emily Brontë's classic, and failed miserably.

'Well, not that little.' Clayton smiled wryly. 'Actually, she was about nine and going through a *Pride and Prejudice* thing and thought *Wuthering Heights* would be the same.'

'It's not.'

'Nope. But she put so much effort into blackmailing me into reading it that I made her listen to the entire book. I was a vengeful little bastard at thirteen.' He chuckled.

'Blackmail? How?' Beth asked, intrigued.

'She caught me and Mike using Angie's favourite china plates as clay pigeons for target practice with Dad's rifle.' He winced. 'Angie found out anyway. Don't know how. Especially when we went to a whole lot of effort to blame it on our youngest brother, Stephen. We even hid the broken pieces in his bedroom.'

'That's awful!' Beth smothered a shocked laugh. 'My God! I'm glad my sister was never that mean to me. Valerie was a saint by comparison.'

'She sounds like she was a character.' Clayton snagged himself another cracker with cheese.

'She was.' Beth sighed. 'I miss her dreadfully.' Beth felt the usual twinge of grief sneak up behind her. Clayton must have seen it because he launched into another tale of childhood mischief. This story involved him and his brothers jumping off the house roof, onto a trampoline and then into the family swimming pool. By the time he'd finished, Beth was near to crying with laughter, her sadness swept away on the cool sea breeze that ruffled their hair and sent the candle flickering.

Later, when Clayton dropped Beth back at her cottage, planting a very soft, gentle kiss on her cheek before leaving, she wondered, just a little, if she could pretend she was someone else for the rest of her trip. Maybe then she could take what Clayton seemed to be offering, take what she desperately wanted to have. She fell asleep with a smile on her face.

'What do you want to order? I'm having the barramundi with lemon risotto. I'd suggest the lamb because it's usually pretty good, or maybe the spare ribs. Yum. Or do you want the fish instead?' Laura asked, perusing the menu in front of her. She was wearing a pair of black-framed glasses today and was a bit sexy-librarian in a casual black jersey dress with a split up the side. When Beth had arrived at the bar half an hour earlier, Laura confessed she'd run out of contact lenses and would have to go to Perth to get more after Christmas, which was only a week away.

Over the past half-hour they'd managed to drink a pint of beer each and Beth was amused by the way Laura's need to talk slowed down by a fraction with each sip of beer, to the point where they'd just shared a few moments of relaxed silence between them.

'Maybe a steak,' Beth mused. 'Not too big, with some green peppercorn sauce on the side.'

'Mashed potato too? I loooove mashed potato. I wish I could make it as well as they do here but I can't. I don't know what they do to it. Maybe it's the butter. Actually, it's definitely the butter.'

'A double serve.' Beth grinned. 'It's the best part and there's no point eating out if you can't eat something naughty.'

'Definitely. Although that philosophy is getting me into a whole lot of trouble lately.' Laura rolled her eyes. 'It's the sole reason I've put on weight since I moved back down here. Well, that and chocolate cake. And the beer probably doesn't help.' She nodded towards the full pint sitting next to her. 'There's something about living in the country that makes comfort eating so easy. Not that you'd have to worry.' She pointed at Beth with the slice of warm bread she'd just buttered before taking a bite.

'Actually, I would dearly welcome a bit of extra weight,' Beth countered. 'I've always been quite small. It has its disadvantages.'

'Tell that to *Cosmo*.' Laura leaned back and rubbed her stomach. 'And to my pot belly.'

'I think it's cute.' Beth chuckled and held up her hand when Laura started to object. 'No, honestly. I wish I had one.'

'Shut up.' Laura gave her a gentle kick under the table. 'So says you, Little Miss Tiny. It's easy to say stuff like that when you're so small.'

'And why is that supposed to be such a good thing?' Beth picked up a hunk of sourdough and dunked it in some delicious locally pressed lemon-infused olive oil.

'Being thin is *always* a good thing.' Laura stated the words with such conviction that Beth was taken aback.

The curvaceous, beautiful woman in front of her actually believed she was unattractive, and not in the casual, temporarily neurotic way most women did after reading the gossip pages in a fashion magazine. She truly believed it. This would not do. After a minute or two of internal debate, Beth made a decision. There was a chance it might backfire but she couldn't have her new friend believing such rubbish.

'Honestly, Laura, it's not. Can I tell you something? It's rather personal but relevant.'

'Yeah. Of course! We've decided to be friends, remember? The more personal the better.' Laura leaned forward and braced her elbows on the table.

'I had breast cancer.'

Laura's eyes went saucer-wide but Beth continued speaking before she could ask the usual questions.

'It was caught very early and it's gone now, hopefully never to return. I opted for a double preventative mastectomy because of my family history, and because I was so thin they couldn't do a reconstruction. There wasn't enough weight on my backside or stomach to take fat from and no family members left who could be suitable donors. My sister had already died from cancer that same year and my parents were long gone. So . . .' She shrugged a little woodenly. 'Sometimes a little extra weight is handy. And right now I wouldn't mind being a little curvier, because at least then I'd feel more like a woman.'

Laura stared at her a few moments, the bread dangling, forgotten, from her fingers. 'You had cancer?'

Beth sighed. This was why she didn't like to talk about it. One mention of cancer and you'd think you'd just read out your own obituary in public. 'Yes. But that's not the point. The point is that once I lost my breasts, I realised how much I relied on them to give shape to my body, as small as they were. I would love to have bigger hips and a cute tummy like yours. They're things that would make me feel more feminine.'

'But —'

Beth levelled Laura with a stern look. 'Don't give me sympathy, please. I really don't need it. What I'd rather have is you admit you are beautiful just how you are and to promise you'll enjoy every bite of lunch followed by a nice big slice of chocolate cake without guilt.'

Laura opened her mouth to speak and then promptly shut it again, her eyes narrowing to scrutinise Beth's chest, covered today in a pretty pale-pink blouse.

'Fake,' Beth supplied before her friend could ask. 'I wear a mastectomy bra with two painfully anatomically correct inserts. They're hideous, really. I'd much rather if they were purple or blue, but unfortunately they're flesh-coloured with fake nipples and are far perkier and larger than my real ones ever were.' Despite the heaviness of the topic, she grinned at Laura over her pint of beer. 'Don't tell me you're actually speechless?'

Laura opened her mouth again like a stunned goldfish, but no words came out. Beth couldn't help but find the situation amusing. Her peals of laughter ended up attracting attention from the nearby tables and brought over the waiter, who had been hovering just out of earshot, ready to take their order.

'It's not funny, Beth. You can't just spring that kind of thing on someone,' Laura grumbled after she and Beth gave their orders, making sure to include two large helpings of chocolate cake for dessert.

'I thought it was,' Beth replied. 'And I'm sorry about springing it on you, but I believe the situation called for it. I couldn't have you talking about yourself that way.'

'Why didn't you go for implants?' Laura asked, looking genuinely confused. 'If you hate the bra so much. Nix that, why even bother with the bra at all? You're tiny. It wouldn't look silly for you to be . . .'

'Flat?'

'Well, yeah, flat on top. You've got great legs, a nice arse, not a lot there, like you say, but it still looks good. It wouldn't be weird at all. If anything, you'd just look more waif-like.' Laura studied Beth with a critical eye.

'In answer to your first question, I just couldn't bear the thought of going through another round of surgery. It can take over a year for reconstruction with implants. It's not as simple as you would believe, and more importantly, I didn't see the point. And to your second question, I guess it's more to make other people comfortable.' Beth shrugged, surprised at how easy she was finding this topic after staying silent about it with so many people back home. Maybe the distance from everything familiar was freeing her up. 'So, to cut short a very long and no doubt far less interesting conversation than the one we could be having short, all I would like to say is: enjoy your curves. They're lovely and that's all there is to it.'

'I guess I'll have to drink to that,' Laura said, revealing her cherubic dimples and clinking her glass to Beth's. 'So, how was your dinner with Clayton the other night?'

Now it was Beth's turn to look disgruntled.

'Fair play.' Laura grinned.

'Touché,' Beth retorted, fighting the shyness that ambushed her, causing her cheeks to warm. 'It was wonderful.'

'So, what did he do? Did you go out somewhere? Which restaurant and what happened after?' Laura asked in a rush.

Relieved that they were on much safer ground, Beth told Laura about Clayton's no-show followed by the romantic midnight picnic in the vines.

'You and Clayton are really hitting it off, aren't you? I mean, it's pretty easy to tell you like him. Even Jeff said —'

'What? Jeff said what?' Beth demanded.

'That he didn't have a look in with you the other day. You'd made your mind up on Clayton already.' Laura popped a bite of barramundi into her mouth. 'Oh wow. This tastes amazing. Here.' She offered a forkful of lemon-flavoured fish to Beth.

'Hmm. I agree.' Beth paused, momentarily distracted as she chewed. 'But Laura, Jeff reminds me too much of a —'

'Naughty kid? He's always been like that. I know he's my older brother but seriously, I sometimes think he's three.' Laura chuckled.

'I was going to say I've thought of him as a Jack Russell,' said Beth and then relayed her theory about people and dogs.

'So, what am I?' Laura leaned forward again, keen to hear the answer, pale-blue eyes dancing.

Beth frowned in concentration. 'You're some sort of very affectionate, intelligent dog. Maybe a corgi.'

'A corgi?' Laura reared back in surprise. 'You sure I'm not a yapping little dog like a chihuahua? I know I talk a lot and it can be annoying.'

'Noooo.' Beth smiled and surveyed her friend's expression, noting again that small hint of vulnerability she'd spotted before. 'No, definitely not.'

'Oh good.' Laura was visibly relieved. 'So, back to Clayton. You think you guys are going to get serious? I know you're on holiday and everything, but do you think you might be interested?'

Beth sighed and shook her head sadly. 'I don't think so, Laura.'

'You mean he doesn't float your boat? Because I know he's my brother's best friend and I've known him since I was a kid, but he still gives me lady moments.' A hint of wistfulness crossed Laura's features. 'Not that he's ever noticed me. Actually, I have to say the whole picnic thing is the most romantic thing I've ever heard. I mean, Clayton's always been nice to his other girlfriends but not *that* nice. He's a guy, you know? They don't usually think of stuff like that.'

'Unless they're feeling guilty for standing you up for their dog?' Beth laughed.

Laura thought for a moment then shook her head. 'No. Even then they don't do anything *that* nice. So, have you slept with him yet?'

Beth did a spectacular job of choking on a succulent mouthful of aged Aberdeen Angus steak.

Laura signalled for the waiter to bring Beth a glass of water. It was delivered promptly and a few minutes later Beth was still flushed but fine.

'So? *Have* you slept with him yet?' Laura asked. 'I hear he's pretty spectacular between the sheets, not that I'd know personally. One of his old girlfriends, Sharon Phelps, is a bragger. When she divorced her husband last year, she told everyone the ex was a flop and that Clayton was much better, even though he was her first and they were only sixteen or something when they did it.'

Beth stared at Laura, dumbstruck.

'It's true,' Laura insisted, taking Beth's silence as disagreement. 'She did say it. And since you're acting like that, I'm guessing you haven't slept with him. Why not?'

'After the conversation we've just had, I think the reason is obvious,' Beth spluttered, trying to keep defensiveness out of her tone.

'So, it's all right for me to have a pot belly and huge thighs but it's not all right for you to have had surgery because of a life-threatening illness?'

'It's not the same thing,' Beth protested, shocked by Laura's abrupt reduction of her lack of breasts to a mundane female body complex.

'Only if you see it like that,' Laura retorted. 'If hot sex with a guy like Clayton is on the table, why not take it? All he can do is say no and frankly, from what you just said, he's really interested in you. Clayton's not the kind of guy to be a bastard about things. You know his mum died from leukemia, right?'

'All the more reason —' Beth started.

'For him to be cool with things. Or at least honest,' Laura finished for her before she continued, her expression earnest. 'Seriously, Beth, jump the man's bones. You're on holiday. You're hot. You're young. Go for it.' With that, Laura delicately popped another morsel of fish between her lips and gestured for the waiter to bring them another two pints of beer.

Chapter 9

Sweat beaded on Clayton's forehead, running down to his eyebrows before dripping onto his eyelashes. It stung but his hands were too greasy to wipe it off. He and his dad had just spent the better part of the afternoon sweltering in the massive corrugated-iron shed that encompassed the majority of Evangeline's Rest's wine-making operation, trying to get a reluctant old back-up generator to work.

Christmas was only a few days away and there would inevitably be the usual round of things going wrong, including a summer electrical storm and a power outage. It happened every year without fail, and the last thing they needed was for the restaurant to lose power on Christmas Eve. Especially not when Rachael was charging two hundred dollars a head for a seven-course degustation menu. Definitely not when his family was holding their annual Christmas Eve party at the house.

He finished tightening a bolt then turned to his father.

Rob's reading glasses, perched on the end of his nose, were incongruous with his old grease-smeared khaki work shirt and shorts. He was holding a filthy, cracked ice-cream container full of greasy nuts, bolts and washers in one hand, sorting through it with the other, his forehead lined with concentration.

'Try starting her up again, Dad.' Clayton stepped back from the generator and reached for a rag to wipe his hands.

Rob didn't respond.

'Dad,' Clayton repeated himself, this time a little louder. Given he was a Hardy male, his booming voice echoed around the massive shed a few times, bouncing off wine barrels and vats of sauvignon blanc before reaching Rob's ears.

'What?'

'Start her up again. It should work now.' Clayton gestured to the generator before grabbing another rag to wipe his face.

'Yeah, sure.' Rob put down the container and turned the fuel valve back on, then tweaked the choke and flicked a switch.

A few moments later they were both rewarded with a healthy mechanical roar. Feeling a mutual sense of accomplishment, father and son shared a pleased nod then simultaneously turned when they heard a vehicle approaching.

A few seconds later, Fred pulled up at the back of the shed in a large green John Deere tractor. Clayton and Rob stared with a mix of dumbfounded amazement as their new farmhand climbed down from the cab, leaving the door open so that the tractor's other distressed occupant was clearly visible.

'Any reason there's a sheep in the tractor, mate?' Clayton was the first to speak. He wasn't sure whether to piss himself laughing or blow up at Fred. The piece of machinery in front of them was only six months old, had cost a fortune and was in no way improved by the frantically bleating ewe.

'Uh, yep.' Fred dusted his jeans off then ruffled a hand through his lank dishwater-brown hair. Clayton couldn't help but notice the liberal smattering of sheep shit on the man's boots.

'So, what is it? Actually, don't answer, mate. Just get her down before she wrecks anything.' Clayton shook his head and handed the rag he'd just used to wipe his face to Rob, who in turn used it to wipe his hands.

'He's not mentally impaired or anything, is he? It's worth checking before I kick his arse,' Rob murmured to Clayton out the corner of his mouth. They both watched Fred climb back up into the tractor cab and attempt what was either a complicated tackle or an amorous courtship. It was hard to tell.

Clayton contemplated the scene for a while. 'Nope. Just an idiot.' He cupped his hands around his mouth and bellowed up at Fred, who was having limited success. 'Put her in the stockyards and then clean out the cab, mate. Better be spotless. You wanna tell me why she was in there in the first place?'

'She was on the road,' Fred called back as if that answered everything while he tried to herd the sheep against the steering column.

'Yeah . . . and?'

'Didn't know where it went, so I brought it back to ask you.' Fred grunted as the ewe won another tackle and bunted him square in the guts.

'You didn't think to drop her over a fence and then come ask?' Clayton yelled over the sound of the ewe bleating at full volume and then berated himself. Stupid question.

'Nope.'

'Is she even ours?' Rob asked with an edge of amazement in his voice. His question was met with a series of loud thumps. The ewe was definitely winning.

Clayton decided that was all they were going to get. He gestured for his dad to follow him back into the shed.

'You *sure* he's not —' Rob asked.

'Nope.' Clayton sighed. 'He's not, but I'd say in the past twenty years he's smoked more weed than a bushfire.'

'So why haven't we given him the sack yet?' Rob's amazement abated and his usual autocratic business sense started to show.

'You got any alternative suggestions, Dad? Because I've been advertising for someone for months now and he's the only bite we've had. Seriously. Economic recession, my arse. If Jeff hadn't told me about Fred, we'd still be up to our eyeballs in back work. He's slow but he gets things done. Mostly,' Clayton amended when Rob looked doubtful.

'Unconventionally, by the looks of it. If that tractor isn't immaculate by tonight, he's gone,' Rob said before grinning reluctantly. 'Most ridiculous thing I've seen in a while. Wanna beer?'

'Don't have to ask twice.'

He followed his dad to the porch, where Rob retrieved two bottles from the fully stocked bar fridge they kept outside for days like this. Clayton accepted his and they both took a seat, Rob groaning and wincing.

'Your back hurtin', old man?' Clayton asked.

'Here and there.' Rob downed half his beer in one gulp.

Built like his son and only in his early fifties, Rob was still in great shape, heavily muscled across his chest and shoulders from the hard work that had inevitably taken its toll on his spine. The only things that visibly gave his age away were the thick lines bracketing his mouth and the faint touch of grey at the temples of his thick curly dark brown hair, cut a half-inch shorter than his son's.

'You didn't get in till late the other night. Any reason?' Rob chugged the remaining half of his beer and smacked his lips in satisfaction.

'Might be.'

'Like that, is it?'

'Might be.'

'This reason coming to the party Christmas Eve?'

'If I have to tie her up to bring her,' Clayton replied with a slow grin.

Rob laughed. 'You sure you shouldn't just take round the tractor and haul her into the cab? Worked for Fred and his girlfriend.'

'I'll take your suggestion on board then ignore it completely.' Clayton's grin turned into a smirk when he saw a disgruntled Fred walking back towards the tractor in the distance. The farmhand's shirt and jeans were covered in muck, no doubt a love letter from his new lady.

'Things seem to have settled down between you and Angie,' he said to his dad with deliberate casualness after a few moments of comfortable silence.

Rob curled his lip. 'Stubborn old bag.'

'That's my grandma you're insulting there.' Clayton shot him a sharp look out the corner of his eye.

'My mum, so I get first dibs.' Rob ran a hand over his jaw, grimacing. 'I don't know why she's being so bloody difficult.'

'Probably because you're being such a prick about things.' Clayton propped his booted feet up on the edge of a half wine barrel full of purple and yellow pansies in front of him.

'*Me?*' Rob leaned forward then flinched again at the twinge in his back. 'You'd think I'd get a say about who gets hired and fired around here. If she'd asked me about Gwen —'

'We wouldn't have doubled our cellar-door sales in the space of two weeks. Face it, Dad, Gwen's great. I don't know what your problem is. She's a good egg. I know she and Mum used to be friends. I remember her reading at Mum's funeral, so I don't understand why you don't like her.'

'It's not that easy, mate.' Rob's defeated tone of voice surprised Clayton. He'd expected his dad to spark at his words, not sound depressed.

'It might be if you tell me what happened, because from what I can see, Gwen doesn't have a problem. It's just you.' Clayton had been living in a domestic cold-war zone for over a week now and had reached the end of his tether.

'You're right about that.' A voice came from inside the house behind them. Both Clayton and Rob twisted around to see Angie standing on the other side of the porch screen door with one hand on her hip. Her expression was stern. Gwen stood behind her with a sad look marring her round features.

'You set me up?' Rob growled at Clayton in a furious whisper.

'Nope. But I gotta go check on Fred.' Clayton scooped up his beer and made a hasty beeline for the shed in the distance.

'Robert?'

Rob ignored his mum and instead glared at his yellow-bellied son's retreating back.

'Robert, are you going to answer Gwen?' Angie demanded.

'Let me handle this, Angie. Thanks,' Gwen interjected calmly. 'Do you mind taking over for me at the cellar door for five minutes or so?'

Rob couldn't hear Angie's reply because by then she'd moved further back into the house, but the sound of the front door slamming shut told him he was alone with Gwen. A few moments later he heard the screen door behind him open and the once-familiar smell of roses hit him fair and square in the nostrils. He flinched. Nearly thirty years on and she was still wearing the same damn perfume.

'Robert. Do you mind if I join you for a minute?' Gwen asked.

'Suit yourself,' he grunted, keeping his eyes resolutely focused in front of him as she sat in Clayton's vacated seat. The wooden chair creaked and he heard the sound of her taking a sip from a cup of tea, but she didn't say anything.

He sneaked a sideways peek. She was dressed like some artsy-fartsy hippy as usual. Her spiky hair was curling in the humidity. Huge earrings made of some sort of blue stone hung to just above her round shoulders, and she was wearing an eye-watering green-and-blue shirt that pooled in her generous lap over white linen trousers.

Something caught his eye. Was that a toe ring? Jesus Christ. What woman in her fifties wore a toe ring? Some people just didn't know how to age gracefully.

'I'll take that as a compliment,' Gwen murmured coolly. Rob realised he'd said the latter out loud. He covered up his embarrassment with a surge of indignation.

'I've got nothing to say to you, Gwen.'

'No? I would have thought the opposite.' She sighed a big, chest-heaving sigh. 'Robert, I understand you're angry with me still. But I'd just like to tell you . . .' She paused as Rob snorted derisively. 'I've never stopped thinking of you as a friend. If I'm going to work here I think it would be good for us to talk. This hostility between us —'

'Hostility? You sound like a TV shrink,' Rob bit out, deliberately disregarding her other words.

'*You* sound like a ten-year-old boy.'

Rob tried to stare her down but her expression was far too knowing. When her face softened in sympathy, he pushed himself out of his chair.

'Conversation's over, Gwen. How about you just stick to your job and I'll stick to mine? Better yet, how about you quit your job and give me back my peace and quiet?' He began to walk away. He had bolts to sort.

'Robert,' Gwen called out after him, her tone softer.

'What?' he glared over his shoulder, swiping his reading glasses off when they began to slip down his nose.

'I genuinely didn't know she was there that day.' Gwen's eyes met his dead on as her hands clasped each other tightly in her lap.

'You bloody well did, Gwen, so don't fucking lie to make things better now.' Turning away from the shock and hurt on her face,

Rob stomped off towards the shed, hoping to hell that Fred had screwed up and left the tractor a mess so he could kick some arse.

Beth leaned against the shower wall, letting warm spray wash over her body while she desperately tried to still her turbulent thoughts. She wasn't successful. Once she'd begun to think about sex and Clayton Hardy in the same sentence, her body, infuriating biological organism that it was, had switched her libido on and juiced it up with a dab of rocket fuel. For three nights now she'd been unable to sleep for dreams that would have her excommunicated from her church back in Skipton for sheer lewdness.

The big question, the only question, was: could she do it? Was she strong enough to face yet another rejection if Clayton couldn't bear the sight of her scars? What if he turned away in disgust and fear, like Greg had? Or even worse, what if he *did* have sex with her but only out of pity? She groaned, vigorously scrubbing her face with her hands. That would be so much worse. It would be completely unbearable.

Things couldn't go on like they were now, though. She had already agreed to accompany him to his family's Christmas Eve party tonight. Didn't that make her a tease of the worst sort if she kept agreeing to go places with him? Wasn't that leading him on?

'I don't bloody well knowww,' she answered herself in a groan. Damn it. Why wasn't there some sort of rule book on this thing?

A small voice in her head told her she was a massive coward if she didn't take what life had just thrown at her. It wasn't as if she could pop down to the supermarket and pick up a man like Clayton Hardy on a whim, along with a loaf of bread and some butter. And, as for her promise to herself to never risk rejection again . . . well, this didn't really apply, did it? This was a holiday thing. Maybe this would even be a way to get over what happened with Greg. All evidence to date pointed to Clayton being a rock. Surely he would be able to take the news, or at least leave her with her dignity if the idea didn't work for him.

Maybe, just *maybe* she could do it. How, she wasn't sure. She'd have to tell him first and then . . . would she be able to turn him on? Greg had been a self-professed breast man. Was Clayton? He'd tried to get her topless the time they'd kissed, and she'd felt his arousal pressing against her, but was that because of the breasts he thought she had?

Beth's experience was sorely limited. She'd always been too shy to talk about these things with friends, and that same shyness had extended to looking them up. Now she regretted her reticence. It would be so much *easier* if people were like dogs. Then her appearance wouldn't matter – it would all be up to pheromones.

She needed a plan. More importantly she needed to do some research before this evening, but how? The cottage still wasn't hooked up to wi-fi, she had no phone coverage, and the thought of being caught looking up sex techniques while using a cafe's Internet service was enough to send her into a cold sweat. There were bookshops in nearby towns, but that would mean standing at a counter buying the book. Worse, what if they didn't have the kind of book she needed, one with diagrams, pictures and clear explanations that she could look at discreetly?

She emerged from the shower and strode into the bedroom, towel-drying her hair. And then there was the issue of how to introduce the topic of her cancer to Clayton without shutting down the evening completely. They would have to be alone, obviously. She would have to keep her wits about her, so probably no alcohol —

'You know, they're not that bad at all. The scars, I mean. I don't know what you were worried about. You could probably use a hedge trim downstairs, though. Well, that's only if you want to. I know a really good lady in George Creek who does the best waxing.' Laura's rush of words took a few seconds to register but when they did, Beth screamed loud enough to shatter glass.

'What? What's wrong?' Laura frantically scanned Beth's dishevelled bedroom for a potential threat. She was standing next to the mirror at the end of the bed holding Beth's mastectomy bra up to her chest like she'd been trying it on, which, given the size of Laura's already impressive cleavage, was a rather humorous thought.

'Laura! What are you doing here?' Beth fumbled with her towel until she'd wrapped it around herself, willing her heart to slide back down her throat and resettle in her chest. It was beating triple time.

'Inviting you over for Christmas lunch tomorrow. I forgot to before,' Laura replied simply, as if it made perfect sense for her to be standing in Beth's bedroom waiting for her to get out of the shower. 'I'm doing the cooking because last year Jeff tried to poison us all with chicken so raw in the middle it could have run off the table. You can put these on if you like, but I don't know why you bother. You know, you really are small enough to go without them. They're bloody weird. Especially the fake nipples. They're always on high beam, aren't they?' She squished the cups of Beth's bra with a fascinated expression.

Beth shook her head, trying to shake some sense into her stunned brain. 'Christmas lunch?'

'Yes. I won't take no for an answer because I don't think you have a decent argument for wanting to spend Christmas alone. You can always cancel if Clayton offers later.'

'Can you give me a minute to think about it? I was planning on having a relaxing day on my own tomorrow.' Beth snatched her bra back. She knew she should berate Laura but in that moment Laura reminded Beth so much of her mischievous sister Valerie that she couldn't.

'No,' Laura said, grinning like the demented fairy of goodwill. 'Can I watch you put it on? I'm fascinated by the whole

transformation thing and I want to see if it makes any difference.'
Her smile slipped to a frown. 'Oh. That's probably invasive, isn't it?
Am I invading your privacy?' She flushed red. 'I am, aren't I? Sorry.
I just got so excited at the thought of having you over tomorrow.
But . . . ah, okay, well, you'll be at the party at Evangeline's tonight.
So I'll see you there!'

'Yes, you will. And I'd be happy to come to Christmas lunch,'
Beth said, softening. To be exasperated with Laura for more than
five seconds was impossible.

'Great!' Laura's expression was back to being cheerful again.
'See you then!'

'Oh, Laura, there *is* something.'

'Yes?'

Beth bit her lip as an idea occurred to her. It was so obvious she
didn't know why she hadn't thought of it before. 'Can you tell me
where the nearest public library is?'

'Who's Jo's new friend?'

Clayton's eyes focused on Beth, who was sitting cross-legged on
the lawn in front of his family home. She had a lap full of puppies and was gently patting Waffles while listening to something Jo
was saying to her. As different as they were in both appearance and
personality, the two women had hit it off the minute Clayton intro-
duced them. While he watched, Beth laughed. Her smile lit up her
face, eradicating the tenseness he'd detected when he picked her up
two hours before. It was about time. He'd been getting worried.

Something was definitely wrong. He didn't know what it was,
but whenever she got within two feet of him, she became jumpier
than a rabbit on Red Bull.

'You in there? I asked you a question. Is that a beer you're drinking or liquid deafness?'

'What?' he finally said to his brother Mike, taking a minute to look him up and down. 'Jesus, mate. What's with the shirt?'

Mike shrugged a broad shoulder and took a seat. 'Nothing. What's *your* problem with my shirt?'

'It's pink.'

Mike theatrically widened his vivid blue eyes, ran a hand over his blond stubbled jaw and shook his head. 'Really? Oh shit, mate! No one told me. Call the police.'

Clayton grunted. 'Don't you have somewhere to be? Where's that blonde you brought along tonight?'

Mike grinned. 'Somewhere. I only met her on the flight over here. Anyway, that brings me back round to my question. Who's the chick with Jo?'

'Not for you,' Clayton growled. 'And you must be suicidal. If Jo hears you use the word "chick" you're gonna be taking your balls back to London in an eggcup.' As he said the words, he thought that it might be a good thing if Mike was incapacitated during his stay. Mike was a good-looking bastard and a notorious man-whore. Clayton didn't want him within a square mile of Beth.

'What's this about an eggcup?' Stephen ambled over and joined them from where he'd just been talking with Scott, their younger cousin who was in charge of the barbecue this year.

Despite the two-year age difference between them, Stephen and Mike were nearly identical, but thankfully only on a superficial level. Stephen was usually quieter, more introspective and reserved, whereas in the shit-stirring stakes, Mike left Jeff crying in the dust.

'I was just asking for the hundredth time who Clayton's new girlfriend is,' Mike enunciated slowly, his expression wolfish.

Stephen raised his eyebrows. 'You two together now, then?'

'Who's together?' Jeff asked, wandering over and taking a seat.

'Clayton and Beth,' Stephen supplied.

'Beth.' Mike rolled the word around his mouth.

'Don't go there,' Clayton growled.

Mike leaned away from Clayton's chair and gaped at him incredulously. 'Jesus, mate. You wanna do anything else to mark your territory? How about going over there and pissing on her?'

'Keep your voice down,' Stephen hissed, shoving Mike and furtively glancing at Jo to make sure she hadn't heard anything.

'Yeah, mate. Or Stephen'll have to sit in the naughty spot for hanging out with the big boys,' Jeff guffawed, lazily taking a pull of his beer.

'Fuck off,' Stephen shot back, but there was no ire in his words. He and Jo had announced their engagement earlier in the evening and he had the air of a contented man about him. 'I'd just tell Jo you're being a shit and she'll come beat you up again.' He, Mike and Clayton all shared a mutual grin as they watched Jeff's smug smile go south.

'So, *anyway*,' Mike charitably changed the topic, 'what's up with Dad? He looks like someone's just told him his dog's died and all the fleas are suing him for breach of contract.' He nodded to the other side of the porch, where Rob was hunkered down in a chair staying uncharacteristically silent while his sister Corrine took the spotlight. Normally Rob was the life of the party. To see his dad this quiet unsettled Clayton.

'Gwen Stone,' Stephen supplied.

'Gwen?' Mike asked, looking first at Stephen, then Clayton and Jeff. They shrugged, scowled and shrugged respectively. 'What's going on there? I thought he would have got over all of that years back. Gwen's a doll. Remember how she used to sneak us lollies whenever Angie dragged us to church when we were kids? What's Dad's problem?'

'Don't ask me,' Clayton muttered. 'Just be bloody thankful that you live on the other side of the planet.' At a glance, Clayton could see that Rob was in a bad way. So far his old man had worked through at least two bottles of wine, which was one too many.

Normally he'd go over and intervene, but he wasn't in the mood to have Rob bite his head off for the hundredth time that week. With luck, his dad would drink enough to either fall asleep or have it out with Gwen once and for all.

As he frowned over that, his eyes returned to Beth, only to catch her running her eyes up and down him like he was a tasty piece of cake and she was starving. Whoa. Where had that come from?

'Any reason you're staring at her from afar and not over there making a move, or is this a new mating ritual I haven't heard about yet?' Jeff asked, cutting into Clayton's thoughts. He looked up to see that his brothers had left to supervise Scott burning the steaks. Jeff had taken Mike's vacated seat.

'I'm not staring.' Clayton settled further into his chair.

'No? Fair enough. But the last time I tried not staring at a woman like that, I got a drink thrown in my face.' Jeff chuckled. 'Looks like she's having a good time.'

Clayton's eyes were drawn to Beth again. She now had one of his young cousins in her lap and was showing him how to pat Waffles gently while Jo put the puppies back in their box. There was something so tender in Beth's expression as she looked down at the kid that it left Clayton feeling a little tight in the chest. It was something he didn't want to think about too much right now.

'Had an interesting experience this arvo. Thought you might want to know about it.' Jeff broke through Clayton's reverie.

Clayton turned to his mate. Jeff was wearing a pair of reindeer horns on his head, which somehow made him look a little demonic rather than stupid. Although the kids had got a good laugh earlier when he'd helped hand out the presents.

'What?'

'I was in the library, returning a couple of books, and I saw Beth reading something up the back. Thought I'd go say hello.'

'Yeah, and?'

'And I walked up behind her, took one look at what she was reading and back-pedalled quicker than a cyclist on a cliff.'

'Yeah?'

'Yeah. Remember that book we used to dare each other to get out of the library when we were kids? The one that Mark Pearson ended up photocopying on the sly and selling to everyone?'

Clayton leaned forward and stared at Jeff with incredulity. 'Not that illustrated *Kama Sutra*?'

'Yeah, that was it.' Jeff's features mellowed into a smile. 'I have a few nice memories of that book.'

'Yeah, so do I. You were saying?' Clayton prompted, not wanting to go down the route of Jeff's adolescent relationship with a photocopied sex manual.

'Yeah, anyway, Beth was studying it like her life depended on it. So caught up she didn't even hear me.'

'Really?'

'Serious.'

'Huh.' Clayton resumed staring across the porch at Beth, his mind whirring. A question bubbled up to the surface and, try as he might, he couldn't stop himself from asking.

'What page was she on?'

Jeff made him wait for the answer while he bit into the hot dog he'd been eating. 'Oral sex, mate.'

Clayton choked on his beer.

'Merry Christmas,' Jeff said with a wide grin, slapping him on the shoulder.

Chapter 10

Beth clenched her hands in her lap, surreptitiously pressing them against her stomach to quieten the butterflies erratically trampolining behind her navel. Her hands were shaking, she had a suspicion she was sweating horribly and some time in the past few minutes she'd lost her voice.

She'd been doing so well up to now. The party had been wonderful – so many people all talking loudly, children running amok, and everyone she'd met had been so friendly. There had been the added wonderful news of Clayton's brother Stephen becoming engaged to his girlfriend, Jo. After the celebration had died down, Beth had spent almost the entire evening in Jo's company, enjoying herself immensely. Later in the evening they'd been joined by Laura and Rachael. She could still feel the residual warm glow of spending time with women her age, women who seemed to accept her immediately without reserve.

If it hadn't been for the strange way Clayton had watched her every move during the latter part of the evening, it would have been perfect.

She'd worried that he'd got drunk and wouldn't be able to drive her home. Worse than that, a drunk Clayton would completely ruin her plans for the rest of the evening. Well, if she had any. Which she didn't.

Her foray into the library hadn't been as useful as she'd hoped. She'd only found one manual, the *Kama Sutra*. Thankfully it was an illustrated copy, but it was a little convoluted and advanced for her needs. She'd flicked through page after page of complex contortions and descriptions while feeling paranoid someone would see her lurking in the back shelves. In the end she had taken pictures of some of the more useful pages with her phone to study afterwards but by the time she had got back home, she had barely enough time to get ready for the party.

She debated waiting until after Christmas to make her move, but she couldn't bear the thought of feeling this way for another day, let alone another week.

By the time Clayton pulled his Jeep to a halt behind her cottage, the tension in Beth's stomach was so tightly wound that she felt faintly ill.

'Do you . . . do you want to come in for another bad coffee?' she asked abruptly, her voice uncharacteristically loud in the night silence.

'Ah. Beth. Normally yeah, but I have to get back to help clean up,' Clayton replied gruffly, appearing genuinely regretful. 'I'd love to but —'

'It would be the euphemism sort,' Beth blurted, her voice still unnaturally loud. 'Sex coffee. No, sex *not* coffee. Hopefully not bad.'

Clayton's eyes widened. 'Come again?'

'Sex?' The word was a sort of squeak. 'There's, ah, there's something I want to talk to you about first but after that . . . if you still want to, definitely sex.' The painful heat of embarrassment burned a fiery trail from her toes to the roots of her hair. It burned even hotter when Clayton didn't reply. Silence filled the car while he stared at her in the dark.

'Or we could just have bad coffee?' she amended weakly.

Clayton cleared his throat loudly. 'No. No. Sex would be great.'

'Oh. Really? All right. Good.' She quickly opened her door before Clayton could do it for her and scrambled out of the Jeep. She didn't want to be that close to him yet. Not until they'd talked about things. Without looking back she scampered around the cottage and frantically searched in her handbag for her key, only managing to get the door open and the lights on when two large warm hands firmly grasped her hips from behind.

The touch was so unexpected that Beth stopped still in her tracks. Shivers ran up and down her spine and her knees went wobbly when she felt the gentle scrape of teeth over the bare skin where her neck met her shoulder.

'C-Clayton?'

A hand curved around her hip to brush over her stomach, pulling her back hard against his body as he began to nibble upwards until he gently, slowly, bit her ear. Beth shivered. His breath was warm, his lips soft, brushing over her cheek like a thousand little kisses.

'Clayton?' She tried to sound firm. The hand on her stomach was slowly stroking back and forward. Her legs began to wobble.

'Mmm?'

'Talk. We need to talk.'

'About what?'

'Stop doing that for a second.'

'This?'

'Oh.' She arched her back as that magical hand of his moved lower, his fingers pointing downwards, brushing, cupping the apex of her thighs.

'Or this?' His hand started to move higher over the curve of her belly.

'Ohhh. No. No, that's why we need to talk.' It took a Herculean effort, but Beth pulled herself away, moving unsteadily across the room to lean against the kitchen counter, arms wrapped around her midriff while she willed her breathing to calm and her voice to return.

She glanced at Clayton and her heart rate sped up again. He was standing in the doorway with his arms crossed over his chest, his heavy-lidded gaze following her movements like a hawk.

'What are we talking about?' he asked lazily.

Beth took a few moments to collect her thoughts, then decided the best way to do this was to be direct. 'Me,' she replied shakily as her eyes ran over his chest. He was breathing as heavily as she was. 'Or more to the point my . . .' She started to say 'breasts' and then stopped when her eyes ran lower, much lower. *Bloody hell.*

'You have an erection,' she blurted.

Clayton peered down with an amused expression. 'Will you look at that?'

'I am and, ahh. Ahh.' Her train of thought derailed as her eyes stayed fixed on the distinct bulge in his trousers. 'Do you always get an erection that quickly? I mean. Do I arouse you? I mean. You don't have to touch me or see me naked to get one? See me topless or . . .'

Clayton shook his head, his eyes crinkling with obvious amusement that did nothing to take away from the intensity of his gaze. 'Nope. Just the thought of sex with you does this.'

'Really? Oh? Ah. So. Do you think you would keep it if . . . I mean, if you didn't see my breasts or touch them? If I didn't . . . If . . .'

'If what, Beth?' He prowled across the room to stand directly in front of her. He wasn't quite touching her physically but his eyes scorching up and down her body were almost the same.

Beth opened her mouth to speak then closed it again when no sound came out.

'Tell you what,' Clayton said slowly, his expression thoughtful. 'How about we conduct an experiment.' He raised a hand and gently ran a blunt fingertip across her lower lip.

'Hmm?'

'Sounds like you've got a thing about your breasts, yeah? That's what caused the problem the other night. You didn't want me touching them.'

'No . . . well, actually, sort of. Yes.' Beth exhaled. 'It's not that —'

Clayton cut her off. 'How about we leave them out of the equation, then? As long as you let me focus on the rest of you, I'm pretty sure I'll manage to keep my *erection* long enough to do the job.' His mouth twitched and Beth's eyes narrowed in suspicion.

'Are you teasing me?'

'Yeah,' Clayton drawled, leaning down and gently kissing the middle of her forehead, then her cheek, then the corner of her mouth.

'This is serious,' Beth insisted, her breath hitching.

'All right. You can be serious and I'll play.'

'But you can't —'

'With all of you but your chest,' he murmured huskily before sealing his mouth over hers, flicking his tongue once over her lips, inviting her response. It wasn't long coming. Unable to help herself, Beth tentatively returned his tongue's caress with her own and was rewarded with a low groan as Clayton grasped her hips firmly, pulling her against him so that she could feel every inch of his arousal against her stomach.

Beth moaned as his kisses turned languid, drugging. The earthy clean smell of him, the taste of him flooded her senses and she barely noticed when his hands slid down her sides and up under her dress to her backside, hands cupping each cheek firmly, finger-tips just touching the crevice in between. Her legs gave way and she made a decision.

'Clayton?' Her back arched and her head fell back.

'Hmm?'

'My bedroom . . .'

'Wrap your legs around me,' Clayton demanded roughly, hitching her up against him.

The friction of him rubbing against her with every step had Beth moaning as the last of her worries fell away. Tangling her hands through his hair, she pressed damp kisses against his lips, his cheeks, his neck and gave herself up to the sensation of being wrapped around a warm, hard man.

She didn't even notice when he lowered her to her bed so they were side to side, or when he slipped a hand under the elastic of her underwear, sliding them off.

She did notice, though, when she felt a finger slide across her clitoris before beginning to probe her sensitive, slick entrance.

'Clayton!' she yelped, trying to pull back in shock at how fast things were moving.

'Hmm?' He leaned forward and tried to kiss her again but she moved her head sideways, feeling the rasp of his stubble against her cheek.

'What are you doing?'

'Playing.' Clayton gently eased his finger oh so slowly inside her.

'Oh.' Her breath caught. 'You don't have to.' She arched her hips to take him deeper.

'Want to.' Clayton gently pushed her onto her back. His thumb sharply flicked over her clitoris again just as he began to insert another finger, leaving her feeling extraordinarily stretched and so hot.

'Oh.' She scrunched her eyes shut as white noise, wonderful

white noise, echoed in her ears, obliterating all thoughts, leaving just sensation, wetness, deep breaths, fullness.

'Hmm?'

'That's nice.'

'Good. How about this?' She felt her thighs being gently pushed wide apart and there was a new sensation, warm and sharply pleasurable flickering across her, causing sparks of heat to shoot to her womb and back again. Beth's back bowed, and her legs automatically spread even further apart. 'Ohhh.'

'Hmm?'

'Yessss.' Her hips came off the bed when she felt those fingers moving faster, the flicking on her clitoris intensely pleasurable, building until it was almost painful. Panicking, she reached out to push Clayton away but couldn't find him. She opened her eyes wide at the sight of his head between her thighs.

'*Clayton!*' she wailed, coming up onto her elbows, shocked and embarrassed. 'You can't . . .'

'Shhh,' he whispered, placing one arm across her hips to keep her still. He increased the movement of his fingers, the flick of his tongue, ignoring her whimper of protest.

She flopped back onto the bed, grasping the sheets in a white-knuckled grip, her heels digging into the bed until she was tense enough to shatter.

'Let go, Beth, I've got you.' His words triggered something in her body. Her legs started to shake, she started to sob and then she screamed as wave after wave of intense pleasure-pain flooded her system, flowing through her veins, encompassing her entire world.

Seconds, maybe years later, she opened her eyes, stunned and disoriented to see Clayton standing at the side of the bed. He was naked. Majestically naked. Amazingly naked. Wide, muscled shoulders and chest led down to a taught stomach and . . .

'You still have an erection,' she murmured dazedly while

watching him roll on a condom.

He grinned widely, his deep brown eyes burning their way up her bare legs to the apex of her still spread thighs and resting there for a moment before meeting her gaze. 'I'd say our experiment's a success so far,' he said huskily.

Beth's brow wrinkled. 'How . . . how precisely do you expect to fit *that* in me?'

'How about we keep playing and find out?'

He came back down on the bed, his body covering hers. The feel of his stomach pressing against the skin exposed by her hiked-up dress was extraordinarily erotic as he began to kiss her forehead, her eyelids, her neck before nibbling on her lips.

Distracted, Beth tried to kiss him back until she felt him settling between her thighs.

'It's just that . . . you're a tad larger than . . .'

'Trick of the light,' he whispered in her ear as he reached down, positioned himself and began to push gently but firmly inside, stretching her until she felt like she didn't have any more give.

'Clayton, I don't think this is going to work,' she whimpered, beginning to panic.

His response was to reach down between them and gently stroke her clitoris while kissing her deeply, hips pushing forward a little bit further every time she moaned until he was fully seated, sweat dripping off his skin. 'So far so good,' he rumbled against her ear, his expression strained, his breath hot on her cheek.

'Yes? Ah. Do you want to move now?' Beth asked, feeling a whisper of the same tension building up from before. She moved her legs restlessly until he reached down and hooked them behind his back, bringing him deeper. They both moaned.

'Yeah. Is that all right with you?' he rasped.

'Yes. Yes, I think so.' Beth tentatively squeezed her internal muscles around him.

He groaned. 'Beth? If you keep doing that I won't be able to go slow.' He began to withdraw, and the sensation of him pulling out had her arching her back to bring him in again.

'Maybe you don't have to,' she whispered.

'Sure?' Clayton pushed back in and Beth moaned.

'Yes.'

At the word Clayton's hips began to rock, touching something deeper inside her, different than before, building sensation until there was nothing else, just this wonderfully big man driving into her, making her feel wanted, beautiful . . .

The second orgasm hit before Beth knew it was coming. Crying out, she tightened her legs around Clayton's sweat-slicked skin and dug her nails into his back, feeling him slamming deep inside, pleasure washing over her again and again just as she felt him shuddering and groaning against her neck before collapsing his full weight on top of her, pressing her into the bed.

They must have fallen asleep, because the clock blinked an early hour of the morning when Beth opened her eyes again.

Every muscle in her body ached and she felt like she had a boulder resting on her chest. A gentle, rumbling snore in her ear quickly alerted her to the fact that the boulder was definitely human, and male for that matter.

'Clayton,' she whispered, bringing limp arms up to run her fingertips across the now cool damp skin on his back.

'Hmm?'

'You're heavy.'

'What?' He raised his head off her shoulder and looked around blearily. 'Oh. God. Sorry, Beth. You all right?'

'Yes. Maybe. I'm not sure actually. I think you may have cut off a lot of circulation to vital parts of my body.' Beth winced. 'And I may need to pee.'

Groaning, Clayton hauled himself sideways and collapsed on his back next to her.

Beth jumped off the bed and ran to the bathroom.

Moments later, she stared at her reflection in the bathroom mirror. What a mess. Her short hair was standing up on end, her cheeks were red with whisker burn and there was an imbecilic smile on her lips.

She quickly did what she could to scrub her face, then brushed her teeth before making her way back to the bedroom.

Clayton was now lying sprawled on his stomach, so she took a moment to admire his broad shoulders, tight backside and tree-trunk legs before moving to the bedside and patting his shoulder. 'Clayton?'

'Yeah?'

'It's Christmas Day.'

'Merry Christmas.' He rolled over again. 'How about you come back to bed and I give you your Christmas present?' He peeked up at her out of one eye and looked so boyishly adorable, Beth felt her mouth twitch with a smile.

'Don't you have to spend the day with your family?'

Clayton groaned. 'Bloody family. Yeah. I do. But I don't want to. I'd rather spend the day with you.' He hooked an arm around her thighs and dragged her down to the bed. 'You wanna get out of that dress and onto me so we can celebrate properly?'

Beth was about to say yes when the implication of what he'd just said hit home. She looked down and the beautiful glow she'd just been basking in evaporated. She was still wearing her dress.

Idiot, idiot, idiot! How could she have let things get to this stage without coming clean with the truth?

How was she supposed to tell the man now, *after* they'd had sex, that she was currently wearing a pair of fake breasts? It was lucky the bloody things hadn't dislodged while they'd been making love. Beth stifled a small humourless laugh. That would have sorted things out nicely.

'Beth?' He pushed himself up into a sitting position against the headboard, unashamedly naked and aroused. 'You're looking pretty spooked. Anything going on in your head you wanna talk about? Would you prefer I stay here for the morning instead of going home? I will if you want.'

'No!' Beth's voice came out too loud in the quiet room. She winced, desperately rallying. 'No. Family is important. You should spend Christmas with them.'

Clayton shrugged. 'So are you.'

'Oh? Thank you.' The rush of pleasure she felt at his words momentarily quelled her panic. 'But I really can't put you out. I have to call my gran soon anyway. She's eight hours behind and will be out all Christmas Day, so . . . I was going to call her after I got back from the party tonight but . . .' She gestured jerkily to the bed.

'You wanna call her now?'

'Yes. I might be a while. So, it might be best, well, I don't want to put you out.' Her words hung in the air and she watched with a miserable sinking feeling as the smile slipped off Clayton's lips.

'That your way of giving me the boot?' His expression shuttered and his mouth formed a thin line.

'No. Yes. No.' Beth pressed her lips tightly together trying to find the right words to say. She felt trapped, wanting him to stay but not wanting to ruin it more by keeping him here and then telling him . . . it was late, the intimacy between them . . . she couldn't get her thoughts straight. She just needed the space to work out how to fix this and then it would all be okay. 'It's not that I want you to go. I enjoyed . . . it was nice and . . .'

'Nice, eh?'

'Yes, but I . . . I need to call my gran and . . .'

'I'll get out of your hair, then,' Clayton said tightly. He swung his legs off the bed and stood up.

'Clayton —' Beth began, but he spoke over her while brusquely pulling his pants on and scooping up his shirt from the floor.

'It's all right, Beth. You've got stuff to do. Call me if you want another *nice* time later. That's how you want it, isn't it?'

'Clayton, I didn't mean to hurt your feelings.' Beth didn't think she could have messed this up more if she tried. She scrambled for something she could say to undo whatever she'd just done. The words that would explain her actions and tell him about her mastectomies were lodged in her throat but she couldn't get them out while he was this angry. What if she told him now and he said something horrible? He'd just helped her feel so sexy and wonderful about herself and she couldn't bear to have that undone. At the same time she hated the idea of hurting him. 'I really didn't mean to hurt you.'

'You didn't.' He impatiently pulled on his shirt, leaving the buttons undone.

'Yes I did. I can see I did. Please just give me a few minutes so you can calm down and I can explain. We really . . . we really should talk. We didn't do that before —'

'Later. You have to call your gran, like you said.' Clayton stalked out of her bedroom and picked up his shoes from the middle of the kitchen floor. Beth vaguely wondered how they'd got there.

'Yes, but —'

'Merry Christmas, Beth.' The front door banged shut behind him before Beth could reply, and not long after she heard the sound of his car reversing away from the cottage.

'Well, you handled that superbly,' she muttered to herself, collapsing in an armchair and putting her head in her hands, fighting the dual urges to smack herself silly and bawl her eyes out.

Even though it was getting late, or early, there were still a few strag-glers sitting around the porch when Clayton returned to Evangeline's Rest.

Historically, Rob gave guests the hint to go home by turning off the porch light around midnight then heading off to bed, but tonight he was humouring them.

Clayton groaned. This was the last thing he wanted, and his mood didn't improve when he got closer and saw that it wasn't guests sitting on the porch – it was his dad and Uncle Les.

'You took a while, mate,' his dad slurred in greeting.

'Yeah.'

'Take a seat. Have a beer.' Les waved to the chair next to his. 'Your dad and I were just shootin' the breeze.'

'Yeah?'

'You all right, mate?' Les asked. At forty-eight, he was Rob's younger brother by four years but stood about half a foot taller, blond and lean. He was also the most even-tempered of the older Hardy siblings, Rob and their sister, Corrine, being known for los-ing their cool on occasion.

Clayton didn't bother to answer. Instead he retrieved a beer from the cooler at Rob's feet and cracked it open.

'I was just tellin' Les about the blight on my landscape,' Rob mumbled.

'Yeah?' Clayton broodily stared out into the darkness beyond the porch lights.

'Yeah. Gwen,' Rob muttered.

Les frowned at his brother in obvious exasperation. 'Mate. You've got to let this go. Gwen isn't bad. Angie and Stephen tell me she's sent cellar-door sales through the roof.'

'Why don't you go back to managing sheep and cows and leave me to take care of the wine?' Rob snapped, leaning to one side and glowering blearily at his brother.

'Yeah, why don't I do that,' Les replied, calmly standing. 'You can handle him?' he asked Clayton.

'Yeah. I'll shovel him off to bed.' Clayton scowled at his dad.

'Good. Merry Christmas, mate. I'll see you tomorrow. You coming to our place for lunch along with this sorry bastard?'

'Should be,' Clayton grunted.

'Good. I'm off, then. Yvette took the kids home hours ago and I want to get a bit of sleep before they wake up at four for their presents.' Les patted Rob on the shoulder and left.

'Didn't think I'd see you again tonight after you took your girlfriend home. Beth, wasn't it?' Rob slurred, pouring himself another glass of wine.

'Neither did I.' Clayton frowned down at his beer. He was still pissed off and confused after being kicked out of Beth's place. Not that she'd call it that. She'd no doubt come up with something all English and polite. She'd kicked him out nonetheless, and for the life of him he couldn't work out why.

Nice. *Nice*, she'd said in that prim-and-proper voice of hers like he hadn't just made her scream. He knew she'd come. Twice. Where did she get off calling his technique *nice* and then acting like she couldn't wait to get rid of him?

'Clayton! You in there, mate? Been talkin' to you for the past five minutes.' Rob banged his hand on the arm of his chair.

'What?' Clayton snapped. He knew he should go to bed, but he could hear Angie talking to someone in the house and he had a suspicion that someone was Gwen Stone.

'I wuz just saying that it'd be nice to get a bit of PEACE AND QUIET AROUND HERE!' Rob bellowed the latter towards the house, no doubt waking everyone up and causing district-wide cattle stampedes.

'Too right,' Clayton murmured, covering his eyes with one hand. 'Dad, don't you think you should get a bit of shut-eye?'

'I would, but *she's* in there.' Rob pointed at the house with a wobbling, accusatory finger. 'It's getting so bad a man can't even get sleep in his own house on Christmas Eve.'

'Then sleep out here. You've had too much to drink, old man.' Clayton moved Rob's bottle of wine out of reach.

'What ya do that for?' Rob gave Clayton an outraged glare.

'You want to drink it? You get up and get it, and while you're at it you can walk into the house, get whatever is bugging you off your chest *politely* and go to bed.' Clayton knew he'd live to regret the suggestion the minute he made it.

'*Politely?* I'm always bloody polite. You want me to go in there and tell *that woman* what I really think?'

'Yeah, why don't you? You're going to anyway. Isn't that what you're working up to?' Clayton snapped.

'Who said anything about me wanting to talk to *her*?' Rob pushed himself to his feet, snatched back the bottle of wine and sat down again. 'I'm just trying to get some peace and quiet.'

Clayton heaved a frustrated sigh and unclenched his fists, rolling his head from side to side. 'All right, old man. I'll leave you to it. See you in the morning.'

'You going to bed?'

'Yeah.'

'Oh. Righto. Goodnight.' Rob sounded so pathetically lost Clayton wanted to give him a hug, but he knew it would be as welcome as a shovel to the back of the head. Instead he ruffled his dad's hair and walked into the house.

'Has he drunk himself to sleep yet?' Angie asked as Clayton closed the screen door.

He'd been right earlier. Both Angie and Gwen were seated at the dining table, nursing cups of coffee which, knowing Angie, contained a generous amount of 'spiritual upliftment'.

'Not yet.' Clayton walked into the kitchen. He'd been so distracted by Beth earlier, he'd forgotten to eat much.

'I kept a plate for you in the oven.'

Clayton smiled for the first time since he'd left Beth's. 'Thanks.'

Angie smiled right back at him.

'I should go,' Gwen said, pushing her chair back and collecting her handbag.

'You all right to drive?' Clayton asked.

'Yes. I'll be fine. I was just waiting to get legally sober.' Gwen flashed a warm, apple-cheeked smile at Clayton but it was drooping at the edges, maybe from tiredness or something else. He was too tired and pissed off to care right now.

'All right. Goodnight, then.' He grabbed the plate Angie had left for him and headed off to his bedroom without waiting to hear their replies.

Rob looked up with a squint-eyed frown at the figure standing in front of him, blocking the warm yellow porch lights. 'What're *you* doing out here?'

'Going home, Robert,' Gwen replied, smoothing her hands over the front of her flowing white shirt.

'Go on, then. No one's stopping you,' Rob sneered then took another gulp from his wine glass. He glared at the ground in front of him, which currently contained Gwen's feet, her *toe-ringed* feet, in some sort of pink strappy shoes. Impractical. He snorted to himself.

'Merry Christmas,' Gwen said softly.

'Nothing merry about it. Not with you around.' Rob waited for a response but none was forthcoming. Gwen's feet weren't walking out of his line of vision either.

'What?'

There was still no response. He raised his eyes, fully prepared to give the woman a piece of his mind but stopped, mouth dumbly open when he saw tears running down her cheeks.

'Oh no! Oh *no*. No, don't do that. What are you doing that for?' he exclaimed, alarmed.

'What?'

'Turning on the waterworks like I'm some kind of bastard. *I'm* the one who should be crying, Gwen. Not bloody you. What right do *you* have to get all upset?'

'You're being very hurtful, Robert.' Gwen's voice was shaky as she reached into the large brown leather handbag hanging off her shoulder and pulled out a tissue, which she dabbed under her eyes.

'No I'm not! I just want you to leave me alone. Leave. Me. Alone.' Rob punctuated each word with a nod of his head as if convincing himself that that was what he wanted.

'Why?'

'What do you mean "why"? *Why?* Because if it wasn't for you—' he began but stopped, his mouth open but no words wanting to come out. Damn it. He could feel himself choking up. He covered it by draining his wine glass.

'If it wasn't for me, what?' Gwen's voice was a little croaky but still firm as she met his eyes directly, challenging him to answer her.

'You knew she was there that day you came out here and crawled all over me, didn't you?' The words ripped from his guts before he could catch them. 'You bloody well knew. You knew Pam would see us and assume that we had a thing going on. There I was being a bloody fool, feeling sorry for you and the whole time you'd set it all up. If it hadn't been for you, Gwen, she never . . . she never would have kept how sick she was from me, she would have got treatment and she'd be alive today. I'll never forgive you for that. You may as well have killed her yourself.'

'Surely you can't mean that,' Gwen whispered huskily, her voice audibly clogged with tears. 'I spoke to Pam about it. She knew you were just being kind. She didn't think anything of it.'

'She must have,' Rob snapped. 'Because if she didn't think you and me had something goin' on after she found you plastered up against me that day, why did she shut me out? Why didn't she want to live?' His last words were torn from his chest; his vocal cords felt like someone had taken a cheese grater to them. He averted his eyes, not wanting Gwen to see his tears, not wanting to feel anything. It was all coming back again, the pain, the overwhelming sense of loss, the anger he'd never been able to vent – and it was too much. Too bloody much.

'Please, Robert.'

'What?'

'Stop it. Stop this. It's not helping you and it's not helping me and it's hurtful. To both of us. For once in your life you're going to be quiet and I'm going to tell you exactly what happened that day and you're going to listen.'

'Why would I do that?'

Gwen set her shoulders back and looked him directly in the eye with a steely grace undiminished by the drying tears that left muddy mascara trails down her cheeks. 'Because I'll resign, giving Angie two weeks' notice on Monday if you do.'

Rob stared at her while his alcohol-laden system processed the enormity of her words. 'You mean you'll quit just like that?' He clicked his fingers clumsily. 'If I listen to you rattle on for a bit?'

'Without saying anything.'

'Without saying anything,' he repeated. 'You've got yourself a deal. Start talking.' He carefully sat his glass down next to his chair and leaned back with arms tightly crossed over his barrel chest.

'Can I sit down while I talk?' Gwen asked warily.

'By all means.' Rob gestured grandly to the chair next to him and waited with barely suppressed impatience while Gwen sat down.

'All right. It's quite simple, really, so I won't waste too much of your time,' she began in a calm voice. 'Robert, firstly I would like to tell you what happened that day before I came out to the farm. I didn't know you were going to be here. I came out to see Pam because John had just broken things off and I was devastated. He'd proposed to me a week earlier. I hadn't told anyone but Pam because I wanted to keep it a secret until I could drive to Perth and tell my parents. I don't know if Pam told you he'd proposed. Did she?'

Rob shook his head, brow furrowing.

'Anyway, that's neither here nor there now. John broke it off and I was devastated. I tried calling Pam but she didn't answer the phone, so I drove out to find her. I knew she wouldn't be far from home with the children being so young. Unfortunately, Pam wasn't home when I got here but you were, and I ended up crying all over you. If you remember rightly, you were very much the gentleman and didn't push me away. I felt so grateful to you for being so kind, Robert. I only meant to kiss your cheek, not your mouth.' Gwen looked down at her hands clasped tightly together in her lap. 'We know how that ended. Pam walked in and got the shock of her life. Knowing how it looked, I tried to fix it and explain what had happened over the phone after you asked me to leave. I'm truly convinced Pam believed me and I'm positive she didn't blame you for what she saw, Robert. She was a wonderful person.' Gwen briefly rested a hand on Rob's arm.

'You don't have to tell me that.' Rob recoiled from her touch.

Gwen features softened in understanding. 'No, I don't. What I do have to tell you is that I'm positive that what you believe is wrong. She didn't keep things from you or refuse treatment because of anything you or I did. She loved you. If anything, I believe she didn't tell you how sick she was because she knew you wouldn't let her do things her way without putting up a fight. She wanted to spend as much time with you and the kids as she could without being sick from medication and surgery that wouldn't have worked anyway. We both know she was too far gone. They found it too late. When she died . . .' Gwen's voice caught on the words. 'I didn't just lose my best friend. I lost a sister. I loved Pam more than anyone and I loved you for loving her, too.' Her voice wavered and she looked away. 'So, there you have it. I have nothing else to say.' She pushed out of her chair and brushed her hands over her ample hips to smooth her shirt. 'Merry Christmas, Robert. I'll give Angie my notice the day after next.'

Rob didn't acknowledge Gwen's words with a reply. Instead, he continued to sit in stony silence until he heard her car door slam and her car drive away. Then he stumbled to his feet and wove unsteadily through the house, collapsing fully dressed on his bed, his feet hanging over the edge.

'You're a stubborn bugger, you know,' Angie growled from the doorway.

Rob grunted.

Angie sighed and walked into the room, roughly yanking off his shoes and socks and pulling a rug over the top of him. 'Fifty-two years old and I'm still putting you to bed. Mum was right. Kids never really grow up.'

Chapter 11

'I don't understand, Beth. You're telling me that you've just had sex —'

'Gran!'

'I do know what it is, you know. I've done it enough. Was known as quite the lady about town when I was younger – before your mother was born, just to put your mind at ease.'

'I really don't need to hear this,' Beth groaned, regretting the call she'd made to Violet the minute Clayton had left. She should have gone to bed and waited until daylight. She would have been a lot less raw and emotional then. Certainly a lot less inclined to blurt out her deepest fears. Her gran had always viewed life through a rather skewed lens and she was in fine myopic form this evening.

'You obviously do, because from what you've just told me you're sadly lacking in education,' Violet harrumphed. 'So, you've had sex with this Clayton character and he left you straight after and you're upset.'

'No. No, it wasn't like that at all. He left because *I* upset him. He thinks I wanted him to leave and I did, but not for the reasons he might think. I insulted him quite badly. I panicked when I realised that I hadn't told him what I should have before —'

'You insulted him? Well, then he must have deserved it because that's not like you at all. What was it like, then? The sex. Was he a bad lover? He must have been if you wanted him gone. You know, I went with this one lad, years ago now, long before Louis and your grandfather, who used to have this thing for pulling my hair. Quite off-putting, it was.'

'No, *no.*' Beth tapped her head to dislodge the image of her gran and another man in bed together. It had been bad enough hearing Violet and Louis chuckling away in their bedroom the past few years. She really didn't want to think of white-haired, respectable, church-going Violet Poole as the village tramp. 'It wasn't like that at all. I had a very nice time. Like I told you, it was what happened *after.*'

'A nice time? Nice is for cakes and picnics, girl. I would hope he made you feel much better than *nice.*'

'All right, then. It was amazing,' Beth admitted, cursing the coils of warmth that swirled in her belly at the memory of just how amazing making love with Clayton had been.

'Good to hear,' Violet said pertly. 'So, what's the problem, then? You know it's getting late where you are? Must be about four in the morning. On Christmas Day, too.'

'Yes, I know it's late. I've already told you *twice* now what the problem is. He still doesn't know about my . . . I haven't told him that I don't —'

'Have breasts? Why should that be an issue? If you made love he mustn't have minded that you didn't have any, otherwise he would have told you. No. Mountain out of a molehill, girl. The rest of you is fine. I've always told you that your legs are lovely. You take after me in that respect. Mine are still good for my age. Louis certainly likes them. And I've told you time and time again that breasts are all good and fine when you're young, but by the time you get to my age they can get so droopy you could tie them into a bow. If you'd only got your chest tattooed like that lady in Dorset I showed you on the Internet, you wouldn't be worried about all this. You'd be showing yourself off to everyone and anyone.'

'No. No! *Tattoos?* You're missing the point!'

'So, what *is* the point?'

'If he finds out I lied and he sees me naked without my mastectomy bra, he'll be horrified. Remember what happened with Greg? How he couldn't handle it? I don't know why, but it would be even worse with Clayton and it's been built up even more now that I messed up my explanation and he left angry. I can't go through that again. It would be awful.' Beth's voice caught when she mentioned her ex-husband's name, but the emotion was more from imagining what it would be like for Clayton to reject her, than remembering Greg's reaction.

'Beth, you may as well face it: your ex-husband was as spineless as a jellyfish. He had some good points but it was obvious he didn't have the strength to tie his own shoes without someone to hold his hand, let alone stand by you when you needed him. In short he was a . . . a *douche bag*,' Violet stated emphatically.

'*Gran!* Where did you hear that?' Beth exclaimed, momentarily shocked out of her depressive panic spiral.

'Some American show Louis and I were watching the other day. It fits,' Violet replied with the smug, self-satisfied voice a senior citizen reserves for the moments they manage to shock a member of the younger generation. 'I can still keep up with these things, you know. Anyway, as I was saying, Greg was a fool. I'm trusting you have more taste than to be with another man like him now. If this Clayton has half a brain in his head, he'll not make a peep when you get around to telling him about yourself, which I'm sure you will do at the first possible moment because there is no point wasting a good man when you've found one. And if he doesn't behave, I have more than enough of my pension money saved to fly down there and have words.'

Beth gave up. 'Thanks.'

'You're welcome. Beth, if you could look at yourself from my age and perspective, you'd see what a waste it is for you to hide away like you have these past years. Don't worry about what you *haven't* got and use what you *have* while you're still young. It isn't so easy to have sex when you get older. I have my new hip and everything, but it's working up the energy, and Louis isn't as young or active as he used to be. Mind you, Viagra —'

'Goodnight, Gran.' Beth spoke over Violet's monologue, cutting her off at the pass before she revealed something that would have Beth avoiding eye contact with Louis for the next decade.

'Oh. All right. It is late there, isn't it? Goodnight and merry Christmas,' Violet said, sounding a little put out.

'Merry Christmas. Love you,' Beth replied, ending the call then curling up on sheets that smelled like Clayton before falling into an exhausted slumber.

'Lionel, if you don't start being reasonable I'm going to go home – and that's saying something. I've had enough men to last a bloody lifetime. Why would I marry you when things are pretty good already?'

Beth looked up from the cookbook she had been studying to the sound of Angie Hardy's voice, loud and strident, echoing through the Rousse home. She met Laura's eyes across the kitchen. Laura had momentarily paused in chattering away about past Christmases and was frozen in a tableau of a demented domestic goddess with a kitchen knife in one hand and a carrot in another.

'Marry?' Laura mouthed, eyes wide open.

Beth's stomach clenched at the thought of seeing Clayton's grandmother. She had come over to Laura's family home for Christmas lunch in an effort to distract herself from her worries about Clayton, not to confront them. She'd barely slept all night and when she had, dreams of Clayton rejecting her in a myriad of horrible ways had played over and over until she got up, armed herself with a big stick to beat off any aggressive wildlife and had taken herself off for a walk in the grapevines. All that did was remind her of the wonderfully romantic dinner Clayton had surprised her with, leaving her with a mixture of resolve and dread that was amplifying by the second in the face of Angie Hardy's presence.

The kitchen door promptly opened and Angie stormed in, pulling out a chair at the old farm table and sitting down, her arms crossed in front of her, eyes drilling into the orange seventies tiles over the sink.

'Hi, Angie,' Laura chirped, looking furtively at the door to the living room, presumably where her father was.

'Marry him. We've been seeing each other for years and he wants me to marry him! We haven't even had time to properly celebrate Jo and Stephen's engagement. And now he wants to steal the limelight!' Angie grumbled, running a hand over her eyes. 'No sleep last night because of my idiot son. Putting up with my grandson stomping around all morning like he's just found out the world's going to end, and now *this*.' She heaved a sigh before looking around, seeing Beth. 'You wouldn't know anything about that, would you?'

'Hi, Angie,' Beth said. 'You said Clayton was upset?'

'Bear with a sore head.'

'What's this about marrying Dad?' Laura finally found her voice. 'Marrying as in "Will you marry me" marrying?' Her eyes lit up and she ran to the kitchen door. 'Dad! Did you just ask Angie to marry you?'

'Yeah, love,' came a distant gruff voice. 'Send her back in here when she's ready to say yes, will you.'

'I'll say yes in my own good time, Lionel Rousse, and that's if I'm going to say it at all!' Angie yelled back.

The term *all bark no bite* immediately came to Beth. 'Ah, did Clayton say anything —'

'For Christ's sake, Dad, just tie her up and take her to the church already! Some of us have a hangover.' Jeff's voice sounded from the next room, his tone pure mischief.

'I've already got enough problems in my life, Jeff Rousse, I'll be damned if I add you to them!' Angie roared back. 'You're giving me good incentive to say no!'

'Yes, Mother.'

Angie pushed her chair back and promptly stomped back into the other room. There was a thud and then the sound of heavy foot-falls on floorboards as Jeff began to laugh hysterically.

'So, are you going to say yes or not?' Lionel's voice cut in after a while.

'I'll think about it. I've got enough relationship dramas on my plate as it is,' Angie said over her shoulder as she walked back into the kitchen, this time looking directly at Beth. 'While I'm on the topic . . . I don't tend to interfere, but if you could drop by and knock Clayton around the head some time soon, I'd appreciate it.'

'I'll think about it,' Beth said, feeling a fleeting moment of pride for not immediately caving in the face of such an amazing woman.

That earned her a nod and finally, a slow smile. 'I think you'll be fine. As for you —' Angie turned to Laura, her voice lowered. 'What do you think? Could you put up with me?'

Laura dropped the spoon she was holding and launched herself at the older woman, wrapping her in an enthusiastic hug. 'I couldn't be happier.'

Angie returned the hug. 'All right then, well, I'll think about it.

Just don't tell my lot until I say so, okay?'

'Promise.'

'That goes for you too. No telling that hard-headed grandson of mine.' Angie looked over at Beth, holding an arm out. 'Come over here and give us a hug. It's Christmas and it's not often I get to be around this many girls at once.'

'All right.' Beth walked over and was immediately enveloped in a three-way hug, feeling her chest swell with emotion. She'd missed this so, so much.

She just hoped her conversation with Clayton wasn't going to ruin it all.

Beth drove to Evangeline's Rest with cold, clammy hands gripping the steering wheel. After two days of mulling over Violet's advice and Angie's order, she had finally worked up the courage to seek Clayton out.

Just as she parked next to the cellar door, she spotted him walking away from her towards the large sheds behind his home. Before she could chicken out, she launched herself from the car. 'Clayton!'

He spun around on his heel, his rugged features momentarily registering surprise. 'Beth? What are you doing here?'

'I'm here to see you. Unless you don't want to see me, in which case I'm leaving now.' Beth stopped dead in her tracks.

When he didn't immediately reply, Beth faltered. 'Okay. I'll just go, then.'

He grunted. 'No. If you have something to say, you can follow me. I'm just off to do the rounds.'

'All right.'

Nodding curtly, Clayton turned and strode towards the large shed again, not waiting for her to catch up.

Beth hurried after him. 'Could you please slow down a little?'

'What?' Clayton stopped and turned around again so suddenly that Beth slammed into his chest.

'We can't all be built like farm machinery,' Beth huffed.

'Farm machinery, eh?'

Beth flushed. 'Maybe that came out more insulting than it should have. I came here to apologise, not to insult you.'

'Really? Could have fooled me.'

'You know, I *was* going to apologise. Now I don't think I want to.' She whirled around and stalked back towards her car, berating herself the entire way. Here she was ready to bare her soul, and the man was being as considerate as mud. There was no way this was going to work. Her earlier anxiety transformed into anger and she welcomed it. It felt so much easier after the past few days she had spent agonising.

'Beth,' Clayton called after her.

'What?' she snapped, while searching through her handbag for her car keys.

'Stop.'

'No. I don't think I will, thank you.' Her fingertips connected with serrated metal and she quickened her pace.

'No, seriously, please wait up.' Beth heard heavy crunching footfalls on gravel and then felt a firm grip on her shoulder. She stopped, her back poker straight.

'I'm sorry,' Clayton said from behind her. 'Can we do this again?'

'Why?' Beth demanded, staring determinedly forward. 'I came here to do the right thing, but it's obvious I had the wrong idea about you. I know I offended you the other night but now I'm wondering if it isn't you who should be apologising for not calling or dropping by for days.'

'Yeah, well . . .'

She felt his hand drop from her shoulder. She felt cold without the contact, which was ludicrous, given how hot the day was.

'Look . . . Can we start again?'

'How do I know you're not going to go into another sulk?' Beth turned and watched his eyes narrow and his nostrils flare at her question. She felt immediately remorseful. 'Hideous choice of words. Yes, I'm willing to start again.'

He drew a deep breath and huffed it out. 'All right.' He snatched her hand from her side in a firm grip and half-led, half-dragged her back towards the shed, this time walking marginally slower.

She might have taken issue with the manhandling but instead was relieved for the few minutes to get her thoughts together before she launched into the speech she'd spent the morning rehearsing.

By the time they reached the shed, Beth was braced to talk. Clayton, however, didn't look like he was going to cooperate in a hurry. Instead he stalked over to an upside-down half wine barrel and took a seat, crossing his arms defensively across his chest.

Beth was left standing in the middle of the large space feeling vulnerable and not liking it one bit. She wrapped her arms around her waist, tightly gripping her soft cotton shirt, and waited for him to say something, anything, to break the silence so she could feel comfortable enough to begin.

When nothing was forthcoming, she turned to leave again. 'This isn't going to work.'

'Wait, Beth. Stay. I'm being a bastard,' Clayton called after her. 'I just don't know what to say. It's not every day a man gets told he's crap in the sack. I didn't take it well the other night.'

'Pardon?' Beth's eyes widened even more as she spun around and stared at him in amazement.

'What? You want me to repeat myself?' Clayton growled.

'Actually yes I do, because I don't understand what you're talking about.'

'Made myself clear enough, I thought.'

'No, you didn't. I thought it was obvious that . . . I thought you would have realised that I had a . . .'

'*Nice* time,' Clayton grumbled. His expression was sulky and would have been humorously out of character if Beth hadn't been so dumbfounded.

'Well, yes. It was nice. Better than nice – lovely, actually. What's the problem in telling you I had a nice time?' she asked, her reason for visiting forgotten for the moment. 'My gran implied that the word "nice" might have offended you but I ignored her. She was right, wasn't she?'

Clayton's features creased into a harsh scowl.

'She was, wasn't she?' Beth insisted, realising that in all her own insecurity it hadn't dawned on her that Clayton might have been just as worried about his own performance. She took a few tentative steps towards him. 'Clayton, I'm sorry if I've hurt your feelings. That's the last thing I wanted. It was just that I was worried about something else and . . .' Her confidence fled at the reminder of why she'd actually come by.

'What?'

'As you know, I didn't manage things too well, but rest assured I had a . . . a wonderful time.'

'That's what I thought,' Clayton grumbled. 'So why'd I get the boot?'

Beth shifted uncomfortably from one foot to the other. 'It's complicated. No, that's a silly thing to say. To tell you the truth, I'm a little worried about going into it all now. I had this all planned and now I don't know what to say.'

Clayton's black mood of the past few days lifted completely as he watched the play of emotions cross Beth's features. She looked comically serious. Her short, fine blonde hair stood out at all angles, no doubt a result of worried fingers, and two lines formed cute little indents between her eyes.

It was dawning on him that there was more at play here than Beth implying he was a mediocre lover, and he cursed his temper. He hadn't reacted this badly to criticism since he was a kid, and it was becoming clear that he'd been a bit of an idiot. Okay, a colossal idiot, and that maybe some of the reason he hadn't gone round to sort things out with Beth was due to sheer embarrassment over his own behaviour.

'Beth. I'm sorry,' he blurted.

Her frown deepened. 'Thank you,' she replied in a distant tone. He wasn't sure she'd heard him and got ready to repeat himself, but she spoke first and near on blindsided him.

'Clayton, I'd like to spend more time with you. I like you a lot and I'd also like to have more sex with you,' she stated in a stern little voice, like a schoolteacher telling her students to do their homework.

'What?' He resisted the urge to stick a finger in his ear and wiggle it around to make sure it was working properly.

'I'd like to spend time with you and, ah, more sex. With you. I had a nice . . . wonderful time and . . .'

'And?' Clayton asked, stunned yet feeling himself physically reacting to her prim declaration.

Beth looked down at her feet. 'The problem is that I haven't been entirely honest.'

'What do you mean?' Clayton asked warily.

She looked around then, her expression clearly uncomfortable. 'It's difficult. Could we maybe go somewhere else to talk about this? Somewhere no one will interrupt?'

'Yeah. All right. Easier said than done right now, though.' Clayton glared at his house, still visible through the large shed door.

He'd had enough of his family. It'd been hell the past few days.

Gwen had quit suddenly the day before, giving two weeks' notice. This had thrown Angie, already in a cranky mood, over the edge and she had declared her immediate retirement from the cellar door, which left Rob picking up the slack. So far sales had plummeted during the mornings when Clayton's dad was on shift. Clayton didn't even want to think of how rude Rob was being to the paying public.

'Surely there must be somewhere?' The desperation in her tone snapped him out of it.

'Come with me.' He stood up and took her hand, this time noticing how soft her skin felt against his. Memories of Christmas Eve flooded back to him.

'Where are we going?' Beth stumbled as he began to drag her out the door and he reminded himself to slow down.

His mind worked frantically. 'My car. If you don't mind waiting for a few minutes, we'll go to my new house. It's quiet and we won't be interrupted. Sound all right?'

He could almost hear the gears grinding in that too-serious mind of hers. 'Yes. Yes, I think that will be okay. As long as you promise to bring me back here so I can drive my car home no matter what.'

'Yeah, sure.' Clayton reached into his pocket for his keys and whistled for Waffles before remembering that she was still holed up in the house with the puppies. God, Beth scrambled his brain.

Chapter 12

Clayton surreptitiously monitored Beth's expression while he drove but he couldn't decipher her mood at all. Bloody women. Why did they have to be so confusing? It was so much easier with animals, even fickle grapevines.

He found himself getting nervous as they approached the thick clump of karri and jarrah trees that backed onto his new house. Beth's opinion mattered whether he wanted it to or not, and he had a gut feeling he wouldn't react well if she was negative about his place, especially given how excited he was about it being almost finished. He'd prefer to show her once it was completely done and his stuff was moved in, but it felt right to bring her here. He hoped the hunch wasn't a bad one.

He'd chosen an isolated location on a high hill that overlooked a large part of the farm. It was far enough away from both his dad's and his Uncle Les's that he wouldn't feel like he was in anyone's face. Or more to the point, that they weren't in his. The view was incredible. Golden grassy hills and a crystal-clear gully dam populated with marron occupied the foreground. After that, row after row of gnarled grapevines with the odd large jarrah tree or red gum spotted here and there demarcated the landscape.

He'd designed the house layout himself. It was a large open-plan log-and-stone structure built around a huge central stripped and polished pine-tree trunk that functioned as both a support and a central feature to the combined kitchen and living area. The floors were warm pine, as were the kitchen cabinets, skirting boards and window frames. All in all he was proud of the place. He'd already brought a large recliner couch and a massive flat-screen TV for the living room in anticipation of the day he could finally say it was finished.

When he'd been desperate for a bit of peace and quiet the past few days, he'd considered borrowing one of the smaller diesel power generators from the winery and moving in early. The place was ninety-nine per cent finished. If it wasn't for Christmas and every electrician in George Creek taking off for their annual holiday, it would be done.

Clayton was so caught up worrying about Beth's reaction that he almost missed her wide-eyed look of amazement.

'Clayton, is this your house?' she breathed as the sprawling structure came into view.

'Yeah.'

'It's so large. Is it just for you?' Beth was already opening her door before he could fully pull the car to a stop.

'Yep.' Clayton grinned with a combination of relief and pride at her reaction. Beth didn't see his expression. She was already skirting around the last of the building rubble he'd yet to clear that was blocking the path to the front door.

'Can I have a tour?' Beth ran her fingers over the ornate wrought-iron flyscreen door he had commissioned a local artist to make.

He was full-on grinning now. 'That's the idea. The door's open.'

If he was looking for approval of his design prowess, he got it.

Beth swept into the large living area, admiring the polished floor-boards, the huge windows and the high ceilings before running her hands lovingly over the slate benchtops in the kitchen.

'It's lovely, Clayton.'

He flushed in pleased embarrassment. 'Thanks. Wanna see the rest? It's just about ready for me to move in. There's only a few more things to go.'

'Yes!' Beth exclaimed. Without waiting for him, she swept down the long hallway just off the living room, unknowingly making a beeline for the master bedroom at the end illuminated in a mid-afternoon glow by floor-to-ceiling windows on two sides.

'This is simply amazing.' Beth turned around in the middle of the room.

'Yeah. I thought it'd be nice to have the space.' Clayton shrugged, his eyes alighting on Beth's pert little backside nicely out-lined in form-fitting jeans.

'That's right. This will be your first house, won't it?' She ran her fingers over a windowpane then turned to study the specially designed cast-iron light fixtures on one wall.

'Yeah, and not too soon. It's taken years to get it built. Beth?'

'Oh and will you look at this? My *goodness*!' Beth caught sight of the ensuite bathroom. It was huge. One wall was taken up by a massive picture window, and the others were tiled in a cool grey-black slate. A large sunken tub sat against the far wall overlooking the spectacular view. Next to it was a tremendously roomy shower screened off by a single curved piece of melded glass with an abstract design, yet another treasure supplied by one of Clayton's local art-ist friends.

'Beth?' he asked again.

'Yes?' Beth walked past him and out the master bedroom door into the study.

'Look at these bookshelves!' She inspected each one with

obvious envy and admiration. 'You know, I always love a room with a lot of books. Not that I have many. I can't fit them in Gran's house, and my ex-husband thought they took up too much space. I do love them, though.' She wistfully ran her finger along a smoothly polished surface.

Clayton beamed. He was particularly proud of this room. It was lined on three sides with the bookshelves that Beth was now caressing. He and Jeff had made them to fit months before. Its west-facing window would make the most of the remaining sunlight at the end of the day when he usually did his paperwork. He'd already installed a simple wooden desk against the window with a large comfortable leather couch to the side and was looking forward to the day he could spend a bit of time getting things done without his dad brooding at his desk behind him.

'May I?' Beth pointed to the chair.

'Yeah,' Clayton replied. 'Beth?'

'Yes?' She sank down into the dark brown leather and ran her fingers over its surface. Watching her absorption in the texture of the couch brought Clayton's mind round to more pressing matters.

'You . . . ah . . . mentioned more sex.' He suppressed a chuckle as the little pixie in front of him turned bright pink, tucked her feet together and folded her hands in her lap primly.

'Yes. Yes, I did. I need to talk to you first, though. Before I start, I need to know something.' Beth's eyes were huge as she looked up at him. With her skin bathed gold in the sunlight shining through the window, she appeared slightly other-worldly and so completely beautiful, Clayton couldn't remember for the life of him why he'd kept his distance the past few days. He must be a complete idiot.

'What do you need to know?' He walked over to the desk and propped himself against it. This was probably going to be one of the usual female things. The whole do-you-find-me-attractive spiel more likely than not, which, coming from Beth, would be worth hearing.

'Did you enjoy yourself the other night? W-would you mind so much if . . . if I was lacking in some areas of my body?' Beth asked, or more to the point stammered, in an accent Clayton could have cut glass with.

'What sort of question is that?'

'A direct one, I hope.'

'Did I enjoy myself? I would have thought it was bloody obvious.' He crossed his arms over his chest, waiting to see where this was all going.

'Maybe, but my scope of experience is probably a little more limited than yours, so I wasn't quite sure. You see, the thing is . . . what I'm asking is . . . did it matter to you that you didn't see or touch my . . . my . . .' She gestured at her chest, which drew Clayton's gaze. He stared. Something wasn't quite right but he couldn't put his finger on it.

Beth cursed the anxiety coursing through her veins. This whole conversation had gone much better when she'd rehearsed it in her head.

In her imagined scenario she would confront Clayton, apologise for her rudeness on Christmas Eve and then, depending on his reaction, tell him about her double mastectomy and then either go back to her cottage to lick her wounds or ask him out for a meal that evening. It had all been perfectly simple.

Instead, she'd managed to proposition him for sex for the second time since she'd known him, run her hands all over his house and draw his gaze to the one area of her body in which she felt distinctly lacking. Damn. The man was now staring at her chest like someone studying a magic-eye picture and not quite seeing the hidden image. His confusion made a lot of sense. In aid of her mission for the day, she'd left off her bra and was subsequently as flat-chested as a twelve-year-old boy.

'Clayton,' she prompted, willing the man to say *something* so she could work out how to proceed.

'Yeah?'

'Would you mind answering my question about my, ah . . .'

'Your what?' he interrupted, raising both brows.

Beth narrowed her eyes. 'You're making fun of me, aren't you?'

'Nope.' He shrugged, his expression serious and maybe a little impatient. 'Just spit it out, Beth. I've gotta say I'm up for having sex with you right now if you want to. Literally.' He directed a pointed gaze down at his straining fly. 'But you sound like you want to get something off your chest, and as far as I see it, you're making a big deal out of nothing. I like sex. I like you.' He slowly looked her up and down from her toes to the top of her head before meeting her gaze. 'I don't see what the problem is.'

Beth squeezed her eyes shut. In all her imagining she'd never thought of this being so difficult. 'There's a big problem!'

'All right.' Clayton said the words in a measured tone. 'All right, I'm getting the idea and it's leaving me a little worried. What are you trying to tell me, Beth?'

'Oh damn.' Beth pinched the bridge of her nose. 'Clayton, I'm just going to have to say this. I'm sorry. I practised this conversation in my mind so many times but I'm making a hash of it.'

'Go on.'

'I have – no, *had* – cancer. I had cancer. And, ah . . . breast cancer.'

The words dropped with the weight of a lead brick and Beth was able to witness for the second time in her life a man going completely pale. She waited for Clayton to repeat her ex-husband's words, to ask about what this all meant for him, but instead he just stayed silent, his expression shuttered.

'So . . . ah. Well.' Beth huffed out a breath. 'I might as well get it all out. I had a double mastectomy. The reason I didn't want you to . . . *well*, the reason we didn't . . . I don't have breasts.'

She watched his expression, waiting for some kind of response, anything, feeling completely naked as her mind planned ahead. With luck he'd stick to his promise and drive her back to her car. If he didn't, she could walk. It shouldn't be that far. Maybe an hour or so and —

'Jesus, Beth. That's some pretty big news.' Clayton finally spoke, his voice husky. 'Ah. Thanks for telling me —'

'But no thanks?' Beth supplied miserably, wrapping her arms around her waist.

'No . . . no, I didn't mean that. You've got to give me a minute here.' He ran his hand over his face. 'You've, ah, you've got to admit . . . well, that wasn't exactly what I was expecting. Not that I *know* what I was expecting.'

'I know. If you'll just take me back to my car —'

'Hold up.' Clayton's voice cut in over hers. 'Hold it a second. What else did you want to tell me? Was that it?'

Beth nodded.

He stood there looking her straight in the eye with an intensity she couldn't drag herself away from. Distantly she heard birds in the nearby trees outside the study window and the creak of the house.

'Are you okay now?'

Beth blinked. 'Yes. Yes, I'm okay now. I just didn't want . . . oh, this is so awkward! The reason I acted so strangely on Christmas Eve is because I hadn't told you I didn't have . . . I hadn't told you about my mastectomies. You can see I'm not wearing the prosthetics today.' She looked down at her chest, letting out a small laugh. It didn't contain a lot of humour. 'I can't imagine this being more awkward right now.'

There was another silence before Clayton spoke. 'Well, I could. You could say something English that makes it sound like I'm crap in bed again.'

Beth let out a shocked laugh. 'I think it was evident how much I enjoyed myself, if you care to remember.'

'Yeah.' Clayton's expression relaxed a little and a faint smile stretched his mouth. 'That was pretty damn good, Beth.'

'It was. I was hoping that we could do it again.'

'I think we could manage,' Clayton said quietly.

'You do?'

'Well, why don't we give it a try and see?'

Beth nodded shyly. 'Okay. How?'

'How about you come here?'

Beth's eyes widened. 'Pardon?'

'You heard me.'

'I'm, ah, not sure if I —'

'You wouldn't be chickening out, would you?' He raised a brow. 'About an hour ago you turned up to my place saying you wanted to have sex, but here you are, looking like you want to back out. Come clean, Beth. What *do* you want? Are you going to fuck me or not?'

Beth stared at him. The sheer challenge in his words, part playful, part serious – it was like a switch flicked in Beth's head and all rational thought turned off. She needed to show him that she was more than the cancer. She needed to create a distance, a definition of herself as a woman who wanted him as much as he'd professed to want her.

She went from zero to sixty in half a second, launching herself at his chest, hands looping around his shoulders and legs wrapping around his waist just before her mouth crashed against his so hard that her lips ground against his teeth.

'Ghmmph!' Clayton stood rigidly still, muscles tensed in surprise at the onslaught before the rest of him caught up and his large hands grasped her backside, hiking her against him as he spun around and slammed her against the wall next to the door.

Beth put all of herself into the kiss. Her tongue sparred

aggressively with his as she bit at his lips, his tongue, then groaned out of frustrated anger and frustrated desire when he returned her aggression, pushing her more firmly against the wall and rocking his pelvis against hers.

Her head thunked back against timber as Clayton bit and nipped his way down her throat. 'Clayton.' She gripped his face in her hands forcing him back to look at her. His eyes were dark with lust, his lips red from her kiss.

'Hmm?'

'Make love to me.'

'Damn straight.' He rolled his hips against her, his hands on her backside, gripping her to him.

Beth moaned as his teeth scraped the side of her neck.

'Now.' She shoved her hands through his hair, returning her mouth to his for another hot, hard kiss, wrapping her legs tighter around his waist, feeling a rush of warmth in her belly as he rubbed against the juncture of her thighs.

Gripping her tightly, he spun around and bridged the distance to the couch, bumping, grinding their bodies together. Lost in his taste, his smell, how good he felt, Beth devoured his mouth, angling her head first one way, then the other. She growled in frustration when the contact wasn't close enough, when she couldn't draw the response she wanted out of him.

'Steady,' Clayton rasped, breaking off the kiss as he clumsily fell backwards, bringing Beth down on top of him.

Arms and legs liberated by the new position, she immediately straddled his thighs, pushing up his shirt, raking her short nails over the ridges of his abdominals. She smiled with satisfaction at his hiss of indrawn breath when her fingers reached the top button of his shorts.

'Undo these,' she ordered, fingers fumbling over the button while she bit and sucked on the thick cord of muscle on his neck, tasting salt and sweat.

Groaning, Clayton roughly moved her fingers, flipping the button open and unzipping his fly. His hard cock sprung free. He wasn't any less intimidating this time, but she was damned if he'd imply she was a coward again. Circling the velvety hard skin at the base of his penis, she ran her fist up to the deep red engorged tip and back down again.

'Jesus, Beth.' Clayton flexed his hips involuntarily. It was all Beth needed to repeat the action two more times, gaining a triumphant rush of power with every movement, every noise he made.

'Take off your pants.' His hands tugged at the waistband of her jeans.

'Not yet.' Beth pumped her fist up and down his length again while she used her spare hand to touch his chest, flicking his small flat brown nipples, watching with narrow eyes as they contracted.

'Not helping, Beth.' He roughly pushed her jeans and underwear far enough down her legs to grasp her bare backside in his hands.

Beth whimpered. The skin-on-skin contact was electrifying. She pushed against him, trying to get closer but was frustrated by her clothing. This wouldn't do. Abruptly breaking free of Clayton's hold, she scrambled clumsily off him and skimmed off her jeans and underwear in one swift movement before launching herself back at him, legs straddling his thighs.

Leaning back on the couch, eyes half-closed, looking down at where their bodies met, Clayton groaned. 'Beth.'

'Hmm?' She ran her hands through his hair and resumed her assault on his mouth, clumsily rubbing herself against him, revelling in how good it felt.

'God, this is killing me to say it, but I don't have any condoms,' Clayton rasped in a pained voice, his hips bucking up against her, shooting sparks to her nerve endings.

'Not an issue,' Beth panted. 'I'm on the pill, and no STIs. I take it you're safe?' Without preamble, she raised herself slightly, grasped his straining penis and positioned herself above him. She'd never been this forward before but it felt right, and she wasn't going to stop now.

'Yeah, but are you sure?' Clayton asked through clenched teeth, already gripping her hips, firmly guiding himself inside her tight heat.

'Hmm . . .' Beth threw back her head and with an abrupt movement pushed her knees wide, sinking deep, fast. It wasn't an easy fit, but any discomfort was chased away by the friction against her clitoris as she began to experiment, rocking her hips, luxuriating in the feeling of being so stretched inside. Clayton's hair-roughened skin abraded the sensitive flesh of her inner thighs and she moaned.

'Oh fuck, oh God.' Clayton's back arched and his eyes clenched shut as Beth lifted herself up and slowly glided back down his length, leaning forwards and bracing her hands on his shoulders.

His groan of pleasure spurred her on. She repeated the movement, this time running her fingertips across his hard chest until they found his nipples again. She pinched them hard just as she took him deep inside, feeling the exact moment his control snapped.

Strong fingers grasped the back of her head to pull her down for a toe-curling, messy, open-mouthed kiss as he roughly angled her forward and his hips thrust hard, pushing deep, in a fast, continuous rhythm, rubbing against her clitoris in a way that turned Beth's blood to liquid fire.

Before she knew it, she was wailing as hot burning shards of pleasure arced from where they were joined to every straining muscle, every cell of her being.

Seconds later Clayton shouted huskily and pulled her roughly against him in a bone-crushing hug. Brain temporarily stunned and overwhelmed from endorphins and adrenaline, Beth passed out in a sweaty, exhausted sleep, the sound of Clayton's strong heartbeat reverberating against her cheek.

*

The sky was a variegated purple and a strong salty sea breeze blew across Evangeline's Rest by the time Clayton finally walked through the front door of his family home. In the distance he could hear the faint noise of Beth's car echoing in the dusky, end-of-day stillness.

He'd offered to follow her home but she'd turned him down and he'd had no option but to let her go. He was actually relieved. A lot had happened in the past few hours and he hadn't yet wrapped his head around any of it. Truthfully, he didn't really *want* to wrap his head around anything right now.

He wandered into the kitchen.

'Where've you been?' Rob demanded. He was hunched over the dining table, reading glasses perched on the end of his nose as he paused in writing something. Whatever he was working on was important – there were enough balled-up, presumably failed attempts next to his left elbow to keep a paper recycling factory in business for a week.

Clayton shrugged. 'Checking out my place.'

'Stick your finger in a light socket while you were there?' Rob pushed his glasses up his nose and frowned at the paper in front of him.

'What? No power yet. What are you talking about?' Clayton asked in confusion.

'Take a look in the mirror. While you're at it, I'd do something about that bruise on your neck if I was you. Either that was a pretty big mosquito, or one of Fred's sheep gave you a love bite.'

Clayton decided that this was his cue to leave the room. He stalked into the laundry to check on his dog.

Waffles was sitting in a large cardboard box under the sink panting and shifting uncomfortably as a barrage of squeaking, squealing puppies fronted up to the milk bar.

'Feeling a bit flat, are we, girl?' He squatted down to pat her head. She rolled her soft brown eyes towards him, her expression a picture of such long-suffering patience that it easily transcended species.

As much at a loss on how to comfort his dog as he had been at comforting Beth earlier, Clayton just gave her another awkward pat before standing up and checking himself in the mirror over the sink.

'*Jaaaaysus Christ*,' he exclaimed quietly to himself, tilting his head to the one side and staring incredulously at the massive hickey on his neck, then at his hair. It looked like he'd grabbed an electric fence while standing in a puddle of water.

All in all, he looked like a man who'd just been well satisfied. The hickey was going to earn him some serious hell from his family, though. Not to mention Jeff. Clayton played back the afternoon, trying to work out when Beth had managed to do the damage, but he couldn't come up with any particular moment. It had all been a wild blur that had left him still feeling a little light-headed. Sex had never been that explosive, that emotional. He'd never felt so needy before, and he wasn't sure if he liked it. He didn't want to think about what had brought it all on, either.

The whole cancer thing had thrown him for a loop. Beth must have been pretty sick if she'd had both breasts removed. Did that mean there was a big chance of relapse? Maybe she even had cancer now and didn't know it. God. His felt like puking after merely contemplating the possibility.

A sharp, entirely unwanted memory slunk to the forefront of Clayton's thoughts: his father, just after his mum died. Clayton had been five at the time. His little brother Mike had snuck into his room late at night, scared at a strange noise in the house. Clayton had crept down the hall to his dad's room to investigate and had been completely unprepared for what he found.

His dad, his invincible childhood rock, had been curled up on the floor sobbing into one of Pam's nighties, every line of his body speaking of wrenching loss. His cries had been a rasping, foreign sound, terrifying for the sheer desolation and loss they conveyed.

Clayton felt himself tearing up at the memory. Somehow, his

mum's death hadn't been a concrete thing until that moment. He'd convinced himself she was just away somewhere and that she'd come back soon. He'd faced the reality of death for the first time that night. Just the fact that his dad had never looked at another woman in the past twenty-nine years attested to how much that kind of loss devastated a person.

And now there was Beth . . .

Waffles' low whine abruptly shook him from his thoughts.

'Whaddya think, girl?' he murmured, wiping the back of his hand over his eyes.

She gave him a doggy grin, the same one she always gave him when he was wound up. He'd always interpreted it to mean, *She'll be right, mate – relax.*

'Yeah, well, that's not much help.' He forced a smile for the dog's benefit, bending down to rub her side then straightening up. A twinge in his back startled him, reminding him all over again of Beth and how wild she'd been. Hell, how wild *he'd* been.

Maybe his dog's unspoken advice *was* a bit of help.

Beth was just in Australia on holiday, wasn't she? Then she'd be gone. What would it hurt if he enjoyed her company a bit more before she left? That had been the plan all along, hadn't it?

He didn't want to even contemplate not seeing her again. Maybe if he could manage to steer clear of any heavy conversation over the next few weeks and just show her a good time, it would all work out. She'd learn to relax a bit, and she definitely needed to do that – the woman was more highly strung than the clothesline on his back lawn – and he'd get to see more of her. More to the point, he'd get to touch more of her, which was a win-win situation if ever there was one.

Buoyed by the direction his thoughts had taken, he headed back into the kitchen in search of something to eat. All the exercise had built up an appetite.

Chapter 13

'Are you absolutely, *positively* sure there isn't anything hiding in those bushes?' Beth frowned dubiously at the white-grey sandy path that cut through a scrubby, saltbush-sprinkled sand dune.

'Yeah, it's fine, Beth. See? I'm not wearing any shoes, so you don't have to worry.' Clayton rounded his Jeep to Beth's side. He was balancing a small foam cooler on one shoulder and had a large black beach towel draped over the other.

'Yes, but you're Australian. You probably have a natural genetic reptile and insect repellent oozing out of your pores right now. Whereas every slimy, slithering thing in the area is probably zoning in on me as we speak.' Beth scanned the ground at her feet suspiciously. Much to her relief, all she could see were ants. There were a lot of them scurrying here and there, but thankfully none of them were interested in her.

'I'll protect you.' Clayton grabbed her hand and pulled her along behind him down the path. He appeared completely oblivious to the heat coming off the sand he was squelching through with bare feet, even though Beth had no doubt it was scorching hot.

'Are you sure this is a good idea?' she asked. 'Why couldn't we just wait until sunset and go for a walk then? I really don't have to swim in the ocean, you know.'

'Yep,' Clayton replied. 'I'm definitely sure. You can't tell me you've never swum at a beach and expect me not to take you. You're in one of the world's surfing capitals, for Christ's sake.'

Anyone would think Beth had admitted to a heinous crime. Until that morning she hadn't even known that Margaret River was a big venue for international surfing competitions, but that wasn't a surprise – a few months ago she hadn't known the place existed.

'Yes. Well, I don't think I'm really lacking in my life for not giving it a go.'

'I'll pretend I didn't hear that. Besides, I can't bring you at sunset for a swim. That's when the sharks feed.'

Beth stopped stock-still, feet digging into the sand and face blanching under her wide-brimmed straw hat. 'Sharks?'

Clayton stopped and heaved what Beth thought to be a thoroughly overdramatic sigh. His expression was veiled by his sunglasses and shadowed by his ever-present baseball cap, but his exasperation was obvious. 'Only at night. Haven't you seen *Jaws*? The girl only gets taken at night.'

'The girl at the beginning, yes. But what about the rest?'

'Only robot American sharks eat like that during the day,' Clayton informed her. 'Australian sharks are a bit more civilised. Feeding time is at six at night and six in the morning. You'll be fine.' He began to tug her along again.

Beth gave up digging in her heels and followed reluctantly behind while scanning the drab, knubbly greenery on each side of the path just in case. She was so distracted by that particular task, she bumped into Clayton's back when he stopped abruptly.

'Oomph.'

'Will you look at that? Perfectly calm, just for you.'

'What?' She gripped his waist and peered around his shoulder. The path had come to an end, opening out onto a blinding white beach leading down to water so calm it could have been glass. 'Oh.'

'I haven't seen it this calm in years,' Clayton breathed reverentially. 'Usually the swell here is great. Come on.' He tugged her past a family with small children who were busy engineering possibly the largest sand castle Beth had ever seen and then further past a few groups of teenagers lying in the sun. All the girls and women seemed to be tanned to within an inch of their lives, a sharp contrast to Beth's white-on-white skin.

'Clayton, I don't think this is a good idea.'

'Thought we got past that,' he replied calmly, setting the cooler down on a patch of sand only a few metres away from the tide line, dropping his towel next to it. He put his hands behind his head and stretched, Beth's eyes following the ripple of muscle across his faintly furred chest and stomach. What were they talking about again? Oh yes. That's right.

'No, I haven't quite *got past that* as you say. I believe you told me this morning we were going to the beach and gave me no choice,' she protested. 'And as you can see, I have no swimsuit.' She gestured to her blue cut-off denim shorts and red T-shirt. She'd left off her bra again because she didn't want to imagine what would happen if it got waterlogged. Not that she intended on going into the water.

'Not an issue.' Clayton shrugged.

Beth had to tamp down an increasingly familiar urge to hit him. 'I'm glad you don't think so.'

She'd revealed her secret to Clayton a week ago, and since the morning after, when he'd appeared at her house bearing a French press coffee maker and some freshly ground coffee, they had spent almost every spare minute they had with each other, mostly making love.

Fully expecting at least one conversation about her cancer and mastectomies, Beth had felt unexpectedly relieved when Clayton didn't mention it. Instead, he'd made her feel incredibly spoiled, showing her around the region, asking her opinion of his competitors' wines, taking her to restaurants and picnics and making love to her like they'd not be able to again. Intense wasn't quite the word for it.

She knew she should be bothered by his seeming unwillingness to talk about things but, then again, it wasn't as if she'd brought it up either. She still deliberately kept a top on whenever they made love. She was thankful Clayton didn't let it get in the way of their enjoyment of each other's bodies. He'd explored every other available inch of her countless times in ways that left her toes curling.

As Violet told her during every phone call home, Beth had far too much seriousness in her life. A bit of fun wouldn't hurt her in the slightest.

Although that didn't mean she wanted to swim in shark-infested water.

'You know I can't swim, Clayton.' She squinted in the bright sunlight reflecting off the sand as Clayton pulled a bottle of sunscreen out of his back pocket and closed the gap between them.

'That's all right. I can.' He gently tugged off her hat and dropped it in the sand then squirted a dollop of sunscreen onto his palm before smoothing it over her nose and cheeks.

'And what happens if there's something in the water and it bites me?'

'Shh or you'll get this stuff in your mouth – and it'll taste bad.' He finished rubbing cream into her face while she frowned at him.

'I'm not a child, you know,' she protested indignantly when he began to smooth cream over her bare arms. 'And I did this earlier today.'

'Yeah, but I like touching you, so shuddup and act like you're enjoying yourself.'

'If I must.' Beth heaved a sigh, suppressing a smile. 'I'm not going in the water, though.'

'Okay.' Clayton shrugged. 'You wanna put some of this stuff on me now?'

'Definitely. You should already be wearing this if you're going around shirtless,' Beth said in a stern voice, then snatched the bottle off him before liberally applying the cream.

'You know, I've got more skin than just my chest,' Clayton reminded her with a deep chuckle a few minutes later after she'd got a little sidetracked.

'What? Oh. Yes, you do. Turn around,' she ordered, flushing with embarrassment and finishing the rest of the job quickly but taking great care. Skin cancer wasn't a laughing matter and she'd read somewhere that Australians had a very high rate of it. She said as much to Clayton.

He shrugged and looked over his shoulder. 'So, you coming in with me?'

'What? I told you I'm not wearing the right clothes.' Beth stepped back and held up her hands to ward him off.

He studied her thoughtfully for a moment. 'You're right. You're not,' he agreed and Beth relaxed.

It was just the moment Clayton had been waiting for, and before she knew it she was thrown over his shoulder and they were moving far too quickly towards the water.

'Put me down!' Beth screamed, reaching down to futilely grasp Clayton's sunscreen-slick back and hips for fear of being dropped.

'Nope.'

'Clayton!'

He was splashing through water now. It was flicking up into her face from the backs of his feet.

'I'm getting wet!'

'That's the idea.'

'Put me down! *Now.*'

'All right.'

Five seconds later she came up spluttering, eyes squinting in fury and ready for murder.

'I can't believe you just did that!' she shrieked, wiping water and sunscreen out of her eyes. 'I could have drowned!'

'Yeah. Especially since you're having trouble standing in waist-high water and yelling at me.'

'That's not the point!'

'Definitely not. Come here.'

'No.' Beth started to wade through the water back to the shore . . . until she spotted movement in the water in front of her. Without thinking she turned around and launched herself into Clayton's arms.

'That's more like it.'

'I'm only here because there's something over there.' She fluttered her hand at the water.

'Really?'

'Don't walk towards it!'

'Seriously, Beth, take a look. It's just a fish.' Clayton lowered them deeper into the water and laughed at her outraged squeal. 'Or it could be a baby shark.'

Beth punched his shoulder. 'Don't you dare laugh about that!' The thought of sharks had her craning her head scanning the water around them for the inevitable triangular fin.

'I tell you what. How about you hold onto me and I'll protect you?'

'How?'

'Old Australian trick. You punch them in the nose.'

Beth regarded Clayton's expression carefully. His eyes were dancing with repressed laughter. 'You're lying. You wouldn't know the first thing to do. I bet you're even a bit scared sometimes.'

'Yep, but let's just pretend and everything will be all right.' His mouth curved into tight smile.

Beth had a sudden feeling that they were now talking about more than swimming and sharks. Their eyes met for a tense moment before Beth bit her lip and looked down at the water. 'If I agree to this whole swimming thing . . .'

'Which we aren't doing at all right now.'

'No. Right now you're assaulting me and holding me against my will. *If* I agree, what do I get later in return?' She wrapped her legs around his waist and deliberately relaxed her death grip around his neck as the water billowed her T-shirt around her, lapping against her chest and back.

'You know,' Clayton said with a thoughtful expression. 'I've got this book, *The Illustrated Kama Sutra*. I reckon there's a few pages out of that we could try that'd make up for me getting you wet.' He waggled his eyebrows.

'You're completely shameless, you know that, right?' Beth laughed, wondering if she should tell him she'd seen the same book.

'Yep.'

'It's a deal.' Beth grinned, thinking that there were a few pages she would like to try out too now that she'd gained a little more experience. 'You had better pray that you're flexible, Mister Hardy.' Her expression turned distinctly wicked.

'Me? Nah, I get to pick the pages. Owner's prerogative.' Clayton gave her a cheeky grin. 'Anyway. You ever been felt-up under water?'

'What!'

'Obviously not. Well, there's always a first time for everything.'

For the life of him, Rob Hardy couldn't work out why he'd gone into the wine business. A smarter man would have stuck to sheep and dairy. At least you didn't get ignorant know-it-alls telling you how to do your job when you were shearing.

How the hell had Angie stuck with this job for the past thirty years? How had she put up with the pretentious city bastards without losing her temper and using them as target practice for an all-in wine-bottle-tossing event?

'You know, I think this one is a little too oaky for my tastes.' An emaciated, impeccably dressed vulture-woman screwed up her face at the chardonnay Rob had just poured her, and he could feel his teeth losing their enamel as he ground them together.

'What about you, Warren? Don't you think it has too much oak?' the woman continued, turning to her husband. The man was an overfed banker type, all tucked-in polo shirt and creased white chinos.

'Too acidic for me.' The banker sniffed. He raised his glass to his nose like he was trying to ingest the stuff through inhalation.

'You want to move on to the reds?' Rob resisted the urge to sneer and forced a wooden smile. He knew he was being less than cordial but he drew the line when some stuck-up city bitch told him *his* wine was *too oaky*.

Still, he was a professional. As much as he wanted to tell vulture lady she could shove her *oaky* up her *arse*, he feigned interest when she waxed poetic over a glass of cabernet sauvignon that had more oak in it that a goddamn English woodland.

He took a covert deep breath and tried to remind himself that these people weren't the be-all and end-all of the wine-consuming public. As a matter of fact, he usually enjoyed dropping by the cellar door.

He'd especially liked it since a series of grape gluts had brought down the exclusivity of the region's wine and the big wineries had started to market to everyday people. Since then, he'd got a kick out of the idea that the couple enjoying a glass of Evangeline's Rest shiraz could as easily be a plumber and his stay-at-home wife as the duo in front of him. After all, the plumber was just the sort of bloke Rob had been before he'd thrown a few grapevines in the ground thirty-something years ago.

He fielded one or two more cringe-worthy critiques before politely waving the couple out the door. As he'd predicted, they hadn't made a single purchase. It wasn't that he usually expected people to – the cellar door was all about raising the winery's profile – but for those two he'd make an exception and get a bit uptight.

'Having a rough one today, are we, Robby?' Barry Kensington, a George Creek native and operator of Have A Go Wine Tours, sauntered into the room and gave Rob a familiar crooked, yellow-toothed grin.

'Bugger off, mate,' Rob said in a not unfriendly growl while loading the used wine glasses into the small dishwasher under the bar. He and Barry had gone to school together, so he didn't feel the need to feign politeness. 'How many do we have today?'

'Just the five of 'em.' Barry shrugged. 'It's a quiet one today. They're all pretty far gone after our last stop and they're hitting the reds, so if you wanna make a few sales that's what I'd push.'

'Righto.' Rob nodded and set out five glasses ready to go.

Usually Angie required the tour operators to call ahead so she could prepare for a rush of visitors, but she'd always made the exception for Barry. It probably had something to do with giving him and Rob a smack around the ear when they were five for sneaking gingersnaps out of the biscuit barrel.

'Angie off sick today?' Barry leaned his heavily tattooed forearms on the bar.

'She's retired,' Rob said with deliberate nonchalance.

Barry reared back in surprise. 'You're shitting me!'

'Nope.'

'God help us. I never thought I'd see the day. What about Gwen? Can't she pick up the slack?'

'She quit. She's only doing the afternoons now for another week.' Rob kept his expression impassive.

'Quit? Why?' Barry said, his expression befitting news of a natural disaster. 'Are you insane, mate? Pay her double. They love her in here.'

Rob shrugged. 'Yeah? I don't think that'll work, somehow. You can't predict women, can you, mate? She got her knickers in a knot over something and wants to go, so what can I do?'

Barry shook his head. 'Unknot them! *Jaysus*, what did Angie say? She and Gwen are tight. I bet Angie flipped her lid at the news. You won't find anyone better than Gwen, mate. Salt of the earth. Salt of the earth,' he repeated dramatically. 'You know, I was surprised when she started here considering how much grief you've given her over the years, but I was happy thinking you'd made up. She's a good old bird. Not that old either, eh?' He gave Rob a gap-toothed leer and gestured to his chest, imitating a large pair of breasts.

Rob found himself feeling unaccountably furious. 'Watch it.'

Barry shifted uncomfortably, hunching his shoulders. 'No harm meant, mate. It'll be sad to see her go. Mind you, she won't be out of work long. Once the word gets out, she'll be snapped up in a minute.'

Rob scowled at that. He'd realised as much himself over the past week. True to her word, Gwen had given two weeks' notice the Monday after Christmas. Since then he'd been going through hell. Angie had been furious, refusing to work at the cellar door and leaving Rob holding the baby.

He'd tried to palm the job off to Clayton but his son had declared a week ago that he was taking a month off work, which left Rob pulling double duty. Given that Clayton hadn't taken a holiday in years and had stood in for everyone and anyone else whenever they'd wanted to take time off, no matter how much it burdened him, there was nothing Rob could say. He just had to suck it up, and between him, Les and Angie they'd manage it. It didn't mean he liked it, though. He liked even less the fact that he had one more week of seeing Gwen when she came in for the afternoon shift. She outright refused to speak to him other than the usual formal pleasantries delivered in that infuriatingly polite way of hers.

It wasn't like Rob hadn't made an effort to acknowledge what she'd said during her little speech on Christmas Eve. He'd spent hours drafting a letter telling her he accepted her apology and asking her to stay on. Instead of reading it and rescinding her resignation, all she'd done when he handed it to her was look sad and say, 'I'd rather hear you say whatever is in this letter, Robert.'

He didn't even know if she'd read the damn thing, because she sure as hell hadn't indicated she wanted to keep her job. There was no pleasing the woman. Saying it or writing it was all the same thing. Why couldn't she be happy with that?

'Off with the fairies there?' Barry interrupted Rob's brooding. Rob knew that the gossiping old bastard was itching to get a bit of dirt he could spread around.

'No. Just thinking about work, mate.'

Barry reached into the back pocket of his jeans for a packet of papers and his ever-present Drum tobacco. Barry had smoked home-rolled cigarettes ever since he turned sixteen. It was a filthy habit and Rob told him as much, like he did every other time he saw him.

Barry shrugged his wiry shoulders. 'The missus left me, mate. I gotta have some pleasure in life.'

'So, where is everyone?'

'Having a pee break.' Barry shrugged. 'Good bunch today. All retired tradies, mostly plumbers.' True to his word they wandered in minutes later laughing raucously and generally making a lot of noise.

For the first time that day, Rob genuinely smiled. He served them, made a killing in sales and then turned back to Barry.

'You off now?'

'Yeah. Tell Gwen if she wants a job they're screaming for some-one like her over at Bella's Leap.'

'I'll do that,' Rob said, through newly gritted teeth. He'd be buggered if Gwen would work for those bastards. He'd pay her double to keep her on. He'd tie her to the damn bar if he had to. Unaccountably, the thought wasn't as unpleasant as it should have been.

Barry shot him a knowing grin. 'And I'd appreciate it if you put a good word in for me, mate. I've got a soft spot for Gwen. She's a real classy lady. Always has been.' With that he walked out the door and promptly lit up the cigarette he'd just rolled, sucking like a vacuum cleaner so he'd be able to finish it before he reached the bus.

Rob scowled through the window at Barry's retreating back.

He and Gwen were going to have to talk.

'So, I was wondering . . .' Beth began as she pulled out of Clayton's driveway.

'Yeah? Watch that car, Beth.'

'I saw the car, thank you very much. As I was saying, I was wondering why you're unattached as yet. You haven't been married before, have you?'

'Nope. You might wanna stick to your side of the road, Beth.'

'I drive on lanes narrower than this every day at home, Clayton. With dry-stone walls either side.'

'Yeah, but not in my Jeep, you don't. Remind me why I let you drive?'

'Because you complained so much about having to scrunch up into my rental. Where am I turning? Here?'

'Left, and stick to the left while you're at it.'

'Yes, sir. We do drive on the same side in the UK, you know. You haven't answered my question.'

'No one ever came along.' Clayton wound down his window and a warm breeze wafted into the car. It smelled like gum trees and baking earth. He tried to relax back into his seat but the sight of Beth peering over the steering wheel like a near-sighted pixie was seriously setting him on edge.

'No one in, what is it? Thirty-four years?' Beth asked, brows raised. 'Why not?'

'I dunno. Ask the local female population.' Clayton shrugged.

'I'd rather ask you. Do I turn here?'

'No. It's a bit further yet.'

'Clayton?'

'Yeah?'

'Am I the same as the other women you've been with? Someone you'll forget about later?'

'Jesus, Beth, just spring that on me, why don't you!'

'It's rather straightforward. Yes or no will suffice. Do I turn here, then?'

'Bit further yet. Watch that bobtail crossing the road.'

'Bobtail? What's a bobtail?' Beth asked, craning her neck to see and momentarily forgetting her line of questioning, much to Clayton's relief.

'That lizard in front of us.'

When Beth had finished swerving the car, Clayton carefully unlocked his hands from the tops of his thighs. 'Actually, Beth, don't mind the bobtail. It's fine. Mind me.'

'You could have warned me!'

'Why? They're harmless and it was a foot long if that.' Clayton sighed. 'It's not like it was gonna do anything other than watch you crash us into a tree. We've got a couple at home that steal Waffles' dog biscuit every morning. Turn here.'

Expression incredulous, Beth slowed down and pulled in to Jeff's driveway. 'That *thing* eats dog biscuits?'

'Yeah. Just by the front porch there would be great.'

'Here?'

'Yep.'

The minute Beth pulled on the handbrake, Clayton held out his hand. 'Keys, please.'

'Pardon?' Beth feigned incomprehension.

'You heard me. There's no way in hell I'm going through that again. At least not in my own car. Jesus. You drive like you're the only one on the road. No wonder I nearly wiped you out that first day we met.'

Beth's eyes narrowed and she pulled the keys out of the ignition and deliberately dropped them into her handbag before climbing down from the Jeep.

'You can have them back when you answer my question from before,' she said pertly just before she slammed her door shut.

Clayton glowered at her retreating back and got out on his side just as Jeff sauntered out to greet them wearing his usual off-work uniform of board shorts and a faded blue T-shirt.

'Fancy seeing you two together.' Jeff made a beeline for Beth, planting a smacking kiss on her cheek. 'When you wear him out, you know I'm available, right?' he said in a loud whisper.

Beth laughed and gave him a sharp jab in the ribs. 'Behave.'

'I second that,' Clayton growled.

'All right, all right.' Jeff grinned unrepentantly and wrapped an arm around Beth's waist. 'I can see we're a bit touchy today. Could have something to do with that bruise you've got on your neck, mate. You should get that checked out. Looks nasty. Oomph.' He grunted when Beth elbowed him again. He gazed down at her with warmth in his eyes. 'Laura's inside doing mystical things in my kitchen. She kicked me out because apparently I DON'T KNOW HOW TO COOK SO SHE'LL HAVE TO DO IT ALL,' he bellowed the latter towards the house while Beth ducked and covered her ears.

'You right, mate? Or would you like to deafen us again?' Clayton exclaimed in exasperation.

'I'm fine now.' Jeff gave Beth's waist another squeeze. 'Sorry, Beth. Didn't think there. Anyway, Laura's chained herself to the stove and needs the company.'

'I can spot a hint when it's directed my way.' Beth turned to Clayton. 'So, I'll be driving you home?'

'Over my dead body.'

'Hey, none of that!' Jeff exclaimed. 'If you kill him I'll have to bury him, and I put my back out the other day digging holes for a new fence, so play nice.' He pushed Beth in the direction of the house and openly admired her backside as she walked away. 'Tell Laura that I could do with a beer out here,' Jeff called after her.

'You'll do with a beer shoved up your arse, you cheeky bastard!' Laura called from the porch before greeting Beth.

From where he was standing next to Jeff, Clayton could hear Laura talking a thousand words a minute and knew Beth would be occupied for a while.

'So?' Jeff nudged Clayton in the ribs.

'What?'

'Come on, mate. I gotta live vicariously through *someone*. I haven't had any action since last year. No time with everything going on since Dad retired, not to mention your sister giving me enough evils every time I see her in public. Thanks to her, every female around thinks I'm the Antichrist.'

'Yeah, about that . . .' Clayton raised an eyebrow.

'Buggered if I know,' Jeff muttered, but he didn't meet Clayton's eyes directly. 'Anyway, what's up with you and Beth? You two serious?' When Clayton's expression turned pained, Jeff leaned over and thumped him on the back. 'I can see this is going to require beer. Come on. If we're lucky Laura hasn't put cyanide in my sausages.'

Chapter 14

It was early morning and the sounds of the local birds' wake-up call drifted through Beth's open bedroom window.

Feeling warm and relaxed all over, Clayton lay on his side with his head propped up on his palm and watched Beth sleep. She was curled up facing him with her hands tucked together beneath her pillow. A short straight hank of hair had fallen over her eyebrows, and her mouth was partially open.

His gaze went lower, taking in her fine frame. She really was a tiny thing. He guessed she could have made a good ballet dancer if she'd wanted to be one. Hell, she might have been one for all he knew. A flash of tenderness washed over him at the thought of a little-girl Beth in a pink tutu, a serious expression on her face as she pirouetted.

He smiled when she made a soft, sleepy sound. He'd worn her out. Again. Or maybe she'd worn him out and he was still so buzzed that it hadn't kicked in yet. He idly smoothed the lock of hair away from her eyes.

They had planned to go out for dinner last night but Beth had sprung him with the page of the *Kama Sutra* that Jeff had caught her reading in the library what seemed like months before. Being an obliging man, Clayton had taken what was coming to him. He smirked at the thought. And then, well, he'd had to pay in kind. He couldn't have the woman thinking she'd got the best of him. He'd done pretty damn well, too, considering how she'd passed out straight after. She was even snoring genteelly. He suppressed a laugh at that. The woman was so English, she even snored with a posh accent.

'What's so funny?' Beth mumbled, opening her eyes enough to peer up at him through her lashes.

'Nothing.' Clayton couldn't resist running a finger over the two little frown lines between her brows.

'Good.' She promptly went back to sleep.

Chuckling to himself and feeling energised, Clayton got up and padded naked into Beth's kitchen to make himself a coffee. The sunrise was a stunning mix of red and pink this morning and he caught sight of a small group of kangaroos grazing near the porch. He debated waking Beth up to show her and then decided against it.

He'd gathered quite quickly that she wasn't her best after just waking. In fact, she was downright surly. On top of that, he was a little worried she'd be scared of the kangaroos rather than happy to see them.

Only the day before she'd recounted a story she'd read in a book about a man being disemboweled by one. Clayton had laughed at that. She worked every day taming psychotic chihuahuas, pit bulls and dobermans without even blinking, but show her a hopping marsupial and she ran a mile. Clayton had a feeling she'd never be at one with Australian nature. Not that she needed to be – she was going home in a few weeks. Thirteen-and-a-half days exactly now. Feeling twitchy at the thought, he waited for the kettle to boil, then made himself a coffee and wandered back into the bedroom.

Beth had kicked off the rugs and was now sprawled on her back, her legs and arms akimbo. The sheet sat low on her hips and her T-shirt had ridden up, exposing most of her flat little stomach and a faint trace of pink that indicated the beginnings of one of the scars on the left side of her chest.

His smile faded and his gut clenched. Beth's chest was a no-go zone. He'd been fine with that. In fact, he'd preferred not to dwell on what she had been through, but now the thought of it triggered a sharp stabbing feeling in his chest. He needed to see more of her, all of her. If someone asked him in that moment why, he wouldn't be able to say. He just knew he had to.

Setting his coffee aside, he sat gingerly on the edge of the bed and reached over with unsteady hands and a pounding heart to gently hike Beth's T-shirt under her arms. She made a noise in her sleep, muttering something under her breath, and he stopped still, adrenaline pumping through his veins, his hand poised in the air, fingers lightly pinching soft cotton. Keeping his eyes on her face he monitored every inward breath, every little exhalation she made, for signs she was awake. *Christ.* He felt like a horny teenager getting his first sight of a girl's boobs, knowing he'd be toast if he got caught. The fact that Beth didn't have any didn't mean anything. In a way, it made what he was doing seem even more illicit.

He focused on what he'd just uncovered. His mouth tensed at the corners and his gut lurched. *Fuck.* He hadn't been properly prepared for this very real physical evidence that Beth had been sick. That she was mortal. That she could have died. Could still die.

Each faintly puckered, symmetrical pink scar began high up under Beth's arms and extended down in a curving diagonal to almost meet in the middle of her chest with an inch to spare. The colour stood out against the pale creamy white skin surrounding it, a stark demarcation of what she'd been through. Clayton reached a shaking hand towards the scar on the left and traced his finger just above it, as if by doing so he could rub it all away. He swallowed loudly past a thick lump in his throat. Did she see these every day and think about what she'd lost? Did she still worry? Did she still have a chance of getting cancer again? *Did she still have cancer?*

The sick feeling turned into a very real cold, clammy need to vomit. The thought of Beth sick, maybe even dying, was untenable. With his heart pounding in his chest, Clayton quickly lowered her T-shirt.

He couldn't breathe. He needed fresh air, and fast. Stumbling to his feet, coffee forgotten, he fled the room.

Beth woke to the smell of fresh coffee. Stretching languidly, she opened her eyes and spotted the source sitting on her bedside table. Clayton must have made it for her. She flopped onto her stomach and grabbed the heavy mug, gulping down a mouthful then grimacing when she discovered it was cold.

'Clayton?'

There was no reply.

'Clayton?' she called out again and got out of bed. Thinking he'd maybe fallen asleep on the porch like he had a few days before, bare feet up on the railing, tousled head lolling to one side, Beth wandered outside. He wasn't there.

'Strange,' she murmured to herself as the first twinge of worry she'd experienced in more than a week wormed its way through her consciousness. She gave herself a mental shake. To worry was foolish.

He couldn't be with her all the time. Even if he was taking a holiday, Clayton had responsibilities. He'd most likely decided to check on things at Evangeline's Rest and hadn't wanted to wake her. Satisfied with this logical explanation, Beth wandered back into the cottage to have a shower.

She pulled her T-shirt over her head as she walked through the living room and tossed it onto her bed, smiling over how relaxed she'd grown with her own nudity.

In the past few years she'd barely been able to meet her own eyes in the mirror, let alone view the rest of herself as a naked whole. A few weeks ago, if someone had told her she'd be standing stark naked in front of a mirror after a night of making love with a man like Clayton, she would never have believed them. This time in Australia had been filled with so many firsts, she'd lost count.

Only days before, she'd visited Laura's beautician friend and got a 'hedge trim', as Laura had termed it. It was her first experience of a bikini wax and she had to admit, it hurt an awful lot less than she imagined it would. It had helped that Laura had come along to take her mind off things, giggling at the funny faces Beth had pulled.

Clayton's reaction had more than compensated for any pain Beth experienced. He'd behaved like she'd given him a belated Christmas present. She grinned at the memory and ran her hands through her hair, which was sticking up at odd angles to her faintly pink face, a casualty of the afternoon she'd spend helping Clayton plant the garden at his new home two days ago.

Her eyes were a deep golden brown. She hadn't seen them that colour for years. Not since before Valerie had died. She knew that it was Clayton's doing. Some time in the past few weeks, she'd managed to fall in love with the big, gruff beast of a man. Intellectually she knew it had been a stupid thing to do but right now, feeling this happy, she couldn't fault herself.

Her eyes drifted lower, to her chest. She turned first one way and then the other, looking at herself properly for the first time in well over a year. Maybe Laura was right and the scars weren't that bad after all. Beth had been lucky enough to get an excellent surgeon. Because she hadn't had a large tumour removed and it hadn't been emergency surgery, they'd been able to keep things relatively neat.

Not that she'd even thought about that at the time.

All she'd been thinking – or, more to the point, fearing – was ending up just like Valerie: one lump removed, then another, then finally the decision for one breast. Her sister hadn't had a chance to consider the other. They'd found cancer in her lymph nodes by then and after that it advanced at a terrifying rate. Beth suspected that Valerie had seen that as something of a blessing. She'd given up the fight not long after, having been worn down by surgery, treatment, sheer exhaustion and fear.

Beth hadn't wanted any of that. Within minutes of hearing her diagnosis and the doctor's recommendations, she'd made her decision. Having already lost her sister to breast cancer, and her grandmother on her father's side, she was in the highest genetic risk category – her breasts had to go.

Violet, the first person Beth told, had been a lifeline in light of Greg's reaction to the bad news. Beth had never once considered that Greg wouldn't support her decision. He was her husband. He loved her. Surely, she'd reasoned, he would understand that this was literally a life-and-death decision, especially after witnessing Valerie's struggle. Unfortunately Greg hadn't viewed it that way. Beth could still remember every nuance of his reaction.

He'd been watching TV when she told him. Manchester City had been playing Manchester United and she'd turned the sound off to get his attention. She'd only just come back from the doctor and had done her best to keep calm as she told him the news.

'Cancer?' he'd repeated, his narrow features paling to an off-white.

'Yes,' Beth had replied, her fists clenched at her sides. She had managed a stiff upper lip these past weeks but she could feel the cracks forming and prayed Greg would say the right thing so she could stay strong.

'Can't be.'

'I've just been diagnosed. I have breast cancer, Greg. You knew it might be a possibility, we talked about it after I found the lump.'

He'd stared at her dumbly. 'Can't be.'

Before Beth knew it he had turned the sound back up and was watching his game.

She'd stared at him, feeling frustration rising but quelling it, knowing that she needed to be sympathetic.

She'd raised her voice, hoping to trigger some form of reaction. 'It would have been nice if you had come to the doctor's appointments with me like I asked.'

'I was busy.'

'Watching football.'

'Like I said, busy.' There was a defensive edge to his voice she had only heard once before, when he had refused to come to the hospital with her when Valerie was sick. Beth felt a sinking feeling. Please don't let it be like that. She needed him.

'The doctor thinks I should have a double mastectomy. With Valerie and my family history he said it was the safest route to go. And I think I agree.' She waited for some kind of acknowledgement – anything – but instead Greg stared resolutely forward, only the pale sheen of sweat on his forehead showing that he might have heard her.

Beth stood there, looking at the man she had been married to almost all her entire adult life and realised in that moment that this was all she was going to get. This was it. Just before the tension inside her reached boiling point he turned down the TV and turned to her. *Thank God!*

'That's where they take your breasts off?'

'Yes. With Valerie dying, I've decided it's the right thing to do.' Her voice had hitched at her sister's name. Valerie had only passed away four months before.

'But they can make you new ones, like Angelina Jolie got or

something?'

Beth shook her head, trying to understand the turn the conversation was taking. 'No, it's not that simple. The doctor said —'

'Can you get bigger ones? Do I get a say in how big they're going to be? Because you could do with being a bit bigger. Never wanted to say it before, but you're a bit on the small side.'

The next moments were something of a blur in Beth's memory. She remembered snatching the TV remote from Greg's hands, she remembered the sound of a state-of-the-art TV screen smashing and she remembered the look of incredulity on his face.

She had given him an ultimatum that day: either he would turn up to the hospital and support her or they were over.

Greg had turned up at the hospital, but he'd arrived at the worst possible time, while a nurse was changing Beth's dressings. Beth had been woozy from pain medication and had felt such an overwhelming relief that he had decided to be there for her that she hadn't thought he wouldn't want to stay. But he had – until he saw Beth's chest and fell apart right then and there. Mumbling apologies and visibly sweating, Beth's husband of seven years had asked for a divorce.

Not immediately able to comprehend his words, Beth hadn't intervened when her attending nurse had bellowed for someone to remove Greg from the ward. Things had only sunk in a few hours later during a short window of time when the pain medication temporarily wore off. Before she'd caught herself, Beth had fallen into a black depression, only wishing for the peace of being buried at Skipton Cemetery next to Valerie and their parents.

If it hadn't been for her gran, Beth knew she wouldn't have survived those first horrible months. Violet and Louis had turned up to the hospital every day without fail, bullying Beth with a resolute cheer and convincing her to move into their cottage so she could return to the land of the living. In the meantime, Louis had dealt with Greg. After confronting Beth's husband and giving him a lecture that was still talked about in Skipton, Louis had taken on the role of go-between, making sure Beth got Charlie and half of everything in the ensuing divorce, as well as providing her with a solid shoulder to cry on when she'd needed it. For Beth, the move back to her gran's had been a welcoming, comforting form of hibernation.

Later, she'd lost herself in her work, because her canine clients couldn't criticise and they loved her no matter what she looked like; in fact, they seemed particularly attentive if she was having a bad day. She only socialised with Violet and Louis's friends, who were well past the age where they'd find Beth's surgery worthy of comment. It had been a comfort to spend time with Violet's cronies. Many of them had survived breast cancer, some of them had undergone mastectomies, and they understood what Beth was going through.

Beth turned away from the mirror and turned on the shower. The past month had felt like waking up from a long sleep to find out the world really was a wonderful place. Thanks largely to Clayton, she was beginning to see herself as young and certainly attractive, if his reaction to her body was any indication.

Smiling at that thought, she leisurely soaped her chest and stomach. She would love to share this with Clayton. She'd never showered with someone before and quite liked the idea of getting soapy hands all over his spectacular body, but that would mean she'd have to be naked too. While it wasn't quite as scary a thought as it had been a few weeks before, she didn't think she was ready for that.

They'd never made love or been involved in any kind of intimacy while she was topless. He hadn't mentioned her breasts since that first day she'd told him about them, let alone asked to see her completely naked. While Beth knew his silence on the topic was problematic, she couldn't deny she didn't feel relieved. After all, while her ego had received some rather lovely attention of late, she didn't quite know how she would handle his reaction if it was negative. Especially since she knew her heart was very much involved.

Greg's rejection had been painful, but she knew now what she'd felt for him had never matured past a need to have what her parents had. It was a pale imitation of the intense joy and at times fear she felt in Clayton's company. Joy because he made her feel so completely cared for, and fear that it would all end too soon. She was leaving in just under two weeks. She wanted to ask him if he wanted her to stay longer, if he felt the same about her as she did for him. She knew she had to, but that would mean talking about her cancer and the chance she could get sick again. She would never forgive herself if she didn't bring it up, but she was having a great deal of trouble working up the courage.

Beth! You've still got time for that. Live in the moment, you silly woman. She cut off her gloomy train of thought, then smiled over how much she sounded like her gran. She knew that's exactly what Violet would tell her, and Beth had to admit she'd be right. If surviving cancer had taught her anything, it was not to second-guess the future. With that in mind, she got out of the shower and began to plan her afternoon.

Maybe she could use Clayton's absence to her advantage. He'd been so wonderfully solicitous, playing tour guide and taking good care of her both in bed and out, that she felt she needed to repay him in some way.

She ran through the options while drying her hair. She had already orchestrated a surprisingly successful demonstration of what she'd learned in her little pre-Christmas research expedition to the George Creek Public Library. Clayton had certainly enjoyed himself if his roar of approval had been any indication. Given how loud he'd been, the entire local area probably knew how much of a good time he'd had.

As wonderful as the experience had been, she wanted to give

him something else, something outside of the bedroom. A thought occurred to her and she grinned. *Yes, that would do nicely.*

Clayton was working on an old Massey Ferguson tractor when Rob found him. Locating his son hadn't been hard – he'd just followed the sound of swearing and the clang of various tools as they were flung around the large shed housing Evangeline's Rest's farm machinery.

'Thought you were on holiday,' Rob said while giving the salt-and-pepper stubble on his chin a pensive scratch, noticing the taut lines of his son's shoulders.

'Make yourself useful and pass me the wrench over there,' Clayton snapped, not even bothering to look up from where he was elbow-deep in greasy machinery.

Rob located the tool and handed it over before peering at what his son was doing. 'I don't think you need to pull that apart, mate. Just give her a grease-up and she'll be fine.'

'Dad, this was hard enough before. With you blocking the light it's bloody impossible,' Clayton growled through gritted teeth as he worked on loosening a particularly stubborn bolt, forearms straining. 'This fucking thing has seized. What stupid idiot forgot to grease it last?'

Rob stepped back so the meagre light filtering into the shed reached the tractor's intestines again. 'You, I reckon.'

'No it fucking wasn't.' Clayton grunted with effort. 'Had to be you or Les.'

'Nope.'

'How the fuck would you know?'

'Because you told me two months ago to leave off doing any maintenance on the old girl here. If I remember rightly, you said you wanted to give her an overhaul.'

'And when would I have had time for that?'

'Oh, I dunno. Looks like you've got enough time now,' Rob replied calmly. He saw the black stare Clayton levelled at him, then realised belatedly just how worked up his son really was. He braced himself for the explosion. It wasn't long coming.

Out of all of Rob's kids, Clayton had always been the one with the calmest temperament, but on the rare occasion when he did lose his cool, it was an event worth paying for ringside seats to watch.

Rob wasn't disappointed today. Growling an impressive list of obscenities, many of them anatomically impossible, Clayton sent the wrench flying until it clanged into the far wall before giving the tractor tyre a kick. He then began to pace up and down the length of the shed, his steel-capped boots kicking any errant piece of machinery, tool or furniture that got in the way, while Rob mentally ran through a checklist of all the things that could have set his son off. He decided to take a punt at the cause when Clayton paused for breath.

'So, how's it going with this woman you've been seeing?'

Clayton came to a halt a few feet away and glared, fists clenched at his side, chest heaving and nostrils flaring.

Rob felt relieved he'd hit the nail on the head first go but was at a loss on how to proceed. He wasn't the world expert on women and relationships by a long shot. 'Just a friendly enquiry.'

'Yeah? Well, keep your friendly enquiries to yourself,' Clayton snarled, scanning the ground, picking up a wrench and returning to his work on the tractor.

'Righto,' Rob said to no one in particular, giving his chin another scratch before taking a seat on an empty ten-gallon drum.

Keeping an eye on Clayton's back, he began to whistle softly to himself while Clayton filled the air with a large number of colourful expletives aimed at the tractor.

Ten minutes later Rob had just decided it might be worth getting a beer if he was going to have to wait all afternoon when Clayton spoke.

'Dad?'

'Yeah?'

'You think of Mum still?'

Rob raised his eyebrows at the unexpected question. 'All the time, mate. Every day. Why'd you ask?'

'No reason.' Clayton went back to banging the crap out of something for a few minutes as Rob waited patiently. The next question, when it came, took the wind out of him.

'If you'd known she was going to die, would you still have married her?' Clayton didn't see the colour leach from his father's features.

Rob opened his mouth to make the only acceptable reply, the expected reply, but Clayton cut him off, his face a picture of abject misery when he turned around.

'Don't get me wrong, Dad, I know you loved Mum and still do, but would you have *married* her if you'd known that you would have six years of happiness followed by almost thirty years of grief?'

'Where's this coming from, mate?' Rob asked in a gravelly voice before noisily clearing his throat.

'Just running a few thoughts through my head.'

'Yeah, right.' Rob rubbed his eyes with a shaky hand. 'Well, I have to say I don't know how to answer you right now, Clayton. I, ah —'

'I'm not questioning your love for her, Dad. You've said you don't regret anything a load of times. What I'm asking is, if you knew the day you met Mum in high school that she'd be dead in less than ten years and that everything that has happened *would* happen, would you still have made the decisions you made?' Clayton's gaze was hawk-like.

'*Jesus,* Clayton, what kind of question is that?'

'Can you just try to answer? It'd mean a lot to me right now.'

'All right. All right. Ah. Honestly? You know your mum and I got together when we were sixteen, so if you'd told me all about it then, I don't think I would have believed you. I was a cocky little bastard. I thought I was immortal. I thought Pam was immortal.' Rob's voice hitched on his wife's name.

'But if you *knew* there was a good chance . . .' Clayton prodded.

'If I knew,' Rob repeated shaking his head. 'I don't know, mate. I just don't know. I'd love to say that I would have done everything the same, but I just don't know. Is that a good enough answer?'

Clayton gave him such a searing, searching look that Rob found himself averting his eyes. There were times when his oldest son reminded him a hell of a lot of his father, Clayton's grandfather. Far too serious for his own good.

'Beth had cancer. Breast cancer,' Clayton muttered.

Rob just stared at him. 'That's the woman you're going out with right now? The little thing that I met at the cellar door and the Christmas party?'

'Yeah.' Clayton roughly ran a hand through his hair, liberally coating it with engine grease.

Rob felt a sharp twinge in his gut at the very obvious pain on his son's face. 'She all right now, though? In remission?'

'Don't know. She said she *had* cancer and said she was okay now, so that makes it sound like she is but I didn't specifically ask if she was in remission.' Clayton shook his head. 'She's had both breasts removed, so I think it was bad.'

Rob winced at that. 'You care for her?'

'Yeah. Fuck. I don't know. I mean, yeah I do, and I thought I was fine with it and all, but after thinking about it, considering what you've gone through, what you went through after Mum —' He didn't finish the sentence, just swallowed convulsively and averted his eyes. Rob had to do the same for a few moments.

'What are you asking me, Clayton?' he asked eventually.

'That's the thing . . .' Clayton began. 'I don't know. She's here on holiday and she'll go home in a few weeks, but it doesn't feel like it's just a fling, and if it's not, where does that leave me? Do I ask her to stay, knowing . . .' He paused again and breathed deeply. 'Knowing she could go the same way Mum did, or do I just let her go?'

'You wanna do that?'

Clayton's lost expression said it all. For a moment Rob wanted to walk over and give him a hug like he would have when he was a boy, but even as a kid Clayton would shrug him off, claiming he was all right when he obviously wasn't.

'What happens if she does get sick and I can't handle it? What happens if I'm one of those men who walks out when he finds out his wife has cancer?'

Wife? Rob thought, but kept it to himself. 'You'd never do that, mate.'

'How do you *know*? Could you predict your reaction to Mum getting sick?' Clayton asked.

Rob slumped on the barrel, his mouth drooping. 'I, ah . . . no, I couldn't. It came out of the blue and if I could do it again . . . I don't know how I would have reacted differently.' Unexpectedly he felt his eyes watering and he quickly averted them.

'You all right?'

'Yeah. Yeah, just give your old man a minute, eh?' Rob sniffed loudly and swiped a hand over his face.

They fell silent. Clayton began to pick up tools, dropping them in the toolbox next to the tractor, giving Rob time to regain his composure.

'You know, I was a kid when she died, but I still remember her like it was yesterday. I remember seeing you together. She loved you. You two were made for each other.'

'Yeah, I know that, mate,' Rob replied, but there was something in his voice that conveyed a lot less confidence than there would have been a few weeks before. Clayton let it go and Rob was grateful.

'You know, Clayton,' he said just as Clayton began to wipe his oily hands on an old rag.

'Yeah?'

'If you're looking for advice right now, the best I can give you is take the good stuff as it comes, and if you're serious about this Beth, ask her every question you can think of. *Every* question. Face it head on.'

Clayton nodded, his expression miserable again. 'Thanks, Dad. I just don't know if I want to hear the answers.'

Chapter 15

Beth was feeling spectacularly proud of herself as she stood in her kitchen, hands on hips, surveying the sparkling counter in front of her adorned with a rack of cooling chocolate-chip cookies. She'd never successfully baked before and had been pleasantly surprised by how relaxing the whole process had been. There was something so comforting in the knowledge that as long as one followed the recipe precisely, everything would work out. She'd managed to do that quite nicely with the help of some kitchen scales she'd picked up from George Creek. They were digital and went to four decimal places. She had experienced some difficulty finding an egg that weighed exactly fifty-five grams as the recipe stipulated, but after that it had been smooth sailing.

Her phone rang and she picked it up absentmindedly. 'Hello?'

'What's a nine-letter synonym for "stretched"?'

Beth rolled her eyes. 'We've talked about this, Violet Poole. Stop wasting your money calling me and get out your thesaurus.'

There was the sound of someone industrially sucking on the end of a pencil.

'Elongated,' Beth sighed.

'Thank you,' Violet said primly. 'How are things going with your young man?'

'I'm not sure today. Good, I think. He's gone out.'

'Where?' Violet demanded. 'And why aren't you with him? I thought you were living in each other's pockets.'

'Out. Somewhere. He does run a winery, you know,' Beth said then quickly changed the subject. 'I baked today.'

'You what?'

'Baked.'

'That's what I thought you said. You never bake.'

'I did today.'

'Are you feeling all right?' Violet actually had the temerity to sound concerned.

'Yes, I'm fine,' Beth snapped. 'What's so strange about me baking?'

'Maybe it's hormones,' Violet mused to herself. 'You're making a nest, aren't you? Louis? Louis! Beth's nest-building. You're not pregnant, are you?'

'What? No!'

'Well, you could be, couldn't you?'

'Gran, I'm on the pill. The chances are next to zero. Baking does not indicate pregnancy. It indicates I'm on holiday and trying something new.'

'Hmm,' was all Violet was going to say to that. 'So, it's all working out? Is it serious with this Clayton, then?'

'Gran . . .' Beth began in a warning tone.

'Well, you're baking all of a sudden. You can't blame me for enquiring. I'll be the one packing up all your things and shipping them off to Australia if you decide to stay.'

Suddenly distinctly uncomfortable with where this conversation was going, Beth fell silent.

Violet got the hint. 'Have you got any more gossip for me?'

'Not since yesterday.' Beth sighed. 'I do have things to do, you know.'

'I'm sure you do. Baking being one of them,' Violet retorted. 'Did I tell you what Bernie Johnston said to me at the Seniors' Club yesterday?'

'No. Do tell,' Beth replied, feeling much better now that they were traversing known territory. Violet and Bernie Johnston had been at each other's throats for decades, and recounting verbal dog fights with her arch nemesis was one of Violet's favourite hobbies – next to actually having the fights in the first place.

Twenty minutes later, the now familiar sound of Clayton's Jeep pulling up behind the cottage put an end to their chat.

'Gran, I have to go now,' Beth cut in on Violet's tale of octogenarian social politics.

'Why?'

Beth rolled her eyes. 'Because Clayton has just arrived and you're bankrupting Louis with this call.'

'Oh, that's all right, then. Talk to you tomorrow.'

'Next week.'

'I love you, you know.'

'I love you too, but that doesn't mean you're getting away with calling every day. Next week. I'll have something decent to tell you by then.'

Violet's sigh could have sunk a battleship. 'All right, then. Louis is waiting to drive us to Morrisons for our cup of tea and a shop anyway.'

'Bye.'

Beth ended the call with no small amount of affectionate exasperation and relief. Elderly she may be, but Violet had the interrogative ability of a Scotland Yard investigator when she thought something was up.

At the sound of the door opening Beth turned around. 'Hello. Just in time.' She grinned widely in anticipation of Clayton's reaction to her newfound baking expertise. Her grin faded when she caught sight of his serious expression.

He must have just had a shower because his hair was wetly curled around his face. Water was still dripping off the ends onto an impeccably ironed navy polo shirt. His mouth was pinched at the corners and his shoulders appeared extremely tense. Even more worrying, he wasn't quite meeting her gaze.

'What's wrong?' Beth asked.

'Beth, we need to have a talk.' His voice was raspy, like he was getting a cold. He still hadn't moved from the doorway.

'All right.' Beth willed her own voice calm as pinpricks of unease danced across the back of her neck. 'What about?'

'You and me,' Clayton said abruptly, meeting her eyes for a few fleeting seconds before looking back over her shoulder.

'Oh? Aren't I supposed to be the one that brings up that line of conversation?' She tried to force some levity into her tone, but it fell flat. She didn't know what was going on, but whatever it was didn't feel right.

'Can we sit down?' Clayton stalked over to the only armchair in the living room, leaving Beth to perch on the edge of the sunny yellow sofa. She sat, watching him warily.

Seconds ticked by, marked only by the loud song of a kookaburra perched on the porch railing outside and the metallic plinking of the oven racks cooling.

'What would you like to talk about?' she asked when the tension became unbearable.

Clayton opened and closed his mouth a few times then groaned, leaning forward, grasping his head in his hands. 'Beth, I don't know how to ask this.'

'What?'

Nothing was forthcoming. Instead he just stared at the floor like he hoped it would swallow him up.

'Tell me,' Beth urged. She'd always been a member of the rip-the-bandaid-off-quick school of thought and right now it looked like bandaid time.

'Are you going to die? No. *Fuck!* That's not what I meant to say.' Clayton stood up with enough force to push the armchair back. It scraped across the floorboards heavily with a grating, obscene noise that echoed around the room.

Beth sat in stunned silence as the reality of someone she cared for voicing her innermost fear out loud washed over her.

'Sorry, Beth, that came out wrong.'

'I guessed as much,' she said in a strangled voice.

'What I wanted to ask . . . What I didn't ask before is if you still have . . . do you still have cancer?' Clayton blurted. He began to pace the room and for the first time since Beth had met him, he seemed vulnerable.

She inhaled a shaky breath. *You should have expected this*, she told herself. 'No. Like I said when I first told you, I *had* cancer. I'm in remission now. I have been for nearly three years,' she answered calmly and watched as Clayton's entire body slumped in a way that would have been comical under any other circumstance. He walked back over to the armchair and sat down heavily.

'Does that answer your question?'

'Yeah,' he said, but there was still something about his expression that told Beth it hadn't completely.

'All right. That's good, then. What brought this on?' Beth felt like she was walking blindly through a minefield.

He shrugged. It was a completely unconvincing gesture.

'Clayton?'

'Give me a minute.'

'All right,' Beth pushed to her feet and walked into the kitchen.

'What are you doing?'

'Making tea. I make tea when I'm stressed and right now I'm a little stressed.'

'Fair enough.'

Beth could feel his gaze burning into her back as she went through the usually calming ritual of measuring leaves and pouring water.

'What are those?' he asked when she placed a few cookies on a saucer.

'Chocolate-chip cookies. They were meant to be a surprise for you because you said you like them.'

She brought her cup and the cookies back to her chair and placed them on the coffee table in front of her. 'Clayton?'

'Yeah?'

'Are you trying to end it? Us?' Beth felt herself go calm the minute the words left her mouth. She had always been able to do this, switch off from anything emotionally hurtful when needed. She'd had to learn how to do it as a child and was spectacularly adept. It was only afterwards, when she had to process, that things turned bleak.

'*What?*'

'I thought it was an obvious question. Are you ending things? Because if you are, I'd rather you just got it over and done with.' She paused for a moment as the hurt feelings she'd put a lid on tried to rise to the surface. 'I won't judge you but I'd appreciate it if you're straight with me. Answer me, Clayton. Are you ending it between us?'

'I don't like where this is going,' Clayton protested in a tight voice, watching her every movement.

'That's unfortunate, because I believe you were the one that started us down this path.' Beth raised her cup of tea to her mouth to hide her trembling bottom lip and grabbed a cookie off the plate, gripping it in front of her like some sort of shield.

Clayton stared at her for a painful few moments before he swiped both hands over his face and heaved a ragged sigh. 'Beth, I'm sorry, I've handled this wrong.'

She looked down at her lap, exhaling slowly. 'No, no you haven't. You just took me by surprise. Although I have to say it wasn't an easy question to hear.'

'Yeah. I get that. I meant to ask you what the chances were that you could still be sick, because you didn't say before and I was worried.'

'I understand.'

'So, now that you've answered me, can we forget we had this conversation? Not the bit where you told me you're in remission, but me putting my foot in my mouth. Can we start again?' He rested his forearms on his knees as he spoke, leaning towards her. Everything about his expression, his body language, was telling her he was earnest.

Setting her cup carefully down on the coffee table, Beth deliberated over Clayton's request. Her gut feeling was to find out what was really going on, because it felt a lot bigger than just one question and an answer, but something stopped her. If she took this any further, when they were both upset, there was a risk things could go horribly wrong. Did she want it to end like this? The answer was a resounding, screaming no. Did she want this awful tension between them for the rest of her stay? Again, the answer was no. Did she want something more than just a holiday fling? That was trickier. Either way, any chance of having anything more could be destroyed if she let this conversation go on . . .

'I can hear you thinking from here,' Clayton said, watching her warily.

'Yes,' she said firmly, her voice loud in the still room.

'Yes, what?'

'Yes, you can start again, but you'll have to do it properly.'

'Yeah?'

'Yes. So, I'll meet you at the door in two minutes.'

'What?'

'The door. You're going back outside and we're starting again.'
She gestured to the doorway.

'When I asked if we could start again I didn't mean —'

'Well, I do, and by the way, you had better notice my cookies.'
Her voice wavered a little but she ignored it.

The absurdity of the situation must have got through to Clayton
because he smiled, despite the worry in his eyes. 'All right.' He
pushed out of the armchair and strode to the door, letting it close
behind him with a bang.

For some daft reason, Beth rushed to the kitchen bench, to the
exact spot she'd been standing when she ended the call with Violet.
She felt nervous tension zing through her body as she heard the door
open.

This time, Clayton came up behind her before she could turn
around and wrapped his strong arms around her waist.

'I missed you today.' He pressed a soft kiss to her neck.

She twisted around and was immediately wrapped in a tight hug.

'I missed you too,' she replied, her words muffled against his
shirt as she soaked up the warmth radiating from his body and
inhaled his wonderfully comforting scent.

'What are those things on the bench?' He rested his chin on the
top of her head.

'Chocolate-chip cookies. Would you like one?'

'Sounds great. How about later, though?' Clayton began to
walk her backwards towards the bedroom.

'Clayton,' Beth protested in a warning tone. As nice as the prospect was, she didn't want to be brushed off with sex.

Clayton gave her a squeeze. 'I'm not good with words, Beth. Just
give me this, all right?'

She began to object but then stopped. Wrapped up in an unbelievably gentle embrace, with Clayton's heartbeat pounding against her ear telling her he wasn't exactly as calm as he sounded, she realised she didn't want to say no.

'All right. As long as I get to pick the page we try out this time,' she said with a feigned long-suffering sigh.

Clayton's relieved laughter shook them both. 'No worries, but if I sprain something you're gonna have to massage it better.'

Rob Hardy had gone through his entire life content in the knowledge that he was a decent bloke who was generally held in high regard by the people in his hometown. He worked hard at it and he prided himself on the way he treated people.

When he and Pam had got together so young, there had been talk, especially after Clayton came along earlier than they had all expected. Then, ever since Pam died, he had been additionally careful in maintaining his standing in the community because he knew that his children were particularly vulnerable in not having their mother. He'd been loath to have his kids stand out and risk being picked on, especially when he'd seen how the town had treated Stephen's fiancée, Jo, who'd been mercilessly teased as a young girl for not fitting in.

Today, however, for the first time in his life, he was dreading the drive through George Creek's neat flower-lined streets. Instead of experiencing the usual pride he felt at seeing the thriving small businesses and the familiar faces he'd known since childhood, he felt his entire foundation shaking beneath his feet. He felt like everyone he passed knew where he was going and what he was about to do, and worse, *why* he had to do it. He didn't like that one little bit.

By the time he pulled up in front of his destination, a small house on a quiet street on the edge of town, the back of his shirt was saturated with sweat and his knuckles were white on the steering wheel. He would give anything at this moment to be elsewhere, but the right thing was the right thing and damned if he was going to be a coward.

He pushed himself out of the car and stalked down a neat garden path leading to a tidy Australian Federation-style home painted cream with green trim. As he walked, he surreptitiously wiped sweaty palms on the legs of his good jeans and glanced down at his shoes to make sure they had a shine.

Gwen answered her door at the second ring.

'Robert?' She was clearly surprised to see him and obviously not expecting company. In fact, she looked like she'd just got out of bed.

She was dressed in a calf-length navy satin robe and was holding it closed at her neck despite the belt around her waist. Her short spiky hair was flattened to one side and she wasn't wearing any of her usual make-up. Not that she needed it. Gwen had always had a baby face. She'd looked sixteen well into her twenties and now, at fifty-two, she looked forty at the most. Only the white in her hair gave her age away.

'Robert, is everything all right? Is this about work? Because my last day was Friday.' She searched his expression.

'Yeah. Well, no. Look, Gwen, can I come in?' he asked gruffly.

'Now isn't really a good time.' Gwen turned her head quickly, darting a glance at the dark interior of the hallway behind her.

It occurred to Rob then that she might not be alone. The thought left him feeling unaccountably pissed off. He'd never thought to ask around to find out if Gwen was seeing anyone. She was Gwen. She couldn't be seeing anyone. When she'd been friends with Pam she'd only ever gone out with that idiot she'd said had broken their engagement. How had he not known about that? Seems there was a lot Pam hadn't told him.

His scowl grew even more pronounced.

'Robert, if you're here to take another piece out of me I'm sorry to say I'm not feeling too obliging right now.'

'This will only take a minute,' Rob said, then realised how impatient he sounded. 'Please,' he added and attempted a wooden smile.

Gwen's expression said he might just as well have announced a fatal illness. 'Now I know something is wrong.' She stood aside. 'Come in, then.'

'Thanks.' Rob followed her into a narrow hallway and then through to a dimly lit living room. He savoured the air conditioning as he took a seat on a sagging white sofa while Gwen walked over to the window and briskly opened the curtains.

'Do you want tea or coffee?'

'Have you got anything cool? A beer maybe?' Rob asked despite the early hour of the day.

'I don't have alcohol in the house, but I'll get you a Coke,' Gwen replied and walked through an archway that Rob presumed led to her kitchen.

Rob used the opportunity to study his surrounds. He was surprised to find the room comfortable and colourful, if not a little shabby around the edges. It looked like Gwen hadn't had a lot of money to spare of late. The white linen sofa cover was frayed on the arms. The faded rag rug on the scratched and battered hardwood floor was the worse for wear, although the presence of a large, scruffy tabby cat sleeping in the middle of it explained the pulls and tears. He gave the cat a wary look and continued his scan of the room. On the far side there was a low table holding a small, old-fashioned boxy TV and next to that sat a picture of Gwen and Pam when they were kids.

He felt a sharp pang of loss when he saw Pam's mischievous grin. His kids had inherited it – his second son, Michael, in particular. Rob shifted his gaze sideways and was surprised to see a photo of himself with Pam and Gwen at his wedding.

God, they'd been so *young*. Just turned eighteen. Pam had been pregnant with Clayton already, not that they'd known it at the time. He was looking at Pam like she was his world and she was looking right back with the same expression. She had been his world. She'd been everything to him.

'I thought you would have cut me out.' He gestured to the photo as Gwen returned to the room holding a tray with a small red teapot, a cup and saucer and a glass of Coke sitting on it.

'Why? I never had any issue with you, Robert. What did you want to talk to me about?' She set the tray down on a scratched spindle-legged coffee table, walked over to hand him his Coke, then took the seat across from his.

Bloody hell, Rob thought, she still even sat the same, back relaxed against the chair, but ladylike with her knees together. She was almost regal, a completely classy lady despite the messy hair and slinky robe. She'd always been a bit of a contradiction. He glanced down at her bare feet to see if she was still wearing that toe ring. She wasn't and he felt strangely disappointed. He caught her eye and cleared his throat noisily.

'Ah, Gwen? I've been thinking about what you said the other night.'

'Yes?' Her expression remained impassive.

'Yeah, and I've got a number of things to say.' Rob ran his sweating palms over his jeans again.

'Go on.' Gwen leaned over to pour herself a cup of tea. Her robe momentarily gaped at the neckline.

'Well . . . ah.'

He cleared his throat again. 'Gwen. I ah . . . I owe you an apology.' He opened his mouth to keep talking but was stymied when no words came out. He tried again and felt a lump form in his throat. *Bloody hell*.

'Robert?'

'I . . . give me a minute,' he croaked, heaving a lungful of air before continuing in a gravelly voice, averting his eyes to the mangy cat on the rug. 'I've treated you unfairly since Pam died and for that I'm sorry.' He met her steady gaze. She seemed neither happy nor sad to hear his words. She just sat there watching him until Rob swore he could hear his own pounding heartbeat echo around the room.

'Do you accept my apology?' he asked when the tension got too great.

Gwen lifted her teacup to her lips in one genteel motion and took a sip before setting it back down on the tray in front of her. It was another minute before she finally spoke in a soft voice. 'It must have been hard for you to come here today.'

Rob nodded curtly.

'I want to believe you're not just saying all this so I'll come back to work for you.'

'I'm not lying to you, Gwen, it'd be nice if you came back to work for us, but that's not why I'm here.'

'All right.' Gwen nodded.

'All right you forgive me, or all right you'll come back to work?'

'To the former. I'll think about the latter,' Gwen said curtly. 'As you can see, I'm not really dressed for visitors, so if you wouldn't mind . . .' She looked at Rob then the doorway, clearly giving him the hint to go, but there was something about the way she reached up and gripped her robe closed again that told Rob she wasn't as cool as she was playing it.

'Oh. Yeah, sure. All right, then.' Relieved that he'd got one of the hardest things he'd had to do in recent memory out of the way so easily, Rob stood up and nodded goodbye.

He'd just made it to the door when a thought that had been keeping him awake every night since Christmas Eve pushed itself resolutely to the surface.

'Gwen?' he called, backtracking to the living room to find the lady in question resting her elbows on her knees, her hands covering her face. She sat up abruptly, her robe falling open and revealing a lot of soft white skin and some kind of thin pale-green nightie, almost the exact colour of her eyes.

'Yes?'

'This might sound like a stupid question, but you knew Pam as well as I did. Probably better in some ways.'

Gwen regarded him warily. 'Yes?'

Rob swallowed hard and opened his mouth, but no words came out. He was disconcerted to feel his hands beginning to shake, so he jammed them in the back pockets of his jeans.

'Robert?'

'I've been thinking about what you said on Christmas Eve and . . . and, well, there's something that's been preying on my mind. You might be able to help me.'

'What is it?'

'If Pam didn't tell me how bad she was or refuse treatment because she was angry with you and me, thinking we were an item . . .' He averted his eyes from Gwen's face as understanding dawned.

'Yes, Robert?'

'What, ah . . .' He swallowed hard. 'What did I do wrong that she didn't tell me?' He felt his damn eyes watering, overflowing as his breath hitched and his chest constricted in a vise as old hurt, unacknowledged for twenty-nine years, tore through the scar tissue he'd built to keep it hidden, spewing out to fill every damn part of his body until he shook with the effort to keep it all contained. He tried to continue, forcing the words out. 'I just want to understand . . .' No more words would come. His chest heaved.

Before he knew it Gwen was in front of him, wrapping soft arms around his body and drawing him against her in a warm embrace that absorbed the first violent sob that racked through him and then the next. Embarrassed, ashamed, he tried to pull away but her hand tangled tightly in his hair, firmly bringing his head down to rest in the crook of her shoulder, enveloping him in the smell of warm female and roses.

'You're safe,' she said gently.

Hearing the words, Rob felt something shatter in his chest as pain washed through his body in crashing waves, coming out in loud raspy wheezing noises as he buried his face against her neck, his tears and God-knew-what-else wetting her skin.

She didn't seem to mind; she just kept stroking his back with one hand and holding his head with the other, making soothing, nonsense-filled murmurs.

Eventually, after the worst of it was over, he realised what he was doing, with whom and where, and tried to pull away but Gwen held firm.

'I have to go,' he mumbled huskily, only now becoming aware that he was pressed up against a female body for the first time in years, decades.

'I'm sure you do,' Gwen replied calmly. 'But not yet.'

'What?' Rob pulled far enough away to squint down at her through eyes still blurry with tears. She was studying him intently. Her expression was serious but there was something else there, something sad, tender and – he was a little rusty but he recognised it. Desire. That's what he saw in Gwen's face. It threw him for a loop. 'Gwen —'

'You're going to come with me.' She moved her hand down and clasped one of his. He hadn't realised it until that moment but he'd been gripping the curve of her hips through the satin of her robe. She felt warm, soft and entirely feminine.

The observation unsettled him. 'What? Where?'

'My bedroom.'

'Why?'

'When's the last time you were held by a woman, Robert?' Gwen met his gaze dead on.

Rob baulked at that. 'Ah. That's not . . . I'm not . . . I've gotta go now.' He tried to pull away again but she held fast to his hand, a gentle smile crossing her features.

'No, you don't.'

'No?'

'No.'

And then he found himself following her through the kitchen, down a small hall and into her bedroom.

It was a cozy room. A lot like Gwen, it was feminine and colourful but without frills. Against one wall sat an old brass bed covered with a mix-and-match patchwork bedspread. The only other furniture in the room was a dark-wood wardrobe, a matching chest of drawers and a small bedside table with a large cut-crystal vase full of blousy pink roses.

'Gwen . . .' Rob began again, stopping still at the doorway, panicking.

'Quiet, Robert.'

She pulled him forward then pushed him gently down onto the edge of her bed. He swallowed nervously, keeping his gaze on the floor, feeling like a sixteen-year-old virgin again as Gwen stood in front of him and dropped her robe.

'Why are you doing this? I've been a right bastard to you,' he asked in a dazed voice as she began to unbutton his shirt. It was embarrassing how quickly his body reacted to such a simple touch.

'Some things are better left a mystery,' she said, leaning down to place a tender kiss on his forehead.

'Right,' Rob said and then shook his head. 'But . . .'

His words were forestalled when she grasped the back of his head and planted a long, lingering kiss on his mouth. She tasted like tea and something sweeter, female, almost unrecognisable after thirty years of self-imposed celibacy.

'Be quiet and enjoy, Robert. You comforted me when I needed it years ago. Let me return the favour.'

Rob's heart jumped and his breath hitched when he felt her fingers run down the bare skin on his stomach.

'Gwen. You should know that I, ah . . . I'm not sure how to go about this,' he said gruffly, his eyes meeting hers, meeting understanding.

'You haven't been with anyone since Pam, have you?' Gwen asked, her tone compassionate.

'No.' Rob muffled a groan as her wandering hand moved lower to stroke fleetingly just above the waistband of his jeans. 'And this better not be some pity thing.'

'No one would ever pity you, Robert. And as for the other thing, well, I hear it's a bit like riding a bicycle.' An edge of mischief entered her tone. 'I doubt you've forgotten.' She reached down, grasped his wrists and raised his hands, firmly placing them on her hips.

Rob groaned out loud. 'I didn't come here for this, but I don't think I want to turn you down.' He flexed his fingers involuntarily, feeling a guilty rush of arousal and pleasure at the softness they encountered.

'I know you didn't.'

'I might be a bit of a disappointment,' Rob said, looking up only to find her eyes twinkling with humour.

'Shh.' She pushed him backwards, and other than the odd appreciative groan, he didn't say much else for quite some time.

Chapter 16

Clayton stretched the tired muscles of his back and surveyed the view from his front porch with satisfaction. It had been a good day to move house and he was pleasantly mellow after they'd all drunk a bottle of champagne to christen his new home. Better yet, he finally had the chance to try out his new barbecue, which was mighty enough to make his fellow men green with envy. He puffed out his chest, looked around him and felt a moment of sheer pride. He'd earned this place. The wait had been worth it and he couldn't imagine celebrating with better people.

'You asked Beth to stick around yet? She's leaving in three days now, right?'

With the exception of his best mate.

Clayton deflated like a balloon, grabbing the tongs out of Jeff's hand to rescue what he could of the quality beef sausages he'd taken so much care in picking out at the butcher's that morning. 'The cows are already dead, mate. You don't have to kill them again.'

Jeff shrugged. 'You want to take over? Be my guest. It's your barbie. So, have you?'

'Has he what?' Stephen asked, ending his call to a wine distributor in London and taking a pull on his beer.

'Asked Beth to stay,' Jeff supplied.

'You think they're that serious?' Stephen asked Jeff, ignoring Clayton's incredulous expression.

'So much for this being *my* housewarming party. I am standing here, you know.' Clayton gave his baby brother a glare that should have felled him at the knees. Stephen ignored it. He'd been on the receiving end of that look for thirty years now and it had lost its effect long ago.

'Yeah, I can see that,' Stephen said, then turned to Jeff again. 'So, is he?'

Jeff looked Clayton up and down. 'He looks pretty serious to me right now.'

'He looks constipated to me,' Stephen returned. 'So, fill me in. I haven't really had a chance to talk to her yet. What's she like?' He nodded towards the paddock in front of the house where Beth, Jo and Laura were sitting on the bank of a distant gully dam, talking while they caught marron for their dinner.

Jeff squinted against the sun's glare and considered the women with a thoughtful frown, then glanced sideways at Clayton. He pulled another beer out of the small fridge they'd installed on the porch earlier in the day. 'Too good for him if he doesn't ask her to stay.'

'What the *fuck*?' Clayton exclaimed to the world at large, throwing his hands in the air.

Both Jeff and Stephen ignored him. 'What's she do?' Stephen asked, scratching the sandy blond stubble on his jaw.

'She's a dog trainer,' Jeff supplied, devilry lighting up his eyes. Clayton had to resist the urge to thump him.

'Oh yeah? Well, there's no shortage of dogs round here. Those puppies Waffles had are gonna need some training soon. They've already torn through a pair of my boots. How long they been seeing each other?'

Jeff furrowed his brow. 'About a month or more now. That right, Clayton?'

'Don't ask me, mate. You've got all the answers,' Clayton said tightly, his blood coming to a slow simmer.

'Yeah. About a month or so,' Jeff said to Stephen while opening his beer with the bottle opener on his key ring.

'Yeah? Rachael and Jo like her,' Stephen replied. 'I noticed them spending a lot of time together at the Christmas party.'

'That's not really a recommendation, mate, on either count,' Jeff said sarcastically, and it was Stephen's turn to glare.

'Don't get yourself in a lather. Laura likes her too.' Jeff back-pedalled fast. 'She's talking of flying over to visit Beth in England later this year. I'm thinking of going along too.'

'Over my dead body,' Clayton stated in a deathly calm voice while plating the done sausages and adding a few more to the grill.

'Mind you, if he asked her to stay . . .' Jeff let the sentence trail off.

'If you two are gonna keep this up, I'm going to bloody well kick you out. You can get your nose out of my business or leave,' Clayton snapped, startling them both. 'My house, my rules, so how about you two go back to telling me how great this place is instead of telling me how to run my bloody life. All right?'

'All right, all right,' Jeff said, backing away dramatically. 'Let's change the topic since you're so bloody touchy. You seen the latest cricket score?' he asked Stephen.

'Nah, mate. Should be on now, though.'

Clayton did his best to unclench his white-knuckled fingers from around the barbecue tongs as Stephen and Jeff wandered inside to check out the score on his new TV.

Normally Clayton would have chewed Jeff's head off for being so nosy, but his jaw had been clenched so tight that he hadn't been able to unhinge it to get the words out in time. Searching for a distraction, anything that would prevent a homicide in the next few minutes, he glanced towards the gully dam and saw the three women returning with what looked to be a full bucket of shellfish. His eyes immediately sought out Beth. Next to the two much taller, more curvaceous women, she appeared tiny and fragile, though he knew she was anything but. The woman was tougher than nails. A lot tougher, he had a feeling, than he was.

It was all very easy for Jeff to imply he was an idiot for not asking Beth to stay, but Jeff wasn't in his position. Over the past month Clayton had been the happiest he'd ever been while simultaneously feeling more conflicted than he'd ever thought possible. Try as he might, he kept coming back to the thought that Beth could suddenly, without warning, get sick and die – just like his mum.

He'd tried to hold it all together enough to sort out his feelings, but he couldn't. He wasn't sleeping. He'd even lost his appetite. For the past week he'd lain awake most nights listening to her dainty little snores, feeling a cold, clammy panic that one night they would stop for good and there wouldn't be a thing he could do about it.

He palm-washed his face, cutting the thought short. Christ, he was a mess. He knew his thoughts were irrational and unreasonable, but that was half the problem. He'd always been the most level-headed bloke he knew, yet here he was acting and thinking like a crazy man. He shook his head and growled under his breath. Jeff had no bloody idea. No idea at all.

Beth listened to her new friends chatter as she tried her best to enjoy herself. She, Laura and Jo were seated out on the porch of Clayton's new house watching the sunset while the men watched cricket inside. Or at least Beth was watching the sunset. Laura was regaling

Jo with a story of the couple who'd rented her second holiday cottage the weekend before.

'So, they demanded a full refund because the birdsong in the morning woke them up,' Laura huffed in disgust.

'Serious?' Jo exclaimed, sipping on the glass of red she held in a long-fingered hand.

'Yeah! And *then* they threatened to write negative reviews on TripAdvisor if I didn't give it to them. I tried to explain that I couldn't exactly put a muzzle on every kookaburra and magpie in the area, but it didn't get me anywhere. Of all the things I expected to have problems with, I didn't expect this. Next I'll have someone complaining that there are too many trees blocking their view or that it's too quiet.'

'So, what did you do? Tell them to get stuffed?' Jo asked.

'No. I gave them the refund and I've regretted it ever since. It was pure extortion but I can't afford negative publicity this soon, you know? Other than Beth, they've been my only guests so far.' Laura bit her lip. 'I was going to talk to Stephen and ask if he could help me put a mention of the dawn chorus on the website so that I don't have this happen again.'

'Right,' Jo nodded bemusedly.

Beth let their conversation drift over her as she took in the astonishing vista before her. In the pink-and-purple light of yet another spectacular sunset, the landscape was eerily unworldly. Breathtaking. The sky reflecting off the water of the gully dam they'd pillaged earlier was prettier than anything she'd ever seen.

A sea breeze, smelling of warm earth, salt and tangy gum trees, bathed her skin and she closed her eyes briefly at the sensation. Far from the grassy, sheepy fug of Yorkshire, this place smelled different, dry and ancient.

Beth remembered a story Clayton had shared late one night a week before. He'd told her there was an ancient haunted Aboriginal burial ground on the property demarcated by a ring of stones, and had then laughed heartily when she couldn't sleep. Feeling entirely indignant, Beth had insisted that he take the side of the bed closest to the door to protect her.

Opening her eyes with a start at the sound of booming male laughter coming from inside the house, Beth smiled at the memory. She was going to miss this. She was going to miss everything about being here. Right now it was all she could do not to cry when she thought about it.

'When are you going home, Beth?' Jo's question snapped her out of her reverie, forcing Beth to turn and refocus her eyes.

In the half-light Jo Blaine was striking. Her face was all angular cheekbones, a wide mouth and dark brown eyes, capped off by a bright red pixie cut. Earlier, when Jo had mentioned she'd recently retired from a ten-year career as an engineer working in West Africa, Beth had been dumbfounded. That was until she saw how at ease Jo was around the men.

'She's off in fairyland, Jo,' Laura said in an amused tone.

'Actually, I was admiring Jo's looks,' Beth blurted and then blushed.

Jo did a bit of blushing herself. 'Thanks.'

'My pleasure. I'm leaving in three days,' Beth answered. Just saying the words brought another wave of sadness.

'Is Clayton driving you to the airport?' Laura asked. 'Is he going to visit you soon or are you coming back here to see him?'

'No. I'm going to drive myself back,' Beth replied, avoiding the rest of Laura's questions. She averted her gaze from Laura's curious expression only to meet Jo's sympathetic one.

'Long distance can be hard but it's doable,' Jo said softly. 'Stephen and I managed it for a while.'

'Really?' Beth asked as a spark of hope flickered to life in her chest.

'Yeah. You guys will have it easier than we did, too. Half the time we were out of contact because the rig phone was down and my Internet was limited. You and Clayton can video call over the net for next to nothing every day if you want.'

Beth nodded noncommittally. So far Clayton hadn't said anything about her leaving. He hadn't said a whole lot about anything, really.

Over the past two weeks he'd become entirely unreadable and extremely intense. While they were together during the day – hiking, swimming and on one very memorable day picking grapes before having another luxurious champagne brunch among the vines – Clayton had been a perfect gentleman, but there was always an edge to him Beth couldn't explain. At night, sex had turned into something frantic that was both emotionally and physically exhausting. Every time was reminiscent of the first time after Beth had told him about her cancer at this very house more than a month before. And he still hadn't asked to see her fully naked. It left her feeling torn between bringing the topic up again and not wanting to ruin their remaining time together if this was all they had.

She desperately wanted to talk to him about the questions he'd asked her weeks before, about her cancer, about whether or not she'd die from it one day, but she couldn't build up the nerve. Greg's rejection had left a lasting impression. She couldn't bear it if Clayton reacted the same way after she laid it all out for him. Especially when her feelings for him far overshadowed her feelings for her ex-husband. She just had no way of knowing if he felt the same way about her.

'Beth?' Laura nudged her with her elbow.

'Yes?'

'You on the planet? I've been talking to you for the past five minutes and you haven't moved.'

'Sorry, Laura.' Beth gave her a tight smile. 'I was just thinking how much I'm going to miss being here.' She had to forcibly bite the inside of her lip to stop herself crying when Laura reached over, wrapped an arm around her shoulders and gave her a tight hug.

'It'll work out, sweetie,' Laura said with such self-assurance that Beth almost believed her. She *wanted* to believe her.

'I don't know —'

'Just remember, if you're expecting him to put his cards on the table, you have to too.'

Beth nodded. 'I know. It's harder than it sounds, though.'

'I'll drink to that,' Jo said from her other side. They clinked their glasses together and Beth allowed herself to be distracted with talk of Clayton's new house, Jo and Stephen's brewery, and Rousse and Hardy family politics.

Later that night Beth woke with a start to find Clayton's face only inches from hers on her pillow. His eyes were open, black in the dark, his expression tortured.

Startled, she took the only sensible option available. She screamed, sitting bolt upright and clutching her chest to stop her heartbeat from running away.

'What are you doing? You scared me!' she accused.

Clayton rolled onto his back and threw an arm over his eyes. 'Sorry,' he mumbled. 'Go back to sleep.'

'Pardon? No. I want to know why you were staring at me.' She tucked her arms around her knees and pulled them to her chest. 'I just closely avoided a heart attack.'

'It's nothing, Beth. I'm tired. Go to sleep.'

Beth ignored him. 'No, it's not nothing, or you wouldn't be acting like you are. What's going on? Are you having nightmares?'

Clayton grunted.

'So, what is it?' Beth demanded. 'I'm not going to be able to get back to sleep if you don't tell me.'

Clayton moved his arm off his eyes and slanted a look at her bare legs. 'Wanna bet?' he asked silkily, challenge in his tone.

'I don't bet.'

'Good, because you'd lose.' He rolled onto his side and began to run his fingers up her calf.

'Clayton,' she said in a warning voice. His touch was already triggering goosebumps on her skin.

'Yeah?' His hand moved higher and he gently but firmly unclasped her hands from her knees so that he could run his fingers along the inside of her thigh.

'I'd appreciate it if you talked to me. I'm worried about you,' Beth said, even as she allowed her leg to fall sideways.

'Nothing to worry about.'

'I don't believe you.' She kept her tone stern but leaned backwards against the headboard of his new bed and closed her eyes all the same as his fingers splayed open, teasing over sensitive skin.

'Hmm?'

'Yes.' Beth parted her legs wider and her breath hitched when his touch got a lot more intimate, fingers gently feathering over her.

'How about we talk later?' Clayton hooked one large hand behind her neck and drew her down for a slow and incredibly possessive kiss just as he gently pushed a finger inside her. Her back arched and she moaned against him.

'Yes?' he purred.

'No,' she groaned, moving against him, asking for more. It was so easy to just lie back and take what he was offering. Her body was screaming for it, sensation pooling warmly between her thighs, flicking off rational thought in her brain.

'*Yes*.' Clayton trailed damp kisses across her neck and nibbled at her ear.

'Clayton.' Beth gasped as he added a second finger just as his thumb found her clitoris.

'Yeah?'

'We . . . we need to talk.'

'Later.'

The determination in his tone triggered a warning in the few working parts of Beth's mind. Fighting the drugging lethargy seeping through her veins, she pulled back and focused on his expression.

The eyes watching her weren't heavy-lidded with arousal. Instead they were narrowed and calculating, almost angry.

All of a sudden his fingers inside her felt like an intrusion and the hand at the back of her neck felt like a restraint.

She jerked away as if scalded. 'Move your hand.'

'What?'

'Move. Your. Hand.' Beth snatched his hand from between her thighs and scooted to the far side of the bed.

'Beth?'

'You just tried to manipulate me,' she accused, pulling on her discarded underwear.

'Excuse me?'

'You don't have a hearing impairment. You heard me.' She stalked around to his side of the bed with hands on hips.

'C'mon, Beth, you're overreacting.' Clayton rolled onto his back and covered his eyes with his arm again.

'No, I'm bloody well not. You were trying to distract me. God knows why, because you won't tell me what's wrong.' Beth's frustration was so tangible she could have worn it as a coat.

'It's late. I'm tired. You're tired. I just spent the day moving house. Do we have to do this now?' Clayton asked in a long-suffering tone.

Beth paused as angry, hurt tears prickled her eyes. 'No, we don't. You're right. We don't *have* to do this now. I *want* to do this now. After what you just tried to do, I think I deserve a little honesty.' She crossed her arms tightly in front of her chest, and tucked her shaking hands into her armpits.

Clayton shifted his arm and glared at her. His position on his back should have invested her with a sense of superiority, but his larger size left her feeling at a disadvantage.

'It's nothing, Beth.'

'Nothing?'

'Nothing.'

'Oh, that's all right, then. I guess I'm imagining things. Overreacting? Maybe I'm even being hysterical?'

'One or two of the above.'

Beth took a step back, reeling under the suppressed anger in his voice, her throat tight. 'Clayton?'

'Yeah?'

'I'm leaving in three days.'

It took him a few tense seconds to answer her. 'Yeah. I know.'

'Do you love me?' she asked, her traitorous memory reminding her she had been in a similar situation once before and that it hadn't worked out well. *Please let this be different*, she thought. *Please let Clayton be different than Greg. Please let him want to stand by me, to accept me for what I am, complications and all.*

'*What?*' Clayton's stunned exclamation would have been hilarious if Beth hadn't been so serious and his answer didn't mean so much to her.

'I asked if you love me. I was quite clear.' Beth tried desperately, unsuccessfully, to stop her voice from shaking. 'I'd like to know.'

'Come on, Beth. You're being ridiculous,' Clayton growled, rolling off the other side of the bed in one swift motion. He snatched his jeans off the floor and yanked them on.

'Oh? Well, ridiculous I may be, but I know I love you.' Beth spoke around the lump in her throat. 'If you don't love me, I don't see the point in continuing this discussion. Or . . . or us, really. Can you? We never finished that conversation we started weeks ago, when you asked me if I was going to die. We've not talked about the fact I've had cancer.' She gripped the hem of her T-shirt, pulling it over her head, standing there topless, damned if she would feel embarrassed. 'Is that what this is about? This? These scars?' She pointed to her chest. 'You've never wanted to see them. You've never mentioned them. Is this the problem?'

Clayton's face visibly paled even as his expression hardened. 'Jesus. *No*, Beth. This is about me wanting sleep. If you'd just put your top back on and wait until morning —'

Beth cut him off, the words coming out in a rush now that she was finally saying them. 'Why? So you can pretend this never happened? Because it did. I had cancer, Clayton.'

He physically flinched at the word and she felt it down to her toes, swallowing past the tears building up.

'We need to talk about it if we're going to try to make things last beyond my return home. It will always be there. It's understandable you have worries. I'm scared every day. The chances of it returning are small but that doesn't mean it's not a fear I live with and will live with every day of my life. I know it's a lot for you to handle, but if we stay together it will be something you'll have to deal with too. Do you want that? Can you do that? I know you couldn't leave Evangeline's Rest, but I've been thinking that it would be possible for me to relocate to Australia if —'

'Jesus Christ! It's two in the morning!' Clayton bellowed over the top of her, his expression furious but she could see the panic there, too.

Beth just stared at him, her eyes huge in her angular little face, lips pressed firmly together. 'Yes,' she said huskily. 'It is, but the answer should be the same whether it's two in the morning or two in the afternoon.'

The moonlight coming through his bedroom window cast every

rigid muscle in Clayton's body in stark relief as he stared at her with the same pained expression he'd been wearing when he frightened her moments before. 'I can't do this now.'

Beth felt his words like a punch to her solar plexus. 'When . . . when you say *this*, do you mean this conversation, or us?'

He stayed resolutely silent.

Beth swallowed loudly, pulling her T-shirt back over her head. 'Okay.' She managed a humourless smile. 'I'll just collect my things.'

Feeling like her heart had been ripped from her chest, Beth finished getting dressed, then walked out the front door and drove away, blindly navigating the dirt track separating Clayton's house from her holiday cottage in the moonlight.

For once she didn't think twice about anything jumping out at her. She was far too numb for that.

Chapter 17

Beth's journey back to Perth from George Creek sped by as she went through the motions of changing gears and changing lanes according to the directions from her rental's satellite navigation system.

She'd stalled as long as possible this morning while packing the car and checking over the cottage, hoping futilely that Clayton would walk through the door, declare his feelings and ask her to stay. Unfortunately, as with much of Beth's life, things hadn't worked out the way she'd hoped. Taking one last look around the place that had been the site of so much happiness, she'd allowed herself a little time to cry. Then she'd pulled herself together enough to lug her tremendously overweight suitcase to the car before driving to Laura's.

Beth bit her lip and fought back tears for the hundredth time as she remembered how heartfelt Laura and Jeff's goodbyes had been. At a complete loss for words, Laura had cried as she'd clasped Beth in a tight hug. She'd only let go when Jeff had insisted it was his turn to say goodbye.

Jeff's expression had been intense as he'd taken in Beth's red-rimmed eyes and downturned mouth before he'd grabbed her in a bear hug and murmured, 'He's an idiot, Beth, but don't be too pissed off at him, yeah? He'll work it out. We'll make sure of it.'

Beth had nodded wordlessly against his chest, holding him that little bit tighter in thanks.

'Good,' Jeff continued gruffly. 'Because we're coming to visit you some time this year, eh? I've never been to England.'

'That would be lovely,' Beth had replied in a choked voice. 'I'm going to miss you.'

'I'm gonna miss you too.' He'd given her another quick squeeze before leaning away so she could see his cheeky grin. 'Does that mean I've still got a chance to get a leg over?' He puckered his lips in a parody of a kiss, effectively lightening the mood as Laura elbowed him in the ribs and Beth smacked him lightly on the arm.

'I'll take that as a maybe,' he'd replied before walking her to her car, giving her one final hug and wrapping an arm around Laura's shoulders as they waved her off with promises they'd pass on her goodbyes to Angie, Rachael and Jo.

Now, standing in line to check in for her flight, Beth was fighting an overwhelming sense of disbelief that something so wonderful could be ending like this. Surely any minute now she'd hear a shout and turn to find Clayton striding towards her. He'd scoop her up in his arms, telling her he loved her, accepted her and that he wanted her to stay.

Unfortunately the daydream proved a heartbreaking disappointment. All that happened next was the woman behind the check-in desk waved Beth forward before extorting an extraordinary sum for excess baggage.

Even so, Beth dawdled the entire way up the escalator and through the departure area until she reached customs. Maybe he'd just been delayed in traffic. Maybe he was just parking the car.

He'd be here any minute. Surely he would.

It wasn't until she got onto the plane that it finally sunk in that the last terrible conversation she'd had with Clayton was just that, their last. That's when the tears started and nothing she did to stop them worked. In the end she gave in and hunched over in her seat, crying into her hands in heaving sobs, ignoring the sympathetic looks and slightly irritated frowns of the people in her row.

By the time the plane landed at Manchester airport more than twenty-four hours later, Beth had managed to pull herself together enough to force a smile as she passed through immigration, ready to meet her gran and Louis. She only had a second's warning after clearing the exit before her gran barrelled into her, enveloping her in a baby-powder-scented hug. Beth closed her eyes and hugged Violet, savouring the feeling of warmth and comfort until Louis cut in.

'Let her go, woman. She has to breathe some time, you know,' he complained, then proceeded to knock the wind out of Beth's lungs with a hug of his own. 'It's been quiet without you around.' His words vibrated through his chest. 'She's been givin' me no end of grief.' He chuckled when Violet narrowed her eyes and imperiously ordered him to push Beth's baggage trolley. For the first time in days, Beth felt a sliver of genuine happiness. These people loved her and accepted her just how she was. This was where she belonged.

'It won't work, you know.'

Beth ignored her gran's words as she poured them both a cup of tea and then crouched down to pat Charlie. Even though it was an hour since she'd arrived home, he was still arthritically dancing around the kitchen, happy to see her. She'd missed him and made sure he knew it, scratching the top of his head, down his back, noticing how frail he'd become. Her heart wrenched at that. She still remem-bered when he'd been a little puppy, eating her shoes and racing out of the house to greet her when she'd come home from high school.

'Ignoring me won't work either.' Violet broke through her thoughts, settling herself down on a chair and training her too-observant gaze firstly on Beth's pale features then lower to her new clothing, which was woefully inadequate for the frigid temperatures outside.

Wanting to give Beth and Violet some privacy, Louis had left to buy a bottle of wine so they could celebrate Beth's return. He'd no doubt stay away visiting friends long enough for Violet to perform an interrogation.

'What do you mean?' Beth kept her expression carefully impassive as she gave Charlie one last pat before taking a seat.

'You've been crying,' Violet accused. 'I can always tell. Your nose goes red and stays that way for an age. You look like Rudolf the Reindeer right now.'

'Did you ever consider it could be sunburn?' Beth asked, feeling her stomach sink. Violet was a bloodhound. If she didn't put her gran off the scent soon, she'd end up giving in to the waves of hurt and sadness that were threatening to drown her. She deliberately bit the inside of her cheek hard and forced a smile. Violet and Louis had sent her on a holiday to cheer her up, and Beth would be damned if she was going to have them feel guilty.

'And I could be Linda Evangelista,' Violet retorted. 'You can either tell me now or later. Either way I'm going to get it out of you.'

Beth raised her teacup to her mouth to hide her frown. 'How about later?'

'When?'

'Later.'

'Later as in this afternoon or later as in tomorrow?'

'Later as in next year.'

'How about this evening?'

'Do we really have to?'

'Yes.'

Beth sighed. 'All right.' Only because she figured she'd be able to claim jet lag and go to sleep before her gran could get to her.

Her plan worked. To an extent. At six that evening, Beth made her way up to her tiny bedroom, feeling completely exhausted. With the exception of Charlie's familiar dog smell, the room was musty after two months of neglect. Standing in the doorway, she took in the narrow single bed with its plain navy bedspread, the tiny white wooden bedside table Violet had owned since Beth was a child and the large, ugly white melamine cupboard that contained all of Beth's worldly goods other than the things still packed in her suitcase.

This was her life. She'd been fooling herself in Australia believing she could have more. This was it.

Skirting around Charlie, who'd waddled through the door after her, she sat down heavily on her bed and studied the photograph of her family on the bedside table. Their smiling faces, obscured by a layer of dust, were now blurred by a fresh round of tears as she gently ran her fingertips over the glass. This time the feeling of loss was so much sharper than it had been in recent years. She wished they could be here for her now. But they weren't and they never would be.

Briskly wiping her eyes with the back of her hand, Beth stood up and began to unpack her suitcase while trying not to notice how her new colourful clothes made everything else in the room appear drab.

This had been her existence for the past three years. A narrow single bed, two more pieces of furniture and a miniscule bathroom off to the side. There was nothing on the plain white walls. Beth hadn't bothered to put anything up. She didn't know why. Maybe it was because she'd always viewed her stay at Violet's as temporary. *Or maybe you've viewed yourself as temporary*, a small voice whispered in her thoughts. She had to sit down to process it. *Did* she see herself as temporary? Four nights ago she'd told Clayton she was scared of dying. It had been the first time she'd ever admitted it and she realised it was true. She was terrified. She'd seen so much death in her life. Too much. Until she'd gone to Australia, she hadn't understood just how much she'd withdrawn from the world. And now, despite how horrible she felt, how much she wanted to curl up in her bed and not wake up for a long, long time, this life she'd built for herself wasn't enough any more. It felt claustrophobic, like a well-furnished coffin. Chest constricting at the thought, Beth peered down at the last item in her case. It was a coffee press. The one Clayton had brought her.

That night, she crawled into bed to fall into a deep and troubled sleep with Charlie snoring loudly in his bed by the radiator and Clayton's gift sitting next to the photograph of her family on her bedside table.

Beth woke with her head pounding and her nose twitching to the rich aroma of freshly brewed coffee. Opening her eyes, she cautiously poked her head above the duvet and saw her gran standing at the foot of her bed wearing a quilted pink dressing gown and a determined smile. 'Are you ready to wake up yet?' Violet asked, coming round the bed and setting the tray on the side table after placing the picture of Beth's family carefully on the floor against the wall to make room. She raised her brows briefly at the coffee press then set it down on the floor as well.

'No,' Beth croaked.

'You will be once you've had your coffee,' Violet said firmly, sitting down next to Beth.

Even though both women were small, the bed was tiny, and Violet ended up sitting on Beth's arm. Beth shifted over and Violet scooted even closer, forcing Beth to either sit up or be sat on. It was an old trick Violet had been pulling since Beth was a young girl.

Distraught over the loss of her parents, Beth had refused to get out of bed her first day at her gran's. She'd wanted to keep sleeping until she woke up to find her parents alive and the nightmare over. Instead of insisting, Violet had said Beth could stay under the covers as long as she needed to. She'd then proceeded to sit on Beth while Louis and Valerie looked on, laughing uproariously while Beth's grief temporarily turned to indignation and then amusement.

No one was going to laugh now. Beth certainly didn't feel like it. She'd just woken up from a dream replaying her last sight of Clayton in painfully vivid detail. Reaching a hand up to rub the sleep from her gritty eyes, she realised she'd been crying in her sleep. Luckily Violet hadn't noticed. She was too busy adding her usual five sugar lumps to her coffee and two for Beth.

'Are you ready for your coffee yet?' Violet held out a china coffee cup covered in delicate rosebuds. 'Because I do have arthritis, you know. I can't hold this thing in the air forever.'

Beth's sigh could have powered a sailing ship for weeks. Keeping the duvet bunched under her chin, she scooted up and sat against the headboard, hunching her knees against her chest. Violet handed her the coffee.

'It's a new blend I picked up when we were in Leeds the other week for my hip check-up,' Violet said proudly, taking a genteel slurp of her tooth-achingly sweet brew. 'I'm going to have to get some more. What do you think?'

Beth put the cup under her nose to smell the aroma. She was fully prepared to tell Violet the stuff was great even if it was mud, but instead she felt her eyes sting with tears. She blinked them back but it didn't work. For her, coffee and Clayton were inextricably intertwined. In seconds, the smell transported her straight back to Australia and what she'd just lost. Beth's vision blurred and Violet had to rescue the mug from her hands before she spilled it.

'I thought something was the matter,' Violet said quietly, a mixture of concern and triumph in her voice.

'Everything's the matter,' Beth whispered and began to sob in earnest as she burrowed her face in her gran's shoulder.

Well experienced in dealing with grieving grandchildren, Violet let Beth cry it out, stroking her hair and calling Louis to bring in a box of tissues. They were delivered along with an awkward pat on Beth's back.

'What have you said to her?' Louis asked.

Violet shrugged, dislodging Beth briefly. 'Nothing to cause this.'

'Should I be worryin'?'

'I'm not sure yet,' Violet replied. 'Beth? Should Louis be worrying?'

Beth managed a wet hiccup and tried to pull herself together. If it had been anyone other than these two she would be mortified, but this was Violet and Louis. They'd seen it all. Violet thrust a tissue into her hand and Beth blew her nose. Before she could answer Louis, Violet did it for her.

'I'll let you know later, love. We should be fine here now.'

Beth didn't see Louis's nod or the concerned frown aimed at her back before he left the room. Seconds later they heard the stairs creak as he made his way down to the kitchen, where he had no doubt been making breakfast.

'Should *I* be worryin'?' Violet asked Beth after Louis was out of hearing.

'I'm not a child anymore, Gran,' Beth protested, wiping her eyes.

'You are compared to me,' Violet countered, smoothing Beth's hair away from her cheek. 'This has got quite long, hasn't it?'

'I hadn't noticed.' Beth pulled away and leaned back against the headboard again, eyes downcast as she studied her hands in her lap.

Unasked questions hung heavy in the air but it was still another minute before Beth cracked.

'We broke up. He didn't love me. He couldn't handle the fact I'd been sick. He wouldn't talk about it and when I tried to bring it up before I left he . . . he didn't say anything. He just let me make a fool of myself. I told him I loved him and he didn't say anything. He just let me leave.' Beth's large watery eyes met Violet's.

'Are you sure he doesn't care for you?' Violet asked. 'Men can be notoriously constipated in the word department when it comes to feelings. Louis is a nightmare. His idea of telling me he cares is frying me extra bacon for breakfast.'

'I'm sure,' Beth replied, tearing up again.

Violet took a sip of her coffee and looked thoughtful. 'How about you tell me exactly what happened and I'll give you a second opinion?'

'I don't know if I can.'

'Try.' It was an order. A sugar-coated one, but an order none-theless. Beth could have resisted it but coming packaged as it did, with an imperiously stern expression, she folded in seconds.

'All right.'

After many stops and starts and another handful of tissues, Beth finished her story to find her gran gazing out the small window next to the bed. It was raining outside. The sky was a dull grey that matched Beth's mood perfectly.

'Is a second opinion forthcoming?'

Violet's brow furrowed slightly but she remained silent.

'Gran?'

'Give it time, Beth,' Violet said eventually, turning a sharp gaze towards her granddaughter. 'From what you said, things ended so quickly. Give it time for you to think, and for him too. If his mother died from cancer like you've said, it may be that he cares for you but he's too scared to admit it. It doesn't sound like there's been any time . . .' She patted Beth's leg. 'You're young. Act like it. You've got all the time in the world. Give it time,' she repeated firmly then stood up. 'Breakfast is ready. I can smell it. Are you coming?'

'Is that all?' Beth croaked, a little dumbfounded.

'It's the best I can do right now. I might have more for you later after I think about it for a while. First things first, though: breakfast. And after that you can give me my present. I know you got me one. I hope it's not one of those tacky plastic boomerang things that Beryl's son got her. She's put it on the mantelpiece and every time I see it I have to try not to cringe . . .' Violet continued chattering about nothing while somehow managing to pull Beth's covers off before hustling her down to the kitchen, where Louis had piled three plates high with bacon, eggs and toast. There was an extra serve of bacon for Beth.

Beth allowed herself to feel miserable for exactly one week after her return to the UK before giving herself an internal kick in the backside and getting on with things. If there was ever something she was good at, it was getting on with things. She updated her website and put an advert out on local radio and in the paper to let the village know she was back and taking on new dogs. She went to see her oncologist and got checked out to make sure everything was all right. After giving her a lecture that ran on for ten minutes about missing her previous follow-up visits, he gave her the all clear. Beth celebrated by packing away her mastectomy bras in a drawer and vowing never to wear them again unless she wanted to, not because she thought she had to.

After calling Laura to ask some fashion advice, she bagged up all of her old clothes and donated them to charity. She then delved into her stagnating savings, drove to Manchester and went on a spending spree that would have sent her to bed with a migraine only a few months before. She had got used to clothes that fitted and flattered her during the past two months, and nothing less would do now. Completely ignoring Violet's suggestions, which were largely designed to flash as much skin possible, she bought a practical yet attractive winter and spring wardrobe featuring fitted jeans and shirts, a number of skirts in warm, bright colours, along with some rather nice brown knee-high leather boots.

At her gran's insistence, and against her better judgement, Beth even visited a make-up counter and had a mini makeover that left her looking like a drag queen. She ended up settling for a basic make-up kit purchased from a very helpful man at the Bobbi Brown counter instead. The difference was subtle but according to Laura and Jeff, who gave her their verdict over a video chat, she looked lovely. She just wished her inside state of mind matched her external appearance.

As fine as she was during the day, she frequently found herself wide awake late at night, experiencing a sense of loss that was simply awful. No matter what she did – read, creep downstairs to watch television or go for late-night walks with Charlie – she couldn't rid herself of her grief and hurt over losing Clayton.

Despite telling herself she was foolish, Beth checked her email and phone every day for the first month to see if Clayton had tried to contact her, only to be disappointed each time. After that first month, she forced herself to face the fact it was well and truly over. Her gran was right: she had to give it time. As much as she wished or hoped that things were different – that Clayton was different – they weren't. He'd made his decision, and it would just take time for her to come to terms with that. She'd offered him everything she had and he'd turned it down. That hurt. It hurt so much that some nights she felt like someone had stabbed her in the chest, but along with the pain came the realisation that she was truly living for the first time in years. Even though she was hurting, she was alive, fully alive and making the most of every minute. Clayton Hardy or no Clayton Hardy, she was moving on.

Chapter 18

'It's simple, mate. Only takes a few minutes,' Clayton growled over the frantic bleating of three hundred sheep.

'Yeah, but . . . I dunno.' Fred looked dubiously at the red tagging pliers in his hand and then down at the lambs sardined in the sheep crush in front of him. 'I don't wanna hurt 'em. I mean, it's not like they're gettin' a choice here.'

'Fred.' Clayton towered over his shorter, skinnier employee. 'Think of it as a sheep-beautification project. They're just plastic earrings.' He was being entirely sarcastic, but Fred was impervious.

Brow creased up in earnest cogitation, Fred nodded. 'Right.'

'Right?'

'Earrings? All right. Yeah. So, how do I do it again?'

Doing his best to hold it together, Clayton calmly demonstrated the process for the third time before he was satisfied Fred understood. That done, he left to see his Uncle Les, who was taking care of separating ewes from lambs.

'I'm off for lunch.' He stood to the side as a ewe skirted past him, white-eyed and bleating frantically, looking for her newly tagged lamb.

Les nodded calmly. 'Take the rest of the day off, mate. I've got it here.'

Clayton began to argue but then heard Fred behind him. The silly bastard was apologising to every lamb he tagged.

'Yeah, I might just do that.' His exasperated gaze met Les's amused, incredulous one as they both turned to watch Fred for a few seconds.

Clayton shook his head. 'You getting this?'

'Yeah. Make sure you tell your dad, eh? You know, keeping this bloke on is worth it just for the laughs. He's a good 'un at heart.'

'Yeah, right,' Clayton replied, scowling as he headed off to his ute. He felt like ripping someone's head off, but that was nothing new. He'd been ready to commit murder for weeks. Eight weeks, to be precise.

It had been two months since Beth had left. Clayton felt like crap and didn't know what the hell to do about it. By rights he should have been relieved. Beth was gone and he could get his life back to normal. Instead, he was furious. It was keeping him awake. In fact, he hadn't slept for months. Ever since that night Beth had walked out his front door and flown back home without a by-your-leave.

And did anyone feel sorry for him? Did anyone understand his side of the story? Hell no. The day Beth had flown out of the country, Jeff had driven to his house, called him a fucking idiot and then left in a cloud of dust. Clayton hadn't heard from his best mate since. Laura was acting like he drowned kittens in his spare time, Rachael and Angie had been vocal with what they thought of him and the rest of his family were avoiding him like the plague. Even his bloody dog didn't want to know him. Instead of coming out on the rounds of the farm with him, Waffles crouched in her box giving him a look that patently said six squealing puppies were preferable to his company of late.

Left to his own thoughts, all Clayton could do was brood.

He couldn't believe that Beth had left him like she had. She hadn't even tried to say goodbye, and it's not like she hadn't had a chance. He'd waited for three days after their fight for her to wake up to herself and realise she was in the wrong, but what had she done instead? She'd told him she loved him then left without another word. Just up and left. She may as well have kicked him in the teeth. She hadn't called, she hadn't messaged, she hadn't emailed. Hell, he would even have appreciated a fucking note sent by courier pigeon. But, no. There'd been stone-cold silence, as if what they'd shared had meant nothing to her. Like he was in the bloody wrong when he knew, he *knew* she'd set him up with that middle-of-the-night conversation. Two in the goddamn morning and she'd wanted to have a deep-and-meaningful about relation-ships and cancer and *dying*. And when he hadn't been able to come up with anything in *her* timeframe, she'd left. Fuck that. He pulled away from the sheep pens and sped towards Evangeline's Rest.

Twenty minutes later, Clayton strode in to the cellar door searching for his dad, intending to make sure Rob picked up some sheep pellets when he went to town that afternoon, only to find the room empty.

'Dad?' he called out. As much as Rob hated working the cellar door, it wasn't like him to leave it unattended.

Hearing a noise from the back storeroom, Clayton skirted around the bar and opened the door, only to get a completely unex-pected eyeful.

His jaw dropped.

His dad had Gwen pushed up against the far wall and was doing a good job of enthusiastically exploring her tonsils while Gwen was kneading Rob's rump like it was today's bread special.

'What the *hell's* going on here?' Clayton roared, watching incredulously as the two of them pulled apart, Gwen with some embarrassment, Rob with an irritated scowl.

'What?' Rob snapped.

'I was gonna ask you the same thing,' Clayton snapped right back.

Rob roughly cleared his throat and turned to Gwen. 'I'll take care of this, love. See you out front.'

Love? Clayton thought. He must be going insane. There was *no way* his father had just used that particular endearment for Gwen Stone. As far as his dad was concerned, she was the Antichrist. Wasn't she?

Gwen brushed past him, smiling. 'Good to see you, Clayton.'

Clayton couldn't help but notice there was a swing in her hips that hadn't been there before.

'What's going on here?' he demanded the minute she closed the storeroom door after her, leaving the two men in privacy. 'I thought Gwen quit.'

Rob flushed a dull red. 'We've renegotiated.'

'Yeah, it looks like it.'

'None of that,' Rob barked. 'You come in here for something specifically?'

Clayton opened his mouth and then realised he'd completely forgotten why he'd gone looking for his dad in the first place.

'I'll talk to you later.' He did a quick about-turn and retreated, sparing Gwen a distracted nod as he exited the storeroom.

Clayton stalked across the lawn separating the cellar door and the main house, his gut churning with equal parts anger and incredulity. His world as he knew it was going mad, and somehow it was all Beth's fault. Things hadn't been like this before she'd turned up with her flat tyre. No, things had been *normal*. Everyone had behaved *normally*. Now his father was groping Gwen Stone, his dog was avoiding him and his best mate was pissed at him.

Fuck. His life sounded like one of those country-and-western songs Angie loved listening to.

Thinking of Angie, Clayton internally cringed as he wrenched off his boots and left them on the porch. So far he'd avoided his grandma's inquisition, but he didn't think that would last long. It was a good thing Rachael had been so busy with the restaurant, or he would have had her to contend with too. Rachael was like a rabid dog heading for a postman's leg when she thought she was onto something, and she'd already asked about Beth more than once.

He reached the house and peered through the screen door just to make sure the coast was clear. Stephen and Jo had returned to their apartment in the city days ago, but Angie was still around and right now Clayton wanted a bite to eat, a glass of water and a visit with his dog rather than to be social. Unfortunately, no one had told Angie that.

'It's not a sweet shop, kiddo. You can open the door,' Angie called out from the dining-room table. Her glasses were perched on her nose. Her white hair was loose around her shoulders and she was unusually dressed up in a black silk shirt.

'You're all dolled up. What's the occasion?' Bracing himself, Clayton slid the door open and stepped inside.

'I'm going to Perth later today to see Corrine,' she replied, shuffling through a stack of papers in front of her.

'Aunty Corrine? Why? What's that?' Clayton asked, glancing over her shoulder on his way to the kitchen.

'A prenuptial agreement.'

'What? For who?'

'Me, actually. Lionel asked me to marry him on Christmas Day and I'm still deciding if it's worth saying yes,' Angie replied matter-of-factly.

'Yeah? You've been sleeping with the man for years. What's to decide?'

Angie's glare should have left him a puddle on the floor but he ignored her in favour of greeting his dog.

Hearing Clayton's voice, Waffles skittered out from the laundry with a raft of chubby puppies yelping and howling in her wake. It was a good few minutes before she calmed down enough to park her backside firmly on his foot, ignoring the progeny already nipping and tugging at her master's socks.

'So, you're talking to me now, are you?' he asked gruffly, gently shifting a puppy out of the way with his toe when it began to gnaw on his ankle with needle-sharp teeth. Waffles thumped her tail on the ground and he distractedly scratched her head while turning his attention back to Angie. 'What's this about a prenup?'

'I own a quarter of the winery. If I married Lionel and then died before him he'd be able to inherit, or at least contest the will.' Angie deftly scooped up a wriggling pup from the floor at her feet and gave it a scratch behind the ear, still studying the papers.

'But he wouldn't. And you know Jeff or Laura wouldn't do anything like that.' Clayton paused. 'Although I can see how it's a sensible move to make sure everything's fair and square. What's this got to do with you turning him down?'

Angie tucked the puppy in the crook on her arm before taking off her reading glasses. 'Things have been working quite well as they are. If you haven't noticed, Lionel and I have been spending a lot more time together over the past few years. I'm debating whether or not it's better to just move in with him instead and forego the whole marriage idea. I'm too old for that anyway.'

'Yeah? You sure he doesn't want to move here instead?' Clayton's chest clenched in panic. Angie moving away? That wasn't right. Evangeline's Rest was named after Angie. To think of the place without her pottering around the kitchen, striding around the winery and fighting with his dad didn't feel right. He'd been in favour of Lionel Rousse and Angie getting together for years but had never once considered that it would mean Angie moving house.

Angie raised both eyebrows. 'Why?'

'Because this is your home.' It was wrong. Angie couldn't leave.

'It was yours too until recently, but you seem to be doing fine.'

'That's different.'

'How?' Angie demanded, but before Clayton could reply she held up a hand. 'No, don't answer that. Change the subject because I can just see you and I getting into an argument. Sometimes you remind me so much of your father it's uncanny.'

'I'll take that as a compliment,' Clayton growled, then forced himself to calm down. He'd had enough dramas of late, he didn't need a pissed-off Angie to be another one.

Angie grunted.

'Speaking of Dad,' Clayton said, just now remembering the scene he'd witnessed. 'What the hell is up with him and Gwen?'

'Hmm?'

'They were all over each other in the storeroom a few minutes ago.'

'Were they, now?' A slow grin spread across Angie's angular features as she placed the puppy back down on the floor in the care of an anxious Waffles, then leaned back in her chair. 'It's about bloody time.'

'What?' Clayton stared at her in amazement.

'You heard me.' Angie shrugged. 'Although I thought you would have sorted out *your* little self-imposed drama before your father managed to get his head out of his backside.'

'I was waiting for this.' Clayton walked over to the fridge and began to collect the makings for a sandwich, hoping he'd be able to get his lunch together and sneak away before Angie got the ball fully rolling. He should have gone back to his place. What the hell had he been thinking?

To Clayton's surprise, Angie didn't say another word. Instead, she went back to her papers while he slapped mayonnaise on half a bread roll and sawed off a chunk of ham to go with it. He'd just taken his first bite when she spoke again.

'Lionel said Jeff has his tickets booked for next month. You going to go see him off?'

'What? See him off? Where? What tickets?' Clayton asked around a mouthful of sandwich.

'For his holiday to the UK,' Angie replied calmly. Only the twitch at the corner of her mouth revealed that she knew exactly what the information was doing to her grandson.

When Clayton had finished choking on his food, he managed a strangled, '*What?*'

'Jeff's holiday to England. Are you going to see him off at the airport?' Angie repeated calmly. 'Didn't you hear me the first time?'

She watched with obvious satisfaction as Clayton's features contorted into an expression of blind fury.

'Close the door behind you when you leave,' she said mildly as he slammed down his sandwich, yanked his phone out of his pocket and started to dial Jeff's number before he got to the door.

Jeff wandered onto his porch at the sound of Clayton's ute skidding to a halt out the front of his cabin. He had all of five seconds' warning before he was doubled over and gasping as a fist was firmly planted in his gut.

'Fuck'n 'ell,' he wheezed. 'Hello to you too.' He stumbled backwards and slumped into one of his rattan porch chairs.

Clayton advanced until he was standing only a foot away, his fists clenched, waiting for Jeff to get back up so he could knock him down again.

'Heard about my holiday, did you?' Jeff squinted up at Clayton while gingerly rubbing his stomach.

'You fucking bastard,' Clayton snarled, moving forward another step but not touching Jeff again. He played too fair to hit a man while he was down. Instead he glared at Jeff in tense silence, his entire body bristling with pent-up rage.

Jeff rubbed his bruised ribs and glared right back. 'An apology would be appreciated. Next time give a man a bit of warning, will you?'

'You don't deserve any goddamn warning. She's *mine*.'

'Could have fooled me,' Jeff returned, his eyes hard. 'If you got your head out of your arse for long enough to look at a calendar, you'd see that she hasn't been *yours* for two months. You let her go. More fool you. Anyway, enough with this shit. You've just ruined my lunch. If I have to deal with you, I need coffee.' He got to his feet and stomped into his house.

'What the *fuck*, Jeff?' Clayton roared at his back, then followed him inside.

'She invited me and I took her up on it.' Jeff poured himself a mug of thick black coffee from his percolator.

'When?'

'When, what?'

'When did she invite you?'

'A few weeks ago. Something like that.'

'You've been talking to her for *weeks*?'

'Well. Yeah.' Jeff added milk to his cup and then gave it a stir. 'All the time. Laura comes over here to call her because my net speed is better, so I see Beth once every few days or so.'

'*You've been seeing her?*' Clayton's bellow shook the cabin's foundation.

'Yeah. Video calls, mate. It's not the Stone Age here, you know. You'd have seen her too if you'd bothered to come around. Oh, just wait.' Jeff slapped his forehead. 'You dumped her, didn't you? And you've been acting like a prick since. My bad. So d'you want a coffee or are you just here to bitch at me?'

Clayton stared at him incredulously.

Jeff couldn't help but notice that his friend looked like shit. Clayton's eyes were red-rimmed, his skin was a sick sort of grey under his tan and he'd lost weight.

'You look like hell,' he said. 'Want some lunch? I've got some of Laura's chicken pie left over.' Jeff plated a serve of pie, put it in the microwave then leaned back against the kitchen bench, crossing his arms over his chest as he watched Clayton pace up and down the length of the living room, expression switching from furious to pained and back to furious again.

'You can't go see her, mate,' Clayton said finally, coming to a stop in front of Jeff, his hands by his side and his shoulders slumping.

Jeff steeled himself against pity. If his mate wasn't such a stubborn prick, he wouldn't be in this situation now. 'Why not?'

'She's my . . . she was my . . . look, you just bloody well can't.' Clayton rammed his hands through his hair, his expression pleading.

'Tickets are booked. I hear planes can fly as far as England these days. Pretty amazing, that. So, yeah. I'd say I can.' Jeff pulled the pie out of the microwave when it chimed and held the plate and a fork out for Clayton. 'You sitting in here or outside?'

Clayton stared blindly down at the plate.

'You put it in your mouth and chew.' Jeff slid the plate onto the breakfast bar.

'Why?' Clayton demanded as he sat down on a bar stool.

'Why eat? Well, if you don't know that, it's a wonder you're alive.'

'That's not what I mean and you know it.'

'It's just a holiday, mate. I like Beth. She offered to show me around.' Jeff shrugged. 'It shouldn't worry you anyway. As far as I can tell, you dropped her because she had cancer a few years back, which makes you a bit of a prick, doesn't it? There's nothing else I can think of. Laura can't work it out either.'

'Jesus Christ!'

Jeff ignored Clayton's outburst and shrugged. 'It's all we can think of. I mean, you two seemed pretty happy, everything was working, wasn't it? I know she told you she loved you. Then you go fuck it up. Laura reckons it's got something to do with your mum dying.' Jeff cocked his head to the side.

'Fuck you,' Clayton snarled and pushed the bar stool back so fast it crashed to the floor.

'No. Fuck *you*, mate,' Jeff replied calmly. 'Sort your shit out with Beth or get over it. My flight's on the fifteenth.' He walked around the bench, picked up Clayton's stool then wandered over to the front door and held it open.

Clayton roared up to Evangeline's Rest for the second time that afternoon and made a beeline back to the cellar door as the image of Jeff's smarmy grin melded with an image of Beth's devastated expression that last night. Jeff and Beth. Jeff speaking to Beth. Jeff holding Beth. Jeff touching Beth. It wasn't going to happen.

'*Dad?*'

'He's gone to George Creek.' Gwen poked her head out from the storeroom with a welcoming smile on her lips that turned quickly into a worried frown when she saw his expression.

Frustrated, Clayton let loose a string of obscenities. He spun on his heel, fully intent on driving to town, finding Rob and telling him that he was looking after the farm for the next week while Clayton flew to England and told Beth what he thought of her covert relationship with Jeff.

'*Not so fast, Clayton Hardy!*'

He stopped cold just outside the door at the sound of his name being bellowed at a volume that would make even Angie wince. He turned around, ears ringing, expression stunned, to see Gwen standing a few feet behind him with her hands on her ample hips.

Pale-green eyes were narrowed and shooting sparks as she bristled with outrage. 'You owe me an apology and you're going to give it to me *now*. I have *never* heard that kind of language before from you, and I never want to hear it again.'

Clayton flushed red. 'Sorry, Gwen,' he mumbled, looking down at his feet feeling all of five years old.

'You should be. Now come back in here right now and cool down for a minute.' She reached behind the bar and poured two small glasses of cabernet sauvignon. 'What's the problem?'

'There's no problem,' Clayton said curtly. 'Look, Gwen. I appreciate that —'

'You're just as bad as your father. You know that, don't you?' Gwen picked up her glass and gulped down a generous mouthful. She held out a glass to Clayton and he took it. 'Sit,' she ordered, pointing imperiously to a bar stool.

Clayton was about to resist again but something stopped him. Maybe it was his fight with Jeff, maybe it was the lack of sleep, but he suddenly felt the need to talk. He needed someone to understand. Hell, *he* needed to understand, because underlying all the anger sloshing around, burning a hole in his gut right now, was a sea of hurt. If Beth had been talking to Jeff, why hadn't she tried to talk to him? He kept coming back to the fact that *she* was the one who had left, *she* was the one who hadn't given him a chance.

He took a seat.

Gwen took the stool next to him, arranged her long, bright blue shirt neatly over her lap then leaned on the bar facing him, her cheek resting on her palm. 'Now. I'll ask again: what's the problem?'

Clayton rested his head in both hands. 'Everything, Gwen. I'm going crazy here.'

'Hmm?'

'Everyone's acting like I've messed up. I know I haven't. I can't have.' He groaned. 'It doesn't make sense. *She* left *me*. Now Jeff's going over there to see her and I don't know what the hell to do.'

'You're talking about that little thing you were going out with over Christmas. Beth?'

'Yeah.'

'Want to tell me about it? It's quiet this afternoon. I don't have any tours due for another hour or so and we haven't had any drop-ins yet.'

Clayton grimaced, picked up his wine and gulped it down. 'You sure you wanna hear it?'

'Yes.'

He exhaled a huge puff of air, slapped his thighs and braced himself. 'Yeah, all right. Can't get any more screwed up than it is already.'

It took Clayton a while to warm up to the topic, but eventually he managed to get it all out from beginning to end, including the last argument he had with Beth. He left out the physical part of the fight they'd had because he didn't think that was anyone's business, but he included the rest: Beth telling him she loved him and that she'd stay, then leaving like her words hadn't meant a thing. While he was at it, he forced himself to tell Gwen about Beth's double mastectomy, her cancer and how he'd been terrified about her dying every night that last month of her stay.

'I didn't sleep, Gwen. I was shit-scared I was gonna wake up and she'd be gone. Every night. But now I wake up wishing she was here and I don't know what to do,' he finished, clenching his hands into fists on the bar.

There was a clink of bottle on glass and the sound of pouring wine before Gwen spoke. 'You know your father blamed me for your mother's death, don't you?'

'Come again?' Clayton reared back in his chair, brow lined in confusion.

Gwen sighed. 'It was a mix-up. Your father blamed me for your mother refusing treatment for her cancer.'

Clayton shook his head, blindsided by this unexpected information. It suddenly felt like the ground had been ripped out from beneath his feet. 'What? Mum refused treatment? Dad didn't say anything about her not trying to get herself better. Why? Why would she do that?'

Gwen sighed, sipped from her glass and looked straight ahead to the racks of bottles arranged behind the bar. 'It's a long story. I'll try to do it justice. A while before your mum died she came home to find your father comforting me after my fiancé broke off our engagement. I'd come out here to see your mum but ended up crying all over your dad. Believe it or not, he didn't dislike me then.' She offered him a faint smile but her eyes were sad. 'And I think I was probably a little in love with him, too. Always had been. Anyway, your mum walked in and saw us together and left. I explained to her what had happened and all was forgiven. I'm sure it would have been forgotten if Pam hadn't been diagnosed with leukemia a few days later. She never told your dad about the severity of her diagnosis or that she'd turned down treatment. Her diagnosis had been made far too late to do anything, and she wanted to make sure she had as much time as possible with your father and you children. When he found out, your dad blamed me for her death. He thought she'd made her choice because she was hurt and angry at him.' Gwen's voice caught. 'It was horrible, Clayton. The shock was incredible when she died. Your father was so heartbroken and wouldn't listen to reason.'

'Yeah, I remember,' Clayton said dazedly, his voice choked. Why hadn't his mum wanted to live? Surely there'd been a chance, even if it was a small one, that she might have survived, that she would be here today. 'Why are you telling me this?'

'Out of all of Pam's kids, you took her death the hardest.' Gwen looked him straight in the eye. 'You didn't speak for over a year afterwards. You were always such a quiet little boy anyway, always so serious, trying to look after everyone. I remember seeing you in town with your dad and the children two weeks after the funeral. Your father was pushing the trolley in the supermarket but it was obvious he wasn't really up for the job. I'll never forget how wrecked he looked. And there you were, five years old with a grocery list in one hand, Michael's hand in the other, doing the shopping.' She smiled sadly. 'I can't help but think you had to be stronger than everyone else, even your father. You've never really grieved for your mum, have you?'

'What?' Clayton managed. He didn't know why but he felt himself tearing up. 'Yeah, of course I have. She's been gone twenty-nine years.'

'And for that entire twenty-nine years you've been doing the right thing, kiddo, but from what Angie says, you've never once really asked any questions about your mum, never wanted to know who she was. You know, both your brothers and your sister have come to me separately over the years and asked about Pam, but not you.' Gwen put a warm hand on his shoulder and he had to resist the urge to shrug it off. Just that one sympathetic touch left him ready to howl. 'I think it's about time you forgave her. It took your dad twenty-nine years to face the fact that Pam chose to die the way she wanted to. Twenty-nine years for him to forgive her and himself. I think it's time you did the same.'

Clayton just stared at her blindly, only half-hearing Gwen's words. His rib cage felt too tight. It was strangling him, compressing everything, his lungs, his heart, up to his throat, where they all formed a plug he couldn't breathe past.

Either oblivious to his predicament or ignoring it, Gwen continued. 'If you care for Beth, if you want a future with her or any other woman, you need to let Pam go. She loved you, Clayton. Sadly, people die – some from lingering illness, some straightaway. You never know when you or the people you care about are going to go. All you can do is take it a day at a time.'

'Easier said than done,' Clayton said huskily.

'That's life, kiddo.' Gwen got to her feet, collected their used glasses and walked around the bar to load them into the dishwasher.

Clayton watched on as she began to line up the wines available for tasting that afternoon, starting with sauvignon blanc and ending with a port.

His thoughts were a jumbled mess, coiling around and tying him in knots. Pictures of his mum and Beth combined until his head ached and his belly hurt. He was flooded with memories of his five-year-old self's determination to take care of everything and everyone, especially his dad. He couldn't remember crying about his mum's death. He'd worried that if he did and his dad or one of the other kids saw him, they'd get upset. Instead, he'd done his best to hold it together by not thinking too hard about things, about the fact his mum wasn't there any more and never would be again. He saw with a flash of clarity that he'd always believed he could stave off anyone else leaving, dying, if he could just hold it all together. If he could just keep going, it would all be fine. It was magical thinking, off-with-the-fairies kind of stuff. But it had worked. It had worked well enough at least because they were all okay, weren't they? Everyone was fine. Well, except he wasn't. And it sounded like his dad hadn't been for a long time either, despite outward appearances.

And now he'd been told his mum had refused medical help. What was he supposed to do with that? Surely she knew his dad would have been there for her. Surely she didn't think that her kids wouldn't have tried to be there for her and help her through it. Clayton would have tried. He would have done anything to show her how much he loved her. He would have shown her it was worth fighting.

Or would you have cut her cold like you did Beth for fear that she could die anyway? a small voice muttered in his subconscious.

He frowned at that. It didn't make sense. He'd only been five when his mum died. He was a grown man now.

A grown man who is still so shit-scared, he let the only woman he ever cared about go, the voice came again. *You let her stand there and lay herself on the line, and you gave her nothing. She showed you her scars and all you could do was tell her to get dressed! Christ, you didn't even say goodbye because you were so scared of seeing her leave you. Better to let it end suddenly and blame it on her than to face the fact she could one day get sick again. Coward.*

He'd let Beth walk away. Hell, he'd *wanted* her to walk away rather than make him face reality. He'd panicked. He hadn't wanted her to talk about cancer. Cancer equalled his mum. Cancer equalled death. Better she left. Better he was miserable without her . . .

He was a fool.

'Don't let it get you down, Clayton. You didn't do anything wrong, and I know what Pam did was out of love. Your mother would be so proud of you if she could see you today.' Gwen's softly spoken words cut through his thoughts and straight to the bone.

'No, she wouldn't,' Clayton said in a choked voice as it all sank in. 'No, she'd say I was the biggest idiot there was.'

Gwen gave him a look so full of compassion, it was painful to see. 'There's always time to make up for your mistakes. People forgive. I know I'm putting myself where I'm not welcome, but the last three decades have taught me that it's better to have one day of happiness with someone you really care about than years of regret.' With that she walked into the storeroom to collect a handful of brochures, tactfully giving Clayton time to regain his composure.

'I've really messed up,' he said to her when she returned.

'Yes, love, but everyone does at some stage or another. It's what you do to fix it that counts.' She leaned across the bar and placed a hand over his clenched fist.

'What if she doesn't forgive me?' Just voicing the words brought a wave of panic so strong it was almost suffocating.

'She will if she loves you. It's not something people can just turn on and off at the drop of a hat.' Gwen smiled ruefully. 'I tried to kill my feelings for your father for three decades and wasn't successful, so I doubt a few months will do it for your Beth.'

'What do I do?' Clayton demanded, his mind frantically working. He couldn't just up and leave the farm. He had to arrange for someone to take over. He had to sort out flights. Hell, he didn't even have a passport. How long did that take? He said as much out loud.

'Forget about worrying. Just get off your backside and go get her back,' Gwen said firmly, patting him gently on his cheek and returning to work just as a group on a wine tour walked through the door.

It wouldn't stop raining, and everything was so green it made Clayton's head hurt. And the roads were so narrow, much narrower than they were at home. He squinted through the waterlogged windscreen and ran through his plan again.

He had to get this right. It had taken him nearly a month to get here, to line everything up, and every day of that month he'd had to fight the urge to pick up the phone and call Beth – but that would have ruined it all. Somehow, he knew if he talked to her in person he'd be able to explain what had been going on in his head that night she'd last seen him and convince her to give him a second chance to get it right. If he tried to do that over the phone, there was a chance she'd hang up, or even worse, hear him out and then tell him she wasn't putting up with his shit anyway. That's what he'd do if someone threw everything he offered them away without a word. And although she was nice, he knew Beth wasn't a pushover. The lady had a spine of steel. It was one of the things he loved about her.

Over the past month he'd replayed their time together over and over again, seeing just how happy she'd made him, how alive he'd felt in her company. He knew he'd been working hard for the past few years. Hell, he'd been working hard since he was a kid, but for a while there, with Beth, it had felt like he was doing it for a reason. He'd had someone to share it with. That day she'd seen his house for the first time and expressed her approval had left him feeling like he'd actually achieved something. It had all clicked together. Unfortunately, he'd been too scared to see it.

He sure as hell wasn't scared any more. Determined would be the better word. Thanks to the Cancer Council in Western Australia and a whole lot of extra research, he was full bottle, at least intellectually, on what Beth had gone through. He wouldn't stick his head in the sand like last time. With Laura's help, he'd learned that she'd had something called a *ductal carcinoma in situ* and had opted for drastic treatment to reduce her risk of getting cancer again down to a small chance, no doubt because of her sister's death. He understood why Beth had made the decision for the double mastectomy, but it still hadn't been easy to hear Laura talk about it. Especially when she'd let slip that Beth's surgery had been the reason her husband had left her. He'd felt like hurling when he'd learned about that.

Clayton couldn't help but draw the obvious parallels between Beth's spineless ex-husband's rejection and his own refusal to talk to her or even look at her when she'd been brave enough to bare all that last night they were together. Never mind these last months of silence. He knew how she must have seen it, and it killed him that he'd hurt her so badly. But he was going to make it right.

Yeah, he knew exactly what he was walking into, or driving towards more to the point, and he was doing it with eyes wide open, knowing it was what he wanted to do. He wanted Beth. He wanted the whole deal, and he'd bloody well get down on hands and knees with a big pink bow around his neck if that's what she needed to believe that he meant it.

He came to an intersection, followed the GPS instructions on his phone and turned left down yet another narrow road. This one had the rock walls Beth had mentioned on either side. The Yorkshire countryside was truly spectacular, but Clayton didn't care. All he wanted to do was reach Beth's place, ask her forgiveness and convince her to give him another go.

Chapter 19

Beth was exhausted. She'd just finished a full day trying to teach Martine, a dogue de Bordeaux puppy with the brains of a pea, not to jump up on his owner, only to work out that the dog was actually quite intelligent, it was the owner that needed help. Now all she wanted was a cup of tea, something to eat and a blessed, elusive night's sleep.

She pulled into the short driveway leading to her gran's cottage only to find a large black Audi blocking her way. It was already dark and raining despite it being spring, so Beth almost rear-ended the thing. Muttering under her breath, she reversed her car and parked down the lane before striding towards the house, shivering in the cold. She'd left her new wool coat at home today thinking she'd have no need for it and was now seriously regretting the decision.

Whoever was visiting Louis and Violet was not in her good books this evening. Not that anyone would be tonight. It was the three-month anniversary of her return from Australia and she'd been fighting an overwhelming sadness all day. She'd never been one for sentimentality, but for the past three months she'd found herself quietly marking each week, each month since her return. It was ridiculous, really. Foolish. She'd told herself as much over and over again.

Maybe it was just Laura and Jeff's impending visit that was bringing it all up again. She couldn't wait to see them, but a small part of her wanted to call them and tell them to cancel their flights – that way she could continue to get over it and on with it.

And she *was* getting on with it. She'd spent the past two weeks looking at various small rental properties in the area and had decided on a cosy little two-up two-down in the centre of the village just off the high street. She was due to sign the lease tomorrow and then it would just be a case of moving in. That wouldn't take long. She only had a few boxes of possessions to shift.

It was high time she started to live her life again as if she was going to live and keep on living. In that vein, she'd accepted an invitation to dinner from Peter Nesbit, a handsome, quiet doctor who owned an endearingly affectionate Bernese mountain dog. She didn't know where he intended to take her, but she'd been quite firm in stating she didn't want to go to the pub.

Keys . . . keys. Her fingers were numb as she searched through her handbag and she levelled another glare at the intruder's car. There was a small Hertz sticker on the back. Who did Violet and Louis know that would rent such an expensive car?

She was still brooding on that particular question when she gave up on finding her keys and decided to ring the bell. Neither Louis nor Violet would hear it, but the visitor might.

The door opened just as she pressed the button. Startled, she took a step back, slipped on the wet doorstep and gripped the doorframe to steady herself.

'Beth?'

Beth stared up with huge round eyes, her heartbeat pounding

and her breath catching. In the dark, with the kitchen light behind him, Clayton was just a large silhouette, but she would recognise that body, that scent, anywhere. The question was, what was he doing *here*? In England? In Skipton? *In her home?*

'C-Clayton? What are you doing here?' she asked in a strangled croak.

'I'm here to see you,' he answered, his voice husky and uncharacteristically uncertain.

'Why?' She took another step backwards, squinting to better see his expression. Her whole body was shivering and she wasn't sure if it was from the biting cold or shock.

'Let her in, boy. She's freezing out there.' Louis's voice came from the kitchen behind Clayton and without any warning Beth was grasped by the hand and hauled inside.

The moment the door was closed, Beth pulled away like she'd been burned. She hurried over to the far side of the kitchen and leaned against a counter, tightly crossing her arms over her chest, tucking her fingertips into her armpits to warm them.

Violet and Louis, seated at the table, were spared a cursory glance before Beth narrowed in on Clayton. She brutally squashed the involuntary warm glow of happiness that kindled in her chest.

He was incredibly handsome. His broad chest was covered by a charcoal fisherman's jumper, his narrow hips and rugby-player legs hugged by blue jeans. He'd had a haircut since she'd last seen him and his face was smoothly shaved, but Beth couldn't help but notice that his eyes were red-rimmed and pinched as if he hadn't slept for some time. Good. A smidgeon of Beth's sanity returned and with it came anger. How dare he turn up after months of nothing? And like this. No phone call. No email. Nothing. Just him. At her gran's house. Filling up the kitchen. Smelling so good she could cry. It wasn't fair. He shouldn't be here now. Not today. She was still grieving their failed relationship. She didn't want any reminders.

'You didn't answer me. What are you doing here?' Her voice sounded harsh even to her own ears.

'Beth! The least you could do is say hello before you start being rude to the boy. Especially after he's come all this way!' Violet exclaimed.

Beth narrowed her eyes at her gran in warning and then turned back to Clayton. A dark red flush covered his cheekbones as he opened his mouth once, twice, but nothing came out.

'Clayton?'

'Beth,' he began. 'I, ah . . .' He ran his hand through his hair, not quite making eye contact. 'Can we talk?'

'Why?' Beth pursed her lips and tightened her arms across her chest.

'Because I need to apologise. This is harder than I thought it would be. I, ah. I was wrong and . . .' Clayton's eyes flickered to Louis and Violet, who were watching proceedings with the air of concerned spectators at a tennis match. 'Is there anywhere we can do this in private?'

Beth took a deep breath and was about to demand to know what *this* was when Violet cut her off.

'The living room is free.'

Beth's eyes widened with incredulity. '*Gran!*'

'On second thought, I have a better idea. Louis, why don't you come and help me with my crossword while we watch the news? We'll go into the living room and leave these two to talk.' Violet gave Louis a pointed stare that said he could either go along with her idea or face dire retribution.

'I don't know . . .' Louis replied, looking from Beth to Clayton and back again warily. Beth was just about to ask him to stay when her gran spoke again.

'Louis.' Violet said his name with the commanding tone of an army general dealing with a subordinate reluctant to go over the top of the trench and fight the good fight.

Louis heaved a sigh, rolling his eyes. 'All right.' He painstakingly got to his feet and turned to Clayton. 'You goin' to do right by my girl?'

'Yeah,' Clayton replied, not taking his eyes off Beth, who was presently dumbfounded in the face of her gran and Louis's treachery.

'Okay, then. I'll be in the next room if you need me,' Louis said with a pointed look at Beth.

'Thanks,' Clayton replied, not taking his eyes off Beth for a second.

'No. Wait!' Beth exclaimed as the living-room door closed with a definitive click. She felt panic rising. She couldn't be alone with him. Not feeling this off-centre. She wanted him gone and this stupid, irrational feeling of hope to wither and die before it took flight, or she'd be a wreck when he left.

Within seconds the sound of the TV turned up to its usual unbearable volume filtered into the kitchen. The noise sat leaden in the room as Beth bit her lip and stared pointedly into Clayton's eyes, willing him to get what he wanted to say off his chest quickly so he could go and she could escape to her room and have a damn good cry.

'What do you want to say to me?' she demanded tightly.

Clayton ran a hand over his jaw. 'Beth . . .'

'Yes?' Beth pursed her lips.

'You know I'm not good with words.' He hunched his shoulders, his eyes pleading. 'I thought it would be easy when I saw you and —'

'Why. Are. You. *Here?*'

'I missed you,' he said simply, his expression pained. 'And I want to say sorry for being a complete and utter dickhead.'

'Yes?'

'And I want to answer that question you asked me.'

'Which question?'

'Whether or not I love you. I do.' He bridged the distance between them, not quite touching Beth but close enough that she had to look up to see his expression, close enough that she could feel the warmth from his body.

'Oh.' Beth's outrage turned a sharp corner into hurt and she felt tears prickle her eyes. Damn it. 'Clayton, it's obvious you're feeling bad, maybe guilty, but I forgive you. Just go home and leave me alone. I'll tell Gran and Louis you said goodbye.' In quick jerking movements she uncrossed her arms, skirted around him before he could reach for her and walked to the door, only to be stopped by his quietly spoken words.

'I love you, Beth.'

Beth's hand tightened over the cold metal door handle, her shoulders tensed.

'Why?' Her voice cracked.

'What?'

She stared resolutely at the door in front of her, refusing to turn and look at him. 'Why? Why now? Why not before? Why do you think you love me now? Why? Three months ago I offered you everything I had and you didn't want it. Why now? Everything's the same, Clayton. I still had cancer. I could still get sick. What's changed your mind?'

It was a tense few seconds until Clayton answered, his voice coming from just behind her as she steadfastly kept her eyes on the wood grain in front of her, trying to keep the tears at bay.

'I won't lie to you, Beth. It took me two months to work it all out,' Clayton said. 'I was miserable without you but the whole time I told myself *you* were the one who hadn't given us a chance by leaving that night like you did. I didn't want to admit that I was the one in the wrong because if I did that, I'd have to admit how scared I was. I was fucking terrified.'

'Of what?' Beth turned around despite herself, finding him

standing only a foot away, his expression a mixture of anger and sadness.

'My mum died when I was a kid. Five years old. There wasn't any warning. She was fine one minute, doing all the normal stuff mums do, and then the next minute she went to the hospital and died. Dad was a wreck. It hurt so much. All I can remember is feeling like everything had fallen to bits. It still feels that way some days.' He averted his eyes, blinking furiously for a few seconds before facing her again. 'After I started to care for you I got terrified that you —' He paused and swallowed hard. 'Christ, Beth. I don't want to lose you. I couldn't handle it.'

'You lost me already, Clayton.'

'I know, and it was the stupidest thing I've ever done. I want to undo it. I *need* to undo it.' Clayton closed the gap between them, placing his hands on Beth's shoulders and hauling her against him. 'I love you, Beth,' he repeated against the top of her head, holding her tense, resisting body tightly. 'Tell me I haven't fucked up completely. Tell me you still love me.' His voice caught at the end and Beth felt the first cracks appear in her defences.

'I'm not sure if I can, Clayton. I don't know if I can put myself through it all again,' Beth said, her voice wavering.

There was a stunned silence and she glanced up at Clayton's face. He looked devastated, mouth turned down, eyes shining unnaturally. 'Christ, Beth. Please tell me you don't mean that.'

'Why did it take so long? You didn't even say g-goodbye.' Beth's voice caught on the last word and her bottom lip started to tremble.

'I'd do anything to take that back if I could. I know there's no reason for you to give me the time of day, but at least believe me when I say that. If I could go back to that night I would tell you that I would do anything to have you stay. I would say that I love you and that no matter what happens in the future, I'll be there.'

Beth's breath caught. 'But you didn't.'

'No, I didn't.' Clayton reached up and wiped his thumbs under her eyes. 'I'm so sorry. And I'm sorry I didn't tell you how beautiful you are. All over. Especially here. You're so brave. I wish I'd told you that.' He leaned back and put a hand on the centre of Beth's chest, his fingers splayed out to cover both of her scars.

The first chest-heaving sob hit Beth unexpectedly and her entire body jerked in Clayton's arms. It was followed by another, then another until Beth couldn't tell when one gasping watery breath ended and another began. All she could do was burrow herself against the comforting warmth of Clayton's chest, clutching him like a life raft in an angry sea.

She was vaguely aware of Louis speaking in concerned tones at some stage, of Clayton moving her backwards until he was sitting on one of the kitchen chairs with Beth still held tightly against him.

'I'm so sorry, Beth,' he repeated again.

'What does that mean? What happens if I learn it's come back? The chance is very small but it's still there. It could come back. I could die. I could go to the doctor's office for a routine visit and come back with the news I've got cancer again. Can you cope with that? Can you *live* with that? Because if you can't I won't – I *can't* be with you. You might as well climb back in your car and drive straight to the airport.' Beth pulled back enough to look him in the eye.

Clayton exhaled like she'd just punched him in the stomach. 'Jesus, Beth. Don't talk like that. Nothing's set in stone. This last month I've been doing research nonstop trying to understand what you've been through. It probably doesn't come close, but it was enough to help me understand what I could do to give you the support you need to fight it if it came back. We'd fight it together. You wouldn't be alone again. I'd never let you go like I did back home. Never again. I've got my eyes open. I know what I'm getting into and I still want to be with you, if you'll have me. Just promise me you wouldn't keep anything from me. You wouldn't have to protect my feelings. Whatever happens, whatever you choose to do, I'll support you. You'd just have to tell me what's going on and what you need.'

Beth sat in stunned silence, her heart beating triple time, her breath caught in her throat.

'I love you, Beth. I'll say it as many times as I need to until you believe me. I didn't say it that night, but you're so, so beautiful to me. The most beautiful, brave, amazing woman I know.' Clayton whispered against her hair. 'Please come back. You offered to move to Australia before. I know I don't deserve it, but I'd do anything to make that work.'

Beth sniffed wetly before shaking her head. 'It's not that simple, Clayton. What if you change your mind again?'

'I won't. I swear. Hell, I'll hand you the shotgun myself if I do anything like that. I want you. I want the lot. I want you with me every day. I want to wake up next to you. I want to drink God-awful coffee with you every morning. I want to see your face before I go to sleep at night. I've never wanted anything more. Please, Beth. Give me another chance. Spend the rest of your life with me?' His hand stroked through her hair before cupping her cheek.

Beth pushed away, bringing a hand up to wipe her eyes as an incredulous realisation dawned. 'Are you asking me to marry you?'

'I was getting to that.' Clayton gave her another tight squeeze before loosening his hold. He slipped his hand between them, reached into his pocket and pulled out a ring and held it in his palm in front of her. It was yellow gold with a small princess-cut diamond surrounded by tiny sapphires. 'It was Mum's,' he said quietly. 'Dad gave it to me just before I left.'

Beth stared at the gold band as potential futures flashed through her mind. Some time in the past thirty minutes, three months of hurt had been put on the back burner, replaced by an overwhelming urge to take what Clayton was offering. He genuinely seemed sorry, he was saying all the right things, and everything she knew about him to date told her he'd rather stay silent than promise something he couldn't see through. But still . . . she couldn't give in this easily. It had been a long, hard road, but she'd finally grasped just how much she was worth and she had to make sure this happened the right way – if it was going to happen at all.

'And?' Beth's stomach cramped with anxiety but her voice stayed firm.

'And, what?'

'Are you going to ask me?' She stuck out her chin.

'Do you love me?' he prompted, relief entering his voice, causing his entire upper body to relax and curve around hers.

'Yes. Are you going to ask me?' Beth repeated briskly, unable to take her eyes off the ring in his fingers as she elbowed him in the ribs.

The booming sound of Clayton's surprised laughter bounced off the stone kitchen walls and drowned out the TV.

'Well?'

'All right. All right. Jesus. You had me going there. Stand up. Yep, like that and sit down again. All right, then.' He managed to switch places with Beth so that she was sitting in the kitchen chair and he was standing in front of her. Well, that was before he dropped to one knee at her feet, his expression turning serious again. 'Beth Poole . . . will you marry me?'

'Oh bugger.' Beth's eyes filled up with tears again. 'You weren't supposed to do that.'

'What did you think I was gonna do? Leave?' Clayton asked incredulously.

'Maybe,' Beth answered, wrapping her arms around her waist, giving herself a reassuring hug and a pinch to make sure this was real. 'Can you ask again? I'm not sure I really caught the first time.'

'Yeah, all right.' Clayton grinned. 'Beth Poole, would you do me the honour of becoming my wife?'

Beth's breath hitched, her heart tripped and she opened her mouth to answer but before she could make a sound, a loud female voice bellowed from the other side of the living-room door.

'*Yes!* Now let us back in there so I can see the bloody ring!'

Acknowledgements

A huge thanks to my wonderful friends who generously shared what it was like to deal with cancer from diagnosis, to treatment, to recovery. Being in your company and listening to your stories has been a truly humbling experience.

Sarah Fairhall, thanks so much for your patience, tact and brilliant sense of humour. Best. Editor. Ever.

And the awesome team at Penguin Australia, thanks so much for all the support and hard work.

Theresa Mathison, Anja Dreyer, Mersedeh Badrian, Jen Hogan and Jo Henrickson, what would a gal do without friends like you? She'd be lost, that's what. Thanks for the reading, the support and the honesty in the shaping of this book.

The mighty Seldons, thanks again for all the fun. A special thanks to Maia for informing me that she's written a book and it will sell more than all the others in the world, so I don't need to be an author anymore. (Oh to have the confidence of a five-year-old!) Go for it, sweetie!

Barbara Winmill, your company is divine. Thanks so much for the countless cups of tea, the wonderful conversation and inspiration. A lady couldn't ask for a better friend.

Rhyll Biest, thanks for making me belly laugh on a regular basis with your take on all things romance and writing.

And finally to all the marvellous bookstores stocking my books and the lovely people who have purchased *Summer Harvest*. I can't thank you enough. You're the best!

Chapter 1

'What the hell?'

Jo Blaine's motorbike helmet bounced off antique pine floor-boards with a dull plastic thud as she took in the state of her Fremantle penthouse apartment.

This was so not the way she'd left it when she'd flown out to her offshore oil job in Mauritania. No way.

There was a rumpled tartan throw rug and a pillow on one of her cream leather couches, a bright-red coffee cup – her favourite damn coffee cup – was sitting on her hand-cut glass-and-jarrah coffee table and the books in her bookshelves looked as if they'd been rifled through.

She took a step further inside, kicking a pair of expensive-looking, size-fourteen men's leather shoes out of her way, and immediately felt a cool breeze against her cheek.

The sliding door leading to the balcony was wide open, letting in the scent of a recent summer shower on bitumen. The sounds of distant traffic and boats going up and down the Swan River filtered in, an incongruous backing track to her growled exclamation.

Definitely not how she'd left it before.

'Hello? Anyone here?' She turned back around, narrowed eyes searching for a coffee-loving, couch-sleeping, male Goldilocks but only saw her massive silver Maine Coon cat, Boomba, who chose that moment to waddle past with a pair of men's undies firmly clasped in his mouth. His fat furry backside moved side to side as he disappeared into the kitchen, where Jo could see stacked Domino's pizza boxes on the counter. Her temper, always on a short fuse after a long, sleepless flight, began to sizzle and fizz as she put the clues together.

She only knew one man with size-fourteen feet. That same man had a key to her apartment and was about to experience the flaming wrath of a jetlagged woman. 'Scott? Where the *hell* are you?' She called out her best friend's name as she kicked off her steel-capped boots and reached into her pocket for her phone. She held it to her ear, hearing nothing but dial tone, feeling herself getting more and more worked up.

Boomba waddled past her again, chirruping around his mouthful. His expression said clearly that as far as he was concerned, she should forget her house invader, admire the thing he'd killed and give him a pat.

'And what the hell are you doing here, fuzz ball?' Jo reached down and plucked the underwear out of his mouth, throwing it away. 'You're supposed to be at Amy's. Want to tell me what's going on?' The cat gave her his usual entitled feline stare and then butted his head into her shin.

'You're no help.' She walked through the living room, kicking a pair of socks out of her way, and stopped short in front of the vibrant blue-and-green abstract painting she'd bought last time she was in town. It was askew, as if someone had knocked it, and she felt something inside her snap.

This was not cool. *Not. Cool.* Her house was supposed to be empty. Her cat was supposed to be at her sister's and there wasn't supposed to be a . . . *man* anywhere within a good twenty metres of her right now, even if he was her best mate. She'd spent the last sixteen weeks surrounded by Y chromosomes and all she'd been looking forward to was a blessedly empty, *male-free* environment.

Scott finally answered, his tone suitably shocked. 'Jo? What time is it over there?'

'It's eight in the morning. I'm home. In Perth. Where are you?'

'*Home?*' Scott's deep voice momentarily took on choirboy heights he hadn't achieved since pre-puberty. 'You're supposed to be on holiday in Brazil!'

Jo squeezed her eyes tightly shut. 'Yes. Home. I cancelled the holiday because I wanted to be *home*. You know, that place I like to come when I'm not on some rusting oil rig in the middle of nowhere? You know that place? The place you were looking after. The place currently being lived in by someone who has feet the size of yours. The place currently containing my cat, who should be at Amy's.'

'Ahh. Yeah. About that.'

'Yeah, about what? What the *hell* is going on?'

There was a moment of silence and then a dull thud as if something had been hit, quite hard. 'I'll explain, but it's probably better I do it in person.'

'What? Why? I just want an answer and I want it now!'

'You'll get one . . . just . . . just stay there. I'll be there in fifteen minutes. We'll get all this sorted out. I'm sorry, Jo.'

Jo scowled, turning around, taking in the disorder and feeling a renewed sense of outrage. 'You bloody well better be. And bring me some goddamn coffee. I haven't slept properly for days and all

I wanted was to have a shower and fall into bed and instead—'

'Ten minutes,' he said with an edge of frustration in his tone that had better not be aimed at her. Given the mood she was in at the present moment, she'd be able to take Scott on one-on-one. They didn't call her Krakatoa out on the rigs for nothing.

Jo hung up, looking around until her eyes settled on her bedroom door.

There was no way Scott would make it in ten minutes, let alone fifteen, and she was *tired*.

Shooing Boomba out of the way with her foot, she headed for her room.

The feeling of tiredness was blasted to smithereens the minute she pushed the door open, took in the contents of her bed and roared with rage. '*Who the hell are you?!*'

'AAGGHH! *Gnph*.' The very naked, very buff and all-over tanned blond man who'd until that moment been sleeping spread-eagled on her bed shouted in surprise, leapt to his feet, tripped over Jo's cat and fell facedown on the floor.

About the author

Georgina Penney first discovered romance novels when she was eleven and has been a fan of the genre ever since. It took her another eighteen years to finally sit in front of a keyboard and get something down on the page but that's alright, she was busy doing other things until then. Some of those things included living in a ridiculous number of towns and cities in Australia before relocating overseas to Saudi Arabia, Bahrain, Brunei Darussalam and currently, Scotland.

In between all these travels, Georgina managed to learn to paint, get herself a Communication and Cultural Studies degree, study Psychotherapy and learn all about Hypnotherapy. In the early days she even managed to get on the IT roller coaster during the early noughties boom, inexplicably ending the ride by becoming the registrar of a massage and naturopathy college. There was also a PhD in the mix there somewhere but moving to Saudi Arabia and rediscovering the bodice ripper fixed all that.

Today she lives with her wonderful husband, Tony, in a cozy steading in the Scottish countryside. When she's not swearing at her characters and trying to cram them into her plot, she can be found traipsing over fields, gazing at hairy coos and imagining buff medieval Scotsmen in kilts (who have access to shower facilities and deoderant) living behind every bramble hedge.